AF512026

WAR OR PEACE IN SRI LANKA

by

T.D.S.A. Dissanayaka

WAR OR PEACE IN SRI LANKA

by

T.D.S.A. Dissanayaka

Popular Prakashan

Popular Prakashan Pvt. Ltd.
35-C, Madan Mohan Malaviya Marg
Popular Press Bldg., Tardeo
Mumbai - 400 034

©T.D.S.A. Dissanayaka

First Printed in September 2004
First reprint January 2005

ISBN: 81-7991-199-3 (3947)

Typeset by Vans Information Ltd., Mumbai

Printed in India
by Nikeda Art (Printers) Pvt. Ltd.
Mahalaxmi Inds. Estate
Unit No. 7-8, 3rd floor
Dainik Shivner Rd. Gandhi Nagar
Lower Parel, Mumbai - 400 013

Published by Ramdas Bhatkal for
Popular Prakashan Pvt. Ltd.
35-C, Pt. Madan Mohan Malaviya Marg
Popular Press Bldg., Tardeo
Mumbai - 400 034.

Respectfully dedicated to my friend, philosopher and guide

BISHOP LAKSHMAN WICKREMESINGHE

(1927 - 1983)

May his courageous voice continue to be heard,
long after he has returned to his Maker

NOTE BY AUTHOR

My fellow Sri Lankans, wherever you may be,

Please do not put your trust in our politicians. Whatever their politics may be, they rarely want to help our nation in her advancement. Instead, they want our nation to help them in their advancement, at any cost, even at the cost of a Civil War.

Please do not demean yourself, like most Sri Lankans do, by being beholden to Presidents, Prime Ministers and Ministers. It is they who should be beholden to you, because they are your servants, not your masters.

Please do not be misled by our State-controlled media which has been reduced to a ludicrous level of sycophancy, irrespective of who is in power.

Politicians of Sri Lanka, condemn me if you must. However please remember, History will absolve me, not you!

T.D.S.A. Dissanayaka
(1938 -)

ACKNOWLEDGEMENTS

This book is essentially a compendium of my six books on our Civil War, namely "The Agony of Sri Lanka" (1983), "The Dilemma of Sri Lanka" (1993) and "War or Peace in Sri Lanka" (Volume I to IV) written between 1995 and 2003. Manmohan Bhatkal, Chief Executive Officer of the Popular Book Depot of Mumbai read them during his frequent visits to Sri Lanka and invited me to write an international edition in five hundred pages, half the combined length of the six original books. In that endeavour Shivani Ganesh, the Editor (English Publications) of Popular Prakashan (Private) Ltd. of Mumbai, was of immense help to me.

Then Manmohan Bhatkal wanted the international edition to be of racy style which can be read in one sitting. I invited him to be the Editor-in-Chief of such an envisaged book. He chopped and changed the text and this three hundred page book is the nett result of our labour! Indeed I am most grateful to him. Vans Information Limited typed the numerous revisions in exemplary manner, under relentless pressure. While this marathan effort was on, Godwin Fernando, my classmate at the University of Ceylon and Director of Research on all my books and S.S Wijesinha, Retired Secretary General of Parliament, and the Chief Moderator of my last ten books rendered yeoman service, as usual. The Nasa Communications in Colombo-3, consisting of A.H.U. Marikkar and his two daughters Rameesa and Rasheeda assisted me splendidly with the logistic support, under tremendous pressure.

Lt. General Nalin Seneviratne, Retired Commander of the Army, Admiral Mohan Samarasekera, Retired Commander of the Navy, Air Vice Marshal Harry Goonetileke, Retired Commander of the Air Force, Rudra Rajasingham, Retired Inspector - General of Police Bradman Weerakoon Retired Secretary to the Prime Minister and W.T. Jayasinghe, Retired Foreign Secretary, checked the scripts for authenticity in their areas of specialty.

This book went into print in August 2004, three months behind schedule, because of the unprecedented volume of work undertaken. Then Jigesh Gangadharan, Production Manager of my Publisher handled the operation with immense skill.

Thus I made my entry into the international scene as an Author. How I survived this ordeal even I do not know !

CONTENTS

Chapter I

SRI LANKA: WHAT WENT WRONG?

At a time when the sun never set on the British Empire, the British were so enchanted by Ceylon, as Sri Lanka was then known, that they called it the 'Pearl of the Orient.' The British raved over its scenic beauty. The British admired the stability of the Crown Colony of Ceylon. Besides, the British admired how fluently the Ceylonese spoke English, adapted to the British public school system, played cricket, and appreciated the finer points of the British way of life. By the same token, the British could never comprehend a complex dichotomy in Ceylon. The English speaking minority and the Sinhala and Tamil speaking majority lived in two separate worlds, of their own making.

Against this background, a very pertinent reference to Ceylon in 1930 was the internal memorandum prepared by Sir Charles Jeffries, later Under-Secretary for Colonial Affairs.

> "Ceylon provides the classic example of how with good sense and goodwill two nations can carry through the extremely difficult and delicate transition from a subject-ruler relationship to an equal partnership.
>
> Ceylon has been the prototype and model for the new Commonwealth hopefully in the latter half of the twentieth century.
>
> In Ceylon we British learnt, by trial and error, the art of Colonial administration. They also learnt the wisdom of learning systematically the art of self-governance, which is essentially a process of trial and error."

Taking all these encomiums into account, the British decided to give special treatment to the Crown Colony of Ceylon. Therefore in 1931, universal franchise became a gift to Ceylon from the British, under the

Donoughmore Constitution. No leader of Ceylon had agitated for it in the Legislative Council. At best there were the lone voices of the Labour leader A.E. Goonesinghe and George E. de Silva, the Member for Kandy. Nowhere in the British Empire was the experiment carried out in the decade of the nineteen thirties.

The first General Election in Ceylon under universal franchise was held in 1931. The new State Council of Ceylon had fifty seats to be filled by election. Forty six seats returned duly elected Members. In the four electorates of Jaffna, Kankesanturai, Kayts and Point Pedro, the Tamil community which accounted for approximately 95% of the voters in those constituencies, boycotted the General Election because they perceived the Donoughmore reforms were inadequate. For example the idealistic Jaffna Youth Congress led by Handy Perimbanayagam wanted self-rule immediately. Others bemoaned that in the last Legislative Council, which was elected on a restricted franchise based on property and educational qualifications, there were eight elected Tamil Members in a Council of twenty nine elected Members. In the new State Council, there were only seven Members in a House which provided for fifty elected Members. Yet others claimed that universal franchise being introduced so suddenly, just three years after it was introduced to Britain, was a disaster. This created the impression, both amongst the British rulers and the Sinhalese, that the people of the Jaffna peninsula where over 50% of the Tamil population of lived according to the Census of 1931, were opposed to universal franchise.

In fairness to the Ceylon Tamil community, it must be added that outside the Jaffna peninsula they participated enthusiastically in the General Election of 1931. For example G.G. Ponnambalam, then a young, up and coming politician who had taken a First at Cambridge and had done brilliantly as a law student at Lincoln's Inn, wanted to contest either the seat of Jaffna or Point Pedro. He could not do so because of the popular boycott. Therefore he decided to contest the seat of Mannar where he was altogether an alien. He lost narrowly to a candidate who was a resident of Mannar. In Colombo North, Dr R. (later Sir Ratnajothi) Saravanamuttu won easily. In Trincomalee, M.M. Subramanium, formerly an elected Member of the Legislative Council, was duly elected. In Batticaloa South, H.M. (later Sir Mohamed) Macan Markar defeated E.R. Tambimuttu, formerly an elected Member of the Legislative Council.

The Burghers, Christians from all ethnic groups and Ceylon Tamils, in that order, were the pampered minorities in the Crown Colony of Ceylon.

They respectively accounted for 0.6%, 9.1% and 11.2% of the population according to the Census of 1931. The British systematically played these minorities against the majority, the Sinhalese Buddhists, who accounted for 64.3% of the population. With the introduction of adult franchise, the Sinhalese found an equitable representation in the State Council. Nevertheless in the Public Service, the British continued to recruit Burghers, Christians and Ceylon Tamils in large numbers and Sinhalese Buddhists as few as practicable. That pernicious policy of divide and rule continued unabated until Independence in 1948 because it was part and parcel of British policy throughout their Empire.

For the first time, in 1931, Ceylon had a Legislature which represented a cross section of our population, besides being elected on the basis of universal franchise. The General Election of 1931 was indeed interesting. The Sinhalese accounting for 69.2% of the population were delighted that three quarter of the State Council consisted of their kind. (In the Legislative Council, half were Sinhalese.) The Sinhalese Christians who accounted for approximately 5% of the population were in clover. Twelve State Councillors were Sinhalese Christians. The Muslims could not understand why they won only one seat when their community accounted for 6.9% of the population. The Indian Tamils who accounted for 12.0% of the population also did not fare too well and won only two seats. The Ceylon Tamils bemoaned that adult franchise was not workable in our nation!

Very significantly the Burgher community which accounted for only 0.6% of the population could not win a seat. Their representatives in the State Council were two of the eight Appointed Members namely Dr. V. R. Schokman and Sir Steward Schneider. However the Burgher community accepted reality. Some Burghers who went to Britain for higher studies or training, never came back. A small number migrated to Australia. After Independence they migrated to Australia, in large numbers.

The British were embarrassed by the boycott of the General Election in the North. Therefore Sir Edward Stubbs, the Governor of Ceylon, used his influence on the Ceylon Tamil community, and in 1934, by-elections were held in the Jaffna peninsula. Accordingly Arunachalam (later Sir Arunachalam) Mahadeva (Jaffna), S. Natesan (Kankesanturai), Nevins Selvadurai (Kayts) and G.G. Ponnambalam (Point Pedro) were duly elected.

The second General Election held in 1936 generated considerable interest in all communities. Universal franchise was accepted by all communities but there were justifiable misgivings about some iniquities. For example the Muslim community was astonished that despite accounting for 6.9% of the population they won no seats in 1936 and just one seat in 1931. The Indian Tamil community accounting for 12.0% of the population, as against 11.2% of the Ceylon Tamil community won only two seats as against eight by the Ceylon Tamils. Quite obviously there was some error in the delimitation of the electorates made by the British. As a first step, Governor Stubbs opted for two Muslims, T.B. Jayah and Razeek (later Sir Razeek) Fareed as Appointed Members.

G. G. Ponnambalam, unquestionably a rising star in the Ceylon Tamil community, had serious misgivings about the preponderance of Sinhalese both in the Board of Ministers and in the State Council itself. All seven Ministers in 1936 were Sinhalese as against five Sinhalese, one Tamil and one Muslim in the last State Council. The Sinhalese accounted for 69.2% of the population. Therefore in a State council of 50 elected Members, there should have been around 35 Sinhalese elected as Members but there were 39. He therefore clamoured for balanced representation. However by 1937, he devised the slogan 'fifty-fifty,' which represented anything but balanced representation.

According to Ponnambalam power should be shared in the ratio fifty-fifty, with parity of status for :

(a) The Sinhalese speaking majority
(b) The non-Sinhalese speaking minorities.

The English speaking minorities, the Burghers (0.6%) and the British (0.2%), ignored the proposal. Therefore Ponnambalam modified his proposal as follows :

(a) The Sinhalese speaking majority
(b) All Tamil speaking minorities.

That proposal worked like a charm on the Tamil community living in the Northern and Eastern Province. In direct contrast, the Indian Tamil community, 12.0% of the population as against 11.2% of the Ceylon Tamils, was lukewarm. They lived amidst the Sinhalese in the Central Province, Sabaragamuwa and Uva and they did not want to antagonise the majority community. Therefore Ponnambalam the demagogue campaigned vigorously in the North and the East and Ponnambalam the brilliant lawyer, articulated his case before the State Council. His address to the State Council was the longest speech ever made in the history of our Legislature. It was no accident that he was looked upon as the uncrowned King of Jaffna.

In direct contrast in the eyes of the Sinhalese, the fifty-fifty proved only one thing. The Ceylon Tamils, especially those from Jaffna, just did not know how to live as a minority.

Those Sinhalese who were enraged claimed publicly that all Tamil speaking minorities, the Ceylon Tamils, the Indian Tamil and the Muslims put together accounted for only 30.1% of the population whereas the Sinhalese accounted for 69.2%. Therefore, how can they clamour for fifty-fifty? The exact parallel today is that the Ceylon Tamils are clamouring for two-thirds of the coastline of the entire nation and one-third of the land mass, while accounting for only one-eighth of the population.

The anger of the Sinhalese was based on two issues. The British played the Ceylon Tamil minority against the Sinhalese majority at every turn. For example the Ceylon Tamils accounted for 11.2% of the population but over one-third of the then prestigious Public Service were from this community. In contrast the Sinhalese accounted for 69.2% of the population but less than one-half of the Public Service was from this community. That was a sore point in the relationship between the two communities which were traditionally hostile to each other, having fought wars for 2,000 years. The Sinhalese were hoping that these anomalies would hopefully be straightened out after Independence and justice given to the discriminated majority community. Now it transpired that under universal franchise, the Ceylon Tamils themselves were attempting to subvert natural justice stemming from simple arithmetic and clamouring for fifty-fifty, a thoroughly illogical proposition.

G.G. Ponnambalam was both an orator and a demagogue. As a demagogue he could appeal to emotional issues with the greatest of ease. He produced the gunpowder, one of two essential ingredients for an explosion. All that was necessary for the Sinhalese was to produce a demagogue who produced the fire, the other key ingredient for an explosion. Hypothetically, if there was a demagogue who advocated Sinhala as the sole Official Language after the British left, then the explosion would certainly have ripped Ceylon apart and the British would not have left us in 1948. Mercifully there was no such demagogue in the Sinhalese community in the decade of the nineteen thirties.

The concept of Sinhala Only was first introduced into the Legislature by J.R. Jayewardene (MSC for Kelaniya) within a month of his swearing-in on May 23rd, 1943. At that time there was no United National Party and no Sri Lanka Freedom Party. (They were formed in 1946 and 1951 respectively.) Nearly everybody of consequence belonged to the Ceylon

National Congress which was a conglomeration of forces, not a political party. Without consulting anybody, J.R. Jayewardene advocated Sinhala to replace English when he tabled the following Motion on June 22nd, 1943.

"Sir, the Motion tabled by me reads as follows :

(a) That Sinhala should be made the medium of instruction in all schools;

(b) That Sinhala should be made a compulsory subject in all public examinations;

(c) That legislation should be introduced to permit the business of the State Council to be conducted in Sinhala also;

(d) That a Commission should be appointed to choose for translation and to translate important books of other languages into Sinhala;

(e) That a Commission should be appointed to report on all steps that need be taken to effect the transition from English into Sinhala.

My motion seeks to displace English from the position which it has held for over 125 years as the official language of this country. Thank you, Sir."

(Source: Hansard)

There was pandemonium in the Legislature. The ensuing bedlam was so great, the Speaker Sir Waitilingam Doraiswamy (MSC for Kayts) adjourned the House. J.R. Jayewardene himself told me so when I was writng *J.R. Jayaewardene of Sri Lanka* in 1977.D.S. Senanayake, the Leader of the State Council, was livid. He sent his son Dudley Senanayake (MSC for Dedigana) to warn J.R. Jayewardene that he would like to break his neck. Dudley Senanayake himself told me when I was writing my first book *Dudley Senanayake of Sri Lanka* in 1973.

J.R. Jayewardene was a brilliant product of Royal College, the Colombo University College (later the University of Ceylon) and the Colombo Law College. He entered the Colombo Municipal Council in 1938 from the New Bazaar Ward and entered the Legislature in 1943 from Kelaniya. Many expected the elder statesman, E.W. Perera, a Christian, to win that seat at the by-election of 1943. However J.R. Jayewardene then 37 years old, a son of a devout Christian father and a devout Buddhist mother, and himself a devout Buddhist campaigned on the basis :

> "Kelaniya is sacred to the Buddhists and this bye-election will be held on a Poya day. How can Kelaniya send a Christian to the State Council?"

J.R. Jayewardene won by a landslide! Thus he too was a demagogue. This information was given to me by Sirisoma Ranasinghe, the Campaign Manager of J.R. Jayewardene and my Publisher in Sri Lanka.

D.S. Senanayake, livid though he was with the proposal of J.R. Jayewardene, quickly got Tamil Members of the State Council to propose amendments. Wherever the word "Sinhala" appeared, the amendment proposed read "Sinhala and Tamil". To calm, ruffled feathers, with the co-operation of the Speaker the proposal of J.R. Jayewardene was deliberately delayed. In due course J.R. Jayewardene himself amended his Motion substituting "Sinhala and Tamil" for "Sinhala". He addressed the State Council on the amended Motion on May 24th, 1944. A superb orator, that day he spoke like a real statesman, and was honoured by a standing ovation by the State Council. Therefore, his entire speech is reproduced at this juncture.

> "Sir, my Motion seeks to displace English from the position which it has held for over 125 years as the official language of this country.
>
> The tragedy that is enacted everyday in our Court, in our Public Departments and in the very lives of our people is very vividly described in that famous book *The Village in the Jungle* which I would advise Honourable Members of this Council to read. There, Sir, a villager from a hamlet in the Hambantota District is brought up for trial in the Courts before an English Magistrate, and after a number of days of trial, during which he does not understand a single word of what passed between the Judge, counsel and other officials, he is sentenced to a long term of imprisonment, and even at that stage does not know what had happened. That tragedy is occurring even today.
>
> It is argued by those who know only English, who have been educated only in English, that if we displace English and make Sinhalese and Tamil the official languages, we will be shutting out a large world of literature, and culture from our people. They little understand that the world of literature is already a closed book to 90 percent of our people. We can today after so many years of English as the official language, measure its achievements in this country. It is true that we have produced a number of famous lawyers, doctors and judges and possibly legislators, but in the field of literature, of science, of culture, we have been entirely barren of achievement.

It was not so when the native language was the language of the Government. I think history records that wise men both from the East and the West came to the shores of Lanka to read the books that were preserved in the sanctuaries of the Buddhist Sangha. If one reads the travels of Hauen Tsang, Marco Polo and Fa Hien and the lives of great Western philosophers such as Dhalke, Rhys, Davids and others, we would find the contribution that this country made to world literature when we had our own language as the official language. (Loud applause)

Therefore I place this motion before the House; and I wish to speak a word of explanation with regard to my desire to include Tamil also. I had always the intention that Tamil should be spoken in the Tamil-speaking provinces, and that Tamil should be the official language in the Tamil-speaking provinces. But as two-thirds of the people of this country speak Sinhalese, I had the intention of proposing that only Sinhalese should be the official language of the island; but it seems to me that the Tamil community, who speak Tamil, wish that Tamil also should be included on equal terms with Sinhalese. The great fear I had was that Sinhalese being a language spoken by only three million people in the whole world would suffer or may be entirely lost in time to come, if Tamil is also placed on an equal footing with it in this country. The influence of Tamil literature, a literature used in India by over forty million and the influence of films and Tamil culture in this country, I thought might be detrimental to the future of the Sinhalese language; but if it is the desire of the Tamils, that Tamil also should be given an equal status with Sinhalese I do not think we should bar it from attaining that position. (Loud applause)

I do not think there will be any difficulty in this House, which is composed of representatives chosen on a universal franchise, in securing the end we have in view. It is the universal franchise that has brought the English-educated and the masses together, and it is the impulse created by the use of the universal franchise, by the ideals created by the grant of the universal franchise, which enabled the people to choose their own rulers, which will ultimately make Sinhalese and Tamil official languages of this country. I would therefore suggest to this House that we anticipate that event, and give it the sanction of our vote and decision. (Loud applaux)

Language, Sir, is one of the most important characteristics of nationality. Without language, a nation stands a chance of being absorbed or of losing its identity. With language, it has a chance of living for centuries. It is because of our language that the Sinhalese race has existed for 2,400 years and I think that composed as we are in this House, on the eve of freedom in a free country we should prepare for a national official language. This House, I am sure, will vote with me that English should be deposed from its position as the official language of the country and Sinhalese and Tamil, the ancient languages of our people, spoken by over ninety percent of our people, should be made the Official Languages of Lanka." (Standing ovation)

The amended motion was carried without a division and J.R. Jayewardene was congratulated by nearly everybody in the State Council, irrespective of whether they spoke in English, Sinhala or Tamil. Besides the amended Motion became the language policy of every political party in Ceylon at the time of Independence and it enhanced the stature of J.R. Jayewardene immeasurably. Accordingly in 1945, he was made Chairman of a Select Committee of the State Council to handle the issue of Sinhala and Tamil gradually supplanting English.

In 1946 the Soulbury Commission was not favourably disposed to the proposal of G.G. Ponnambalam on the fifty-fifty policy. He was asked awkward questions such as whether he received a mandate from the Indian Tamil community and the Muslim community and if so why these communities have not made any such proposal to this Commission. Lord Soulbury insisted that even then the Sinhala speaking majority accounted for 69.2% of the population and all Tamil speaking minorities put together accounted for only 30.1%, thus the concept of fifty-fifty was not based on reality. Lord Soulbury even emphasised that G.G. Ponnambalam who took a First in the Natural Science Tripos at Cambridge University would find no difficulty in understanding this elementary arithmetic. That was British sarcasm at its best!

Indeed the proposal for fifty-fifty presented by the all powerful All Ceylon Tamil Congress was rejected altogether by the Soulbury Commission.

In terms of the Soulbury Commission, the unitary form of Government which prevailed since the Colebrook-Soulbury Cameron Commission of 1833, was advocated. It was easy for Lord Soulbury to come to that conclusion because there was no proposal whatsoever for a Federal structure. For example during the Donoughmore Commission in 1928 the Kandyan leaders proposed a Federal system. Ceylon to be divided into three regions: the Kandyan Provinces for the Kandyan Sinhalese, the Maritime Provinces for the Low-Country Sinhalese and the Northern and Eastern Provinces for the Tamils. Lord Donoughmore rejected the proposal outright, exactly the same way Lord Devonshire did in 1923. Nevertheless Lord Soulbury recognised the problems of the minorities. To protect their rights he incorporated Section 29 of The Soulbury Constitution which read as follows :

"No such law shall :

(a) prohibit or restrict the free exercise of any religion;
(b) make persons of any community or religion liable to disabilities or restrictions to which persons of other communities or religions are not made liable to; or
(c) confer on persons of any community or religion any privilege or advantage which is not conferred on persons of other communities or religions; or
(d) alter the constitution of any religious body except with the consent of the governing authority of that body."

Thus a basic flaw was that Section 29 (c) did not explicitly protect the language rights of the minorities to the same extent that it protected the religious rights of the minorities. No doubt a Bill of Rights as proposed by G.G. Ponnambalam would have been better.

In 1946 the United National Party (UNP) was set up to contest the General Election of 1947 under the Soulbury Constitution. The hierarchy of the UNP was basically as follows:

D.S. Senanayake (President), Leader of The State Council and Minister since 1931

S.W.R.D. Bandaranaike (Vice President), Minister since 1936

J.L. (later Sir John) Kotelawala (Vice President), Minister since 1936

Sir Arunachalam Mahadeva (Vice President), Minister since 1942

T.B. Jayah (Vice President), Member of the State Council since 1936

Dudley Senanayake (Joint Secretary), Member of the State Council since 1936

J.R. Jayewardene (Joint Secretary), Member of the State Council since 1943.

To conduct the first General Election under The Soulbury Constitution, the State Council was dissolved as of July 1947. With the dissolution, some important Bills lapsed. One such was the Bill on Official Languages as recommenced by a Select Committee under the Chairmanship of J.R. Jayewardene. After much deliberation that Select Committee recommended that Sinhala and Tamil be the Official Languages of Ceylon commencing 1957. Also that English be retained till then, while Sinhala and Tamil will be used progressively till the transition is duly completed in a time frame of ten years.

In his wisdom D.S. Senanayake envisaged a new Dominion of Ceylon where the Sinhalese and the Ceylon Tamils, who had fought each other for centuries, and all other communities would continue to live in peace as they were now doing.

He had many confidante from the Ceylon Tamil community. In the realm of politics they were Sir Arunachalam Mahadeva, Professor C. Suntharalingam who had a double First from Oxford and Sir Ratnajothi Saravanamuttu, a former Mayor of Colombo. In the prestigious Ceylon Civil Service his confidante were K (later Sir Kanthiah) Vaithianathan and P. Saravanamuttu, the younger brother of Sir Ratnajothi. In the Mercantile sector it was Adigar Arumugam Sellamuttu. That was common knowledge and the Ceylon Tamil community, especially the 25% of them who lived amongst the Sinhalese, greatly appreciated the leadership of D.S. Senanayake.

Besides, D.S. Senanayake handled with exemplary skill the complex dichotomy of the English speaking *elite* and the Sinhala speaking *hoi polloi* and their totally different sense of values. Without any doubt D.S. Senanayake was from the English speaking elite. (So were S.W.R.D. Bandaranaike, J.L. Kotelawala and Sir Arunachalam Mahadeva, to mention a few.) D. S. Senanayake was a distinguished product of S. Thomas' College. It was no accident that he gave both his sons English names though they were born when the father was battling the British and was locked up for his trouble! When his sons were ready for University education he opted for Oxford and Cambridge. Both were admitted to Cambridge because they chose the Natural Science Tripos. Notwithstanding these Western predilections D.S. Senanayake had no illusions that political power resided in the Sinhala and Tamil speaking *hoi polloi*, not in the English speaking *elite*.

The results of the General Election were as follows :

UNP	42
Independens	21
LSSP	14
Tamil Congress	7
Ceylon Indian Congress	7
Communist Party	3
Labour Party	1
Total	95

(Source: Department of Elections)

The ethnic breakdown was 68 Sinhalese, 13 Tamils, 7 Indian Tamils, 6 Muslims and 1 Burgher, which was more or less commensurate with the breakdown of our population according to the Census of 1946. The only exception was the Indian Tamil community which was still under - represented in Parliament due to a faulty delimitation of electorates. In accordance with the Soulbury Commission, the British Governor, Sir Henry Monk-Mason Moore, called upon D.S. Senanayake to form the first Government of Ceylon. Prime Minister D.S. Senanayake did so with characteristic wisdom. The key UNP members, as listed in page 10 but barring Sir Arunachalam Mahadeva who lost his seat in Jaffna to the charismatic G.G. Ponnambalam, were appointed as senior Cabinet Ministers. Sir Arunachalam was offered an Ambasssadorship, Washington or New Delhi. He opted for the latter. To bring in the Tamil component into the Cabinet, two former members of the prestigious Ceylon Civil Service, Professor C. Suntheralingam (Independent - Vavuniya) and C. Sittampalam (Independent - Mannar) were duly appointed.

Thereafter, to broadbase the Government, the Prime Minister invited G.G. Ponnambalam to join his Cabinet, which he ultimately did in September 1948. Altogether five of the seven Members of Parliament from the Tamil Congress joined the Government. S.J.V. Chelvanayakam, MP (Tamil Congress -Kankesanturai), the Deputy President of the Tamil Congress thought it was a penny wise pound foolish policy. He was deeply suspicious of the motives of Prime Minister D.S. Senanayake. That assessment was shared by C. Vanniasingham M.P. (Tamil Congress - Kopay). The two of them joined the Opposition. Thus the Tamil Congress was split asunder.

The Prime Minister was widely respected for the development work which he initiated as Minister of Agriculture and Lands in the first and second State Councils. However S.J.V. Chelvanayakam was suspicious when D.S. Senanayake brought in landless Sinhalese peasants into the Tamil speaking District of Vavuniya in 1936 and to the Tamil speaking District of Trincomalee in 1938, when the restoration of the Vavuniya tank and the Kantalai tank were duly completed. In 1936 D.S. Senanayake did offer land in the District of Vavuniya to the landless peasants of the District of Jaffna but there were no takers. The landless in the District of Jaffna were just not interested in transmigration to the God forsaken District of Vavuniya. They were primarily interested in giving a good education to their sons and thereafter seeking employment in the then prestigious Government Service. It was only then that D.S. Senanayake brought in

Sinhalese from Mirigama, his electorate and Kegalle his son's electrorate. Even then, the only Sinhalese who accepted the challenge in the virgin jungles of Vavuniya were roughnecks from these two electorates. Somehow they turned out to be good colonists. In 1938, D.S. Senanayake did not offer land to the landless peasants in the Tamil speaking District of Trincomalee. Instead he brought in more Sinhalese roughnecks from Mirigama and Kegalle, also Balapitiya and Waskaduwa, where the Sinhalese are rather aggressive by nature. Thus the demographic pattern began to change in those districts as reflected in the statistics given overleaf

District of Vavuniya			
Census	Sinhalese %	Tamils %	Muslims %
1931	8.1	82.7	9.2
1946	16.1	75.3	8.6

District of Trincomalee			
Census	Sinhalese %	Tamils %	Muslims %
1931	10.1	50.2	34.9
1946	20.7	44.4	30.0

(Source: Department of Census and Statistics)

In February, 1948, just one week after Independence, Prime Minister D.S. Senanayake triumphantly announced his dream irrigation project, Gal Oya, in the Tamil speaking District of Batticaloa. To accelerate work, the contract was awarded to Morrison Knudsen Inc. of San Francisco which had become world famous by virtue of its work in the Tennessee Valley Authority, initiated by President Franklin D. Roosevelt of the United States. It was widely rumoured that the Prime Minister would bring in tens of thousands of Sinhalese peasants into the Gal Oya valley when the construction of the giant dam was completed in 1951.

Therefore S.J.V. Chelvanayakam advised G.G. Ponnambalam that the Tamil Congress should not join the UNP Administration but instead vote with the UNP from the Opposition. In December 1948 S.J.V. Chelvanayakam became even more suspicious when the Prime Minister moved in Parliament, The Ceylon Citizenship Act. Admittedly every sovereign nation has to define who its citizens are. For example, were the British expatriates in Ceylon free to become citizens of Ceylon, if they chose to? What was the citizenship of 12% of the population who were Indian Tamils? Were they citizens of India or citizens of Ceylon?

In 1948, the basic qualification for citizenship for aliens anywhere in the world was five years as a permanent resident. For example, Ceylonese who had lived in the UK for five years were eligible for British citizenship. The Burghers who migrated to Australia needed permanent residence of five years before becoming citizens of Australia. The plantation labour from South India had lived in Ceylon for 75 years or more. However all except those whose parents were born in Ceylon were disenfranchised in terms of The Ceylon Citizenship Act of 1948. For example, the seven Members of Parliament from the Ceylon Indian Congress suddenly lost their right to re-contest their seats in the next Parliament and this Party could not conceivably win one seat at the next General Election, scheduled for 1952, at the latest. S.J.V. Chelvanayakam was livid. In his eyes the Sinhalese were an unjust majority. His battle cry was "Today it is the Indian Tamils. Tomorrow it will be the Ceylon Tamils". In his perception, the Ceylon Tamils could live with dignity and self respect only in a Federal set up, not in a unitary form of Government. Accordingly, in January 1949, he formed the Federal Party. The inaugural Convention was held in Trincomalee. He was elected as Founder President, C. Vanniasingham M.P. (Tamil Congress - Kopay) as Vice President and Senator E.M.V. Naganathan, a well known family doctor in Colombo, as General Secretary.

By 1951 Prime Minister D.S. Senanayake and the Leader of the House S.W.R.D. Bandaranaike were at loggerheads. These two leaders had two different political philosophies. D.S. Senanayake was pro-Establishment whereas S.W.R.D. Bandaranaike was anti-Establishment ever since his days at Oxford. D.S. Senanayake was a visionary. His vision was – how to obtain Independence from the British without bloodshed. S.W.R.D. Bandaranaike was also a visionary. His vision was what Ceylon should be after Independence. For example, he advocated a bloodless revolution with power shifting from the over-privileged *elite* to the under-privileged *hoi polloi*.

What the Leader of the House S.W.R.D. Bandaranaike had learnt at Oxford was intellectually similar to what Prime Minister Jawarharlal Nehru of India had learnt at Cambridge, Prime Minister Liaquat Ali Khan of Pakistan had learnt at the London School of Economics (of the University of London) and President Manuel Roxas of the Philippines had learnt at Harvard. However Prime Minister D.S. Senanayake was a high school drop out though he was unquestionably a very able Prime Minister. Thus he was devoid of an intellectual base which is a priceless asset for any Prime Minister or executive President. (Prime Minister Sirima Bandaranaike and President Ranasinghe Premadasa were also high school drop outs. They too were unquestionably able. They too had the same deficiency, namely the absence of an intellectual base.) Prime Minister D.S. Senanayake and Leader of the House S.W.R.D. Bandaranaike were getting further and further apart since Independence. To compound the crisis, the Prime Minister courted disaster when he began to groom his son Dudley Senanayake, a Cabinet Minister since 1947, as the next Prime Minister at the expense of the heir apparent S.W.R.D. Bandaranaike, a Minister since 1936 and the Leader of the House since 1947. Finally Bandaranaike left the UNP in anger in 1951 to form his Sri Lanka Freedom Party (SLFP). The next General Election was scheduled for sometime in1952 but before that Prime Minister D.S. Senanayake died suddenly in March 1952,when he suffered a massive stroke while on horseback. He was succeeded by Dudley Senanayake who won the emotionally charged General Election of 1952 by a landslide.

In the context of national unity, a cardinal policy of the late Prime Minister, the UNP and the Tamil Congress received a massive mandate in the Northern Province and the Eastern Province at the General Election of 1952. S. Natesan (UNP) defeated S.J.V. Chelvanayakam (Federal Party) at Kankesanthurai and was made a Cabinet Minister. V. Nalliah (UNP) won Kalkudah and was also made a Cabinet Minister. Most leading candidates from the Federal Party for example Dr E.M.V. Naganathan (Jaffna) and A. Amirthalingam (Point Pedro) lost badly.

At the General Election of 1952, like at the General Election of 1947, every political party, large or small, advocated Sinhala and Tamil as the Official Languages of Ceylon. All Parties advocated a gradual change except the SLFP which pledged to do so in 24 hours. Since 1952 S.W.R.D. Bandaranaike had to languish in the political wilderness, although he was the Leader of the Opposition. However in 1953 the *harthal* (stoppage of work) organised by the LSSP to protest against the removal of the rice subsidy became violent. The Army had to open fire several times and during that crisis Prime Minister Dudley Senanayake was taken ill with a chronic stomach ailment which he got during times of stress. He resigned and was taken to London for medical attention. He was succeeded by the Leader of the House, Sir John Kotelawala, who can best be described as a playboy. In fairness to him, he was a good freedom fighter and a capable Cabinet Minister but was totally impervious to the winds of change in Ceylon.

Later in 1953 Prime Minister Jawarharlal Nehru of neighbouring India enunciated his language policy in the Lok Sabha, the Lower House of the Parliament of India. He said,

> "Today English is the Official Language of India. It is spoken in every State in the Union. Twenty five years from now an Indian language has to take the place of English. Today Hindi is spoken widely but only by 42% of our people. For example Hindi is spoken widely in North India but is hardly spoken in South India. It is only when Hindi is spoken throughout South India that we can perceive it to be the Official Language of India. In my judgment that will take one generation, hence my reference to twenty five years. We cannot do so any earlier."
>
> *(Hansard: October 1953)*

There was hardly any response in Ceylon to that policy decision except by S.W.R.D. Bandaranaike. He explained to his audiences what Prime Minister Jawaharlal Nehru had said in the Lok Sabha. He then said that whereas in India only 42% spoke Hindi, in Ceylon 72% spoke Sinhala. Therefore he concluded :

> "*Mama Aga Methi unoth*
> *peya visi hatherakin*
> *Sinhala pamanak, Sinhala pamanak*
> *Apey rajaya bashawa keranawa*"

(If I become Prime Minister in twenty four hours Sinhala only, repeat Sinhala only, will be made our Official Language.)

That was the ultimate of being a demagogue but it was the principal theme of campaigning by S.W.R.D. Bandaranaike in 1954. He drew massive and enthusiastic crowds wherever he went. It was clearly a populist move amongst the Sinhalese. Therefore at the annual Convention of the SLFP in December 1954, he proposed that henceforth Sinhala only be made official policy of the SLFP. That proposal was accepted with much enthusiasm.

In direct contrast, throughout 1954 Prime Minister Sir John Kotelawala, in his customary pithy language, said repeatedly at public meetings amongst the Sinhalese,

> "Those of you who want to start a communal racket like the SLFP do not know what it entails. The UNP composes of all communities who inhabit the Island, as reflected in its name. As long as I am head of the UNP the principle of parity of status for Sinhala and

> Tamil which we adopted when our Party was formed in 1946, will remain."

Amongst the Tamils, he dropped some bricks in characteristic style, while addressing meetings in Jaffna and in Delft in 1955. It resulted in a backlash amongst the Sinhalese and a giant protest rally in Anuradhapura was held outside the sacred Sri Maha Bodhiya.

Quite clearly S.W.R.D. Bandaranaike was scoring heavily with his Sinhala Only policy. Therefore, within the Working Committee of the UNP there was much agitation led by J.R. Jayewardene, Leader of the House, to change the language policy of the UNP. Sir John Kotelawala resisted those moves but finally yielded to the populist move amongst the Sinhalese. The UNP formally adopted the Sinhala Only policy, proposed at their annual Convention held in Kelaniya in January 1956 by J.R. Jayewardene who was the Member of Parliament for Kelaniya. That proposal was carried by acclamation. All elected Tamil MPs from the UNP stormed out of the Convention and immediately resigned from the UNP. Sir John Kotelawala wound up the Convention with a political somersault, incompatible with his personality, claiming,

> "I want Sinhala to be the sole official language of Ceylon as long as the sun and the moon last."

Thus in a short space of two years, the two largest political parties amongst the Sinhalese changed their language policy radically by strictly adhering to democratic norms. However both the SLFP and the UNP were unmindful that they had sown the wind and would have to reap the whirlwind. In fact the only political parties which acted with wisdom on the sensitive language issue were the Marxist LSSP and the Communist Party. The LSSP campaigned in all nine Provinces on the premise of parity of status for Sinhala and Tamil, which was their language policy since the inception of their Party in 1935. Dr Colvin R. De Silva, earlier Member of Parliament for Wellawatte-Galkissa, went a step further and campaigned on the basis,

> "Either we will have two languages and remain one nation, or we will have one language and become two nations!"

In the North and in the East mass support shifted visibly in favour of the Federal Party, which had fared disastrously in the General Election of 1952 and even S.J.V. Chelvanayakam had lost his seat. Now he was looked upon as a prophet for having predicted so accurately the behaviour of the Sinhalese in respect to the Tamils. At the General Election of 1956 the complex dichotomy of Ceylon, the English speaking *elite* and the Sinhala and Tamil speaking *hoi polloi* each living in a world of their own making, underwent a cultural revolution. The UNP Administrtion under Prime Minister Sir John Kotelawala had come under many Western influences both cultural and otherwise. In the prevailing mood of the electorate and a campaign spearheaded by the *Maha Sangha*, S.W.R.D. Bandaranaike was swept into power by a landslide.

In Parliament Prime Minister S.W.R.D. Bandaranakie himself initiated the Official Language Act of 1956. The Bill was supported enthusiastically by the SLFP and allies in Government and the UNP in Opposition. Thus the gunpowder (fifty-fifty) and the fire (Sinhala Only) were put together. The explosion ripped Ceylon apart. Sri Lanka has not yet recovered from that explosion and whether it ever will is largely a matter of conjecture. The first ever Sinhalese-Tamil riots took place when the Official Language Act of 1956 became law. In 1957, it was obvious that a riot at a national level would take place at any moment. It was against that background that Prime Minister S.W.R.D. Bandaranaike and S.J.V. Chelvanayakam began negotiating for some kind of equitable solution. They reached an honourable agreement which was known as the Bandaranaike-Chelvanayakam Pact. That Pact was assailed by the *Maha Sangha* who had brought Bandaranaike to power in 1956. It was also assailed by a section of the UNP led by J.R. Jayewardene who was not a Member of Parliament because he was trounced in Kelaniya in 1956.

On the issue of the reasonable use of Tamil, in the North and in the East, J.R. Jayewardene claimed that Prime Minister S.W.R.D. Bandaranaike was betraying the Sinhalese! Therefore he proposed a protest march from Colombo to Kandy which would culminate at the sacred Temple of the Tooth where they would pray for the Sinhalese!!

The behaviour of Prime Minister S.W.R.D. Bandaranaike was even more revolting. Under relentless pressure, without even consulting S.J.V. Chelvanayakam, he publicly tore up the Bandaranaike-Chelvanayakam Pact in March 1958. He did so in the presence of hundreds of members of the *Maha Sangha* who were occupying the lawns of his private residence in Rosmead Place and had refused to leave till he abrogated the Pact. Two months later, Sinhalese-Tamil riots broke out at the national level. It was fought with savage fury, as reflected in the following citation for the Ceylon Police Medal for Gallantry.

"On the 30th May 1958 at about 4.00 p.m. Inspector D.D.S.K. Ranasinghe and six Policemen encountered a motorised unit of about 600 thugs armed to the teeth on the Kebittigollewa Road at Mahadivulwewa. His jeep was fired upon and his party was attacked by shotguns and sand bottles. Taking cover behind his jeep, Inspector Ranasinghe and his men held this entire mob at bay with rifle fire.

The motorised elements of the mob consisted of eight Land Development vehicles, two Euclids from the Padaviya Scheme, a water bowser, a vehicle with petrol and another with explosives. An examination of these vehicles revealed huge amounts of dynamite in four gallon tins, hand grenades and Molotov cocktails by the hundreds, guns, swords and deadly weapons. These vehicles were manned by about 500 to 600 Land Development labourers. I personally examined these explosives and weapons. Never in my career had the Police come across such a vast quantity of death-dealing explosives.

In the capture of this armed convoy, 71 men were killed by fire in a Police cum Military action whilst 26 others were injured. 393 rioters were taken into custody whilst about 100 escaped.

The plan of this convoy, as revealed by some of the prisoners who were taken into custody, was to attack Anuradhapura by dark where they would be received by supporters in the town who were ready to cut the power lines. Having destroyed the Police Station they were next to kill the Tamil refugees in the protective camp at the Kachcheri. There were over 3,000 Tamils at the time in Anuradhapura.

By this heroic action in combating this army of thugs, Inspector Ranasinghe has prevented the destroying of hundreds of lives and saved Anuradhapura from a blood bath. It is a miracle that this Police party is alive today. Without doubt the achievement of this Inspector can be recorded as the bravest incident of preventive action ever recorded in the history of the Ceylon Police Service.

Therefore I recommend in the strongest possible terms that Inspector D.D.S.K. Ranasinghe be awarded the Ceylon Police Medal for Gallantry, our highest decoration for gallantry, and he be promoted to Gazetted rank on the basis of an exceptional measure.

C.C. Dissanayaka MVO, CPM, OStJ

Acting Inspector-General of Police"

The newly promoted Assistant Superintendent of Police D.D.S.K. Ranasinghe was not the only recipient of the coveted Ceylon Police medal for Gallantry in 1958. The same high honour was bestowed on Bertram

Weerasinghe, Acting Superintendent of Police, North Central Province. Both were Sinhalese Buddhists and both were functioning in strict accordance with the Police Ordinance. The Police Department was indeed proud of these two officers. So was their *Alma Mater*, Royal College.

I had unlimited access to S.J.V. Chelvanayakam, the leader of the Federal Party because his son Chelvanayakam Vaseeheran was my classmate. He was one of my closest friends, and when we were young I was a frequent visitor to his parental home and he to mine.

I well remember S.J.V. Chelvanayakam repeatedly telling me in 1958,

> "Jungle*, you and my son Vaseeheran have been very good friends ever since you both were tiny tots. That way you got to know me. Can you now see why I am advocating Federalism? If I fail to achieve it, sometime in the next generation, the Tamil community will clamour not for Federalism but for a separate State."

I was then a 20 year old undergraduate at the University of Ceylon. I was amazed how accurately S.J.V. Chelvanayakam had predicted the relationship between the Sinhalese and Tamils. His basic thinking was as follows :

1. Before the British unified Ceylon, there was no kingdom that united the entire Island from Point Pedro to Dondra Head.

2. When the Portuguese arrived in the sixteenth century there were basically three Kingdoms :-

   a) Kotte (Sinhalese)
   b) Kandy (Sinhalese)
   c) Yalpanam (Tamils)

3. Culturally the Sinhalese and Ceylon Tamils are two distinct races which for over two thousand years had their own Kingdoms. (The Indian Tamils had no such Kingdom. They were merely plantation labour brought in by the British.)

4. In the modern world the Sinhalese and Tamils can live together in peace and with dignity as two different entities only within a Federal system.

---

* *The famous Police Officer C.C. "Jungle" Dissanayaka was known by that nickname since his days at Royal College. His son, the Author, inherited that nickname during his days at Royal College. Thus the nickname "Jungle" still causes much confusion in Sri Lanka with many confusing father for son and vice versa.*

5. It is a pity that the Tamil community did not clamour for a Federal set up before The Soulbury Commission. Instead the Tamil community clamoured for fifty-fifty which was totally unrealistic.

After the ugly racial riots of 1958, Prime Minister S.W.R.D. Bandaranaike attempted to mollify the Tamils with a Special Provisions Bill which was presented to Parliament in August 1958. By August 1959 nothing had happened and in September 1959 the Prime Minister was assassinated. His eventual successor, his widow Prime Minister Sirima Bandaranaike, shelved the proposal. Much worse, she unleashed a period of blatant discrimination against the Ceylon Tamils. There were hundreds of examples. Two episodes distressed me deeply and personally, because they pertained to two life long friends of mine.

When my class at the Faculty of Science at the University of Ceylon graduated in 1961, five students obtained Firsts. Ganesh Chanmugam (Mathematics) was clearly the winner of the English Universities Scholarship. In practice most of our scholars opted to study at Oxford, Cambridge or London. Ganesh Chanmugam opted to study at Cambridge.

However the Ministry of Education had other plans. They claimed that since 1961 the qualifications to win the English Universities Scholarship was obtaining a First and passing in Sinhala at the GCE (Ordinary Level). Therefore they awarded the scholarship to V.K. Samaranayake (Mathematics) who was the runner-up under normal circumstances. Little did the Ministry of Education know that Chanmugam and Samaranayake were classmates and close friends ever since their days at Royal College. Samaranayake not only turned down the Government scholarship but also castigated the Ministry of Education for having discriminated against his friend Chanmugam. (In professional life Professor V.K. Samaranayake, now Professor of Computer Science at the University of Colombo, has a long and distinguished record of standing up to unnecessary interference of the Government in University life.)

The Ceylon team for the Asian Games in 1962 held in Jakarta, Indonesia, consisted of sixty one athletes, boxers, cyclists, marksmen, swimmers, table tennis players and wrestlers and nineteen officials. Somehow the Captain was not announced and everybody had assumed that it would be Nagalingam Ethirveerasingham of Jaffna, who had won a gold medal at the last Asian Games where I was his room mate and was a finalist at the Olympic Games. Apparently the Government of Ceylon, the principal financier of the team, had other ideas. However every senior member of our team refused to captain the team if the obvious candidate was overlooked. Ethiriveerasingham was finally appointed and went on to win a silver medal, easily the best performer in our team.

Not surprisingly Ethirveerasingham, who had graduated from the University of California, Los Angeles, emigrated to the United States. In the other example, Chanmugam graduated with a First from Cambridge and also emigrated to the United States. He went on to become a much respected Professor. That indeed became the trend in the Tamil community. As such, Ceylon lost some of her best professionals in every conceivable walk of life.

After winning at the General Election of 1965, Prime Minister Dudley Senanayake revived the Special Provisions Bill for Tamils which was in the Order Paper for 1958, and was proposed by Prime Minister S.W.R.D. Bandaranaike. When he presented it in Parliament, the Leader of the Opposition Sirima Bandaranaike protested strongly! She led a march to Parliament and that became unruly. It resulted in the Police opening fire and a member of the *Maha Sangha* being killed. To compound the crisis, the LSSP which so courageously stood for parity of status for Sinhala and Tamil in 1956 did a complete about turn. Shamelessly they spoke against the Special Provisions Bill for Tamil and voted against the Bill!

S.J.V. Chelvanayakam was convinced that the Sinhalese and Tamils could not resolve their differences easily. However the Federal party trusted Prime Minister Dudley Senanayake but not the Sinhalese.

At the General Election of 1970 Prime Minister Sirima Bandaranaike was swept into power by a massive landslide. The coalition of SLFP-LSSP-Communist Party won 117 seats in a Parliament of 160 thus securing a two-thirds majority, a pre-requisite to change The Soulbury Constitution. Very wisely the Prime Minister Sirima Bandaranaike set up a Constituent Assembly to effect Constitutional changes within two years. By the same token Prime Minister Sirima Bandaranaike very unwisely embarked on a suicidal policy of standardising marks to enter our Universities.

The tiny Jaffna peninsula had a population of approximately 50% of all Ceylon Tamils, based on the Censuses of 1901 to 1981. By virtue of these Censuses the Jaffna peninsula has by far the highest density of population in the entire island. On the other hand the Jaffna peninsula has an impoverished soil and has a very low rainfall. There are no rivers anywhere near the Jaffna peninsula. The water table is high but is contaminated with sea water. Thus, even in modern times, tube well irrigation is not possible. Besides in the Jaffna peninsula there is no industrial base and no prospect for oil. Therefore since the nineteenth century parents have invested heavily in education and thereafter employment in the salubrious Sinhalese speaking areas. It is largely a matter of opinion whether the school network in the District of Jaffna or the District of Colombo was better organised. For example, the prestigious schools in Jaffna, St John's College, Chundikuli and Jaffna College, Vaddukodai, earlier called the Vatticotta Seminary, were established in 1823 as against the prestigious schools in Colombo, Royal College (1835) and S. Thomas' College (1851). The Uduvil Girls School, complete with a hostel was set up in 1824. The Catholic school St Patrick's College, Jaffna was set up in 1856 as against St Benedict's College, Kotahena (1865) and St Joseph's College, Colombo (1896). The Methodist schools, Jaffna Central College and Hartley College, Point Pedro were established in 1816 and 1853 respectively as against Wesley College, Colombo in 1874. Likewise the Church Missionary Society of London set up Chundikuli Girls' School in 1896 whereas they set up Ladies' College, Colombo in 1900. The Catholic nuns set up Holy Family Convent, Jaffna in 1861 and Holy Family Convent, Colombo in 1903. When the Colombo Medical College was set up in 1872 approximately half the students were from Jaffna. When the Technical College was established in 1902 and the Colombo University College in 1921, approximately half the students were from Jaffna. This produced some tantalising results. For example, in 1971, 72.6% of our population were Sinhalese and 11.8% were Sri Lanka Tamils whereas the breakdown in the well known professions were as follows :

Professions	Sinhalese	Tamils
Accountants	305	360
Doctors	2,469	1,961
Engineers	716	475
Lawyers	2,815	1,121

(Source : Census of 1971)

These figures reveal to what extent the Tamil community was oriented towards the well established professions for at least two generations and not due to any favouritism as perceived by some Sinhalese. However since 1967, when the GCE (Advanced Level) examinations for even Science subjects, eg. Botany, Chemistry, Physics et cetera were conducted not in English but in Sinhala and Tamil, there were ugly rumours that Tamil students were favoured by Tamil examiners, who were basically

University lecturers. It was no rumour that, Professor E.O.E. Pereira, Vice Chancellor of the University of Ceylon had complained bitterly to Prime Minister Dudley Senanayake, his close friend since their days at Cambridge, that he had serious misgivings on the marking of Tamil scripts of those seeking admission to the Faculty of Engineering. Professor Pereira, who was a much respected Dean of the Faculty of Engineering since its inception in 1950, had an impeccable reputation as a just man who was good to his students and staff alike. Besides he was a Burgher, thus neutral in the conflict between the Sinhalese and the Tamils. Therefore the Prime Minister had no alternative except to have the Government inquire into this scandal. It resulted in one Professor being compelled to resign. Against this unsavoury background, in 1970 the newly elected Sirima Bandaranaike Administration bemoaned that there were too many Tamil students and too few Sinhalese students in our Universities, namely University of Colombo, University of Peradeniya, University of Kelaniya, University of Jayawardenapura and University of Moratuwa.

In 1967, admission to our Universities was strictly on marks, with the interview helping those who were borderline cases but had shone in sports and other extra curricular activities. For example, in 1964, Chandrika Bandaranaike, the daughter of the incumbent Prime Minister, sought admission to the Faculty of Science of the University of Ceylon and failed in her examination. She was clearly University material by virtue of her grades at St Bridget's Convent. Therefore in 1965 she entered, The Aquinas University College run by the Roman Catholics, and in 1967 she left for France to pursue University education on a scholarship awarded by the Government of France. In fairness to her it must be stated that her mother was not the Prime Minister of Ceylon when she was awarded this scholarship.

In 1970 the remedial action the Sirima Bandaranaike Administration should have taken was to set up within five years a University in Jaffna complete with a Faculty of Medicine and a Faculty of Engineering. Then there would be more vacancies for Sinhalese undergraduates in the already existing Universities in and around our major population centres, namely Colombo, Kandy and Moratuwa. Instead the Government immediately opted for the standardising of marks, giving a high cut off point for schools in the Districts of Colombo and Jaffna, on the premise that these two Districts had the best educational schools in the nation. The new policy was not even listed in their election manifesto earlier in 1970.

The youth in the District of Jaffna were outraged and rebelled against the Government. By the end of 1970, a Tamil Youth Front led by Ponnadurai Sathyaseelan was established to fight for their rights. In 1971, it became the more sophisticated and armed Tamil New Tigers (TNT) led by Chetti Thanabalasingham, which caused havoc in the Jaffna peninsula. In the power struggle within the TNT, Velupillai Prabhakaran liquidated all his rivals including Thanabalasingham and set up the dreaded Liberation Tigers of Tamil Eelam (LTTE) in 1975. Prime Minister Sirima Bandaranaike set up a Jaffna Campus of the University of Sri Lanka initially with a Faculty of Science and a Faculty of Arts. That could not contain the rebellion by the youth.

In 1973 while writing *Dudley Senanayake of Sri Lanka* I interviewed S.J.V. Chelvanayakam several times. He repeatedly told me :

> "I am losing my struggle for Federalism because of Bandaranaike, his widow and J.R. Jayewardene (then Leader of the Opposition). I have always told you that if I fail, then the Tamil people will ask not for Federalism but separatism.
>
> "Can you see what the militant Tamil youth are doing? Whereas I advocated peaceful methods such as *satyagraha* and *hartals*, they advocate violence."

In 1975 the LTTE assassinated Mayor Alfred Duraiappah of Jaffna who belonged to the ruling SLFP. According to the LTTE the Mayor was a traitor and therefore Velupillai Prabhakaran himself assassinated him. Thus began the ascendancy of the LTTE.

As the ethnic problem became more and more grave, the Tamil United Liberation Front, a conglomeration of all political parties in the North and East had their first annual Convention in Vaddukodai on May 14th 1976. There they unanimously adopted the following resolution proposed by S.J.V. Chelvanayakam (President of the Federal Party) and G.G. Ponnambalam (President of the Tamil Congress).

> "The First National Convention of the Tamil United Liberation Front meeting at Pannakam, Vaddukodai on this 14th day of May 1976 hereby declares that the Tamils of Sri Lanka, by virtue of their great language, their religions, their separate state over a distinct territory for several centuries until they were conquered by the armed might of the European invaders and, above all by their will to exist as a separate entity ruling themselves in their own territory, are a nation distinct and apart from the Sinhalese.

Therefore this Convention announces to the world that the Republican Constitution of 1972 has made the Tamils a slave nation ruled by the new colonial masters, the Sinhalese, who are using the power they have wrongly usurped to deprive the Tamil nation of its territory, language, citizenship, economic life, opportunities of employment and education, thereby depriving all the attributes of nationhood of the Tamil people;

And taking note of the reservations in relation to its commitment of the setting up of a separate state of Tamil Eelam expressed by the Ceylon Workers Congress as a trade union of the plantation workers, the majority of whom live and work outside the northern and eastern areas.

This Convention resolves that the restoration and reconstitution of the free sovereign, secular socialist state of Tamil Eelam based on the right of self determination inherent to every nation has become inevitable in order to safeguard the very existence of the Tamil nation in the country.

The Convention further declares :

(a) That the State of Tamil Eelam shall consist of the people of the Northern and Eastern Provinces and shall also ensure full and equal rights of citizenship of the State of Tamil Eelam to all Tamil speaking people living in any part of Ceylon and to Tamils of Eelam origin, living in any part of the world who may opt for citizenship of Tamil Eelam;

(b) That the constitution of Tamil Eelam shall be based on the principle of decentralisation so as to ensure the non-domination of any religion or territorial community of Tamil Eelam by any other section;

(c) That in the State of Tamil Eelam, caste shall be abolished and the observance of the pernicious practice of untouchability or inequality of any type based on birth shall be totally eradicated and its observance in any form punished by law;

(d) That Tamil Eelam shall be a secular State giving equal protection and assistance to all religions to which the people of the State may belong;

(e) That Tamil shall be the language of the State but the rights of Sinhalese speaking minorities in Tamil Eelam to education and transaction of business in their language shall be protected on a reciprocal basis with the Tamil speaking minorities in the Sinhala State:

(f) That Tamil Eelam shall be a socialist State wherein the exploitation of man by man shall be forbidden, the dignity of labour shall be recognized, the means of production and distribution shall be subject to public ownership and control while permitting private enterprise in these branches within limits prescribed by law, economic development shall be on the basis of socialist planning and there shall be a ceiling on the total wealth that any individual or family may acquire.

This Convention directs the Action Committee of the Tamil United Liberation Front to formulate a plan of action and launch without undue delay the struggle for winning the sovereignty and freedom of the Tamil nation.

And this Convention calls upon the Tamil nation in general and the Tamil youth in particular to come forward to throw themselves fully into the sacred fight for freedom and to flinch not till the goal of a sovereign socialist State of Eelam is reached."

I well remember meeting S.J.V. Chelvanayakam in mid-1976 while on home leave. Again he told me :

"Jungle, I told you several times that if I fail with Federalism, then my community will opt for separatism. What I never dreamt was that it will happen in my lifetime.

"Please understand that G.G. Ponnambalam and I have come together. It is the two of us, not Velupillai Prabhakaran, who sponsored the Vaddukodai Resolution. However both of us are now terminally ill. It will be Velupillai Prabhakaran and his LTTE who will attempt to usher in the State of Tamil Eelam. To say the least, non-violent methods are alien to them."

That was the last of the many long conversations I had with S.J.V. Chelvanayakam at his residence in Alfred House Gardens, Colombo-3. He was dying when I met him for the very last time in 1977, in Jaffna. His voice was hardly audible and he was emaciated. However, he was still defiant.

"Jungle, I hear you are writing a book on J.R. Please write that J.R. will win by a landslide, also that the Tamil people in the North and the East will never allow him to rule Sri Lanka.

"Our people created so many problems for S.W.R.D. They will ferment even more trouble for J.R."

S.J.V. Chelvanayakam slipped into a coma the following day and died two days later. I remained behind in Jaffna to attend his funeral, which drew the largest crowd seen in Jaffna in living memory.

The General Election in 1977 was indeed crucial for the nation. Prime Minister J.R. Jayewardene set up a world record by winning 143 seats in a Parliament of 168 seats. He campaigned to abolish the socialist frolics of Prime Minister Sirima Bandaranaike which had ruined our nation. In the North, the TULF which campaigned on the basis of adopting the Vaddukodai Resolution, won all 14 seats. They won a staggering 68.3% of the popular vote which was substantially more than the massive poll of the UNP in any of the seven Sinhala speaking Provinces. In that there was a special message to the Sinhalese. On the other hand, in the Eastern Province the TULF won only three out of ten seats and a popular vote of 33.1% whereas the UNP won five seats and 41.1% of the popular vote. In that there was a special message for the Ceylon Tamils.

An economy based on free enterprise was introduced in 1977 and has thrived since then. As such, 1977 was a watershed in the evolution of our nation. Whatever people may say of the language policy of J.R. Jayewardene, millions justifiably pay tribute to him as President of Sri Lanka for his economic programmes, namely the open market economy, the massive development projects notably the Mahaweli Project and the Free Trade Zones.

I served him as an Ambassador continuously for his entire tenure of office of twelve years. Periodically he sent for me whether I was stationed in Indonesia, in our Ministry of Foreign Affairs or in Egypt. Whenever he spoke to me of our ethnic problem, he prefaced his question as follows :

"So 'Jungle' according to you J.R. Jayewardene cannot solve our ethnic problem?"

"Excellency, you are absolutely correct. Your name is associated with the slogan *Sinhala Only*. Such a person cannot solve this problem."

"Who in your opinion can?"

"Excellency, The late Prime Minister Dudley Senanayake could have but I cannot think of anybody in contemporary Sri Lanka."

He then proceeded to ask me some complex questions about our vexed ethnic problem.

As the years rolled by, the hatred the Tamils had for the Sinhalese and *vice versa* grew beyond manageable proportions. The first crisis was during the elections to the District Development Councils (DDC) in 1981. The DDC were set up by President Jayewardene as a first step towards devolution of power. Therefore much importance was attached to the DDC elections in Jaffna which was welcomed by the TULF. The UNP also filed their list of candidates. The LTTE ridiculed the very concept of the DDCs. During the run up to the elections the LTTE opened fire and killed three Policemen, from the large contingent sent from Anuradhapura, Colombo and Kurunegala. That night the magnificent Public Library in Jaffna, perhaps the finest in Sri Lanka, went up in smoke. It was largely believed that this was a crude retaliation by the Police, some of whom knew no better. The intelligentsia both in Sri Lanka and abroad were appalled and castigated the Government of Sri Lanka for this crime, which was publicly condemned by President Jayewardene himself. Many Cabinet Ministers who led the UNP campaign in Jaffna took some of their ruffians to Jaffna because their law abiding supporters refused to risk their lives and limbs in the violence stricken Jaffna peninsula. During the DDC elections ballot boxes suddenly disappeared, a phenomenon unheard of in Sri Lanka since Independence!

Thus the authority of the Government in the Jaffna peninsula was very much in doubt. The LTTE, with their cadres trained in India and Lebanon, was gaining in strength daily, the TULF was losing strength daily and the President was negotiating only with the TULF. It was a matter of time before there was a Civil War.

At the Presidential Election of October 1982, President J.R. Jayewardene was expected to win by a landslide. His achievements pertaining to the economy were indeed impressive. The open economy supplating the socialist frolics of the previous regime, the accelerated Mahaweli project, the Free Trade Zone earned kudos for him. 1977 was justifiably a watershed in the economy and President Jayewardene was the architect of all these magnificent successes. He won with a huge majority.

After his landslide victory in 1982 he did even worse. He said it was unsafe to hold a General Election because there was a Naxalite threat to Sri Lanka. Nobody, not even our Police or our Intelligence, had ever heard of such a threat. The Cabinet was never informed of any such threat. Only President Jayewardene knew all about it! Because of this mysterious Naxalite threat the President wanted the General Election cancelled and instead to have a Referendum to extend the lifetime or Parliament from six to twelve years. He won that Referendum and to ensure it he wanted the Government Parliamentary Group to submit to him undated letters of resignation. The Naxalite threat disappeared as soon as the Referendum was won!

In the meantime on the ethnic issue, the nation was drifting towards a Civil War the combatants being the Government of Sri Lanka and the Tamil terrorist movements.

Chapter II

THE TERRORIST MOVEMENTS

On May 22nd 1972, when Sri Lanka became a Republic, the militant Tamil youth rose in defiance against the new Constitution, causing convulsions in the Jaffna peninsula. One year earlier the JVP, the militant Sinhalese youth, had risen in defiance against the Government and their insurrection shook the nation to its very foundation.

The militant youth, both Sinhala and Tamil, were educated, being beneficiaries of the free education system and were unemployed, being victims of a stagnant economy. To the Sinhala militant youth the panacea for all evil was a Marxist State even more radical than that envisaged by the well established Marxist parties in Sri Lanka. To the militant Tamil youth the panacea was a State of Tamil Eelam. In their radicalism the youth, both Sinhala and Tamil, chose modalities outside the framework of democracy. They both claimed that within such a framework it was impossible for them to obtain any redress let alone salvation.

The militant youth in the Jaffna peninsula were raised in an environment of continuous confrontation with the Government. Since 1956, the boycott of schools, the picketing of Government offices, hoisting black flags and performing *satyagraha* was a way of life for them. It happened year in year out except during the three years 1965-68 when the Federal Party was a component of the Dudley Senanayake Administration. For generations, the Jaffna youth was docile, however since 1956 they became progressively defiant. As the possibility of redress for grievances receded still further, in recent years the opinion in the Tamil community gradually gravitated towards secession. In their radicalism the militant youth clamoured for secession with recourse to terrorism. In fact the first terrorist to be taken into custody was Ponnadurai Sathyaseelan, President of the Unemployed Graduates' Union. He was arrested on February 23rd, 1973 by Sub-Inspector A. E. Perampalam of the. Criminal Investigation Department of the Police (CID).

Sathyaseelan confessed to a conspiracy to assassinate the Minister of Post and Telecommunications, C. Kumarasuriar, around the time Sri Lanka became a Republic. He and Mavi Senathirajah, President of the Tamil Youth Front (TYF), had met at the cycle repair shop, with three other conspirators. They decided to manufacture hand bombs in the privacy of the Kondalady Vairavar Temple and subsequently to attack the visiting Minister with them. Somehow the Temple authorities got wind of this and tipped off the Police but Sathyaseelan and others had already fled.

Thereafter Mavi Senathirajah decided to tamper with high tension electric towers with a view to plunging the entire Jaffna peninsula into total darkness on Republic Day. He, Sathyaseelan and Kasi Anandan accordingly approached Jeyam, a former employee of the Ceylon Electricity Board, with a view to forcibly collapsing the high tension electric towers at Murungandy. On May 21st 1972, they together with Vellupillai Subramaniam alias Maniam, went by car to Mankulam juction, walked two miles to Murugandy and removed the nuts and bolts in several towers. Somehow they did not collapse immediately but did so a few days later thus having the desired effect on Jaffna. Maniam was eventually arrested by Inspector T. I. Bastianpillai of the CID.

About that time Sathyaseelan decided that V. Kumarakulasingham Chairman, Village Committe of Nallur, and a supporter of the Government should be exterminated. The task was assigned to Sivarajah, Sabaratnam and Thanpalasingham, all from the TYF. Sivarajah and Sabaratnam hijacked a taxi in Tinneveli and when the taxi driver S. Ulaganathan, resisted they shot him dead and put his body into the luggage compartment. Then they proceeded to Nallur, entered the home of Kumarakulasingham and shot him at point black range. Thereafter the taxi with the body of its former driver was consigned to the flames.

On September 17th 1972 Velupillai Prabhakaran led a bomb attack at a carnival held at the Duraiappah Stadium. It was an attempt to assassinate Mayor Alfred Duraiappah of Jaffna a staunch supporter of the Sirima Bandaranaike Administration. The following month Prabhakaran unsuccessfully led a raid on a commercial establishment in Stanley Road, Jaffna.

Then Sathyaseelan decided to murder A. Thiyagarajah. Mavi Senathirajah provided him with two 38 revolvers and ammunition. Sathyaseelan, Jeevarajah, Niranjan and Boopathy Balavedivetkaran had some target practice in the Visvamadu forest before leaving for Colombo. The plan was for Boopathy and Jeevarajah to enter the home of Thiyagarajah and for the latter to shoot him dead at point blank range. The shooting at point black range was not fatal due to poor marksmanship. Following their return to Jaffna they were all arrested by Inspector Bastianpillai and Sub-Inspector Perampalam. Shortly thereafter the cycle shop of Amerasingham was raided and several packets containing chemicals to manufacture explosives were removed.

The Tamil United Front (TUF) a conglomeration of all Tamil Political Parties in the North and the East, protested from public plarforms at what they called 'the arbitrary arrest of youth' and called Inspector Bastinapillai and Sub-Inspector Perampalam traitors. From the same platform the youth leaguers threatened these two Police Officers with death. A few months later at the annual session of the Federal Party held at Mallakam, A. Amirthalingam their General Secretary exhorted the Tamil youth to rise up against the Government. He said that all he could offer them immediately were assaults by the Police, threats by the Army, jail, torture and even death but eventually, the birth of the State of Tamil Eelam.

By 1974, 41 TUF youth leaguers were detained at Welikade Jail under Emergency regulations. However violence erupted again when Prime Minister Sirima Bandarnaike was due to visit Jaffna on October 5th, 1974. For nearly a month the TUF campaigned to boycott the visit. Just before the Prime Minister arrived the Tamil New Tigers, a militant group within the Tamil Youth Front led by Chetti Thanabalasingham systematically unleashed violence. Hand bombs were lobbed into the jeep of the Kankesanturai Police Station. Dynamite was ignited in the home of V. Ponnambalam, a member of the Communist Party and the interpreter of the Prime Minister during her forthcoming visit. Dynamite was ignited and thrown into the Chenkathanai Railway Station causing extensive damage, in an attempt to assassinate Mayor Alfred Duraiappah. Bombs were exploded in the Grand Bazar, Jaffna, causing more panic than damage and CTB buses set on fire with impunity. Shortly after the return of the Prime Minister to Colombo, explosives were detonated in the office of the Deputy High Commissioner for Sri Lanka in Madras and the Maha Bodhi Headquarters in Madras. Among those who were convicted was a youth leaguer Raju Kandeepan, son of A. Amirthalingam. In rapid succession dangerous chemicals were stolen from the laboratory of Urumpirai Hindu College and Rs. 91, 000 stolen from the Multi-Purpose Co-operative Society of Tellippalai, in raids led by Prabhakaran.

On January 3rd 1975 several TUF youth leaguers including Ponnadurai Sathyaseelan detained in Colombo under Emergency regulations were released to appease the TUF. It was timed for the by-election at Kankesanturai. They returned to Jaffna by train and crowd of several thousands led by S. J. V. Chelvanayakam and A. Amirthalingam gave them a heroes' welcome at the Railway Station. An even bigger reception awaited Mavi Senathirajah, the President of the TUF Youth League, when he returned to Jaffna in like manner.

Ever since the youth leaguers were released from detention in January 1975, brazen disregard for the law became a way of life in the Jaffna district with robberies of Banks and Co-operative establishments being rampant. With Sathyaseelan deciding to emigrate and Mavi Senathirajah turning out to be a moderate, the Tamil New Tigers became the dominant element in the quest of a separate State of Tamil Eelam. The other radical elements joined the Tamil New Tigers in May 1975 to form the Liberation Tigers of Tamil Eelam (LTTE). Vellupillai Prabhakaran exterminated all rivals to become the leader of the LTTE.

The LTTE began their activities with military training in the Vavuniya district in the farms of the Tamil Refugee and Rehabilitation Organisation (Those farms in due course came under the management of the Gandhian Movement). Though fanatics and callow youth, they themselves realized their limitations in being unable to shoot accurately even at point blank range.

The training had just commenced when Prabhakaran decided to exterminate Mayor Alfred Duraiappah who was a thorn in the flesh of the radical elements. On July 27th 1975, when the Mayor customarily visited the Krishna Kovil in Ponnalai he fired at him at close range. The assailants then overpowered the chauffeur and fled in his car, while the Mayor lay dead in a poul of blood.

This episode gave much publicity to the LTTE in general and Prabhakaran in particular.

After completing their basic training, the Tiger Movement turned their attention to the robbing of banks, their principal source of financing, and attacking the police, the principal threat to their existence. In March 1976 in a daring raid the People's Bank at Puttur was robbed of Rs. 668, 000 in cash and jewellery. In rapid succession followed raids on the Multi Purpose Co-operative Societies in Puloly and Madagal. The haul in the former was Rs. 350,000 and in the latter, chemicals sufficient to manufacture 30,000 hand bombs.

A Police team consisting, amongst others, of Inspector Pathmanathan, Constable Karunanidhi and two Constables bearing the same name of

Shanmuganathan were detailed to investigate into the robbery at Puloly. Of them PC Karunanidhi was also having a significant role in the Duraiappah murder case. PC Karunanidhi was shot dead in Mavadipuram on February 14th 1977, the two PCs named Shanmuganathan were shot dead at Inuvil on May 18th 1977. Inspector Pathmanathan narrowly missed death when explosives thrown at his car blew off two doors. An attempt was also made on the life of Inspector Kumaru, Personal Assistant to the Superintendent of Police, Jaffna, who was handling many confidential matters pertaining to these investigations.

With more and more Tigers being trained in Vavuniya, they became even more daring. Early in 1978, Uma Maheshwaran and a few of his associates visited the home of K. Kanagaratnam (TULF—Pottuvil) in Kollupitiya, shortly after the MP had crossed over to the UNP. They shot at him at point blank range. *A coup d'grace* was fired into his head when he was lying on the ground writhing in pain and bleeding profusely from a bullet wound in his chest. Miraculously the MP did not die. By another miracle the assailants got away by taxi while people in the neighbourhood including me, rushed to the scene on hearing the sound of gunfire followed by the wailing of a woman.

Inspector Bastianpillai and Sub-Inspector Perampalan who were investigating into the attempted murder of Kanagaratnam, were tipped off that Uma Maheswaran was hiding in a farm in Murunkan, not far from the Roman Catholic shrine at Madhu. According to this confidential information, the farm was in the middle of the jungle which is not unusual in the Vavuniya district. On April 7th 1978, Inspector Bastianpillai, Sub-Inspector Peramapalam and Sergeant Balasingham were on the offensive. In Murunkan as they came near a watch tower of the Tigers perched high in the trees and well concealed by the foliage, Uma Maheswaran and other terrorists opened fire killing Inspector Bastianpillai and Sergeant Balasingham and injuring Sub-Inspector Perampalam. The body of Inspector Bastianpillai was then mutilated savagely. Sub-Inspector Perampalam while escaping, fell into a well and was shot dead by Sellakili a notorious terrorist. Thereafter the terrorists killed the chauffer of the Police vehicle and set it on fire having removed the radio equipment.

In May 1978, the Tigers finally shot and killed Inspector Pathmanathan at his residence in Jaffna. In June Inspector Kumaru, who had just retired from the Police, was shot dead in broad daylight at the Velvettiturai Bazaar. Four days later A. Arulampalam, former MP for Nallur, was shot at but escaped without injury. In July there were four daring robberies, two from CTB buses, one from a van when a traveling salesman was robbed of Rs. 15,000 at gun point from the Thinnaveli Post Office. In September a CTB bus was hijacked and set on fire; then followed a robbery of school teachers' salaries in Point Pedro.

On September 7th 1978, some Tigers traveled on the Air Ceylon flight from Kankesanturai to Ratmalana. On board they fixed a time bomb to detonate approximately half an hour after the aircraft landed at Ratmalana. The aircraft was due to be ferried across to the hangar at the Katunayake International Airport from Ratmalana and the plan was to create a spectacular explosion over the City of Colombo and chaos on the ground with the falling debris. Providence however stalled this wicked plan. The crew decided to delay their departure and when the explosion took place and completely gutted the aircraft, it was still on the parking apron.

Shortly thereafter, a taxi was hijacked, the driver put into the luggage compartment and the vehicle used to rob the Kopay Multi Purpose Co-operative Society of Rs. 30,000. On December 5th, 1978, the Tigers carried out their biggest raid hitherto in the Jaffna peninsula. They raided the People's Bank at Nallur and robbed over Rupees one million in cash. Police Constables Kingsley Perera and Satchithanadan who were on guard duty were shot dead and another Policeman injured in the exchange of fire. In March 1979, the Tigers waylaid a bus at Killinochi and robbed mail bags containing Rs. 20,000.

While the Rule of Law was thus negated, it was indeed significant that the leadeship of the TULF said absolutely nothing. No sympathy whatsoever was extended to the families of the dead Policemen and nobody of consequence from the TULF attended their funerals. Equally disturbing was that none of these murders, attempted murders or serious crimes were solved. No culprits were apprehended as little or no evidence was forthcoming.

Of the few informants, S. A. Emmanuel of Chankanai, Thaadi Thangarajah of Kondavil and A. Krishnagopal of Velvettiturai were shot dead by the Tigers. T. Poopalasingham of Chunnakam and A. Sivarajah of Thondamannar gave vital information pertaining to the Avro incident and the Nallur bank robbery respectively. They were the next victims of the execution squads.

Early in 1979 the Tigers shot and killed PC Gnanasamabandan of the CID who was investigating into the Avro incident, PC Sivanesan who was investigating into the murder of Inspector Kumaru, and Inspector Guruswamy who gave evidence against the Tiger Movement before the

Sansoni Commission. A few months later S. Swarnarajah and his wife who were due to leave for the Middle East were killed in Thondamannar as suspected informants of the Army.

Friend and foe alike agree that President Jayewardene was by nature cautious and took a long time to arrive at a policy decision, because he painstakingly weighed the pros and the cons. Since his assumption of office as Head of Government, first as Prime Minister and later as President, his carefully thought out strategy was to evolve an honorable political solution to the Tamil problem within the framewaork of a unitary State. This would have entailed weaning the TULF away from separatism. That was no easy task especially after the TULF had polled over 68% of the votes in the Northern Province and had won all 14 seats in that Province. Necessarily, a solution would take time and already negotiations for the District Development Councils were taking an inordinately long time.

However it was impossible for President Jayawardene to be patient any more with the terrorist movements, whether it be an organization within or without the TULF. He therefore hand picked Brigadier T. I. Weeratunge, Chief of Staff of the Army, and sent him to Jaffna with the following mandate:

> "It will be your duty to eliminate, in accordance with the laws of this land, the menace of terrorism in all its forms from the Island and more specifically from the Jaffna District. I will place at your disposal all resources of the State. I earnestly request all law abiding citizens to give their co-operation to you. This task has to be performed by you and completed before 31st December, 1979."

Brigadier "Bull" Weeratunge had a good reputation as a field commander. He was trained at the Royal Military College at Sandhurt and the National Defence College at New Delhi. In 1979 his appointment as Commander of Security Forces in the North carried powers which had hitherto never been given to a Military Officer. He superceded all civilian officials in the North including the Government Agent. Besides, the newly enacted Prevention of Terrorism Act with wide powers of search, arrest and detention, immeasurably increased the authority of the Army and Police.

In a few months it was more than evident, that the strategy adopted by Brigadier Weeratunge worked. There were no more murders by the Tigers and even the incidents caused by them decreased sharply and then were obviated altogether. In 1980 the situation was just as stable and the Brigadier reverted to his substantive post at Army Headquarters in

Colombo. Thereafter the complex apparatus of the Security Force Headquarters in Jaffna was whittled down and later dismantled altogether.

In the meantime the terrorist movements went into hiding or took refuge in Tamil Nadu in India. They were not so foolhardly as to have taken on a fully armed brigade. They recognized their limitations in being trained in Vavuniya and hence sought training facilities abroad. Besides, they had their own problems.

The Marxist leanings of Uma Maheswaran who was trained by a Marxist-oriented guerilla organization in Lebanon and his subsequent weakness for women annoyed the abstemious Prabhakaran. These considerations resulted in Uma Maheswaran breaking away from the Liberation Tigers of Tamil Eelam (LTTE) and forming the Peoples Liberation Organisation of Tamil Eelam (PLOTE). Thereafter, 16 of his associates left for training in Lebanon. The training was arranged by a London based Marxist and Eelam supporter, Eliathamby Ratnasabapathy.

In the meantime, another component of the terrorist movement, the Tamil Eelam Liberation Organisation (TELO) led by Thangadorai and Kuttimani was based in Madras. Both were well known smugglers and with their knowledge of the underworld of Tamil Nadu they arranged for training facilities there. In a clever manouvre they recruited retired instructors in the Indian Army who were Tamils. Well knowing that their pensions were small, they paid them handsomely and simultaneously aroused Tamil sentiments in them.

In this manner, 46 Tigers including Thangadurai, Kuttimani, Jegan and "Oberoi" Thevan from the TELO, Prabhakaran, Charles Anthony alias Seelan, and Sellakili from the LTTE were trained in guerilla warfare in Tamil Nadu. It must be emphasized that this training was done surreptitiously and without the knowledge of the Government of India and the Government of the State of Tamil Nadu.

About this time Eliathamby Ratnasabapathy was instrumental in forming the Marxist-oriented Eelam Revolutionary Organization of Students (EROS) which established offices in London, Madras and finally in Jaffna. Others formed the General Union of Eelam Students (GUES) which also established offices in London, Madras and Jaffna.

The terrorist movements showed their newly acquired professional skill with two daring robberies in January 1981. The LTTE under Prabhakaran and TELO under Thangadorai teamed up to rob a pawn broker in Kurumbachitty of nearly Rs. 1,000,000. A few days later in another combined operation the LTTE and TELO raided the People's Bank at Neerveli and robbed it of over Rs. 8,000,000. It was hitherto the biggest bank robbery in the history of Sri Lanka and resulted amongst other things in the entire Board of Directors of the People's Bank tendering their resignations.

The first victim of the professionally trained terrorists of the PLOTE led by Uma Maheswaran was R. Balasundaram, a UNP stalwart from Kilinochchi. He was shot dead towards the end of 1980. The PLOTE was quiet till May 1981 when the election campaign for the District Development Councils had gathered momentum. On May 25th 1981 the leading UNP candidate, A. Thiagarajah, former Tamil Congress MP for Vaddukkodai, was shot dead with a view to disrupting the DDC elections. On May 31st, 1981 the day before the election, the PLOTE shot and killed two Police Constables who were on patrol at Nachimakovilady. It incensed the Police contingents brought in from other districts for election duty as such violence was altogether strange to them. They went on the rampage and amongst other things set on fire the splendid Public Library in Jaffna. The PLOTE thus achieved their objective of disrupting the DDC elections. In July 1981 Sunderam, the deputy of Uma Maheswaran led a daring raid on the Annakottai Police Station, in the quest of arms and ammunition. The raid was successful and casualties included two Policemen dead and two more injured. In rapid succession followed a raid on the Watakachchi farm to rob a jeep.

In October 1981 Brigadier Weeratunge was promoted Major General and assumed duties as Commander of the Army. That week the LTTE ambushed an Army jeep on the Kankesanturai Road near Jaffna and killed two soldiers. They were the first Servicemen to be killed by the Tigers. The following week the PLOTE carried out a lightening raid on the People's Bank at Kilinochchi when the Armed Forces and Police were deployed in the Anuradhapura area, which Queen Elizabeth was visiting. The loot was a staggering Rs. 40 million.

Thus Tiger activity in 1981 surpassed its peak performance of 1978 and 1979. To the Army and the Police two aspects were obvious. The Tigers were professionally trained terrorists and were short of arms, hence they took away even superannuated shotguns during their raid on the Annakottai Police Station.

Mercifully the Eelam Movement also had its serious set backs in 1981. In October a routine Navy patrol swooped on a launch about to leave from the Manalkadu beach. On the beach were three well known smugglers Thangadurai, Kuttimani and Jegan, the entire leadership of TELO. Following their arrest 24 of their professionally trained terrorists were arrested. Kuttimani was charged with the murder of Police Constable Sivanesan at Valvettiututai in 1979.

The trial attracted much publicity and when the death sentence was passed Kuttimani attempted to play the role of a martyr. Addressing the Court from the dock he said

> "After I am hanged I wish to donate my eyes, so that though my body is dead at least my eyes will see the birth of the new State of Tamil Eelam for which I have sacrified my life." Perhaps this was a propaganda effort inspired by his TULF lawyers. In real life Kuttimani was anything but a hero. When arrested he attempted to commit suicide on Manalkadu beach. In jail he squealed, resulting in many of his associates being arrested. Besides he was convicted on his own confession.

The TELO, bereft of leadership and professionally trained terrorists for all intents and purposes ceased operations. However they indulged in intensive propaganda, to give a halo of martyrdom to Kuttimani who incidentally was not executed but had his sentence commuted to imprisonment for life. Late in 1982, a feeble effort was made to resuscitate the TELO. Two murders were attempted. Both were amateurish attempts reminiscent of the pre–1979 era.

Thus ended the role of the most ruthless of all Tigers. The TELO had a hallmark, to kill the victims with a bullet in the head at close range. They had struck terror in the Jaffna peninsula and were merciless on Police informants. They were responsible for the deaths of Emmanuel, Thadi Thangarajah, Krishnagopal, Swarnarajah and his wife. They were just as severe on the Police having murdered Inspectors Pathmanathan, Kumaru and Guruswamy and Constables Gnanasambandan and Sivasesan.

In November 1981, the Army systematically arrested 12 hard terrorists of the PLOTE. In February 1982 a Navy patrol boat arrested Anton Ampalagam, a key figure in the PLOTE. Ampalagam squealed and it resulted in many of those who has taken part in the raid on the Annakottai Police Station, Wattakachchi farm and Kilinochchi Bank robbery, being arrested. About that time the Army opened fire and killed Karthan and the LTTE executed Sunderam, who ranked second only to Uma Maheswaran in the hierarchy of the PLOTE. As the hostility between the LTTE and the PLOTE increased, Uma Maheswaran fled to India and took with him his surviving lieutenants Somasundaram Satheswaran alias Kannan and Thurairajah Sivanesawaran alias Kakka.

Of the terrorist groups barring the LTTE, the PLOTE had the highest casualties. The survivours were restricted to periodic forays with amateurism of the pre–1979 vintage. However their destructive nature was reflected in 1982 when they killed a soldier at the Kurikatuwam Ferry, a Policemen in Vaddukkodai, an informant at Chulipuram, robbed the Victoria College, Chulipuram, and attacked three examination centers. At Kokuvil they were truly embarrassed publicly when a lone Police recruit guarding a G.C.E. (Ordinary Level) examination center opened fire causing the terrorists to flee.

With the fluction of time the PLOTE became more and more subdued and confined their activity to the District of Vavuniya which was the power base of Uma Maheswaran. Operating from the farms of the Gandhian Movement they carried out a series of robberies of weapons in that district resulting in Army patrols being strengthened.

In direct contrast, the LTTE, the parent body of the terrorist movement and the one favoured most by the TULF, was gaining in strength. On the one hand their principal rival PLOTE was reduced to a shambles, on the other their leadership and the professionally trained cadres were intact.

The leadership of the LTTE consisted of Prabhakaran, Charles Anthony alias Seelan and Chelvanayatam alias Sellakili in that order. They had over 20 terrorists trained in India and an armoury of 4 machine guns, 12 rifles, 21 repeater shot guns, 3 shot guns and 2 revolvers.

In March 1982, Prabhakaran left for India to exterminate his sworn enemy Uma Maheswaran. They exchanged fire in Pondi Bazaar, Madras, resulting in Uma Maheswaran, Kannan and Kakka of the PLOTE and Prabhakaran and Ragawan of the LTTE being arrested by the Tamil Nadu Police. It was indeed significant that A. Yogeswaran M.P. (TULF-Jaffna) and Chelvanayakam Chandrahasan, son of the late leader of the TULF, both lawyers by profession, rushed to Madras to defend them. They interceded with the Government of Tamil Nadu requesting that the arrested terrorists not be extradited to Sri Lanka.

In view of these developments the LTTE was subdued for a few months. They became operational again in July 1982, when they ambushed and killed a Police patrol at Nelliaddy. Then they stepped up their activity with an attempt to blow up a Navy convoy at the Ponnalai causeway. That exercise was strategically timed for the visit of President Jayewardene to Jaffna, during the campaign of the Presidential election of 1982.

While the terrorist movement thus gathered momentum within Sri Lanka, another vicious movement gathered momentum abroad. It was the vilification of Sri Lanka by overseas Tamils carried out via the mass media and via the grapevine.

Since the 1958 racial riots there was an exodus of Tamil professionals. As the years rolled by they became respected citizens in foreign countries. Abroad they enjoyed a standard of living they could not dream of in Sri Lanka but in their hearts there was a love-hate relationship with Sri Lanka. On the one hand they hankered for the land of their birth, on the other they looked upon themselves as having been driven out of the land of their birth. In reality they had left of their own volition due to acute problems of insecurity.

When Jaffna became restless with the adoption of the first Republican Constitution in 1972 and the mood changed from the clamour for federalism to secession, the overseas Tamils launched their publicity campaign to discredit Sri Lanka. Simultaneously they began to finance Tamil organizations in Sri Lanka.

Initially the propaganda directed by the overseas Tamils was on grounds of racial discrimination. The charge was indeed valid during the S. W. R. D. Bandaranaike Administration and the Sirima Bandaranaike Administration of 1960–65. However during the Dudley Senanayake Administration of 1965–70 it was obviated almost altogether. The position was nearly as good after Prime Minister Sirima Bandaranaike was returned to power in 1970. However the overseas Tamils were oblivious to recent changes in Sri Lanka and became obstreperous.

A cursory gance at the Census of 1971 would reveal that 72.6% of all Sri Lankan were Sinhalese and 11.8% were Sri Lanka Tamils. However the breakdown in the professions were as follows:

	Sinhalese (%)	***Tamils (%)***
Civil Servants	71.41	8.3
Doctors	50.1	39.0
Engineers	59.2	39.6
Lawyers	68.3	36.2
Accountants	48.1	48.2

Thus there was hardly any evidence of discrimination. However the strong objection of the overseas Tamils, was valid about the standardization of marks at the University Entrance Examination.

In 1970 the Sirima Bandaranaike Administration brought in a system of weightage of marks whereby students, be they Sinhala, Tamil or otherwise, from the districts that were underdeveloped were given preferential treatment in admission to Universities. For instance students from the Mullaitivu District, which is Tamil speaking, or the Monaragala District which is Sinhala speaking, needed fewer marks than those in the Jaffna or Colombo districts to gain admission to any University. This system proved both workable and acceptable. Then in 1971, standardization of marks was introduced to the Sinhala and Tamil media which resulted in blatant discrimination against the Tamil students. In 1977, Prime Minister J. R. Jayewardene scrapped this system because it was unjust.

Following the adoption of the Vaddukkodai resolution in 1976, the strategy of the overseas Tamils was to damage the good name of Sri Lanka through a three pronged attack directed politically, economically and at the Human Rights record. To achieve this, Eelam lobbies were set up in every Western capital and in every major city in the West which had a Tamil population.

Following his magnificient victory in 1977 when Prime Minister J. R. Jayewardene, as he then was, made a strenuous effort to maximize foreign aid for the many development projects he had in mind, the Eelam lobby stepped up its campaign of vilification. In the aftermath of the racial riots of 1977, in the first month of the J. R. Jayewardene Administration, they disseminated horror stories to blacken the image of the new Government. Suffice it is to state that the foreign aid received by the J. R. Jayewardene Administration was unprecedented since Independence and was the highest amongst the Third World nations on a per capita basis. By the same token the campaign of vilification had no impact on foreign investments in Sri Lanka. From next to nothing it increased to Rs. 314 million in 1978, to Rs. 1,748 million in 1979, to Rs. 3,413 million in 1980. Tourism likewise made a steady growth from 103,204 visitors in 1975 to 153,665 in 1977 and 321,780 in 1980.

On the other hand the Eelam lobby was successful in damaging the reputation of Sri Lanka in the sensitive field of Human Rights, with the skillful manipulation of the media.

Whenever the Police and the Army cracked down on the terrorist movement there was a wave of horror stories about Sri Lanka. In direct contrast, when the Tigers killed Policemen or Servicemen, altogether 37 were killed between 1977 and 1983, there was not a word in the foreign media.

Such lopsided publicity did have the desired effect from the viewpoint of the Eelam lobbies and several Non-Governmental Organisations began to finance Tamil organizations. For instance the Gandhian Movement whose farms in the Vanuniya district were used to train terrorists, received generous assistance from NOVIB (Netherlands), Christian Aid (UK), Bread for the World (Federal Republic of Germany), NORAD (Norway) amongst others. Such overseas benefactors were supporting this Movement, quite oblivious to their nefarious activities. They naively believed that the "Gandhian" Movement stood for the principles of Mahatma Gandhi, the Apostle of Non-Violence, and were engaged in a programme of village settlement schemes, pre-school projects and distribution of milk food.

For instance NOVIB donated a jeep, 4 vans, salaries for 100 employees, 350 tons of milk food and gave a grant of Rs. 150,000/- to develop the farms at Palamoddai and Kallaru. Quite clearly their motivation was altruistic.

However that did not apper to be the motivation of Dr. S. Rajasunderam, General-Secretary of the "Gandhiyan" Movement who wrote to various Eelam lobbies abroad as follows:

> "Israel is the showpiece of Western ideals in the Middle East. Eelam can be showpiece of the ideals of Mahatma Gandhi in the Indian Ocean. In terms of local and Indian politics this developments is most appropriate."

In 1981, the "Gandhian" Movement received Rs. 55,000 from Christian Aid and in 1982 the contribution was increased to Rs. 453,000. Bread for the World donated Rs. 1,650,000 in 1981 and Rs. 2,279,000 in 1982. With such financing the "Gandhian" Movement which began in 1976 in Vanuniya spread its activities to the Batticaloa and Trincomalee districts. In the meantime Era Vasudevan, a manager of a "Gandhian" farm, became the leader of the TELO group of Tigers in Batticaloa and Sandadiya, the Rehabilitation Officer of the "Gandhian" Movement, became a key figure in the PLOTE of Uma Maheswaran. Besides, in 1981, S. A. David, President of the "Gandhian" Movement, and Dr. S. Rajasunderam, made at strenuous effort to bring about a rapproachement between Uma Maheswaran and Prabhakaran.

In the meantime every now and then Eelam lobbyists abroad staged a publicity stunt geared to attract the attention of the media. Perhaps the most successful of them was the gimmick of Krishna Vaikunthavasan, a London-based lawyer and Eelam supporter. In October 1978 he impersonated Foreign Minister A. C. S. Hameed to address the UN General Assembly for a few minutes. Embarrassed security guards hustled him away from the rostrum after he had spoken a few sentences. However from the viewpoint of the media it was a sensational story at the expense of Sri Lanka.

In May 1979, in an even more vicious publicity stunt, geared exclusively to the media, was carried out successfully in Massachusetts, The Tamil Eelam Association of America is based in Sommerville, Massachusetts, is a small and a politically inconsequential city of 84,000 people including 300 Sri Lanka Tamils. Somehow they inveigled Mayor Eugene C. Bruce, to protest against harassment of Tamils in Sri Lanka. They also manoeuvred Marie Howe, the Representative of Sommerville in the State Legislature of Massachusetts, to table a lengthy resolution in that Assembly denouncing the manner in which Tamils are treated in Sri Lanka. Marie Howe could not locate Sri Lanka on the map of the world, when I personally administered that test on her while on a routine visit to my American *Alma Mater* Harvard University situated nearby. She was however well aware that such a resolution was not binding on the State Legislature of Massachusetts. Moreover by tradition, such resolutions are never debated but merely adopted as a courtesy to the Representative who tabled it. Thus this resolution was "adopted." In another publicity stunt, Governor Edward J. King of Massachusetts, who also did not know where Sri Lanka was situated, was inveigled into declaring May 22nd 1979 as Tamil Eelam Day in that State.

The Department of State of the Government of United States looked upon these developments not without amusement. Formal announcements were made disowning any responsibility on the part of the Government of the United States in these antics. However from the viewpoint of publicity, Sri Lanka had suffered yet another set back.

By 1980, the Eelam lobbies had taken stock of their performance. Quite obviously they had little or no impact on the inflow of foreign aid and foreign tourists that poured into Sri Lanka or foreign investments which had come in on a scale hitherto unprecedented in Sri Lanka. However the Eelam lobbies did strike a chord of response on Human Rights issues. The Prevention of Terrorism Act was in particular made to appear a draconian legislation under which the Army and Police had the licence to go on the rampage and which they gladly did.

By 1980 expatriate earnings had overtaken rubber as the second largest source of foreign exchange. It was in vogue for young people of all communities to go abroad for a few years and to remit their savings to Sri Lanka. Such employment was readily available in the Middle East where over 80,000 Sri Lankans worked but increasingly difficult in the Western countries which accounted for another 100,000 including immigrants who had opted to renounce their citizenship of Sri Lanka. These difficulties stemmed from rigid visa regulations which are now part and parcel of Government regulations even in Australia, Canada, New Zealand and the USA, countries which have been created through immigration from abroad. However based on Western concepts of liberalism, all Western nations deliberately leave open a loopholp in their rigid immigration laws, for political refugees.

Some ingenious Tamils living abroad exploited this loophole to maximum advantage to blacken the image of Sri Lanka and simultaneously to help their relatives and friends. Such persons traveled on pre-paid tickets or were recruited through employment agencies in Jaffna and on arrival at their distinations applied to be "political refugees." Newspaper publicity and support from Human Rights organizations were drummed up to bolster the application. Whether the applicants were successful or not, the publicity was detrimental to the good name of Sri Lanka.

When the applicant was not successful, the matter was referred to Court, again with much Press publicity, and if still unsuccessful to the High Court and eventually to the Supreme Court. During this time consuming process of a few years the "political refugee" was as a rule allowed to work and thereby achieved his objective of earning some money abroad.

This technique reached unprecedented proportions in July 1981 when nearly 400 Sri Lanka Tamils who had left Colombo by Aeroflot flights to Moscow en-route to East Berlin turned up in West Berlin seeking "refugee status." An ingenious employment agency had spotted a loophole in the immigration regulations in the Federal Republic of Germany (West Germany) which is liberal in granting refugee status to defectors from the German Democratic Republic (East Germany). The authorities were particularly liberal in interpreting this regulation in West Berlin and hence the sudden appearance of 400 "political refugees" not from East Germany but from northern Sri Lanka. Amidst much publicity, which tended to exaggerate out of all proportion the ethnic problem, these "political refugees" were sent back to the land of their birth in two chartered flights from Luftansa.

In mid-1981, racial tension mounted with the escalation of violence by the terrorist movemenst. In June 1981when Prime Minister R. Premadasa visited London for the opening of the Sri Lanka Exhibition, to celebrate fifty years of adult franchise, there were ugly scenes created by Eelam supporters. There were similar disruptions later in June 1981 when President J. R. Jayewardene visited London for the Royal Wedding. In July 1981 there was the fiasco of "political refugees" in West Berlin. With the President, the Prime Minister and the nation insulted, in London, any volatile incident at home was sufficient to spark off another racial riot. Finally the eruption took place on July 30th 1981.

During the raid on the Annakottai Police Station, two Constables were killed, one was a Muslim and the other a Sinhalese. Following the funeral of PC 13534 Jayaratne Banda, in Kurunegala there was rioting in that town. The violence spread quickly to the Western and Southern Provinces and to Sabaragamuwa. In the midst of sporadic acts of violence, for the first time in the history of communal riots in Sri Lanka, there was premeditated and organized violence. It first erupted in Sabaragamuwa, in Ratnapura, Kahawatte and Balangoda, then in Negombo and Panadura.

Bus loads of trained saboteurs appeared suddenly from nowhere. They were armed with jerry cans containing petrol. They set fire to Tamil commercial establishments and quickly disappeared into nowhere.

Following the racial riots of 1981, the reaction of President J. R. Jayewardene was exemplay. Even in public he took a conciliatory attitude towards the Tamils. The President was particularly severe on anybody in the UNP who adopted, in public, a hostile attitude towards the Tamils. Dr. Nevile Fernando (UNP-Panadura) was first cautioned, then warned and finally expelled from the UNP for his public statements hostile to the Tamils. This resulted in militant Sinhala elements being critical of the President, but he brushed them aside. Even the militant *Maha Sangha* (Buddhist clergy) were brushed aside.

On his own volition President J. R. Jayewardene initiated a dialogue between the Government and the TULF to work out an honourable settlement to the Tamil problem. At these periodic discussions the Government was represented by the President, the Prime Minister, the leaders of the Tamil community in the Cabinet, K. W. Devanayagam, Minister for Home Affairs and S. Thondaman, Minister for Rural Industrial Development, the leaders of the Muslim community in the Cabinet, M. H. Mohamed, Minister of Transport, and A. C. S. Hameed,

Minister for Foreign Affairs, and representatives of the younger generation in the Cabinet, Gamini Dissanayake, Minister for Mahaweli Development, and Ranil Wickremasinghe, Minister for Youth Affairs, Sports and Employment and Education and Lalith Athulathmudali, Minister or Trade and Shipping. The TULF was represented by A. Amirthalingam, Leader of the Opposition, M. Sivasithamparam, President of the TULF, all senior TULF Members of Parliament, Professor Jayaratnam Wilson son-in-law of the late S. J. V. Chelvanayakam, and Dr. Neelam Thiruchelvam, a party intellectual and son the late M. Thirunchelvam who was a Cabinet Minister in the last Dudley Senanayake Administration. A battery of senior officials was co-opted. I was one of them.

The deliberations were carried out without any publicity whatsoever in an atmosphere of cordiality, with the President reiterating his desire to satisfy Tamil aspirations the Tamils within the framework of a unitary form of Government.

A donation of Rs. 1,000,000 from the President's Fund, the largest donation ever made from that Fund, was given to rehabilitate the Public Library in Jaffna. The Government paid compensation whenever people were killed or property damaged in the racial riots of 1981. The scope of activity of the two new Universities in Jaffna and Batticaloa, where the medium of instruction is Tamil, were enlarged and substantial grants made from the exchequer.

The TULF was not ungrateful for these acts of statesmanship which incidentally were lost on the Eelam propagandists abroad. However the TULF was increasingly critical of the slow progress in implementing the District Development Councils Act of 1980. The TULF repeatedly protested that the funds earmarked for the DDC were woefully inadequate to implement these plans. Besides the TULF wanted the District Minister to be elected by the DDC and not appointed by the President as stipulated in the Constitution. The negotiations on these matters were painfully slow and frustrating.

In the meantime President J. R. Jayewardene sought re-election and the terrorist movements was again on the warpath. On October 20th 1982, the President was re-elected by a comfortable majority. On October 27th the LTTE led by Seelan, in the absence of Prabhakaran, carried out a commando style raid.

The Chavakachcheri Police Station is on the Jaffna-Colombo road. It is a two storey building with the Charge Room and the desk of the Officer-in-Charge downstairs, the singlemen barrack upstairs and in the out-house.

On numerous reconnaissance missions the Tigers had observed the location of the armoury, the strong box (which contains the ammunition and the machine guns), and the nature of its locks.

Just before the break of dawn on October 27th 1982, a hijacked minibus silently approached an out-house of the Police Station. A few Tigers took up positions to seal off the road while about fifteen Tigers carrying Sub-Machine Guns (SMG), Self-Loading Rifles (SLR), carbines and rifles approached the Police Station in combat formation. A Police sentry noticed some unusual activity and before he realized what was happening there was a hail of bullets and he was injured. Another sentry opened fire and was promptly killed by SMG fire.

With military precision, the Tigers stormed into the building under cover of SMG and SLR fire. The main force captured the Charge Room while a support force went upstairs. In the Charge Room the Tigers shot at anybody who got in their way. Two Policemen were thus killed. A Police suspect who went berserk in the lockup was silenced for ever. Then with explosives, the armoury and strong box were opened. The arms and ammunition were systematically whisked into the minibus which had reversed into the Police compound.

In the meantime, the support force which was upstairs to stall the Policemen there, opened fire and injured two Constables. One of them was shot through his hand and to save his life leapt out of the balcony. In the process he broke a leg. Two Constables escaped unhurt by hiding in the toilet. However one courageous Policeman, Constable Weerakoon, grabbed a repeater shot gun and opened fire thrice, wounding two terrorists.

A Tiger rescue squad immediately evacuated their wounded which included Seelan who was shot in the knee while directing operations in the Charge Room. Sellakili who took over command then ordered a strategic withdrawal before all the ammunition was loaded into the minibus. Thereupon the Tigers clambered into the vehicle which sped away.

A detailed inquiry into this raid revealed that PC Kandiah, who was in the Charge Room died in the brave performance of duty. However the Policemen in the out-house had acted in a cowardly manner. They were armed and the minibus which was used by the Tigers was initially parked just outside the out-house. Yet not one Policemen there opened fire in defence when their Station was under siege.

With the Presidential election over, the Government stepped up its campaign against terrorism by taking into custody not only terrorists but also those who aided and abetted terrorism. Accordingly, the Rev. Phillip Singarasa and the Rev. A. S. Singarayar, two Roman Catholic priests, were arrested. Allegedly they had helped to deposit part of the loot from the Nallur and Neerveli Bank robberies with finance companies and in fixed deposit accounts. Likewise, Dr. M. Nithiyanathan, a lecturer at the University of Jaffna, and his wife Nirmala, who allegedly gave shelter to Seelan after he was seriously injured during the raid at Chavakachcheri, were arrested. Early in 1983, the leaders of the "Gandhian" Movement, S. A. David and Dr. S. Rajasunderam, were arrested. Indictments were filed against them in the High court and the subject is now sub-judice.

Against this background, the TULF publicly revealed its attitude towards the terrorist movement. The dreaded terrorist Kuttimani, who was in the Death Row of Welikade Prison convicted of murder, was nominated as the TULF Member of Parliament for Vaddukoddai.

In March 1983, the Commissioner of Elections announced by Gazette notification that the Local Government elections for the entire island and 18 by-elections for Parliamentary seats would be held on May 18th. Thus a mini-General Election was scheduled for May 18th 1983, and the campaigning was brisk.

In the Jaffna peninsula power was wielded by the TULF and the LTTE. The TULF was enthusiastic about the election whereas the LTTE opposed to it. Thus the atmosphere was charged with the LTTE threatening the TULF and the UNP.

On the morning of April 29th 1983, K. V. Ratnasingham the principal UNP candidate for the Urban Council of Point Pedro, was watching Television at the residence of a friend. Sri Lanka was playing a Test Match against Australia at the Asgiriya cricket ground and when play was adjourned for lunch, he left for his home for lunch. While walking on the main road he was ambushed opposite the Point Pedro Rest House by several youth on cycles. They fired two shots into his head killing him instantaneously. They left behind a death sentence issued by the LTTE and cycled away without any undue haste.

Two hours later S. J. Muttiah, the principal UNP candidate for the Chavakachcheri Urban Council, had some youthful visitors at his home. They came on cycles, fired several shots into his head, left behind a death sentence issued by the LTTE and cycled away.

Around 5 p.m. that day, the van belonging to the principal UNP candidate for the Velvettiturai Urban Council was stopped near the town by some youth. Thinking the candidate was in the van they fired into it and killed V. Rajaratnam, the body guard of a UNP stalwart in the Jaffna District.

As the shock waves traversed through the Jaffna peninsula, all UNP candidates announced their withdrawal. Thus only the TULF candidates were left in the fray.

Leaflets issued by the LTTE stressed the need to boycott the elections to embarrass the Government. Further the leaflets claimed that the TULF was a failure and achieved nothing through the District Development Councils in which the TULF had placed much faith, in order to obtain redress for the Tamil community. The leaflets, which were issued in the name of Prabhakaran, further threatened all Tamils who were supporting the Government. This was emphasized in a separate set of leaflets sent to Tamil Policemen in the Jaffna peninsula.

Despite these threats the TULF continued its campaign in the Jaffna peninsula and wherever they fielded candidates. From every public platform A. Amirthalingam said that he was proud of the acts of heroism and defiance of the youth who were fighting to set up the State of Tamil Eelam. However he appealed to the "boys," as the Tigers are affectionately referred to in Jaffna, to act with foresight in their struggle. He drew a parallel to the IRA which regularly contested elections in Northern Ireland and mentioned that a MP in the British Parliament from the IRA had fasted to death in prison to attract worldwide attention for their struggle. Amirthlingam stressed on the importance of elections in the struggle for freedom. This infuriated the Tigers who disrupted a meeting of Amirthalingam in Jaffna on May 8th by shooting in the air and setting his car on fire. That resulted in many TULF candidates withdrawing from the election.

The Tigers then stepped up their campaign against the election by placing parcel bombs strategically in the Jaffna peninsula. The bomb placed before the headquarters of the General Union of Eelam Students (GUES) at 62 Clock Tower Road, Jaffna, criticized that organisation for its recent mishandling of events in the peninsula. Another bomb was placed before the offices of the *Saturday Review* the strident English newspaper which advocated the cause of the TULF at the forthcoming election. It carried a threat for misleading the general public. Another bomb placed near the office of *Sutantiran* carried a tirade against Uma Maheswaran.

On May 18th 1983 where the local Government elections were held, the Tigers experimented with their new home-made grenades. Seven explosions were heard in Jaffna, Chavakachchceri , Point Pedro and Velvettiturai where the election was conducted. The message was loud and clear. Polling was reduced to almost nothing throughout the day.

Anticipating more violence, the Army and Police arranged elaborate security precautions. Every polling booth had on the outside a guard of five soldiers carrying T-56 Chinese assault rifles and five armed Constables, on the inside. Besides, every hour the polling booths were visited by mobile patrols of the Army and Police.

Around 4.15 p.m. an Army patrol had visited the polling booth at Sivaprakas Maha Vidyalaya at Kandermadam which was guarded by five soldiers from the Raja Rifles and five armed Police Constables. Shortly thereafter, Private Somasiri reported to Corporal Warakapitiya that he had observed some suspicious movements not far from the polling booth. The Corporal had hardly instructed Private Somasiri and Private Bandara to keep the area under surveillance, when suddenly Seelan launched a grenade and machine gun attack from behind a parapet wall.

When the attack was launched the security personnel had no pre-determined defence worked out. Corporal Jayawardene guarding the front entrance was shot dead while trying to seek cover, Private Aluvihare who was with him took cover in the polling booth. Private Somasiri got into the toilet and opened fire with his T-56 assault rifle. Corporal Warakapitiya and Private Bandara took cover behind the toilet and opened fire. Constables Abbas and Tilekaratne ran out of the polling booth and took up positions behind the toilet. Constable Thavarajah hid in the nearby Kovil.

Seelan then directed their fire on the toilet whereupon Corporal Warakapitiya and Constable Abbas escaped from the rear compound with the injured, Private Bandara, Constable Tilekeratne and Constable Premadasa. However Private Somasiri with commendable courage ran out of the toilet, took command of the polling booth and repulsed the attack with the assistance of Private Aluvihare and Constable Ranbanda. In the meantime Sellakili crept up to the dead body of Corporal Jayawardene and removed his T-56 assault rifle and two magazines. With that accomplished Seelan suddenly called off the attack.

The Tigers suffered no losses but the Security Forces had many casualties besides, many displayed cowardice. Hitherto the general public in Jaffna looked upon the Security Forces either with fear or passivity. Now their attitude was that of unconcealed contempt. They were of the opinion that the Security Forces were no match for the Tigers whose military skill was admired. Besides the Raja Rata Rifles went on the rampage on the night of May 18th, further reinforcing the impression that the soldiers were good only in the attack of defenceless civilians.

The Army promptly withdrew the Raja Rata Rifles to their base in Anuradhapura. After a preliminary inquiry, six soldiers were dismissed. 90 soldiers deserted the regiment. They too were promptly dismissed. Six officers in the ranks of Lieutenant and Captain, who were in sympathy with the deserters, had their commissions withdrawn. The Lieutenant Colonel was compulsarily retired.

In the mean time the PLOTE of Uma Maheswaran had observed that a jeep from the Sri Lanka Air Force base at Vavuniya drove down daily to town to purchase provisions. On June 1st 1983, the vehicle left with Leading Aircraftsman Kulasiri in the front seat, Aircraftsmen Ratnasiri, Ranjan and Gunsekera in the rear seats.

In Vavuniya town L/AC Kulasiri got down to make the purchases. Two youth then appeared from nowhere and shot at the airmen in the rear seat. A/C Ratnasiri leapt out of the jeep and returned the fire injuring a terrorist named Ramanathan. More terrorists entered the fray and in the exchange of fire A/C Ranjan was injured. Then L/AC Perera who was in the driver's seat and without weapons crept into the rear compartment to pick up the T-56 assault rifle of A/C Ranjan. Just then a hand grenade was lobbed into the jeep by the terrorist leader Sithamparananathan.

The explosion ripped open the jeep and also the abdomens of L/AC Perera and A/C Gunasekera. It was a fearful sight to see their entrails scattered all over the jeep. Incidentally the foreign press which of late had taken upon itself the task of defending Human Rights in Sri Lanka did not say one word about the right to life of these young airmen, the sight of whose mutilated bodies could make even strong men weep in public and made me vomit.

L/AC Perera and A/C Gunasekera were buried with full Air Force honours in their respective home towns of Minuwangoda and Kandy. Following the funerals, rioting broke out in 40 towns with the Kurunegala and Trincomalee districts being badly affected.

In Vavuniya rioting broke out on June 1st itself. Besides Sinhala people who account for about a quarter of the population of that town tipped off the Police resulting in Ramanathan and Sithamparanathan being arrested in a few hours after a shoot out at Kovilkulam.

With the Vavuniya incident the racial tensions escalated rapidly. In the Trincomalee district the Sinhala population was of the opinion that the Tamils would evict them forcibly to create the State of Tamil Eelam. Hence they took a pre-emptive strike and the Tamils retaliated. The Sinhala people had the tacit support of some sections of the Armed Forces, the Tamils had the open support of the TULF. There was a wave of violence from June 11th to 15th and a second wave commencing June 26th. The tension was so great that Rear Admiral Asoka De Silva, the Commander of the Navy, was posted to Trincomalee with wide powers similar to those given to Brigadier Weeratunga in 1979. Rear Admiral De Silva, who was trained at the Brittanica Royal Naval College at Dartmouth and the National Defence College in New Delhi, had an excellent reputation as a Naval Officer throughout his distinguished career. He contained the violence within a few days.

The tension throughout the country was further accentuated by student unrest. In mid-May there was a Sinhala–Tamil clash amongst the students at the University of Peradeniya. It resulted in many Tamil engineering students leaving for Jaffna and Batticaloa, whereupon the Universities of Jaffna and Batticloa went on strike. By early June half the Tamil students who left the campus had returned and on the night of June 6th 1983, there was a fracas in the James Peiris Hall. Two Sinhalese students, W. A. D. T. Wickramasinghe and A. Ekanayake, assaulted two Tamil students, K. Dayaparan and, A. Suverndran. Following a disciplinary inquiry Wickramasinghe and Ekanayake were suspended, resulting in Sinhalese students boycotting lectures. The boycott escalated into a strike which in turn fuelled the racial tension within the campus. The strike in Peradeniya evoked sympathy strikes in the Universities in and around Colombo.

In this charged atmosphere, the Tamil Eelam Liberation Front (TELF) led by Dr. S. Dharmalingam and Kovi Maheswaran called for a *harthal* on July 1st in protest against the harassment of Tamils in the Trincomalee area. Since its inception in 1981 as an alternative to the TULF, the TELF was ineffective. However this *harthal* was a complete success, besides most children kept away from school. In addition the TELA, an off-shoot of the TELO led by "Oberoi" Thevan set on fire the *Yal Devi*, the Colombo-Jaffna express train, at Kondavil. They also set fire to CTB buses at Annakottai and Puttur. Dr. S. A. Dharmalingam and Kovai Mahesan were arrested the following day under the Prevention of Terrorism Act. The TELA than issued an ultimatum that unless these two prisoners are released by dusk on July 4th they would retaliate. The ultimatum issued in the form of posters was ignored, whereupon on July 5th around noon,

15 youth armed with revolvers and knives entered the office of the Divisional Superintendent of Mails in Jaffna and caused extensive damage to Government property. On the following day similar damage was done to the Post Office in Thinneveli and the day after to the Office of the Assistant Government Agent in Tinneveli.

Shortly after midnight on July 5th 1983 a commando squad of the LTTE led by Seelam dressed in Army uniform and carrying machine guns walked into the house of Thambiah Ramanathan in Kokuvil. Having woken him, they said they were from the Army Camp at Gurnagar and they wanted to borrow his Delica Van because their jeep had broken down at the Thavadi junction. Obligingly Ramanathan took out his vehicle and handed over the switch keys.

By 2.30 a.m. the Van with Seelan, Sellakili and others on board arrived at the quarry office of the Kankesanturai cement factory. At gun point, the security guards and a time keeper were tied up. The Tigers then ambushed the storekeeper and at gun point took his keys away. When they left five minutes later they took with them the following items:

> 5 Plunger type exploders, 1 Pneumatic drill, 2 Avometers, 200 metres of cable wire and the miscellaneous equipment

By 4.30 a.m. the van was returned to Ramanathan who was politely thanked for the use of his vehicle.

Thereafter, with unfailing regularity the terriorist movements consisting of the LTTE of Prabahkaran, the PLOTE of Uma Maheswaran, its off shoots in the Batticaloa district, and the TELA, led by "Oberoi" Thevan, systematically unleashed violence.

On July 15th 1983, Brigadier J. G. Balthazar, Commander of the Security Forces in the North, who had bided his time, launched his counter offensive. He had information that Seelan, the most wanted terrorist next to Prabhakaran, was operating from a house in Meesalai near Chavakacheri. The Sandhurst trained Brigadier who had seen action in the Congo with UN Forces, worked out a complex operation. That evening the Army ambushed and killed Seelan amongst others.

This was indeed a grievous blow to the LTTE. During the past two years Seelan had a leading role in the robbery from the pawn broker in Kurumbachitty and the People's Bank at Neerveli. He organized the killing of the first soldiers to die in Jaffna peninsula, just a week after General Weeratunge took command of the Army. He executed Sunderam, his opposite member in the PLOTE led by Uma Maheswaran. He led the attack on the Chavakachcheri Police Station, the polling booth at Kandaramadam and the Cement Factory in Kankesanturai. He was responsible for the murder of UNP candidates and the disruption of the Local Government elections in the Jaffna peninsula just two months earlier. No terrorist, not even Uma Maheswaran or Prabhakaran, had a record of banditry comparable with Seelan. His usefulness was such that when he was injured in the raid at Chavakachcheri and was surreptitiously sent to India for treatment, the LTTE was subdued till he returned to the Island. Now he was dead. The five pellet marks on his left knee cap, received during the raid in Chavakachcheri, bore testimony to his identity. Further testimony was the obituary announced by the LTTE though the medium of posters. They swore vengence on the Army.

On his part Brigadier Balthazar stepped up the campaign to ambush Sellakili. In his assessment the TELO had, for all intents and purposes, been silenced; only a splinter group TELA led by "Oberoi" Thevan was operational. With Uma Maheswaran seeking refuge in India, Sunderam killed by Seelan, Karthan killed by the Army and twenty six under arrest, the PLOTE was effective only around their base in Vavuniya and Batticaloa, where an affiliate group was operational. However the LTTE was fully operational, the only casualties being Prabhakaran who was arrested in Madras and Seelan killed a few days ago. Thus Sellakili was now the prime target.

In the recent past Sellakili had assisted Seelan in the raids on the Chavachcheri Police Station, on the polling booth at Kandaramadam and on the Kankesanturai Cement Factory. Some years earlier Sellakili had a leading role in the raid on the People's Bank in Tinneveli and Puttur, the murder of Inspector Bastianpillai and his staff and of P. C. Karunanidhi, the first Policeman to die at the hands of the Tigers.

The escalation of violence by the Tiger Movement and the TELF was to pressure the TULF into resigning their seats in Parliament by August 4th 1983. When the current Parliament first sat on August 5th 1977, after the General Election of 1977, in terms of the Constitution it would automatically dissolve at the end of six years if not dissolved earlier. President J. R. Jayewardene was re-elected for a second term on October 20th 1982. Instead of having a General Election he called for a Referendum seeking extension of the Parliament for another six years. The people voted as follows:

Yes 3,142,223 No 2,065,983

Thus the lifetime of the Parliament was extended for six years using the unorthodox methodology.

The Tamil speaking areas, especially the Jaffna district, voted heavily against the Referendum. The LTTE and the TELF was of the opinion that the TULF should resign their seats in Parliament at the end of the six years. This brought about a head–on confrontation between the moderates and the radicals in the quest of the State of Tamil Eelam. The final decision was to be taken at the forthcoming annual Convention of the TULF.

The General Council of the TULF met at the residence of its President, M. Sivasithamparam (TULF — Nallur) on June 18th 1983 and adopted the following resolution.

(a) To request the Government to find a political solution to the Tamil problem by recognizing the right of self-determination.
(b) The TULF to continue its struggle to establish a State of Tamil Eelam through non-violent means.
(c) The TULF condemns the action of militant youth who have been a threat to duly elected members of local bodies.
(d) The TULF condemns the atrocities caused by the Raja Rata Rifles in Kandermadam on July 18th, 1983.
(e) The TULF requests the Government to withdraw troops from the North and to revoke the Prevention of Terrorism Act.
(f) The TULF will hold their annual Convention in Mannar on July 23rd and 24th 1983.

Against the background of this resolution the Parliamentary group of the TULF met at the residence of A. Amirthalingam in Colombo on June 27th. There it transpired that V. N. Navaratnam M. P. (TULF–Chavakachcheri) was adamant on resigning his seat on the following premises:

(a) He was elected by the people of Chavakachcheri in 1977 for a period of six years.

(b) The people of Chavakachcheri voted overwhelmingly against the Referendum to extend the lifetime of the Parliament by another six years.

Navaratnam who was a MP continuously since 1956 further stated he would re-contest Chavakachcheri.

In 1981 A. Yogeswaram M. P. (TULF— Jaffna) was of the opinion that the TULF should contest the DDC election in June 1981 in the teeth of opposition from the LTTE. Now he claimed that in two years the DDC has achieved absolutely nothing and was a farce, because the Government had not provided adequate funds. He said that the assessment of the LTTE was vindicated and he was personally in favour of resigning his seat and boycotting the ensuring by-election.

During the many crises in July 1983 the new Marxist parties in the Sinhala areas, the JVP led by Rohana Wijeweera and the NSSP led by Vasudeva Nanayakkara, revealed their hand. Both parties had received a severe drubbing in the recent exercise of the franchise. At the Presidential election held on October 20th 1982. Wijeweera received an ignominous 4% of the votes and Nanayakkara 1% as against 53% by President J. R. Jayewardene and 39% by his principal rival, Hector Kobbekaduwa of the SLFP. At the Local Government elections of May 18th 1983 the JVP could not gain representation in any Municipal Council or Urban Council. The NSSP fared even worse and Vasudeva Nanayakkara could not win the Eheliyagoda seat in the Parliamentary by-election despite support from many parties. Indeed it was very clear that the JVP and the NSSP were heading in the same direction as the Trotskyite LSSP and the Communist Party, namely total eclipse and eventual extinction.

The JVP and the NSSP however had previously displayed a marked predilection for violence. In 1971 they were responsible for the insurrection which cost over 18,000 lives. With conventional methods of achieving power beyond their reach, their predilection for violence was once again evident.

At a public meeting held at the New Hall on July 6th Dr. Wickramabahu Karunaratne, the Secretary of the NSSP, and a Lecturer in the Faculty of Engineering at the University of Peradeniya complete with a doctorate from Cambridge University said,

> "The youth in the Tamil and Sinhala areas should join together in overthrowing this ... (expletive deleted) Government of ... (expletive deleted) J. R. Jayewardene."

Rohana Wijeweera who spoke next echoed the same sentiments. At another meeting Dr. Karunaratne protested on behalf of the NSSP on the arrest of S. A. David and Dr. S. Rajasundaram, the leaders of the Gandhian Movement. Thus the NSSP became the first party in the Sinhala speaking areas to show sympathy for the LTTE.

During the student unrest at the University of Peradeniya Wijeweera and Dr. Karunaratne attempted to make political capital by fomenting anti-Government sentiments. That surprised nobody. What surprised everybody at Peradeniya was the solicitous attitude Wijeweera and Dr. Karunaratne took towards the Tamil students.

The clamour for a State of Tamil Eelam evoked no positive response whatsoever in the Sinhala speaking areas except from the JVP and the NSSP. However across the Palk Strait the reaction was very different. It evoked emotion and generated support.

A. K. Shajahn of Madurai attempted self-immolation within the premises of the Office of the Deputy High Commissioner for Sri Lanka in Madras. He poured kerosene over himself and set himself ablaze but a sentry was able to douch the flames and rush him to hospital. Immigration officials at Meenamabakam Airport, acting of their own disuaded Indian nationals from traveling to Sri Lanka for duty-free shopping, on the premise it was unsafe to visit Colombo.

On the initiative of M. Karunanidhi, President of the DMK, Leader of Opposition and former Chief Minister of Tamil Nadu, an all party conference was summoned for June 19th 1983, in Madras. It was attended by all parties except the ruling Anna DMK. The conference decided to agitate for Tigers being given asylum in Tamil Nadu and to call for a public meeting in July 2nd, at Shenoynagar, Madras.

The protest meeting at Shenoynagar was sponsored by the DMK, the Dravida Kalakam led by V. R. Veeramani, the Kamraj National Congress led by P. Nedumaran, the Muslim League led by Abdul Lathiff and the several Marxist parties. It was attended by over 10,000 people. The gathering was addressed by Karunanidhi, Veeramani, Nedumaran and Abdul Lathiff, amongst others. They all stressed solidarity with the Tamils in Sri Lanka and expressed admiration for the militant youth whom they claimed were forced to take up arms. Karunanidhi further stated that unless Prime Minister Indira Gandhi took action soon to give some redress to the Tamils in Sri Lanka, the DMK would be compelled to create a situation that would force her hand.

At first, the ruling Anna DMK led by Chief Minister M. G. Ramachandran took a cautious stand. However they were soon compelled to take a stand against the Government of Sri Lanka, to prevent the Opposition from stealing a march over them in the State elections scheduled for early 1984. Thus the entire spectrum of political opinion in Tamil Nadu was orchestrated against the Government of Sri Lanka. To achieve this state of public awareness the following course of action was taken:

1. The mass media gave wide coverage to events in Sri Lanka with recourse to mixture of truths, half-truths and untruths. The mass

media was particularly severe on the Armed Forces and Police who were stationed in the Tamil speaking areas.

2. Over 150 organisations submitted protests to the Chief Minister of Tamil Nadu.
3. The DMK launched a campaign for the collection of two million signatures for a memorandum seeking UN Forces to be stationed in Sri Lanka, on the same lines as in Cyprus.
4. Politicians from all political parties in Tamil Nadu spoke emotionally in the State Assembly about the Tamil problem in Sri Lanka.

Prime Minister Indira Gandhi was scheduled to visit Tamil Nadu on July 20th 1983, to open a nuclear plant at Kalpakkam. In view of the tension in Tamil Nadu, caused by events in Sri Lanka, on July 18th the Government of India indicated to the Government of Sri Lanka, through diplomatic channels, its concern for the safety of Indian citizens in Sri Lanka. By the same token the Government of India assured the Government of Sri Lanka that it had no intention of interfering in the domestic affairs of Sri Lanka.

About this time the Government of Sri Lanka was hauled over the coals by the news media in the entire Western world. The influential Amnesty International released their report on Sri Lanka and it was a tirade against the Government on the violations of Human Rights.

The report of Amnesty International claimed that political suspects in Sri Lanka had been held incommunicado under the Prevention of Terrorism. Act and tortured both in Army camps and Police Stations. Amnesty International claimed that in some cases detainees have been kept in solitary confinement for more than eight months after arrest and that torture included hanging victims upside down with hooks, beating them with metal bars and driving needles under the toe-nails and finger-nails.

In one of several specific allegations its stated that on April 10th 1983 K. Navaratnarajah, a terrorist from Trincomalee, died in custody at the Army camp at Gurunagar after being held incommunicado for two weeks. At the autopsy 25 external injuries and 10 internal injuries were found on his body and the coroner had passed strictures accordingly.

In one of several less specific allegations, it was stated that at the Army camp at Elephant Pass, suspects were kept chained to iron grills for as long as six months. That at several Army Camps suspects were made to crawl on broken glass and had chilli powder inserted into various sensitive organs.

The Government issued a rebuttal which was published by every daily newpaper in Colombo. It was however ignored by the media abroad. Amnesty International in the past had been critical of successive Government of Sri Lanka especially for the manner in which the accused in the 1962 *coup d'etat* were treated and the insurgents were handled in 1971. They were now hypercritical of the manner in which the current Government was handling those who were arrested for agitating for a separate State of Tamil Eelam.

The findings of Ammesty International was drummed up by Eelam lobbies around the world. Noisy demonstrations complete with extensive media coverage were held in Boston, London, Paris, Sydney and Toronto. In the State Assembly of Massachusetts, Marie Howe tabled a resolution on the alleged violation of Human Rights in Sri Lanka. The Eelam lobbies gave that resolution wide publicity, craftily making it appear that it represented international support for their cause.

With the communal problem quite obviously worsening, President J. R. Jayewardene summoned a Round Table conference on the terrorist problem and sent invitations to all parties represented in the Parliament. The Conference was scheduled for July 20th 1983 and for one reason or another all parties in the Opposition, namely the TULF, SLFP, MEP and the Communist Party declined. The invitation was accepted only by the ruling UNP and its ally, the Ceylon Workers' Congress which accounts for just one Member of Parliament.

As the crucial week-end of July 23rd – 24th 1983 approached, it was increasingly clear that the TULF would decide at their annual convention to be held in Mannar, that their Members of Parliament resign their seats. In fact on July 21st, when they last assembled in Parliament, V. N. Navaratnam the long standing Member for Chavakachcheri delivered an emotional farewell address and the Leader of the Opposition exchanged words with the Prime Minister on the futility of a Round Table Conference.

Incidentally, my dear friend Brigadier J. G. Balthazar was very keen to have me as his guest for the week-end July 23rd/24th. We have been close friends ever since we were members of the Sri Lanka Atheletics team, some twenty five years ago. I knew his birthday and it was not in July. Therefore I was wondering why he wanted me at his camp at Gurunagar, Jaffna, during the next week-end because I had already spent a glorious week-end with him earlier in July. That was when I escorted to Jaffna the correspondents of BBC, *The Times of London* and *The New York Times,* all of whom were based in New Delhi and all were hostile to Sri Lanka. President Jayewardene was gracious and offered them travel on Air Force helicopters

Despite the intense political activity in Mannar on Saturday 23rd July 1983, Jaffna was quiet that day. It was in fact just another day at the Army Camp at Gurunagar. That evening Brigadier Balthazar and his staff routinely had dinner in the Officer's Mess while the other ranks had their dinner in their quarters. They then watched television, their only recreation in the evenings. Later in the evening Brigadier Balthazar excused himself and left for his office with his Duty Officer, Major F. C. J. De Silva. He also left word for his Intelligence Officers to join him. In the privacy of his office he directed Major De Silva to activate the Commandos and the special troops who were to lay in ambush for Sellakili that night. The Intelligence Officers were detailed to brief the detachment which would leave Gurunagar at mid-night. H-hour was 0100 hours and target area was not far from Kondavil. The code name for the patrol was Four Four Charlie.

In the meantime a routine patrol Four Four Bravo was scheduled to leave Gurunagar (code name Four Four) at 2200 hours. It was from the C Company of the First Battalion of the Sri Lanka Light Infantry based at Madagal about 20 miles away. It consisted of a detachment of 15 soldiers led by Second Lieutenant A. P. N. C. De S Wass Gunawardene. The instructions of the Brigadier were that the patrol should be back in Madagal before mid-night if necessary shortening the prescribed route:

> Gurunagar — Jaffna — Naga Vihara — Nallur — Kopay — Urumpirai — Kondavil — Kokuvil — Jaffna — Kaliyankadu — Madagal.

Second Lt. Gunawardene received the instructions from Major De Silva who further emphasized that the patrol must be in Madagal Camp by midnight. Four Four Bravo left Gurunagar and was in radio contact every five minutes All reports indicated that Jaffna was quiet.

In the meantime Sellakili who had sworn to avenge the death of Seelan had made a careful study of the Army patrols. He had observed that the maximum intensity of such patrols was between 2000–0200 hours. Every night they covered the main roads Palali — Jaffna, Kankes anturai — Jaffna, Point Pedro — Jaffna, Kankesanturai — Jaffna, Point Pedro — Jaffna while covering other roads. Also the convoys traveled about 75 — 100 yards apart.

On the night of July 23rd 1983 he deployed a platoon of about 25 terrorists in battle dress at Tinneveli on the Palali — Jaffna road, at a point where the road was dug up to install new telecommunication equipment. Near one such excavation four mines were placed. The plunger stolen from the Kankesanturai Cement Factory was placed on the balcony of a nearby house. The wiring was then connected. Machine gun nests were placed near the exploder and across the road. The machine guns (SMG) were once the property of the Chavakachcheri Police Station.

The main force, consisting of the "killer squad" and the "cut off party" was located 75 — 100 yards behind and on both sides of the road. Sellakili himself was there. Everybody was armed with SMG and repeater shot guns, also from Chavakachcheri, the T-56 Chinese assault rifle from the raid on the polling booth in Kandermadam and a SLR of Indian manufacture. Besides the "killer squad" had with them an arsenal of home-made hand grendades.

At 2328 hours the radio at Gurunagar cackled,

> "Four Four Bravo for Four Four. We are now leaving Urumpirai junction. Absolutely nothing to report. The town is very quiet."

The Army convoy consisted of a Jeep and a Tata half truck. In the Jeep was Second Lt. Waas Gunawardene sitting next to the driver Private N. A. S. Manatunge. In the rear seat were Lance Corporal G. D. Perera and Privates S. S. Amarasinghe, S. P. G. Rajatillake, K. P. Karunaratne. The Second Lt. had a SMG and the others SLRs (Self Loading Rifles). All except the driver carried a hand grenade. In the half truck was Sergeant S. I. Thelakaratne in the front seat with Corporal G. R. Perera at the wheel and Private A. J. R. Fernando between them. In the rear were Corporal R. A. U. Perera, Lance Corporal Sumathipala, Privates M. B. Sunil and D. N. A. D. Manapitiya all seated, Privates G. Robert and A. J. Wijesiri standing in the look-out position.

Within five minutes of leaving Urumpirai the jeep was slowing down near Tinneveli because of the obstuction on the road due to the installation of telecommunication equipment. As it was passing the excavation on the road, the exploder set off the mines. There was a thunderous explosion, followed by a hail of machine gun fire on the jeep and a still fiercer barrage on the half-truck.

Despite the concussion due to the explosion and injury sustained by machine gun fire Second Lt. Waas Gunawardene leapt out of his jeep and pulled out his hand grenade. Before he could lob it he was mowed down by machine gun fire. The driver Pte Manatunge was injured by machine gun fire. He staggered out of the vehicle and was killed. The explosion had injured Pte Karunaratne, Pte Rajatillake and Pte Manatunge. They somehow scrambled out of the vehilcle and attacked the enemy with hand grenades before being killed. L/Cpl C. D. Perera was probably not injured. He stormed out of the Jeep with his SLR blazing and pursued the enemy. His dead body was found quite some distance from the jeep.

On seeing the explosions around the jeep, Cpl G. R. Perera who was driving the half truck applied the brakes sharply. It resulted in Pte Robert and Pte Wijesiri in the look-out position falling on top of the others. The vehicle came in for heavy fire from both the "killer squad" and the "cut off party" thus taking fire from four sides. It killed Cpl. Perera in the driver's seat, Ptes Robert, Sunil and Wijesiri in the rear compartment and all but killed Pte Manapitiya. Sgt. Thelakaratne and Pte Fernando who were both injured scrambled out of their seat, took cover from the vehicle and opened fire on the enemy. Pte. Fernando was soon killed while Sgt. Thilakaratne kept on firing till a home-made grenade blew off one hand and all but blew off one foot.

Cpl. R. A. U. Perera and L/Cpl Sumathipala kept on firing and the latter in addition lobbed his grenade. In his dying moments Pte Manapitiya gave his grenade to the L/Cpl Sumathipala who changed their magazines and kept up the pressure on the enemy. At one stage they alighted from the vehicle and kept on firing at the enemy in two different directions, thus pinning them down.

In the meantime, the radio operator at Gurunagar was constantly calling,

"Four Four for Four Four Bravo can you hear me?"

"Four Four for Four Four Bravo can you hear me?"

At 2340 hours a message was sent to Brigadier Balthazar that radio contact with the patrol was lost and that a sentry had heard gunfire and explosions in the distance. The Brigadier who was still in civilian dress rushed into the radio room. Having checked on the information he alerted the Army camps in Madagal, Palali, Thondamanar and Valvettiturai. The Brigadier then cancelled the ambush prepared for Four Four Charlie due to leave at mid-night and instead sent them in search of the missing patrol, Four Four Bravo.

At 0009 hours the radio at Gurunagar cackled,

> "Four Four Charlie for Four Four
> Have located Four Four Bravo.
> Both vehicles destroyed. All dead
> Repeat both vehicles destroyed. All dead
> Location . . ."

About that time Cpl R. A. U. Perera (subsequently given a battlefield promotion) telephoned from the Kondavil CTB Depot. Having fired till his ammunition was almost exhausted he ingeniously retreated. In view of injuries in both legs he had removed his boots, made tourniquets with the boot laces and had run to safety. He gave the exact location of L/Cpl Sumathipala (subsequently given a battlefield promotion), who likewise had fired till his ammunition was almost expended, and thereafter had retreated and was lying injured.

Brigadier Balthazar and his staff rushed to the scene. On arrival they found Sgt. Thelakaratne still alive but bleeing profusely from the loss of a hand and one foot dangling from its skin. He was rushed to hospital but died on admission.. L/Cpl. Sumathipala was also rushed to hospital and was pronounced out of danger. Cpl. Perera was then dispatched to hospital. Thereafter the dead were removed.

Thus ended patrol Four Four Bravo of July 23rd, 1983 a day which will surely go down into the annals of history of the Sri Lanka Army. The Army can indeed be proud of this patrol which fought so bravely against fearful odds and had inflected many casualties on the enemy and had even killed Sellakili. Of those who made the supreme scarcifice for Sri Lanka, the nation could proudly say,

> "They shall not grow old,
> As we that are left grow old
> Age shall not weary them,
> Nor the years condemn
> At the setting of the sun
> And in the morning."

"WE SHALL REMEMBER THEM"

Chapter III

THE CIVIL WAR

As the word got around about the ambush at Tinneveli it invoked anger in the Sinhalese people and fear in the Tamil people. The General Cemetry in Colombo, where the dead soldiers were to be buried with full Military honours, was the epicenter of one storm on Sunday 24th July 1983. Jaffna was the epicenter of another storm, for that morning the Sri Lanka Light Infantry had gone on the rampage to avenge the 13 deaths.

Earlier in the day there was much controversy as to what type of funeral should be accorded to the dead soldiers. Major General "Bull" Weeratunge, the Commander of the Army, who had arrived in Jaffna that morning, and the entire Army contingent in Jaffna were opposed to the funeral being held there. That left two options open. The first was to hand over the dead to the next-of-kin for funerals in the respective hometowns and thereby risk 13 separate riots. The second was to bury the dead in Colombo under Emergency Regulations and to face the consequences in the city. During the communal riot of 1958, 1977 and 1981, Colombo was amongst the last places to be effected. It was not affected at all in the communal riot of 1956 or in the insurrection of 1971. Therefore it was decided, at the highest levels, to have the funeral at the General Cemetry in Colombo with full Military honours. The next-of-kin were duly informed.

The Army drew up a detailed plan for the Military funeral which was to be attended by the President, the Prime Minister and the Cabinet. By 2 p.m. Brigadier Kenneth Pereira, Director Logistics at Army Headquarters, who was in charge of funeral arrangements had added the final touches. An Air Force aircraft would bring the dead bodies to Ratmalana Civil Airport. Thereafter A. F. Raymonds the well known undertaker, would prepare the bodies for burial in sealed coffins because many of the bodies were mutilated. That would be done at their funeral parlour. The cortege would then be taken to the General Cemetry for burial at 5 p.m. The *Paansakula* ceremony (final Buddhist rites) was to be peformed by Buddhist priests from a nearby temple. Brigadier Pereira had pleaded with the Buddhist priests to avoid any inflammatory utterances in their sermon and on second thoughts, he decided to omit the sermon altogether. Brigadier George Thevanayagam who was in charge of Military ceremonies had arranged for funeral parties, from several regiments. The Army band was to be in attendance and the last post was to be sounded by buglers from the Sri Lanka Light Infantry.

By 3 p.m. the Deputy Inspector-General of Police (Metropolitan Range), Edward Gunawardene, took over command of the Police arrangements at the cemetery. With charactristic skill he left nothing to chance and kept in readiness a riot squad from the Borella Police Station.

By 5 p.m. there were no signs of the dead bodies. This caused the weeping relatives and their Members of Parliament to plead that the bodies be handed over to them. They claimed that their grief was compounded by the fact that they were denied their obligations of arranging the funeral in a manner compatible with time-honoured family tradition. As their clamour increased, the crowd also increased. It included over 3,000 slum dwellers from adjoining Wanathamulla.

By this time the dead bodies, clothed in new uniforms and wrapped in polythene bags had barely reached the Army camp at Palali, 20 miles from Jaffna. Procedural problems at Jaffna had caused the inordinate delay. After an emotional farewell from troops stationed at Palali the funeral flight, an Air Force Avro, took off from the Palali Air Force Base, at 6.05 p.m.

In the meantime the helicopter bringing General Weeratunge to Colombo returned to the Gurunagar Army Camp on a Presidential directive. The President wanted the General to spend the night in Jaffna in view of a rampage by the troops that morning, which had caused many deaths. As punishment, 29 soldiers were summasrily dismissed from the Army.

By 7.20 p.m. when the Avro arrived at Ratmalana the crowd at the cemetery had increased to over 8,000. Besides the crowd had taken up the cry of the next-of-kin to hand over the dead bodies. As the crowd became more restive they began to fill the graves with sand to forcibly prevent a burial. It was followed by a hail of stones and vituperations. They then broke the equipment to be used at the funeral and hurled it at the Police. The projectiles descended on may senior officers, amongst others on A. C. A. Gaffor, Senior Superintendent of the Police. The 300 pound giant almost fell into a half closed grave. After he regained his balance he took out his revolver and fired a few shots in the air. That failed to quieten the crowd. When the crowd became restive again there was another stream of obscenities and a hail of stones and Police Sergent Welikala was seriously injured. At that point the riot squad was called upon to fire tear gas. A baton charge followed. Thereafter the Police withdrew and the Army handled the crowd control operation.

By 8.30 p.m. the cortege had left Ratmalana Airport for the cemetery under a heavy Army and Police escort. In view of the upheaval in the cemetry Brigadier Pereira, who had earlier amended the programme for the funeral, radioed directing the cortege be diverted to Army Headquarters. Then the Minister of Internal Security T. B. Werapitiya, and a retired Deputy Inspector-General of Police, and General Sepala Attygalle, a former Commander of the Army and now Secretary, Ministry of Defence, left for 66, Ward Place, the residence of the President situated less than a mile away. On hearing their report the President cancelled the Military funeral and decided to hand over the dead to the next-of-kin at Army Headquarters. The decision was duly conveyed by Brigadier Pereira over the public address system at the cemetery around 10 p.m., whereupon the weeping relatives left quietly and the restive crowd left in an unruly state.

Anticipating further trouble Edward Gunawardene rushed the riot squad from the cemetery to seal off the Ward Place — Kynsey Road juction near the private residence of the President. The crowd that dispersed along D. S. Senanayake Mawatha marched up to Borella junction, less than half a mile away and smashed up Nagalingam Stores, a leading Tamil establishment. It triggered off a chain reaction around Borella junction which is the intersection of five main roads, D. S. Senanayake Mawatha, Baseline Road, Cotta Road, Ward Place and Maradana Road. The rampaging mob, which suddenly mushroomed to about 10,000 set on fire any Tamil building. It included the Borella flats where some Sinhalese people lived. The next targets were leading Tamil houses in the neighbrourhood. The home of. J. A. Selvaratnam, retired Superintendent of Police C.I.D., on Kurruppu Road, the home of the leading surgeon Dr. A. S. Thavarasa off Cotta Road, were set on fire. Air Force troops from the nearby Guwan Pura were rushed in to assist the Police. Their presence saved the home of Air Commodore C. E. Puvimanasinghe in Rodney Place, from a similar fate.

The much respected Inspector-General of Police, Rudra Rajasinghem, himself a Tamil, was directing Police operations at Borella. Meanwhile the Police repeatedly fired tear gas shells. The intensity of the firing was so rapid that the effects of the tear gas was felt by the sentries at the residence of the President a quarter mile away. After exhausting their stocks of tear gas shells, the Police opened fire in the air with rifles. That finally caused the mob to disperse. They did so in the direction of Dematagoda, Maradana and Narahenpita. Soon those areas were smouldering. So was Thimbirigasaya which is adjoining Narahenpita and Grandpass which is adjoining Maradana.

The Fire Brigade had arrived in Borella but in the height of the drought the water pressure in the hydrants was insufficient. Thus Borella was aflame for hours and the Borella Police Station had become a virtual refugee camp.

President J. R. Jayewardene summoned a meeting of the Security Council for 9.30 a.m. that morning. The Security Council consists of the President, the Minister of Internal Security, the Secretary to the President, the Secretary of Defence, the Service Commanders and the Inspector-General of Police. While this meeting was still in session at the President's House, earlier known as Queen's House the official residence of the British Governor, barely 100 yards away the Ambal Cafe, a Tamil establishment in the Bristol building was aflame. The fire quickly engulfed the entire building. Soon Sarathas, a leading Tamil clothier on York Street just 100 yards away suffered the same fate. In rapid succession Tamil shops down Baillie Street right in front of the President's House were set on fire. By the time the Security Council adjourned their meeting and the President enforced a curfew in Colombo, every Tamil establishment in the Fort shopping area was aflame. The rioting spread to Olcott Mawatha, opposite the Fort Railway Station. Ananda Bhawan, a *thosai* boutique, Rajeswari Stores, an oilmen store and Ajantha Hotel, all Tamil establishments were set on fire.

By 10 a.m. the slums of Colombo in Wanathamulla, Slave Island, Maradana, Narahenpita, Hattewatte, Kirillapone, Canal Bank, Grandpass, Modera, Kotahena and Mutwal erupted with savage fury. Slum dwellers armed with crow bars, kitchen knives roamed the streets inflicting death and destruction on Tamils.

On the previous night Wellawatte and Dehiwela, which contain the largest concentration of Tamils in Colombo, were unharmed. Now the mob from Canal Bank roamed these areas setting fire to Tamil homes and destroying Tamil shops. Looting followed.

Mobs from Slave Island and Maradana stormed into the Fort and at the Bo Tree Junction turned into Gas Works Street and Forth Cross Street which had a preponderence of Tamil establishments. They caused extensive destruction till Inspector Gererad Ignatius opened fire and contained the mob. Earlier another mob had entered the Main Street and reduced the Tamil shops there to a shambles, till Inspector Ignatius opened fire and brought the situation under control. He was promoted to rank of Assistant Superintendent of Police, at the first available opportunity.

The slums in Grandpass and Kotahena erupted about the same time and R. C. N. Gunesinghe, Assistant Superintendent of Police, himself opened fire at Panchikawatte and Armour Street. Kotahena was particularly badly affected and the Police opened fire again in Armour Street, also in Bonjean Street and Pickering Road and baton charged in Lukmanjee Square.

Meanwhile slums in the centre of the city, Narahenpita, Hattewatte and Kirillapone erupted and the violence spread to the middle class residential areas of Anderson Flats, Elvitigala Falts, Torrington Flats, and Thimbirigasyaya. Later the violence spread to Sulaiman Terrace, Buller's Road and Gregory's Road in the exclusive residential area of Cinnamon Gardens. By now the Canal Bank abutting another exclusive residential area of Park Road erupted. Around 12 noon distress signals were received at Police Headquarters and in the Ministry of Foreign Affairs that the home of R. M. Abhyankar, Deputy High Commissioner of India, was attacked. The Inspector-General of Police and I rushed there separately. The Vienna Convention clearly spells out the protection given to foreign diplomats. While the IGP handled the security aspects I handled the diplomatic aspects. Mercifully it was not the home of Abhyankar but that of his neighbours which were attacked. Another house on Park Road that was attacked was that of Ambassador C. Gunasingham, till recently High Commissioner for Sri Lanka in Singapore, and now a senior official in the Presidential Secretariat.

By now the entire city of Colombo was aflame. The suburbs of Ratmalana, on the south, Kadawatte and Kelaniya in the north and Nugeogda, on the west had also been attacked by rempaging mobs. Particularly revolting in the outburst of violence in Kadawatte was the fate that befell a passenger who was fleeing from Colombo in an ambulance. At the Kiribathgoda Junction the mob stopped the ambulance and he claimed to be a Muslim. But his foreskin proved otherwise and he was burnt alive.

The curfew declared by the President was to be effective from 6 p.m. in Colombo. It was advanced to 4 p.m. and later to 2 p.m. In view of the violence in Kelaniya, Kadawatte and later in Negombo the curfew was extended to the Gampaha district. As the violence spread to Kalutara town the Kalutara district was also subject to the curfew. The mob at Kalutara was particularly fierce. When the well known TKVS Stores was attacked, the owner fled upstairs to seek refuge but as the fire spread he jumped out of a window. A man of much wealth and with many enemies, he was got hold of physically by the mob and unceremoniously tossed into the inferno.

The rioting hitherto was by leaderless mobs. In the afternoon the violence took a different turn. There was organized violence by gangs which were quite obviously trained and who operated with military preceision. Their targets were the economic bases of the Tamils in Colombo and their homes.

The organized violence first erupted around 12 noon at Ratmalana, which has the largest concentration of factories in Sri Lanka. Mobs attacked Jetro Garments and Tata Garments situated on Galle Road. Both factories were completely gutted. They then attacked Tamil houses in the Soysa Flats. The housing estate has nearly 500 flats of which 92 were occupied by Tamils. Of them 81 were systematically broken into, household effects tossed out of the windows and then set on fire. The mob was armed with electroral lists used at the 1982 Presidential election, which was available to any citizen on the payment of a small fee.

W. A. Samarawickrema, Senior Superintendent of Police, Mount Lavinia opened fire and there were casualties but the mob turned into Borupana Ferry Road, on the landside, and Maligawa Road on the seaside. The Ponds factory, the S-lon pipe factory, Reeves Garments, Hydro Garments, Hyluck Garments and AGM Garments were consigned to the flames. The next targets were Manhattan Garments and Poly Pack on Kandewela Road. Further afield on Attidiya Road the mob proved its attack was premeditated by leaving alone the Indian factories such as Kundanmals, Oxford, and Bakson Garments. They set fire to the Tamil owned Berec factory and Mascons Asbestos plant. In this manner the organized violence accounted for 17 factories in Ratmalana and by evening the trained squads wound up their activity by setting on fire Tilly's Beach Hotel in Mount Lavinia after it was evacuated by occupants and staff.

In the meantime a train from Galle made an unscheduled stop at Attidiya Road in Ratmalana. The communication cord was pulled again when the train was abreast of Brighton Hotel in Wellawatte.

At each point trained squads were discharged. Shortly thereafter they demonstrated remarkable skill in destroying homes. They smashed up windows whenever they were closed, thus ensuring ventilation, they then broke the roof and from the roof top poured in petrol followed by a lighted taper.

Tamil homes were thus systematically consigned to the flames. Such homes were identified with pin point accuracy using electoral lists. In attacking shops the trained squads responded to three commands in Sinhala.

1. Kada (break)
2. Adha (Haul)
3. Gini (set fire)

During this process there was no looting whatsoever.

Wellawatte and Dehiwala were exposed to mob fury in the morning. The second wave of violence was of considerably larger magnitude. In Ratnakara Road, Dehiwala, there were 53 houses, with 26 Sinhalese houses and 27 Tamil houses. The Sinhalese houses were unharmed. 27 Tamil families lived in 24 houses owned by Tamils and 3 owned by Sinhalese. The 24 Tamil house holds were set on fire. The other 3 households had their moveable property thrown on to the road and then set on fire so as to prevent the houses being damaged.

After sometime the entire Galle Road from Bambalapitiya to Ratmalana looked as if it was a part of a war-torn country. One of the tragic features that day was the role of the Army. They were of passive deportment and merely looked on nonchalantly. Likewise in the Pettah, Maradana and Kotahena the Army merely looked on while fresh violence erupted.

The Tamil owned Maharaja Organisation is the largest commercial establishment in Sri Lanka next to the Upali Group. They lost six factories in Ratmalana, including Ponds, S-lon and Berec. By evening their Head Office in Bankshall Street and their new subsidiary Hettiaratchi Brothers, which still bore its Sinhalese name, were set on fire. Barring the Maharaja Organisation the largest Tamil commercial establishments in Sri Lanka were St. Anthony Hardware Stores, K. G. Industries and Easwaran Brothers. They were also situated in Grandpass. They were all consigned to the flames.

In view of the upheaval in the city, at the Welikade Jail the prisoners were confined to their quarters that afternoon. Within the Jail the maximum security is in the Chapel Section which is a three storey building accommodating 850 prisoners. The terrorists incarcerated there consisted of 35 prisoners, 6 convicted and 29 awaiting trial. They were all on the ground floor.

Shortly after 2 p.m. a large group of prisoners from the upper floors rushed down, overpowered the guards, removed their keys and locked the Chapel Section from inside. These prisoners were armed with makeshift iron rods which they had ripped off from the railings on their floor. What followed is perhaps best described in the findings of K. C. Wijewardene, Chief Magistrate, Colombo, who presided at the inquest.

> "On the evidence recorded by me, it is quite clear that on July 25th 1983 there had been a general unrest in the upper floors of the Chapel Section which had ended up in a riot. These prisoners had stormed into cells B3 and D3 on the ground floor. Violence had erupted, resulting in the death of 35 prisoners. There is no evidence, to identify any suspect, from amongst the prisoners who had so stormed into the wings. There is evidence that some prisoners had attempted to curb the violence by assisting the authorities. None of the Prisons officers or the Army Officers summoned to the scene thereafter could have done anything under the circumstances to prevent that attack. They have all been completely overpowered. None of those prisoners, who were eye witnesses to the incident have volunteered to give evidence before me today. The two who have testified are not eye witnesses and have admitted that they had seen nothing. I have perused the post mortem reports of the 35 deceased prisoners tendered before me and I hold that all deaths are cases of homicide, resulting from a riot in the prison. I therefore direct the Officer-in-Charge of the Borella Police Station to conduct further investigations and . . ."

Among those who were killed that day were Kuttimani, Thangadorai and Jegan. All of them were convicted of murder, sentenced to death and subsequently had their sentences commuted to life imprisonment. The autopsy of all deceased indicated that they were killed by blows with blunt weapons on the head and that none of the bodies were multilated.

Another distressing feature that day, in terms of the Vienna Convention, was the damage suffered by the staff of the High Commission of India. The clerical staff of this Mission lives in Wellawatte and many of them have Tamil names or Tamil sounding names. Their homes were subject to mob fury when the slums in the Canal Bank area erupted that morning. The High Commission evacuated these families to Hotel Taprobane. Later when the homes of the diplomatic staff were threatened they were evacuated to the Hotel Oberoi. That evening when First Secretary M. J. Abrahamas was returning home with his clerk K. V. Iyer, his car was set upon by hoodlums at Bambalapitiya and the vehicle set on fire. Iyer was hospitalized while Abrahams received out patient treatment.

The fire in Baillie Street near the President's House was still raging in the evening and some of the staff in the High Commission in the adjoining building feared that the Mission itself would be gutted. The Fire Brigade was taxed well beyond their resources but priority was given to the blaze in Baillie Street upon a request by the Ministry of Foreign Affairs. Once the fire was douched I visited the staff of the High Commission, first those in hospital, then those in hotels. Then my wife Marlyn joined me in calling on those who were still in their homes. Even in the face of adversity they were truly gracious. There was no recrimination on their part. In my knowledge of diplomacy they were truly worthy representatives of a great nation. The Government of Sri Lanka on its part was quick to fulfil its obligations under the Vienna Convention. Security arrangements were accorded the highest priority and compensation amounting to Rs. 1,267,000 was paid as early as practicable.

The violence which erupted on Monday 25th July was principally in the Western Province with Colombo and its suburbs being particularly badly affected. According to Police Headquarters, the violence in the rest of the Island that day was as indicated below:

District	*Murders*	*Arson*	*Looting*	*Mischief*
Galle	—	35	2	—
Kegalle	—	17	—	1
Trincomalee	—	21	—	—
Vavuniya	—	14	2	—

On Tuesday, 26th July 1983, Colombo was still smouldering. Kandy which had been remarkably quiet the previous day suddenly erupted in the afternoon. Around 2.45 p.m. the Delta Pharmacy on Peradeniya Road was ablaze. Shortly thereafter another Tamil shop near the Laksala building was set on fire. The violence spread to Castle Street and Colombo Street and was brought under control by the Police. However one hour later a marauding mob armed with petrol cans and Molotov cocktails suddenly appeared. In rapid succession Tamil shops in Colombo Street, Trincomalee Street, Kings Street and Castle Street were subject to their fury. It was a miracle that only one Tamil was killed. Having thus ravaged Kandy the mob traveled to Gampola which suffered a similar fate. That evening a curfew was imposed in the Kandy district.

That night the persistent rumour in Trincomalee was that the Naval Base near Karainagar Jaffna was razed to the ground. Jaffna had been captured by the Tigers and that the Naga Vihare, the Buddhist shrine in Jaffna, desecrated. That incensed the Navy and over 80 sailors broke barracks and went on the rampage. They stormed through Dockyard Road, causing much damage there as well as in Main Street, Central Road, North Coast Road and on Thirugnasambandan Road where they even attacked the Sivan Kovil. They accounted for 170 acts of arson before returning to their barracks. The Tamil population retaliated killing two Sinhala people, one outside the Sivan Kovil and the other in Ambuvalipuram.

Rear Admiral Asoka De Silva, the Commander of the Navy, arrived by air in Trincomalee on the morning of July 27th. With his typical sagacity he brought the situation under control. Thereafter with characteristic firmness he hounded out of the Navy 81 sailors who had gone on the rampage. They were dishonourably discharged without the formality of a Court Martial.

On Wednesday 27th July 1983, Trincomalee was relatively quiet except for the murder of a Tamil nurse and her domestic at Weliverikulam. Kandy was still smouldering and violence had spread from Gampola to Nawalapitiya and was contained in Hatton due to the skill of G. Ariyasena, Assistant Superintendent of Police. However violence erupted in Badulla which had hitherto been quiet.

Around 10.30 a.m. a motor cycle belonging to a Tamil was set on fire in front of the clock tower. The Police quickly brought the fire under control and Badulla remained calm though there was a sudden influx of strangers into the Bazaar area. Shortly after 12 noon organized mobs went rampaging and set stores and goods on fire. There was no looting whatsoever. Thus Bazaar Street was aflame. R. C. Dias, Assistant Superintendent of Police, Badulla, opened fire. He observed that the dead and injured were moved away with professional skill while the organized mobs continued with their destruction. Thereafter the rioting spread from the shopping area to the residential area. The homes of many Tamils including those of the much respected lawyer, S. Nadarajah and the much respected surgeon Dr. C. Sivagnam were set on fire.

In view of the escalation of violence P. Mahendran, Deputy Inspector-General of Police, requested the Army Training Centre in Diyatalawa for troops. By the time the troops arrived Yogan, a Tamil businessman who was a well-known Tiger sympathizer, had opened fire from his home resulting in two Police Constables being injured. The Army returned the fire. There were many casualties due to the firing as well as by lynching by an irate mob. For example, Yogan and his family were lynched.

Sellasamy Nadar, another Tiger sympathizer and his household met with a similar fate.

Those who organized the violence in Badulla were seen leaving for Hali-Ela, Bandarawela and Welimada in buses and vans in which they had arrived and other vehicles which they had commandeered in Badulla. By evening those towns were ablaze. By nightfall rioting had erupted in Lunugala. One of the casualties there was a Roman Catholic nun who was shot and subsequently succumbed to her injuries. Incidentally she was a Sinhalese.

In Colombo the relative calm on Wednesday 27th July 1983, was shattered by two major outbursts of violence. At the Fort Railway Station the Jaffna Express was leaving that morning several hours behind schedule. Just as the train was pulling out from platform No. 1 the Railway Security found a package of cartridges on the train. The train was stopped and troops were called in for the search. The Jaffna Express stops en-route at many large Sinhalese towns such as Kurunegala and Anuradhapura, hence the passengers were both Sinhalese and Tamil people. During the search one Tamil passenger attempted to run away. He was mistaken for a Tiger and set upon by angry Sinhalese passengers and killed. Then the Sinhala passengers attacked Tamil passengers, on the pretext they were Tigers. Altogether 11 Tamils were consigned to the flames on the rail track itself. Some were dead, others were still alive when the inceneration began!

Following the prison riot on Monday 25th July 1983, all the terrorists incarcerated in the Welikade Jail were removed from the Chapel Section and accommodated in the Youthful Offenders Building. That evening when the hard core prisoners in the Chapel Section went for dinner they overpowered their guards, rushed to the Firewood Chopping Section armed themselves with axes and firewood and then attacked the terrorists in the Youthful Offenders Building.

> "Subsequent Magisterail enquiry found, that the Prisons officers and Army personnel, who had been summoned from their points of duties outside the Prison gates, had done all in their power to quell the riot, and prevent harm to fellow prisoners and a mass-scale jail break. But the very magnitude of the mob and the swiftness of the attack had rendered their efforts futile as far as the deceased prisoners are concerned.
>
> Both the Army personnel, and the Prisons officers, had found that the intended mass-scale jail break had hindered the full

utilization of their forces in coming to the rescue of the deceased and injured prisoners.

However, the prompt and efficient steps taken by the special standby unit of the Army, serving under witness Major Sunil Peiris, of the Commandos had effectively prevented the Jail break referred to. They helped to quell the mob which might otherwise have even caused the death of other prisoners in the Building of Youthful Offenders who have fortunately survived. The action of this officer and those working under him deserve special commendation.

I find that the death of all 18 prisoners have been caused as a result of a riot in the prison. . . . "

On Thursday, 28th July 1983, Badulla was still smouldering and the rioting had spread from Lunugala to Passara. Fresh violence had erupted in Nuwara Eliya and Chilaw and had been brought under control by the Police. However Colombo, Kandy and Trincomalee were calm. The curfew imposed on an all island basis from 2 p.m. to 5 a.m. commencing the previous day was effective, by and large, and it appeared that the nation would return to normalcy by the following week.

Despite this carnage President J.R. Jayewardene did not address the nation on Monday 25th July or at the latest on Tuesday 26th July 1983. In his first month in office, he had made a speech in a Parliament on august18th 1977 within hours a minor racial riot breaking out in Anuradhapura and Kurunegala. That was when he said *inter alia.*

"When acts of violence were committed, it does not matter who committed them, whether they were Sinhalese or Tamils whether they were UNP supporters or SLEP supporters. They will be prosecuted in our Courts"

"Some of you want to shrik my responcibilityu but I do not intend to do so. To my mind all citizens irresepective of their race, irrespective of their elected to protect all our citizens and we shall do so"

(Source: Handsard)

Now even some UNP supporters were thinking about whether the President was actually shirting his responsibility. Finally he addressed the nation belatedly on Thursday 27th June 1983 at prime time. The President looked both sad and weary. He said,

"It is with deep regret and sorrow that I address you today. When I see the destruction around me, the spate of violence that has arisen, it is very, very distressing. This violence has been aimed particularly against the Tamil people, and it has been caused by the deep ill–feeling and the suspicion that has grown between the Sinhalese and the Tamil people for several years. When there is distrust, when there are grievances, it is easy to lead this violence, and we feel that there is an attempt to lead this violence for the purpose of destroying the political and economic progress that this Government has been able to ensure for our people.

It was from 1956 that this suspicion between the Sinhalese and the Tamil people first began. In 1976, for the first time a movement for the separation of our beloved motherland, the separation of a united Lanka into two nations, was also accepted. The Sinhalese people will never agree to the division of a country which has been a united nation for 2,500 years.

At first, this movement for separation was non-violent. But since 1976 it became violent. Violence increased and innocent people were murdered. Members of the Armed Services and the Police, politicians who did not agree with the movement for violence, whether they were Sinhalese or Tamil, were assassinated. It has grown to such large proportions that not a few but hundreds have been killed during this movement. Because of this violence by the terrorists, the Sinhalese people themselves have reacted. I feel that the movement for separation should have been banned long, long ago. I have also been a member of the Governments which are responsible for not banning it. I thought that in the All-Party Conference which I summoned a few days ago, which we were unable to hold, firstly, because all the parties did not accept my invitation, and secondly because of the violence and the curfew around us, I thought that at that conference I should say that we intend to implement the 1977 manifesto of the United National Party, which sought to solve some of the political problems, that arose, and once we did that, we would also ask the consensus of opinion to make the division of the country illegal.

Unfortunately, we could not hold that conference. But the Government has now decided that the time has come to accede to the clamour and the national request of the Sinhalese people that we do not allow the movement for division to grow any more.

The Cabinet, therefore, this morning decided that we should bring legislation, firstly, to prevent people from entering the Legislature if they belonged to a Party that seeks to divide the nation. Secondly, the legislation will make Parties that seek to divide the nation illegal or proscribe them. And once they are proscribed, the Members cannot sit in the Legislature. We will also see that those who belong to this Party or those who advocate the separation of the country lose their civic rights and cannot hold office, cannot practise any profession, cannot join movements or organizations in this country.

We are very sorry that this step should be taken. But I cannot see, and my Government cannot see, any other way by which we can appease the natural desire and request of the Sinhalese people to prevent the country being divided and to see that those who speak for division are not able to do so legally."

That afternoon Prime Minister Indira Gandhi telephoned President J. R. Jayawardene, and spoke of the repercussions in India caused by events in Sri Lanka. She inquired whether the President would receive Foreign Minister Narasimha Rao as her Special Envoy. The President readily agreed and six hours later a Boeing 737 of the Indian Air Force arrived at the Bandaranayake International Airport. Foreign Minister Narasimha Rao was greeted warmly on arrival by Foreign Minister A. C. S. Hameed. The Indian delegation even left for the President's House where they stayed as personal guests of President J. R. Jayewardene.

On Friday 29th 1983 July Foreign Minister Narasimha Rao had breakfast and a long discussion with the President. There was another round of talks that morning with Foreign Minister A. C. S. Hameed.

The rioting had hitherto caused much death and destruction and had also caused untold hardship to Tamils. Over one third of all Tamils in Colombo were displaced from their homes and were in Care and Welfare Centres, euphemisms for Refugee Camps. Such Centres were set up by the Government to give temporary relief to over 64,000 Tamils in Colombo, who were displaced from their homes.

Everybody, even children knew that the Sinhalese goons were responsible for the catastrophe, yet the President did not even refer to it. The President conveniently forgot to say that those responcible for this bloodshed will be tried under the Penal Code. Of course many openly criticized the President behind his back. More significantly, several criticized him to his face. The nett result was that President J.R.Jayewardene lost forever his reputation of being a firm leader.

While some Sinhalese people had behaved like barbarians and had committed terrible atrocities such as burning alive Tamils, many Sinhalese people helped at the Care and Welfare Centres on a voluntary basis and many thousands of Sinhalese homes gave shelter to Tamils.

Ironically even the dregs of life who behaved like barbarians did not forsake their friends. The Sinhalese hard-core prisoners who slaughtered terrorists in the Welikade Jail did not harm any hard-core Tamil prisoners. The Sinhalese slum dwellers did not harm any Tamils from the same slum.

With Friday 29th July 1983, being the third consecutive quiet day in Colombo, many Tamils were visiting their relatives and friends at the Care and Welfare Centres or doing their shopping. Such crowds were particularly large outside the Care and Welfare Centre at the Ratmalana Airport and in the Pettah.

In the Pettah vendors had brisk sales as life in the city was fast returning to normal. Around 10.30 a.m. that calm was shattered by gunfire. On Gas Works Street two Sinhalese youths collapsed with gun shot wounds. While Inspector U. H. Shelton who was on duty there rushed them to hospital, a crowd of 5,000 gathered and many pointed towards the Adam Ali Building from where they claimed the gunfire had emanated. The restive crowd then began to shout that the Tigers had opened fire. When the Army and Navy noticed some movement in that building situated at 136, Fourth Cross Street, facing Gas Works Street, they opened fire with their SMGs and SLRs.

The Adam Ali Building stood in splendid isolation as almost every other building on Fourth Cross Street had been set on fire on Monday 25th July. This building had been spared by the mobs as it was owned by the Borah community. Now the building was surrounded by Saladin Armoured Cars, encircled by the Army, Navy and Police while a lone helicopter sprayed it with machine gun fire.

R. C. N. Gunasinghe, Assistant Superintendent of Police spoke over his loud speaker in Tamil, English and Sinhala, in that order, and asked all Tamils in the building to surrender or else the Saladin Armoured Cars would open fire. Two innocuous and thoroughly frightened Tamils who looked incapable of violence then emerged. They were arrested. Thereafter the Commandos fired one burst from their T-56 assault rifles. In the absence of a response they stormed into the building together with the

Police. A meticulous search was made. There were no weapons and no ammunition. All they found were 25 Borah men, women and children frightened to death. The only Tamil in the building was a domestic servant hiding behind the overhead water rank. Through fear he had temporarily lost his faculties of speech.

In the meantime rabble rousers spread the word that the Army and Tigers were locked in mortal combat. The story spread like wildfire and frightened city workers fled for their life. Those who owned cars drove at break neck speed on both sides of the road as well as on the pavements. Others clambered on any type of vehicles, cars, buses, lorries, vans and trishaws. Some even traveled in luggage compartment of cars. While office workers behaved in this pitiable manner the slums of Colombo erupted again. Slum dwellers came out armed with axes, crow bars, iron rods and kitchen knives. Their children came out with bricks and stones. They all came out with fire in their eyes to kill the Tigers.

That day there were six tigers in Colombo. They were all in the Dehiwela Zoo!

After some time the slum dwellers waiting for the Tigers ran out of patience. They then stopped the vehicles fleeing from Colombo to search for Tamils. Tamil vehicles were set ablaze and even defenceless Tamils were promptly attacked.

Near the Dehiwela bridge Lionel Karunasena, Assistant Superintendent of Police and a former Asian Games athlete, opened fire with his SMG when slum dwellers on the Canal Bank set upon fleeing Tamils. About the same time for the same reason, Lal Ratnaike, Assistant Superintendent of Police, opened fire at the Canal Bridge near the Wellawatte Spinning & Weaving Mills. He later ordered a baton charge at Thimbirigasyaya. When the Narahenpita slums erupted Ratnaike opened fire again at the Mahawatte Junction.

A short while later A. C. A. Gaffoor, Senior Superintendent of Police and genial giant who had earlier that day saved five Tamils from a certain death, opened fire at Kirula Road. That was when he saw a mob setting a Tamil on fire, alive. The poor victim grappled with the flames before he succumbed to his burns.

In the Pettah Henry Silva, Superintendent of Police, opened fire when looters attacked Dam Street and Sea Street. In the meantime on Attidiya

Road, Tamils, who were fleeing from Ratmalana were trapped. By the time a Police patrol led by Chief Inspector Mohamed Mohideen who had displayed considerable gallantry on Monday that week, arrived at the scene, 11 Tamils were burnt alive. One of the first abandoned vehicles he looked into was a burcher's van which happened to travel on Attidiya Road on its way to the Mount Lavinia beef stall. On board were two Tamils and three Muslims. They were all butchered.

That day Kandy was quiet and Foreign Minister Narasimha Rao who arrived by helicoptor was able to see for himself the damage in that city. Trincomalee and Badulla were also quiet but organized violence erupted in Nuwara Eliya. About the time the Muslims had adjourned for their Jumma prayers, Ganesan Sores and Sivalingam Stores the largest Tamil establishments in Nuwara Eliya were attacked and set on fire. It triggered off a chain reaction which engulfed the Bazaar Street and Lawson Road.

There were also sporadic acts of violence in the Kegalle and Matara districts which were the areas of heavy fighting during the JVP insurrection of 1971. In the Kegalle district the violence spread from Dehiowita to Deraniyagala and was finally contained by the Police at Avissawella. In the Matara district Deniyaya and Morawake were badly affected. There was also fresh violence in Chilaw.

That evening the Government had information that the panic was generated by the JVP terrorists. The word was quietly passed within the Army. The soldiers promptly flexed their muscles. The time for apathy and nonchalanace was over. The Army had fought pitched battles with the JVP during the insurrection of 1971. Those memories still lingered.

With the Army backing the Police to the hilt, the curfew was rigidly reforced even though it was extended continuously over the weekend, from 2 p.m. on Friday till 5 a.m. on the following Monday. Except for the violence in Nuwara Eliya which spilt over to Kandapola and Hawa Eliya with renewed fury and the organized violence in Matale where the bazaar area and the residental area occupied by Tamils was flattened, the nation in general and Colombo in particular was quiet on Saturday 30th July 1983. That night the JVP, NSSP and the Communist Party were proscribed for alleged complicity in the riots. By Monday 1st August the law and the order position was almost normal. The violence unleashed throughout the Island following the ambush is tabulated below.

District	*Deaths*	*Arson*	*Looting*	*Mischief*
Badulla	52	838	630	378
Chilaw	2	161	20	22
Colombo	227	2720	1712	2165
Gampaha	7	216	58	53
Jaffna	70	40	13	1
Matale	3	1131	838	112
Matara	4	220	31	119
Kalutara	6	115	70	97
Kandy	31	1065	132	274
Kegalle	24	490	195	167
Nuwara Eliya	22	194	29	184
Vavuniya	4	23	7	16
Trincomalee	17	643	22	65
Other District	2	257	78	16
Total	**471**	**8077**	**3835**	**3769**

With the law and order situation well under control the biggest problem facing the J. R. Jayewardene Administration was the supply of food and essential goods. It was handled admirably by Lalith Athulathmudali, the Minister for Trade and Shipping. He was assisted by Bradman Weerakoon and Dharmasiri Pieris, two senior civil servants of exceptional ability. There were no shortages whatsoever except for cigarettes. Appparently during the riot, the retail outlets for cigarettes had gone up in smoke.

The visit of Foreign Minister Narasimha Rao to Sri Lanka on Friday 29th July 1983, helped to give the Government of India a clear picture of what happened in Sri Lanka. It was obvious to the visiting dignitary, that President Jayewardene was striving to bring the situation under control as quickly as possible and to prevent the massacre of innocent Tamils. By the same token it was obvious that passions had been roused to dangerous levels. In fact during this visit information was received from Paris that communal violence had erupted within the Sri Lanka community in that city. After several days of tension a Sinhalese student was got hold of by some Tamils and was thrown out of a sixth floor apartment. He died. When that violence in Paris subsided, the toll was 3 Sri Lankans dead, 13 in hospital and 39 in Police custody.

After the return of her Foreign Minister to New Delhi, Prime Minister Indira Gandhi made a statement in the Lok Sabha about the unfortunate events in Sri Lanka. She emphasized that the Government of India stood for the territorial integrity of Sri Lanka and for non-interference in the domestic affairs of Sri Lanka. She alluded to the traditional friendship between the two nations and the deep concern of both the Government and the people of India in the tragedy that had befallen Sri Lanka. She appealed in particular to the people of Tamil Nadu for restraint, as their passions had been roused due to the plight of Tamils in Sri Lanka. Prime Minister Indira Gandhi added that she had offered President Jayewardene whatever assistance Sri Lanka needed in the present crisis and that his request was for assistance of a humanitarian nature.

Accordingly, in the next few days chartered civilian aircraft from India brought in supplies of medicines and dry rations for the refugees. Chartered civilian ships were made available for the transport of refugees from Colombo to Jaffna. India was the first of several friendly nations to offer her hand of friendship to Sri Lanka in her hour of need. President Jayewardene was generous in his praise of the Government of India in general and Prime Minister Indira Gandhi in particular.

However, the reaction in Tamil Nadu was very different. The leader of the DMK, M. Karunanidhi, a former Chief Minister and now Leader of the Opposition, was strident in his attacks on Sri Lanka. He echoed the sentiments of Tamil radicals in Sri Lanka. Dr. S. Janarathanan, who resigned his post of chief Whip in the Tamil Nadu Government to protest over events in Sri Lanka called upon the Government of India to militarily intervene in Sri Lanka. When that request was ignored he called for a black flag demonstration when R.Venkataraman next arrived in Madras. Political opinion in Tamil Nadu ranging from the sublime to the ludicrous and the mass media was orchestrated against Sri Lanka. A *harthal* (stoppage of work) was observed on August 2nd. All parties including the ruling Anna DMK led by Chief Minister M. G. Ramachandran participated. Thousands of protest meetings were held throughout the length and breadth of Tamil Nadu by a cross section of political parties.

As passions were further roused in Tamil Nadu, Dr. Janarathanan resigned his membership of the Anna DMK and set up an office of the TULF at his residence. Karunanidhi resigned his seat in the State Legislature as a mark of protest. To internationalize the cause of the Sri Lanka Tamils, he organized a campaign to collect two million signatures for a petition to be placed before the UN. The petition sought UN intervention and UN Peace Keeping Forces to be stationed in Sri Lanka in a manner similar to the presence of such troops in Cyprus. P. Nedumaran, leader of the Gandhi

Kamraj National Congress, organized a sacrificial foot march from Madurai to Rameswaram and to sail across the Palk Street by boat in a token protest. The protest terminated on the beach at Rameswaram when the Indian Navy made its presence felt.

The ruling Anna DMK was restrained and did nothing to embarrass the Government of India. However the political climate in Tamil Nadu being openly hostile to Sri Lanka, the Anna DMK in one way or another echoed popular sentiments. As a dignified protest all Ministers in the Tamil Nadu Government wore black shirts for one month. One of them S. Ramachandran was a member of the Indian delegation to the UN General Assembly. Surprisingly the Government of India allowed him to bring up domestic affairs of Sri Lanka before the UN. Amassador I. B. Fonseka, Permanent Representative of Sri Lanka to the UN, was devastating in rebuttal.

When the racial riots broke out, the international Press corps suddenly descended upon Colombo. They were an assortment of amateurs, nincompoops and professionals. I handled the few professionals and ignored the others. The professionals, were given interviews with the President, and taken to Jaffna in Air Force helicopters at the height of the crisis. To the best of my knowledge none of them misreported the unforunate events in Sri Lanka. In fact many of them have given me invaluable assistance in writing my books.

As for the others the less said the better. They were only interested in increasing the circulation of their newspapers with horror stories from Sri Lanka.

For instance the *London Guardian* reported as follows on July 27th 1983,

EYES GOUGED OUT IN SRI LANKA GAOL
(From David Beresford in Colombo)

While accounts of massacres are circulating widely among Sri Lanka's Tamil population, it is the massacres in the Welikada goal which are attracting the most attention. There is particular interest in circumstances in which two alleged guerilla leaders were killed.

The two men, Sellarasa "Kuttimani" Yogachandran leader of the Tamil Eelam Liberation Organisation and a political writer and Ganeshanthan Jegenathan had been sentenced to death last year for the murder of a Policeman. In speeches from the dock, the two men announced that they would donate their eyes in the hope that they would be grafted on to Tamils who whould see the birth of Eelam, the Independent state for which they were fighting.

Reports from the Batticaloa gaol, where the survivors of the Welikada massacre are now being kept, say that the two men were forced to kneel and their eyes gouged out with iron bars before they were killed. One version has it that Kuttimani's tongue was cut out by an attacker who drank the blood and cried: "I have drunk the blood of a Tiger."

The verdict at the autopsy was that Kuttimani had extensive injuries on his skull which was battered by a blunt weapon. According to the verdict of the Coroner, which is a public document, there were no other injuries of significance. It was my unpleasant duty to take those foreign journalists, who preferred to believe rumours rather than the verdict of the autopsy, to the morgue. They were invited to open the eyelids of Kuttimani and satisfy themselves.

Another bizarre report emanating from Colombo at the height of the Press censorship, was on the United Press International wire service of August 2nd 1983. The despatch read as follows:

COLOMBO VERY NERVOUS

Colombo (Stewart Slavin reporting)

"With calm returning to burned-out streets in Sri Lanka after a week of ethnic violence that left at least 239 people dead, the Government cracked down on Marxist parties and published reports that it feared an attack from neighbouring India.

Government sources said fears of foreign intervention following the violence between the majority Buddhist Sinhalese and minority Hindu Tamils prompted a request for pledges of military assistance from Pakistan, Bangladesh, Britain and the United States.

They said Pakistan and Bangladesh had responded positively while the US and British Embassies were awaiting instructions from their Governments."

I noticed that Slavin was monumentally naïve about politics in South East Asia, though he was South Asia Manager of the United Press International. He was wondering around Colombo sporting a baseball cap and in fact at first I mistook him for a baseball correspondent! When I telephoned him to inquire whether he had sent this blasphemous dispatch, he swore he had not. I then sent him with my compliments, the relevant portion of the UPI tape complete with his name. Of course I had him deported on the first available aircraft and simultaneously made available a visa for any professional and experienced journalist from United Press International to replace him. They accepted the offer meekly.

The insidious propaganda of the Eelam lobby was even more blasphemous. The LTTE led by Prabhakaran had made it public that the ambush at Tinneveli on July 23rd 1983, was their massive reprisal for the killing of Seelan on July 15th. Yet Ratnam Nithiananthan, a virulent London-based Eelam propagandist, came on a BBC Television programmed on July 25th and said,

"According to reliable information received by me, the Army raped three girls at the Tinneveli Teacher Training College last week. They took them in an Army lorry and . . . . The ambush was to teach the Army a lesson for desecrating Tamil womanhood."

The Eelam supporters throughout the world drummed up this rape story. It is still believed by Tamils in all parts of the world except in the Jaffna district. There it was dismissed as arrant nonsense.

The Eelam propaganda was designed to whip up hatred against Sri Lanka. It was now without any sense of proportion. For instance. Tamara Kunanayakam, a Geneva based Eelam propagandist who works part time for the World Council of Churches, sent the following telex to the Assembly of the World Council of Churches held in Vancouver, Canada on July 29th.

> "Just received news that Velvettiturai town has been razed and all inhabitants killed.
>
> Navy has killed 1,000 in Trincomalee
>
> Two refugee camps in Colombo have been attacked
>
> Food supplies of Jaffna are being blocked by the Army
>
> Our sources of information are UNDP, Colombo, NORAD Colombo and Tamil Information Centre, London."

The UNDP publicly denounced this statement as being blasphemous. This communication was a talking point at the Assembly in Vancouver till the leadership of the Roman Catholic Church and Protestant Churches in Sri Lanka enlightened them.

From the view point of news there was very little to report about Sri Lanka in August, except that the nation fast returned to normal and the Sixth Amendment to the Constitution outlawing separatist movements was duly passed in Parliament. However abroad, the propaganda against

Sri Lanka continued unabated both in the media and on the grapevine. It was indeed distressing to observe the extent to which the nation was vilified and insulted.

1983 was indeed the worst years in the history of Sri Lanka since Independence in 1948. The riots caused incalculable damage to our multiracial society. For example, according to the Government of Sri Lanka 64,000 Tamil residents of the city of Colombo were accommodated in Welfare Centres, euphemisms for refugee camps, during the riots. According to the Census of 1981 the Tamil population of the city was 165,952. Thus one in every three Tamils in Colombo was a refugee!

The foolish amongst the Sinhalese, indeed there are a surprisingly large number of them in the context of the tenuous relationship between the Sinhalese and Tamils, perceived that driving away the Tamils was one sure way of teaching them a lesson. Such pitiable Sinhalese were indeed incapable of even comprehending that causing the Tamils to flee to the Northern and Eastern Provinces will surely create the sovereign State of Tamil Ealam. Indeed the LTTE has sworn to create such a state with recourse to terrorism and the Government of Sri Lanka had pledged to prevent it at all cost.

Economically Sri Lanka had suffered immensely from the recent riots. The ethnic holocaust had cost the nation Rs. 5 billion according to conservative estimates. The riots were in July and by September 1983 the cancellation of tourist reservations for the winter season November 1983/March 1984 was staggering. By September 1983 the giant multinationals Harris and Motorola, who were due to set up factories in the Free Trade Zone at Katunayake had decided not to commence operations in Sri Lanka. So had a number of less well known foreign companies who hitherto had serious intentions of investing in Sri Lanka.

Another distressing development was in respect of foreign aid. In 1977, shortly after his inauguration President Jimmy Carter of the United States had enunciated the principle that in apportioning US aid to foreign countries, the Human Rights record of the recipient nation would be given serious consideration. By the early eighties Australia, Canada and the Scandinavian countries had decided to follow suit. Now in September 1983 our Diplomatic Missions in Canberra, Ottawa, Stockholm and Washington were alerting our Ministry of Foreign Affairs that curtailment of aid to Sri Lanka from those countries was a distinct possibility. This was confirmed by our Mission to the UN in Geneva which handles Human Rights issues. In October 1983, Foreign Minister A. C. S. Hameed left for the UN General Assembly in New York and more importantly to sound fellow Foreign Ministers. His findings were even more adverse. If there were to be a repetition of July 1983, Aid giving nations would write off Sri Lanka altogether, like they had already done to Kampuchea.

It is India, not the Aid giving countries in the West, that is the critical foreign component in the ethnic equation. In the frequent messages exchanged through usual diplomatic channels, the view point of the Government of India came through clearly as follows:

1) The Government of India will never allow the creation of a sovereign State of Tamil Eelam, because such a secession in Sri Lanka may result in Tamil Nadu seceding from India.

2) The Government of India cannot remain a silent spectator while Tamils are facing genocide in Sri Lanka, because that will inflame passions in Tamil Nadu, the home of over 50 million Tamils.

3) Therefore the Government of India favours a just and durable peace with the Tamils living in harmony with the Sinhalese.

India was not alone in her concern for our Tamils who had suffered immensely during the several racial riots for example one in 1977 another in 1981. Australia and Canada acting on purely humanitarian grounds gave the much sought after permanent resident status to those Tamils who were displaced as a result of the recent violence and wanted to begin new lives abroad.

A visible change in the recent political scenario in Sri Lanka was that the Tamil community in the Northern Province in particular, was by and large disenchanted with the Tamil United Liberation Front (TULF). The TULF had received a massive mandate at the General Election of 1977 and won all 14 Parliamentary seats in that Province. Now in the Northern Province the performance of the TULF was looked upon with disdain while the representatives of the terrorist movements were affectionately referred to as "the boys." This gravitation towards "the boys" was further accentuated when The Sixth Amendment to the Constitution became law in August 1983. The Sixth Amendment outlawed all separatist movements and called upon all holding public office to take an appropriate oath. The TULF Parliamentarians refused to take that oath and thereby forfeited their seats. This caused a political vacuum in the Tamil speaking areas which was filled, by "the boys."

Another development of significance was the role played by the Tamil expatriate communities in Australia, Canada, New Zealand, the UK and the USA. In 1983 their numbers would have been in excess of 100,000 and they contributed generously to the coffers of "the boys." Besides they helped to blacken the name of Sri Lanka in the foreign media with a mixture of truths, half-truths and un-truths.

No commentary of events in Sri Lanka after the ethnic holocaust of 1983 is complete without some reference to developments in Tamil Nadu, India, the home of 55 million Tamils out of a global population of approximately 60 million Tamils. This southern State of India, which at the closest point is only 35 kilometers away from northern Sri Lanka, was incensed at the atrocities committed by the Sinhalese on the Tamils in Sri Lanka. The outpouring of grief was spontaneous and it was obvious that the people of Tamil Nadu, let alone their Government, were more than willing to materially help "the boys."

The first peace initiatives began shortly after the ethnic holocaust of July 1983. The Special Envoy of Prime Minister Indira Gandhi of India, Ambassador Gopalswamy Parthasarathy, Chairman of the Policy Planning Commission arrived in Colombo in August 1983. He was a State guest and resided at President's House. I was assigned to his staff by the President who had been informed that he and "Jungle" Dissanayaka used to play bridge together. It was the other "Jungle" Dissanayaka, my father who was a bridge friend! Ambassador Parthasarathy, who was an Oxford educated Brahamin from Madras had several meetings with the President, on the one hand and the former Leader of the Opposition, A. Amirthalingam, on the other. After lengthy private deliberations he produced a draft known as Annexure C to be discussed in New Delhi where the President was due to meet the Prime Minister of India, at discussions during the Commonwealth Summit. (A. Amirthalingam was also in New Delhi.) Annexure C was accepted by all the three leaders. Accordingly the following joint communique was issued in New Delhi.

> "The following proposals have emerged as a result of the discussions in Colombo and New Delhi and are appended for consideration by the All Party Conference. These proposals are in the context of the unity and integrity of Sri Lanka and will form a basis for formulating the agenda of the All Party Conference.
>
> (1) The District Development Councils in a Province be permitted to combine into one or more Regional Councils, if they so agree, by decisions of the Councils and approved by Referendum in that district

(2) In the case of the District Councils in the Northern and Eastern Provinces respectively, as they are not functioning due to the resignation of the majority of members, their union within each Province to be accepted.

(3) Each Region will have a Regional Council if so decided. The convention will be established that the leader of the party which commands a majority in the regional Council would be formally appointed by the President as the Chief Minister of the Region.

(4) The President and Parliament will continue to have overall responsibility over all subjects not transferred to the regions and generally for all the matters relating to the maintenance of the sovereignty, integrity, unity and security and progress and development of the Republic as a whole.

(5) The legislative power of the Region would be vested in the Regional Councils which would be empowered to enact laws and exercise executive powers in relation thereto on certain specified listed subjects including the maintence of Internal Law and Order in the Region, the Administration of Justice, Social and Economic Development, Cultural matters and Land policy. The list of subjects which will be allocated to the Regions will be worked out in detail.

(6) The Regional Councils will also have the power to levy taxes, cess or fees and to mobilize resources through loans, the proceeds of which will be credited to a Consolidated Fund set up for that particular Region to which also will be credited grants, allocations or subventions made by the Republic.

Financial resources will be allocated to the Regions on the recommendations of a representative of the Finance Commission appointed from time to time.

(7) Provision will be made for constituting High Courts in each Region. The Supreme Court of Sri Lanka will exercise appellate and constitutional jurisdiction.

(8) Each Region will have a Regional Sevice consisting of:
   (a) Officers and other public servants of the Region and,
   (b) Such other officers and public servants who may be seconded to the Region. Each Region will have a Regional Public Service Commission for recruitment and for

exercising disciplinary powers relating to the members of the Regional Service.

(9) The Armed Forces of Sri Lanka will adequately reflect the national ethnic composition. In the Northern and Eastern Regions, the Police forces for internal security will also reflect the ethnic composition of these Regions.

(10) A Port Authority under the Central Government will be set up for administering the Port of Trincomalee. The area which will come under the administration of the Port Authority as well as the powers to be assigned to it will be further discussed.

(11) A national policy on land settlement and the basis on which the Government will undertake land colonization will have to be worked out. All settlement schemes should be based on ethnic proportions so as not to alter the demographic balance subject to agreement being reached on major projects.

(12) The Constitution and other laws dealing with the Official Language, Sinhala and the national language, Tamil be accepted and implemented as well as similar laws dealing with the National Flag and Anthem.

(13) The Conference should appoint a committee to work out constitutional and legal changes that may be necessary to implement these decisions. The Government would provide its Secretariat and necessary legal offices.

(14) The consensus of opinion of the All Parties Conference will itself be considered by the United National Party Executive Committee and presumably by the executive bodies of the other Parties as well, before being placed before Parliament.

President Jayewardane had last been in New Delhi in March 1983 for the Non-Aligned Summit and during his visit in December 1983 he saw for himself how greatly the image of his Government had been tarnished. Upon his return to Colombo he informed the Government Parliamentary Group, led by Prime Minister R. Premadasa, that nobody he had met in New Delhi had believed the version of his Government but they had all believed the version of A. Amirthalingam, the leader of the TULF.

Following the racial riots of July 1983, there was a flood of applicants from Tamil youth to join the LTTE and other terrorist organizations such as EROS, PLOTE, TELO, EPRLF etc. Till July 1983, terrorist activity was by and large confined to the Jaffna peninsula. Now it had spread to the other districts in the Northern Province namely Mannar, Mullaitivu and Vavuniya. According to the Intelligence reports so meticulously prepared by Cyril Herath, the newly appointed Deputy Inspector-General of Police (Intelligence), the terrorist organizations were spreading their tentacles to the Trincomalee District where Tamils, Sinhalese and Muslims lived roughly in equal numbers. He added that the terrorist organizations would spread further southwards to the Batticaloa district, where of late local fishing vessels were frequently visiting foreign freighters anchored just beyond the horizon and returning with medium sized boxes. In this manner arms were being smuggled into Batticaloa. Herath, probably the best Intelligence officer the nation has yet produced, had a habit of falling foul of successive Governments because of his unswerving loyalty to the truth. Now his reports were studied with great interest because of their amazing accuracy. He even gave the exact location of LTTE training camps in Tamil Nadu in India.

Thus in 1984, the basic strategy of President Jayewardene was to contain militarily the growth of the Tamil terrorist movements and simultaneously work out a political solution. At the time of recent riots the Army under the command of Major General T. I. "Bull" Weeratunge amounted to only 12,000. The President directed that the strength of the Army be doubled and authorized similar increases in cadre for the Air Force and Navy if that became necessary. Above all, President Jayewardene initiated a round table conference for all political parties, whether they be represented in Parliament or not, to evolve a viable political solution to the vexed ethnic problem. Known as the All Party Conference it began on January 10th, 1984 with following parties participating.

United National Party
Sri Lanka Freedom Party
Tamil United Liberation Front
Tamil Congress
Federal Party
Communist Party
Lanka Sama Samaja Party
Mahajana Eksath Peramuna
Ceylon Workers Congress
Democratic Workers Congress

Thus the entire spectrum of political opinion in Sri Lanka was represented at this Conference. Furthermore, the *Maha Sangha*

(Buddhist clergy) who traditionally play a critically important role in matters pertaining to Buddhism and the Sinhalese race were invited to participate. Therefore as a matter of courtesy, religious dignitaries of all other faiths were also invited.

In essence, the proposals placed before the All Party Conference by President Jayewardene was a document frequently referred to as Annexure C. It had its roots in the District Councils Act of 1980 which the TULF had supported enthusiastically and resulted in the elections for District Councils in 1981. Unfortunately the District Councils were treated lightly by many members of the Cabinet of President Jayewardene and such Councils were all but dead by 1984. Annexure C was perhaps the best compromise any Sinhalese leadership could offer the embittered Tamils in the aftermath of the riots of 1983. Besides it had the benedictions of the Government of India. However President Jayewardene found that his Cabinet was opposed to it. Therefore he jettisoned it, much to the chagrin of India.

The first round of serious negotiations at the All Party Conference began on January 11th 1984, with the formation of two committees. One was to examine the grievances of all ethnic groups, the other to examine the causes for the holocaust of July 1983 and devise the means to eradicate them. The mood at the Conference was somber, yet radiating goodwill. However the LTTE observed the occasion in a typical manner. They attacked the Police Station at Point Pedro, the northern most point in Sri Lanka, and killed two Policemen. They were later horrified to learn that both Policemen killed were Tamils. A few days later the PLOTE kidnapped 12 students from the University of Jaffna who were on hunger strike, whereupon the Government imposed a curfew. In the meantime the UNP and the SLFP, the two largest political parties in Sri Lanka which have alternatively formed Governments in Sri Lanka, were quarrelling at the All Party Conference. The main problem at the Conference was devolution of power in the Tamil speaking areas. The SLFP accused President Jayewardene of trying to impose his will on the Conference and accused the TULF of encouraging Indian interference in our domestic affairs. On February 6th 1984, the SLFP walked out of the All Party Conference thus creating much turmoil. There was more turmoil that week when the LTTE attacked the Police Station at Chunnakam and snipers from EROS killed some soldiers near Achuvelly. Thereafter the TULF whined that ten Tamil shops in Achuvelly had mysteriously caught fire and accused the Sri Lanka Army of sabotage.

To streamline work on security matters, in March 1984, President Jayewardene appointed Lalith Athulathmudali, Minister of Trade & Shipping since 1977, to the new portfolio of Minister for National Security. His new appointment was well received in political circles in Sri Lanka. It was heralded by the terrorist movement with a spate of violence in Jaffna resulting in a curfew being imposed. One of the first edicts issued by the new Minister of National Security was to establish a Naval surveillance zone covering our territorial waters off the coast of the North-Western Province, the Northern Province and the Eastern Province. The explicit purpose of this zone was to prevent Tamils illegally traveling to India, where according to our Iintelligence reports they were being trained as terrorists and to prevent their subsequent return. Thereafter Athulathmudali left for India to explain to his peers there, the misgivings of the Government of Sri Lanka. He invited me to join his delegation and also obtained permission from the President for me to work half a day daily in the Ministry of National Secirity.

Another development of consequence during March was the tirade against India delivered in the course of a debate in our Parliament. A Member of Parliament well known for his eloquence accused India of giving succour to Sri Lankan Tamil terrorists in Tamil Nadu. He then sarcastically invited India to invade Sri Lanka. Had this angry outburst emanated from a backbencher it would have been conveniently ignored by the Government of India. However the tirade was delivered by Prime Minister Premadasa himself!

For three days there was an ominous silence from New Delhi. Then the spokesman for their Ministry of External Affairs stated publicly that since Independence in 1947 no Prime Minister of a foreign country had ever insulted India in this manner. Thereafter, the spokesman refuted the allegations on behalf of the Government of India.

On May 6th 1984 the All Party Conference reconvened and many were wondering what response would emanate from the terrorists. On May 8th the EPRLF kidnapped USAID official Stanley Allen and his bride Mary who were based in Jaffna and threatened to execute them unless a ransom of Rs. 50 million (approximately US $2 million) was paid and 20 Tamils held in remand prisons for terrorist offences were released. This episode resulted in many Aid Missions in Colombo immediately recalling all their experts based in the Northern Province while the Government of Sri Lanka began immediately to negotiate the release of the Allens. They were unconditionally released within a few days after Washington had applied much pressure on New Delhi which in turn applied pressure on

Madras. However the following week EPRLF units supported by the TELO and TEA stormed the Batticaloa jail to secure the release of Rev. A. Singarayar, a Roman Catholic priest, and Nirmala Nithiyanantha, a lecturer at the University of Jaffna, who were due to stand trial shortly for terrorist offences. They were the most prominent of the 20 prisoners whose release the EPRLF had demanded in their original ransom note pertaining to the Allens.

About this time President Jayewardene was working out new initiatives within his foreign policy. He had secretly negotiated with Israel for their anti-terrorist experts to train our combat troops and also to provide them with modern arms. The political price for the package was allowing Israel to have an Interests Section in Colombo as the two countries did not have diplomatic ties. The President agreed and retaliation from the Arab world was swift. Kuwait refused to issue work permits for our housemaids, Saudi Arabia cancelled their aid for the Mahaweli downstream project, Iraq cancelled some substantial orders for our tea and Sudan refused to accept the credentials of our Ambassador who was based in Cairo.

The strategy of President Jayewardene was to accommodate the Indian factor within our domestic politics and simultaneously woo the traditional enemies of India, namely China and Pakistan and those who could influence India decisively, especially the United States and the United Kingdom. In exchanges through normal diplomatic channels, China and Pakistan had expressed their solidarity with Sri Lanka and offered arms to fight the terrorist menace. Accordingly, State visits to both countries were scheduled for June 1984. A State visit to the United States of America and an official visit to the United Kingdom were scheduled for July 1984. The State visit to China was very successful indeed with the Government of China bending over backwards publicly to assist Sri Lanka. The State visit to Pakistan, postponed by a few months because of the ill health of President Zia-ul-Haq, achieved the same result. The State visit to the United States of America and the official visit to the United Kingdom were just as cordial. However, both nations continued to enforce their arms embargo on Sri Lanka, because of its poor Human Rights record in 1983. They exhorted the President to solve the ethnic problem through negotiation and delivered a clear message to India about the sovereignty of Sri Lanka. The latter was vital because in many quarters in Colombo there was the lurking fear that India would invade Sri Lanka.

In fact the TULF and the overseas Tamils were hoping this would happen in July 1983. The Government of India at the highest levels, India emphasized both privately and publicly that she had never entertained such illusions in the past and will never contemplate such an adventure in the future. However all manner of politicians in India, some mere voices in the wilderness, others not without influence, have advocated the Military option. Therefore the signals emanating from Beijing, Islamabad, London and Washington were indeed well received in Colombo and clearly understood in New Delhi.

The first serious attempt to negotiate an honourable peace was in November 1983. However, without the far reaching reforms embodied in Annexure C, the All Party Conference summoned by President Jayewardene for January 1984 turned out to be a ritual of sophistry. The farce went on for eleven long months. In the meantime the numerical strength and the military skill of the LTTE increased by leaps and bounds. On his part President Jayewardene doubled the sanctioned strength of the Armed Forces but they could not contain the LTTE who had made the North and the East ungovernable. On May 14th 1985, the LTTE unleashed their first retaliatory raid on the heartland of the Sinhala speaking areas it was on the sacred *Sri Maha Bodhiya**, in Anuradhapura.

The impact of this crime on the Sinhalese was indeed staggering. For once they clamoured for a negotiated settlement with the LTTE. Thus it was opportune to embark an a second attempt to negotiate for a durable peace. Accordingly a meeting was arranged through the courtesy of the Government of India. It was held in Thimpu, the capital of Bhutan, which is not easily accessible because it is located at high elevation in the Himalayas. Somehow President Jayewardene missed the mood of the nation and offered to negotiate on the basis of the defunct District Development Councils Act of 1980. Much worse, the delegation of Sri Lanka consisted only of officials. I was one of them but at the last moment was replaced by Ambassador C. Mahendran, a superb diplomat and more importantly, a Tamil. It was led by H.W. Jayewardene, the eminent lawyer and younger brother of the President. After its inevitable collapse, the Government of Sri Lanka once again began serious talks with India. The first of such discussions took place in New Delhi between H.W. Jayewardene and Foreign Secretary Romesh Bhandari, of India, who had organised the talks in Thimpu.

The new round of talks in New Delhi in August 1985 laid the foundation for more detailed discussions. Shortly thereafter, M. Sivasithamparam,

* *The Sri Maha Bodhiya is a Bo tree which has grown from a sapling brought from Buddha Gaya 2,500 years ago. Lord Buddha had attained Enlightenment under that Bo tree.*

the President of the TULF together with A. Amirthalingam arrived in New Delhi for consultations with Foreign Secretary Romesh Bhandari and others. On August 4th 1985, they had already written to Prime Minister Rajiv Gandhi as follows:

> "The fundamental basis for any solution to the Tamil problem will be the recognition of the right of the Tamil people to rule themselves in their traditional homelands. In our view such a devolution of power is an absolutely necessary pre-requisite for peace.
>
> As you are aware serious inroads have been made into these trational homelands of the Tamils with State-aided Sinhalese settlers. That has been a way of life ever since Independence and even before. It is analogous to Isreal planting Jewish settlers in occupied Palestine. The pernicious policy of State-aided Sinhalese peasants encroaching on our traditional homelands must stop forthwith."

On October 3rd 1985 President J.R. Jayewardene wrote to Prime Minister Rajiv Gandhi as follows:

> "..
> .... and we have been receiving reports from reliable sources that there is regular movement of weapons, explosives and manpower from Tamil Nadu to Sri Lanka, particularly after the ceasefire became operative. It is between Rameshwaram and Point Calimere and also from points north of Calimere including Vedaraniyam and Nagapattinam that much of this movement took place.
>
> "If it is in any way possible to increase your Coast Guard patrols in Indian waters to prevent these movements from taking place, it would be of great assistance to us; it will also help in a long way to resolve the major problem of terrorism that faces us. We have to increase our defensive mechanisam much more to make detections and ultimately to stop this illegal traffic. This requires large expenditure of capital in training of personnel which will take quite a long time. If you consider it useful I can send my Commander of the Navy or his representative to brief your relevant officials in this problem that faces us.
>
> With kind regards and hoping to meet you in the Bahamas."

It was at the Commonwealth Summit in Nassau, Bahamas, that President Jayewardene first gave Prime Minister Rajiv Gandhi definitive evidence of LTTE activity in Tamil Nadu, India. It was a CIA report which was handed over to the President by General Vernon Walters, the Ambassador at large of President Ronald Regan of the United States.

A report most damaging to India, it clearly spelt out LTTE activity undertaken with the knowledge of Chief Minister M.G. Ramachandran of Tamil Nadu. By then the LTTE had thirty five training camps in Tamil Nadu in the districts of Anna, Chegalpattu, Madurai, Puddukkotai, South Arcot, Salem, Thanjavur, Tiruchi and Ramanathapuram. The LTTE supply bases were in the districts of Atiruchi, Coimbatore, Dharmapuri, Madurai, Periyar, Padukottai, Tanjavur and Rameshwaran. Coimbatore was the principal supply base for arms, ammunition and explosives; Dharmapuri for explosives and Periyar for uniforms. Tuticorin was a haven for smugglers, Tanjavur had their communication centre and Tiruchi the hospitals for the wounded. Nagapattinam was the coastal area from where professional smugglers ferried arms and ammunition across the Palk Strait to Sri Lanka. President Jayewardene indeed surprised Prime Minister Rajiv Gandhi who pretended that he had never heard any of this before. The President assured him that General Vernon Walters would personally hand over a copy of the report on his next visit to New Delhi. The President also emphasised that Sri Lanka would like to have a team from the Commonwealth to investigate into happenings on both sides of the Palk Straits but India promptly vetoed that proposal.

In early 1986, Prime Minister Rajiv Gandhi sent Minister of State, P. Chidambaram, as his Special Envoy with a proposal he had received from the TULF. (He was at Harvard in my time. As of May 2004 he is the Minister of Finance). In essence it was a proposed Constitutional amendment which was to replace the unitary form of Government with a Union of Regions, to carve out the Sinhala speaking electorate in the Trincomalee district and fuse it with the Sinhala speaking Polonnaruwa district of the North-Central Province, to join the Sinhala speaking areas of the Ampara district with the contiguous Sinhala speaking Moneragala district of the Uva Province, the balance areas in the Eastern Province to amalgamate with the Northern Province. Thus the Tamils would have a Tamil speaking North - Eastern Province and the Sinhalese an expanded North-Central Province and an expanded Uva Province. It was indeed an interesting proposal with one flaw. The proposed North-Eastern Province would have two-thirds of the coastline and one-quarter of the land mass of Sri Lanka for just one-eighth of the population.

President Jayewardene gave that proposal considerable thought and rejected it because of that flaw. In direct contrast, since 1995, President Chandrika Bandaranaike Kumaratunga has advocated this proposal as the basis of negotiation with the TULF and other Tamil parties in Parliament.

In April 1986, Prime Minister Rajiv Gandhi sent Minister of State P. Chidambaram and Minister of State, K. Natwar Singh, as Special Envoys to persuade President J.R. Jayewardene to accept the proposal he had rejected three months ago. The President explained that the proposal was indeed attractive to India because carving out a lingustic Province in Sri Lanka was very similar to carving out lingustic States within India, which were successfully achieved by Prime Minister Jawaharlal Nehru in the early years of Independence.

For example in 1952, the intermittent clashes in Central India were obviated when a Telugu speaking State of Andhra Pradesh, was carved out of the Madras Presidency, the State of Mysore and the State of Hyderabad. To quote another example, in 196o the Bombay state was bifurcated to the Gujarati speaking State of Gujarat and the Marathi speaking State of Maharastra. That obviated the earlier intermittent clashes between the Gujarati and Marathi speaking populations. However the President wanted it explained to Prime Minister Rajiv Gandhi how careful and wise his famous grandfather had been on the threat of secession to India. At the General Election of 1957, in Tamil Nadu the Dravida Munetra Kazagam (DMK) led by C.N. Annadurai contested for the first time. The DMK was formed in 1953 against the background of the Government of India declaring that Hindi will be the sole official language of India after twenty five years. In the anti Hindi fervour the DMK campaigned on the basis that if they win, the Madras State as Tamil Nadu was then known, will secede from the Union of India. The Congress won a massive 75% of the votes and the DMK the balance 25%. However Prime Minister Jawaharlal Nehru was perturbed and in 1957 itself he brought in The Sixteenth Amendment to the Constitution of India which made it illegal for any recognised political party to advocate secession from India. Thus at the General Election of 1966, when the DMK led by C.N. Annadurai won by a landslide in Tamil Nadu, the cry of secession had already become a forgotten chapter. President Jayewardene then explained that India was now recommending a linguistic North-Eastern Province, in the very area of the State of Tamil Eelam advocated by the TULF in the Vaddukkodai resolution of 1976 and currently by the LTTE. To Special Envoy Natwar Singh, a former. Commissioner of India to Pakistan, that message was indeed clear and he did not pursue this subject any more.

During that visit of two Special Envoys, on May 3rd 1986, the LTTE attacked decisively with a spectacular explosion on board the Air Lanka Tristar flight UL 501 London-Colombo-Male, when it was on the parking apron at the Bandaranaike International Airport. The transit passengers had already boarded the ill-fated aircraft, when a time bomb in one of the crates transporting meat and vegetables to tourist hotels in the Maldive Islands blew the Tristar apart. It was a fearsome sight with debris scattered all over the tarmac within a radius of 100 meters of the ill-fated Tristar. The death toll was 16 including 13 foreigners. In June 1986, the Eelam Revolutionary Organisation of Students (EROS) triggered off explosions in Colombo at the Central Telegraph Office and at the Ceylon Cold Stores Ltd., a well known Company since British times. Thus the war had come to Colombo.

The next encounter President J.R. Jayewardene had with Prime Minister Rajiv Gandhi was in Bangalore at the SAARC Summit held on November 15th - 16th, 1986. By then India had no fresh proposals for a negotiated settlement. Perhaps for that reason the Prime Minister of India brought Prabhakaran for a private dialogue with the President. That too was an exercise in futility. However, in Bangalore President Jayewardene for the first time proposed the trifurcation of the Eastern Province, with one segment for Tamils, one for Sinhalese and another for Muslims. In due course it was turned down by the TULF. Therefore the two Special Envoys of Prime Minister Rajiv Gandhi, Natwar Singh and P. Chidambaram visited Colombo on December 17th 1986 to meet the President. Natwar Singh suggested that the District of Ampara in the Eastern Province be de-linked and merged with the Province of Uva. President Jayewardene listened sympathetically. Then Chidambaram suggested that the balance of the Eastern Province be merged with the Northern Province. President Jayewardene emphatically turned it down and again repeated the example of how Prime Minister Jawaharlal Nehru created linguistic States but never left room for secession. At the end of the day "the December 19th" proposals turned out to be as follows,

(1) The Eastern Province minus the District of Ampara will constitute the new Eastern Province.
(2) The concept of Provincial Councils is acceptable.
(3) The Northern Province and the new Eastern Province will have separate Provincial Councils.
(4) At a subsequent date the Government of Sri Lanka will consider merging the Northern Province and the new Eastern Provinces

after consulting the opinion of the people in the new Eastern Province.

(5) Sinhala and Tamil will be the Official Languages of Sri Lanka.

(6) The Government of Sri Lanka will consider the appointment of a Vice-President from one of the minorities.

(7) The Muslim Members of Parliament from the Eastern Provinces many be invited to India for further discussions on the truncation of the Eastern Province.

Unfortunately nothing transpired from "the December 19th" proposal. Therefore commencing February 1987 the President began to exercise the Military option, much to the chagrin of India. Perhaps the following message dated February 12th 1987 and delivered to the President by J.N. Dixit, High Commissioner for India in Sri Lanka, reflected the tensions in the Indo-Sri Lanka relations at that time.

"Top secret. For President Jayewardene from Prime Minister Rajiv Gandhi.

"I am very concerned and distressed over the military operations launched by Sri Lanka's security forces, particularly in the last 48 hours. It appears to be a definite move away from a political solution. You will agree that this is a dangerous political signal that is being transmitted. There is still time to get back to the negotiating table, but the present trends are rapidly closing that option. I would earnestly suggest that you kindly consider the serious implications of these happenings. It would be in every body's interest to halt the military operations immediately, as you will agree, it will be difficult for India to persuade the militants to resume political negotiations in the current circumstances. Your ambiguity on the December 19 proposals and the military solution that you seem to be seeking lead us to believe that you have rejected the non-violent path of Mahatma Gandhi. I would humbly request you to consider a negotiated settlement, as the violence can only lead to more violence, hatred to more hatred, pushing a lasting solution well out of reach. Escalating violence will compel us to think afresh about the whole situation, consequent on Sri Lanka's rejection of the path of negotiations.

I am sending this personal message to you over this channel to ensure its total confidentiality. Warm regards."

President Jayewardene was annoyed with that despatch. He therefore chose to ignore the displeasure of Prime Minister Rajiv Gandhi and directed his Service Commanders to prepare for "Operation Liberation" to defeat the LTTE militarily in the Jaffna peninsula. In March 1987 Prime Minister Rajiv Gandhi sent Cabinet Minister Dinesh Singh as his Special Envoy to plead for a ceasefire. President Jayewardene responded positively and the LTTE responded by killing 130 Sinhalese civilians at Habarana on the highway Colombo – Trincomalee and EROS killing 150 in a bus station in Colombo during the rush hour. Therefore President Jayewardene had no alternative except to exercise the Military option. That decision was communicated to Prime Minister Rajiv Gandhi in no uncertain manner by Bernard Tilakaratna, our High Commissioner in India. According to him the Prime Minister of India clearly understood the predicament of President Jayewardene and raised no objections whatsoever.

Accordingly, before dawn on May 26th 1987, the largest Military operation, undertaken upto that time by the Armed Forces of Sri Lanka was launched from Palaly. Brigadier Denzil Kobbekaduwa led the 3rd Brigade on the land route Palaly — Thondananar — Manalkadu — while Colonel Wijaya Wimalaratre took the more difficult coastal route Palaly — Velvettiturai — Point Pedro. The Vadamarachchi sector was liberated within three days of fighting and the Sinhalese were jubilianrt!

Sri Lanka

Kankesanturai
Point Pedro
Palaj
Jaffna
Punkudutivu
Delft
Kacnchativu
Elephant Pass
Punakery
Mullaittivu
Dhanushkodi
Talaimannar
Mankulam
Mannar
Pulmoddai
Manta
Kuchchaveli
Madhu
Vavuniya
Nilaveli
Kabithigollewa
Uppuveli
Trincomallee
Marichchukkadi
Medawachchiya
Horowupothana
Mutur
Anuradhapura
Mihintale
Kantale
Maradankadawala
Kalpitiya
Vakarai
Gal Oya
Habarana
Giritale
Kekirawa
Puttalam
Sigiriya
Polonnaruwa
Passikudah
Kalkudah
Galgamuwa
Dambulla
Chenkaladi
Batticaloa
Udappuwa
Nikaweratiya
Elahera
Cheddipalaiyam
Chilaw
Kurunegala
Matale
Kalmunai
Kuliyapitiya
Elkaduwa
Aluthnuwara
Marawilla
Polgahawela
Wattegama
Weragantota
Ampara
Giriulla
Kandy
Peradeniya
Kegalla
Mawanella
Minipe
Inginiyagala
Negombo
Ambepussa
Bibile
Katunayake
Veyangoda
Gampola
Pussellawa
Lunugala
Ja-Ela
Gampaha
Nawalapitiya
Badulla
Hendala
Kelaniya
Nuwara Eliya
Passara
Colombo
Awissawella
Nanuoya
Ella
Lahugala
Pottuvil
Sri Jayawardhana
pura Kotte
Hanwella
Hatton
Maskeliya
Bandarawela
Moneragala
Ratmalana
Kesbewa
Haputale
Wellawaaya
Panadura
Horana
Ratnapura
Koslanda
Balangoda
Pelmadulla
Opanayake
Kalutara
Kumana
Matugama
Rakwana
Tanamalwila
Beruwala
Moragala
Kataragama
Bentota
Deniyaya
Urubokka
Tissamaharama
Elpitiya
Wirawila
Ambalangoda
Morawaka
Kirinda
Hambantota
Hikkaduwa
Akuressa
Hakmana
Ambalantota
Tangalle
Galle
Weligama
Matara

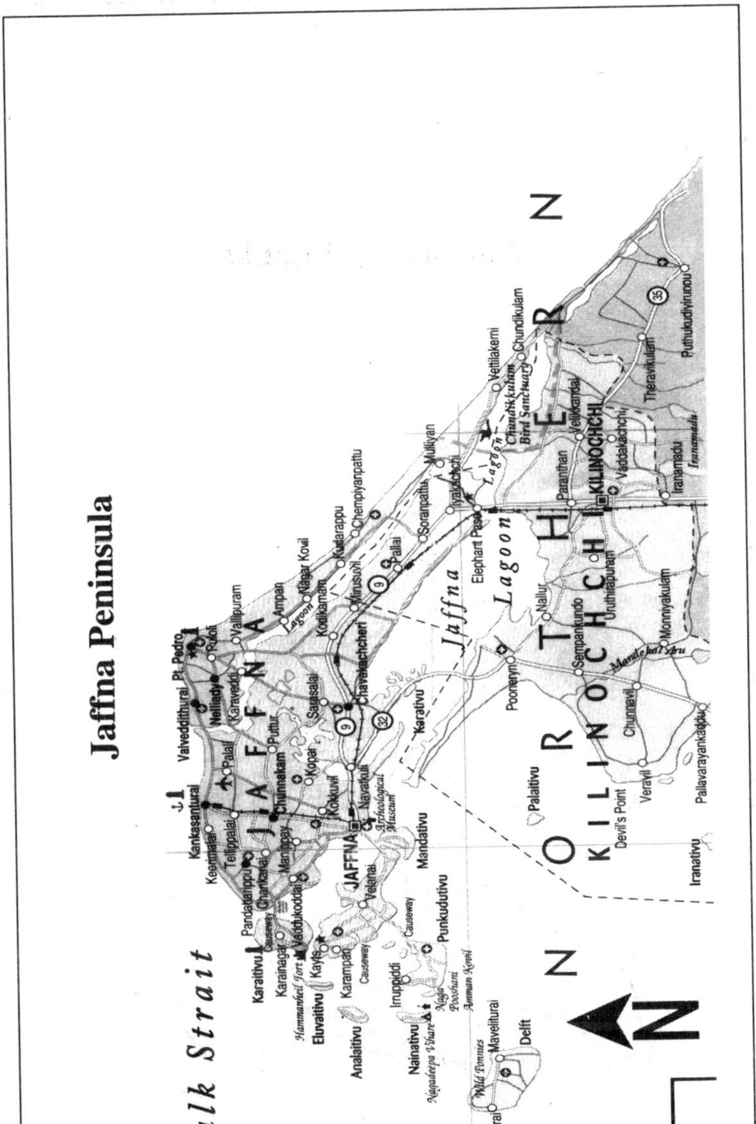
Jaffna Peninsula
Palk Strait
JAFFNA
Jaffna
Lagoon
NORTHERN
KILINOCHCHI
Kankasanturai
Keerimalai
Tellippalai
Palali
Valveddithurai
Pt. Pedro
Point Pedro
Nelliady
Karaveddi
Vallipuram
Ampan
Nagar Kovil
Kudarappu
Chempiyanpattu
Mulliyan
Vettilakerni
Chundikulam
Chundikkulam Bird Sanctuary
Puthukudiyiruppu
Theravikulam
Iranamadu
Vaddakachchi
Vellikandal
Paranthan
Elephant Pass
Iyakachchi
Soranpattu
Pallai
Mirusuvil
Kodikamam
Chavakachcheri
Sarasalai
Puttur
Kopai
Chunnakam
Kokkuvil
Navatkuli
Archeological Museum
Mandativu
Kayts
Velanai
Punkudutivu
Causeway
Irruppiddi
Nainativu
Nagadeepa Vihare
Naga Pooshani Amman Kovil
Analaitivu
Eluvaitivu
Karaitivu
Karainagar
Hammanheil Fort
Vaddukoddai
Pandatarippu
Chankanai
Manipay
Karampan
Delft
Maveliturai
Wild Ponnies
Peiyaturai
9°30'
Karativu
Poonerynn
Sempankundo
Uruthirapuram
Nallur
Monniyakulam
Mandekal Aru
Chunnavil
Veravil
Devil's Point
Palaitivu
Pallavarayankaddu
Iranativu
Iranamadu
N

Northern Sri Lanka

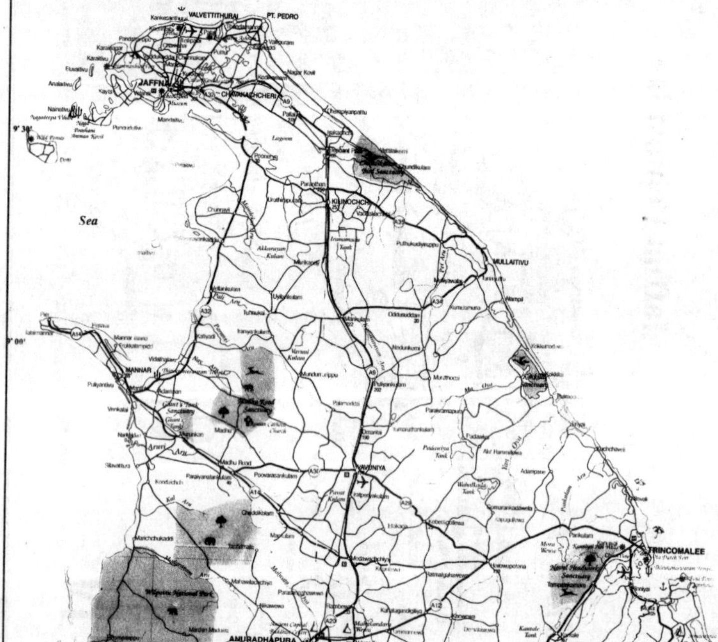

Chapter IV

THE INDIAN INTERVENTION

On May 31st 1987, the very controversial, High Commissioner of India in Sri Lanka J.N. (Mani) Dixit, called on President J.R. Jayewardene at his residence and conveyed a personal message just received from Prime Minister Rajiv Gandhi. The gist of that message transmitted by telephone to India House was taken down by Mani Dixit on the back of an envelope he had with him. It read as follows.

"Uncle,

1. Deeply disappointed and distressed by "Operation Liberation".
2. Your latest offensive in Jaffna is contrary to our understanding.
3. Please do not force us to review our position.

Love to Aunty from Sonia and me.

Rajiv"

The following day Mani Dixit called on Lalith Athulathmudal, Minister of National Security and all but gave an ultimatum. India had strong objections to the Armed Forces of Sri Lanka capturing the city of Jaffna as it would inflame passions in Tamil Nadu. Like most Sri Lankans, Lalith Athulathmudali detested Mani Dixit. However, according to me, Mani Dixit. was by far the ablest foreign Ambassador based in Colombo at that time. I predicted that one day he would be the Foreign Secretary of India. My prediction was laughed at by my colleagues in the Ministry of Foreign Affairs. The factual position was that he was appointed Foreign Secretary in 1991 immediately after serving as High Commission of India to Pakistan.

An infuriated Lalith Athulathmudali passed on the ultimatum from India to the President. Later that day Mani Dixit called on Foreign Minister

A.C.S. Hameed, who also admired the ability of the controversial High Commissioner of India. Mani Dixit sought permission for a flotilla of about twenty boats under the banner of the Red Cross of India to bring in food and medicine to the beleaguered city of Jaffna which was then under siege by General Ranatunga. An astonished Hameed passed on this Note to the President. It read as follows:

> "The population of Jaffna is already suffering extreme hardship under the five month old blockade imposed upon them by their own Government thus becoming the victims of an all out Military assault as part of what has been described as a "fight to finish". Thousands have already been killed in the ethnic conflict and hundreds more are dying as the defenseless civilian population is subjected to sustained strafing and bombing from the air and artillery shelling from the large number of old and new military camps. Although attempts have been made to keep this tragic story from the world by a communications blockade and by sealing off Jaffna from the rest of the world, reports are already filtering out of large scale civilian deaths, property damage leaving thousands homeless and acute shortages of food, medicines and shelter. Even hospitals have become targets leaving the population without adequate medical facilities. In response to this tragic situation, and motivated by humanitarian considerations, the Government and the people of India propose to send urgently needed relief to Jaffna through the Indian Red Cross. These supplies will be sent by sea to Jaffna starting June 3rd, 1987. The supplies will be inspected by the Indian Red Cross. The Sri Lank a Red Cross is invited to join in this inspection. The convoy will be on a humanitarian relief mission, will not be armed nor will it have any armed escort. Representatives of Indian media and international media will be invited to accompany the boats to Jaffna so that they can report on the relief operation. Personnel of the India Red Cross will accompany the relief convoy to distribute the supplies directly to the persons needing relief. We hope that the Sri Lanka Red Cross will co-operate and participate in this humanitarian mission. The concurrence of the Government of Sri Lanka may kindly be conveyed urgently so that relief can reach the long-suffering citizens of Jaffna without further delay".

President Jayewardene summoned an emergency Cabinet meeting to be held that evening. The Cabinet in general and Prime Minister Premadasa in particular was incensed that the Government of India, was interfering in the domestic affairs of Sri Lanka. Therefore on June 2nd 1987 the following, Note was duly delivered to the Ministry of External Affairs in New Delhi, by High Commisioner Bernard Tilakaratna. High Commissioner Dixit was summoned to our Ministry of Foreign Affairs in Colombo and the same. Note was handed over to him in keeping with normal diplomatic pratices. That note read as follows:

> "The Government of Sri Lanka denies the allegations contained in the first two sentences of the message from the Government of India dated 1st June and wishes to state that these allegations are unfounded. While pointing out that the tragic situation in Sri Lanka would not have become acute as at present but for the patronage of separatist terrorism by the State of Tamil Nadu, a constituent of the Republic of India, the Government of Sri Lanka wishes to point out that neither has the Government of Sri Lanka solicited any humanitarian aid nor does the situation prevailing in the North require any assistance from any outside source as the Government of Sri Lanka is in a position to meet all the requirements. As professed, if the Government and the people of India want to be of assistance, the Government of Sri Lanka would consider receiving relief supplies intended for the Jaffna area purely in the interest of good neighbourly relations. The modalities of supply and distribution, it is suggested, could be worked out by the representatives of both Governments."

Notwithstanding this note of June 2nd, and the much publicised order by the President to the Navy to interdict any flotilla from India attempting to violate our territorial waters, which was given wide publicity in the media, the following day a flotilla of 19 Indian fishing boats and small vessels laden with food, medicines and kerosene sailed from Rameshwaram for the Jaffna peninsula. Three hours later the flotilla was apprehended by a flotilla of the Sri Lanka Navy under the command of Captain Mohan Samarnsekera, Commander of the Northern Naval Area just outside our territorial waters. After a lengthy harangue, which was witnessed by foreign journalists on board the flotilla, the boats reversed their course and returned to Rameshwaram. The following day High Commissioner Tilakaratna was summoned to the Ministry of External Affairs in New Delhi. He is truly an expert on India having had four postings in that nation. That day he was expecting some kind of complaint pertaining to events of the previous day. Therefore he took with him his Depty High Commissioner Ambassador C.D. Cassie Chetty. Much to his surprise he was informed that in the next three hours a squadron of Antanov – 32B cargo aircraft from the Indian Air Force would be over Jaffna to parachute food and medicines urgently needed in the peninsula. He was further advised that the Antanovs would be escorted by Mirage-2000 jet fighters, whose pilots were under orders to return fire if any of the Indian aircraft were fired at.

Natwar Singh, Minister of State for External Affairs, who read this riot act then told the High Commissioner of Sri Lanka,

> "Bernard, the Delhi traffic is awful. You will not have the time to get to your High Commission, telephone Colombo and return. Therefore please use my telephone and get through to your Ministry of Foreign Affairs immediately."

That was indeed a novel way of conducting diplomacy. However in view of the extenuating circumstances High Commissioner Tilakaratna accepted the offer and conveyed the shocking news to Foreign Secretary W. T. Jayasinghe in Colombo who in turn got through to Foreign Minister Hameed. In the meantime, at the Ministry of External Affairs of India, Natwar Singh, who was appointed Minister of External Affairs as of May 2004, was apologizing profusely.

> "Bernard I did not know that you came here withour your lunch. Please let me order some sandwiches for you. Would you like tea or coffee with it?"

While they were having this snack and chatting as old friends, the strongly worded protest from Sri Lanka was transmitted by Foreign Secretary Jayasinghe to High Commissioner Tilakaratna by telephone in the same unorthodox manner. It was promptly conveyed to Natwar Singh, Minister of State for External Affairs in New Delhi over sandwiches and coffee! Such is the love-hate relationship between India and Sri Lanka.

That evening June 4th 1987, the Government of India had the audacity to air drop the forty tonnes of food, medicines, kerosene oil, etc. which were on board the flotilla. Eight Antonov-32B cargo aircraft of the Indian Air Force from their bases in Bangalore and Tambaram near Madras with an escort of four Mirage-2000 jet fighters flew over the city of Jaffna around 1700 hours and made the air drop. Around 1pm. that day Mani Dixit called on Hameed and handed over a Note indicating the flight path of the IAF aircraft and that the Mirage fighter pilots were under strict instructions not to open fire unless their aircraft were fired upon by the Armed Forces of Sri Lanka. Hameed handed over a note which was prepared by W.T.Jayasinghe. Then he exhibited his anger in no uncertain manner.

Predictably the Government and the people of Sri Lanka were infuriated. Mani Dixit who was informed of the air drop in advance had on his own initiative moved his entire home-based staff to the Hotel Lanka Oberoi, a five-star hotel which was a joint venture between the Oberoi group and the Government of Sri Lanka. Later he induced Indian businessmen to do likewise. After the airdrop he did not rule out the possibility of Sri Lanka severing diplomatic relations with India. Therefore he personally gave the order to destroy confidential documents of the High Commission. They were taken to his official residence, "India House" in Colombo and consigned to the flames.

President Jayewardene was indeed livid but refined. He refused even to talk to Mani Dixit for nearly one month. He summoned Benard Tilakratna from New Delhi for consulations and it was widely rumoured in the Ministry of External Affairs of India that Tilakaratna would not return for a long time. (That is a well established diplomatic practice of showing anger to the host nation). Prime Minister Premadasa was anything but refined. Besides he loathed India. Therefore he raved and ranted in public, against India. Foreign Minister, Hameed informed SAARC Headquarters that he would be boycotting the SAARC Foreign Ministers Conference scheduled to be held in New Delhi later that month.

Indo-Sri Lanka relations had thus reached its lowest point ever. President Jayewardene was furious. However he was assured by President Ronald Reagan of the United States and Prime Minister Margaret Thatcher of the United Kingdom that they were applying maximum pressure on India. Therefore President Jayewardene was hoping for a miracle and it came in the form of a message received by Gamini Dissanayake, Minister for Lands and Mahaweli Development, from his friend N.Ram the Editor of the Madras based "Hindu". Ram was a confidante of Prime Minister Rajiv Gandhi, Gamini Dissanayake and the LTTE. Those proposals were examined with a mixture of circumspection and suspicion. Thereafter a cautious President authorized Gamini Dissanayake to respond privately but to state that he was doing so with the benedictions of the President himself. Thus a channel of communication was opened and by July 1st 1987, the President condescended to talk to Mani Dixit. Lalith Athulathmudali, was even more frosty when he condescended to speak to Mani Dixit the following day. In the meantime, the affable Bernard Tilakaratna was treated with much respect in New Delhi and even dined privately with his friends Rajiv and Sonia Gandhi. That was a second channel of communication which remained open consistently. The third was between Gamini Dissanayake and Mani Dixit.

Since 1986, I was our Ambassador to Egypt. My friend Lalith Athulathmudali used to telephone me daily at Cairo during those difficult days. He was so enraged whenever he referred to India, that I had to intervene saying,

"Lalith, in our age group you are the best Presidential candidate that Sri Lanka has to offer. If all goes well one day President Lalith Athulathmudali will have to negotiate with India. How the hell can you do that, if despite your education at Royal, Oxford and Harvard you use a string of epithets to describe Mani Dixit, Rajiv Gandhi and even his mother!"

Another day he telephoned me saying,

"Jungle, I am telephoning you about that secret arms deal which you negotiated with Egypt and which I signed in Cairo last year. Please tell your friend Field Marshall Abu Gazala (the Minister of Defence of Egypt) that I will invoke it."

"Okay Lalith. No problem"

"Brigadier Denzil Kobbekaduwa who came with me to Cairo is greatly impressed with those Fahd armoured cars. He says that they are better than the Buffel aromoured cars from South Africa and which were used in the battle for Vadamarachchi. So please ensure that we have those Fahd armoured cars before the next battle for Jaffna."

"Lalith, when will that be?"

"Sooner rather than latter, if I am allowed to decide"

In Colombo, anti-Indian demonstrations and anti-Indian propaganda were commonplace. Against that background Prime Minister Rajiv Gandhi summoned his friend Bernard Tilakaratne for a private chat. In strict confidence the Prime Minister had asked Tilakaratna to inform President Jayewardene, that India was still willing to help Sri Lanka if the Government of Sri Lanka was willing to help the Tamil community to achieve their political objectives within the framework of a united Sri Lanka. Bernard Tilakaratne was convinced that Indian Intelligence was systematically tapping his telephone. Therefore after returning to his residence, he pretended to go out for a walk. In reality he walked to the residence of a friend of his from where he telephoned President Jayewardene. They spoke in Sinhala as a further precaution. A few hours later Dixit telephoned Foreign Minister Hameed seeking an urgent appointment. Thus began the negotiations which culminated as the Indo-Sri Lanka Accord.

The first draft of the Indo-Sri Lanka Accord was prepared by Gamini Dissanayake and Mani Dixit and was based on "the December 19th proposals". It was submitted to the President within 24 hours and he in turn showed it to Prime Minister R. Premadasa and Lalith Athulathmudali who promptly opposed it. By the same token the President showed it to Ronnie De Mel, the Finance Minister, who promptly endorsed it because he had consistently complained that sooner rather than later Aid-donors will cut back on their grants unless the war was brought to an end.

Mani Dixit dispatched the draft to New Delhi with his own shrewd observations that "Gamini Dissanayake is promoting peace, Lalith Athulathmudali is promoting war and both are being promoted by President Jayewardene." How true!

The objections to the drafts prepared by Mani Dixit and Gamini Dissanayake were many. For example, Lalith Athulathmudali was vehemently opposed to giving parity of status to Sinhala and Tamil as Official Languages of Sri Lanka. So was the Minister for Health and Buddhist leader Gamini Jayasuriya who threatened to resign from the Cabinet. The compromise solution was to give parity of status to English, Sinhala and Tamil. English was the language of the elite and the language in which Cabinet meetings were conducted despite the Official Languages Act of 1956! That mollified Lalith Athulathmudali who had won seventeen prizes at Royal College, mostly for English and went on to become the President of the Union at Oxford University. Like President Jayewardene he took pride in his oratorical skill in English. Privately they both bemoaned the deteriorating standards of English in Sri Lanka and both blamed our politicians for it! Whenever they said so, I laughed uproariously at them and they looked upon me pitifully! They both said that I could write any number of books on political science but could never ever become a politician! How true!!

Language, the devolution of power and the merger of the Northern Province and the Eastern Province, be it truncated or otherwise and the utilization of land especially in the Eastern Province through which the largest of Srilankan rivers, the Mahaweli, flows were all hyper-sensitive issues. They caused almost intractable problems and therefore the initial draft was changed almost on a daily basis. Thereafter President J.R. Jayawardene took the unprecedented decision to allow the High Commissioner of India to address the Cabinet. Since Independence, no High Commissioner/Ambassador has had this honour.

Apart from expressing general reservations about the Agreement and lack of faith in Tamil militants, the Cabinet Ministers raised the following specific doubts:

1. The people of Sri Lanka do not trust the Prime Minister or the Government of India as far as the ethnic problem is concerned.
2. India cannot implement any fair compromise, because India will always support the Tamils, because it is subject to pressure from Tamil Nadu.

These objections were handled with amazing skill by Mani Dixit. Infact after the meeting was over, many were heard to remark "Why cannot Sri Lanka produce Ambassadors like Dixit?"

The salient points of the proposed Accord were as follows:

a) The Northern and Eastern Provinces will be merged into one Province temporarily. A referendum will be held in the Eastern Province after one year to determine whether the population there wish to retain or reject that merger.

b) There will be an immediate ceasefire between the Armed Forces of Sri Lanka, who will be confined to their camps, and the Tamil terrorists, who will within one week surrender their arms to an Indian Peace Keeping Force.

c) Elections for the Provincial Council of the North-Eastern Province will be held before the end of 1987.

d) The State of Emergency will be lifted in the North-Eastern Province by August 15th 1987 and an amnesty will be granted to all those held prisoner under the Prevention of Terrorism Act.

e) Tamil and English, hitherto recognised as national languages, will be accorded the same status as Sinhala, the official language.

f) At the request of the Government of Sri Lanka, the Government of India will render all Military assistance to implement this Accord.

At the request of President Jayewardene, Dixit left for New Delhi with the latest draft. At the request of Prime Minister Rajiv Gandhi, Dixit maintained a shuttle diplomacy between New Delhi and Colombo with a Boeing 737 of the Indian Air Force placed at his disposal. In the meantime President Jayewardene and Prime Minister Rajiv Gandhi were communicating daily on their hot line.

There was considerable opposition to the proposed Indo-Sri Lanka Accord. Within the Cabinet, Prime Minister R. Premadasa, Lalith Athulathmudali, Gamini Jayasuriya, and Mrs. Wimala Kannangara, were openly critical. On the other hand the LTTE was just as critical of the Accord. When Prime Minister Rajiv Gandhi arrived in Colombo on July 29th to sign the Accord there was rioting throughout the city and in many parts of the Island. Altogether 40 people were killed, over 100 injured and many Government buildings set on fire by angry Sinhalese. In fact a 24 hour curfew was declared and the Accord was signed while the city was ablaze. Prime Minister Premadasa, several Cabinet Ministers and the Leader of the Opposition Anura Bandaranike, a close friend of the Gandhi family boycotted the function. On July 30th 1987 when the departure ceremonies for Prime Minister Rajiv Gandhi were being conducted and he was inspecting a guard-of-honour from the Sri Lanka Navy, a rating raised his rifle like a club and attempted to hit the visiting Prime Minister on his head.

That day a massive Task Force from India under the command of Lt. General Depinder Singh, General-Officer-Commanding Southern Command, arrived in the Jaffna peninsula and elsewhere in the Northern and Eastern Provinces. Initially the troops were from the 54th Infantry Division under the command of Major General Harkirat Singh. The General established his headquarters at Palaly while his Divison was quickly deployed in the Jaffna peninsula. In rapid succession, the 47th Infantry Brigade (Brigadier J. S. Dhillon) was deployed in Vavuniya, the 76th Infantry Brigade (Brigadier Kulwant Singh) in Trincomalee and the 91st Infantry Brigade (Brigadier Inder Dhar) in Batticaloa. Initially the Indian Peace Keeping Force (IPKF) was well received by the local population, who were under the impression that their ordeal was over and peace would be restored shortly. The presence of the IPKF was viewed with misgivings by our Armed Forces who were now confined to their barracks in accordance with the Indo-Sri Lanka Accord.

While massive Illuyshin–76 aircraft of the Indian Air Force were transporting as many as 1,000 troops daily from the Southern Command of India to Sri Lanka, General Harkirat Singh was experiencing difficulty in persuading the LTTE to surrender their arms, in accordance with the Indo-Sri Lanka Accord. The repeated complaint of the LTTE was that they could not conceivably take any steps without consulting Prabhakaran who was still in India. Prabhakaran was virtually under house arrest in New Delhi and reportedly swearing vengance on Prime Minister Rajiv Gandhi. As no surrender of arms was taking place without Prabhakaran, the Indian Air Force flew him from New Delhi to Jaffna via Madras, where General Depinder Singh spoke to him at length. By now the senior officers of the IPKF had seen for themselves the intransigent nature of the LTTE cadres. Upon his return to Jaffna Prabhakaran swore that no arms would be surrendered to the Government of Sri Lanka. Finally General Depinder Singh managed to prevail upon him that without the handing over of arms (the General was particularly careful to avoid the word surrender) the President of Sri Lanka could not conceivably sign the amnesty stipulated in the Indo-Sri Lanka Accord. This argument convinced Prabhakaran who reluctantly agreed to hand over LTTE arms to the IPKF. Later that afternoon he addressed a massive rally in the courtyard of Amman Kovil at Sudumalai. He said:

> "My beloved and esteemed people of Tamil Eelam. Today there has taken place a tremendous turn in our liberation struggle. This has come suddenly, in a way that has stunned us, and as if it were beyond our power to influence events. Whether the consequences of this will be favourable to us, we shall have to wait and see".

> "You are aware that this Agreement, concluded suddenly and with great speed between India and Sri Lanka, without consulting our people's representatives, is being implemented with expedition and urgency. Until I went to Delhi, I did not know anything about this Agreement. Saying that the Indian Prime Minister desired to see me, they invited me and took me quickly to Delhi. The Agreement was shown to us after I went there. There were several complications and several question marks in it. The doubt arose for us whether, as a result of this Agreement, a permanent solution would be available to the problems of our people. Accordingly, we made it emphatically clear to the Indian Government that we were unable to accept this Agreement".

> "But the Indian Government stood unbudging on the point that whether we accepted or did not accept the Agreement, it was

to declare here that under no circumstances and at no point of time will I contest elections or accept the office of Chief Minister. The Liberation Tigers yearn for the motherland of Tamil Eelam."

On the following day, August 5th 1987, at a public ceremony in Jaffna, which was televised both by Rupavahini and Doordarshan, Yogaratnam alias Yogi, a well known terrorist of the LTTE, in a symbolic act placed a revolver on a table which was flanked by General Sepala Attygalle, Secretary of Defence, and Major-General Harkarat Singh. General Attygalle responded on behalf of the Government of Sri Lanka in handing over the amnesty, signed by President Jayewardene.

On the night of August 10th 1987 a Fast Attack Craft, the Israeli built Dovra P-457 (Lietutenant Commander W.D. Ariyadasa), spotted a relatively large boat within Srilankan territorial waters. The First Officer on the night watch, Lt. T.J.L. Sinniah himself a Tamil, thought it was an Indian trawler that had strayed into Srilankan territorial waters. Therefore he contacted them on International Communication Channel 16. Repeated calls evoked no response. Therefore Lt Sinniah had no option except fire across her bows. Barring the searchlight on PT-457, it was pitch dark. Lt Sinniah observed that the boat was painted in battle grey and was well camouflaged. By that time the warship SLNS *Abeetha* (Commander D.K. Dassanayake) had come alongside. When the captured boat was searched the booty included radio equipment both VHF and UHF, radar, machine guns and AK-47 automatic rifles, above all the LTTE leaders Kumarappah, the brother-in-law of Prabhakaran who was in charge of the Sea Tigers, then in an incipent stage, Pulendran, the LTTE leader in the Trincomalee area who was wanted for the slaughter of 127 Sinhalese near Habarana, on the Colombo-Trincomaee road, and Haran the LTTE leader in Mannar, amongst others. The captured boat was brought to the port of Kankesanturai under a heavy Naval escort under the command of Commander Dassanayake. By mid-morning all radio stations in Sri Lanka announced this dramatic news.

As anticipated, the LTTE protested that under the India-Sri Lanka Peace Accord the President of Sri Lanka himself had given a general amnesty even to LTTE prisoners in jails. Now, one week later, Navy intercepts one of their boats and takes as prisoners some of their leaders. The LTTE loudly claimed that they must be released. Prabhakaran himself interceded with General Harkarat Singh because some of his principal lieutenanats were involved. On the other hand, Lalith Athulathmudali, well knowing the lacuna in the India-Sri Lanka Peace Accord, held his ground. He merely produced an authentic copy of the Accord and referred to the relevant portion. He sent such copies to everybody who mattered in the Jaffna peninsula, in our Armed Forces, in the IPKF and even in the LTTE.

The initial reaction of the IPKF was that under the Amnesty granted by the President even terrorists who were incarcerated under the Prevention of Terrorism Act of 1980 were released. By the same token they appreciated the legal point raised by the Minister for National Security who they knew was an eminent lawyer. The prisoners were treated well by the IPKF and by our Navy. The following day there was a coded message at Palay AFB nearby that the prisoners should be brought to Colombo in a special Air Force aircraft. Major General Jayantha Jayaratne, the Security Forces Commander in Jaffna and a schoolmate of Lalith Athulathmudali, was directed personally by the Minister to escort the prisoners to Colombo. The prisoners swallowed their cyanide capsules just before boarding a SLAF aircraft for Colombo and all twelve of them died. Later that day the LTTE executed an equal number of prisoners-of-war and publicly dumped their bodies before the IPKF office in Jaffna. Thus for the first time the IPKF saw for themselves how the LTTE operated in reality!

The new session of Parliament was due to open on Tuesday 18th, August 1987 and would soon discuss the Thirteenth Amendment to the Constitution. Therefore the President wanted to meet the entire Government Parliamentary Group that morning. The meeting was scheduled for 10 a.m. in Committee Room A. By all accounts, security was very tight. However, from nowhere, a grenade suddenly fell on the head table where the President and Prime Minister were seated, rolled several feet and exploded under the chair occupied by Lalith Athulathmudali. He was bleeding profusely and his schoolmate, Dr. Ranjit Attapattu, Minister of Health, who rushed to his side to give him first aid thought he would not live for more than a few minutes. He was rushed to the nearby Sri Jayewardenepura Hospital and taken direct to an emergency operating theatre where, a team of medical specialists led by the eminent surgeon Dr. K. Yoheswaran, battled for nearly twelve hours to save his life. His pulse was so low that periodically they wondered whether he would survive. It was a miracle that he did. He spent one month in the Intensive Care Unit and was transferred to a room for another month. Thereafter he spent one month convalescing in Cairo, in my residence.

As the days rolled by, General Harkarat Singh and his staff became more and more wary of the LTTE. Quite obviously the LTTE was reluctantly complying with the requirement of surrendering their arms. What started as a mere trickle admittedly gathered momentum. Yet only a fraction of their arms was surrendered. Their frequent excuse was that the EPRLF, EROS, PLOTE, TELO et cetera were also not surrendering the bulk of their arms. Therefore if the LTTE were to hand over their arms they would be annihilated by their rivals. In the meantime, every now and then Indian soldiers were being blown up by mines which the LTTE and other terrorist organizations had laid for the Sri Lanka Army!

This unsatisfactory state of affairs continued for about a month, when the Government of Sri Lanka and the media both domestic and foreign were constantly asking awkward questions about what the IPKF was achieving in Sri Lanka. Based on Intelligence reports and the observation of his senior officers General Depinder Singh was increasingly of the opinion that the LTTE would never hand over their arms voluntarily. He envisaged a show down with the LTTE and accordingly prepared his strategy. He envisaged Indian warships from the Eastern fleet to be moved into the Palk Straits, half the fighter and bomber aircraft from the Southern Command of the Indian Air Force to be made available, in the event of contingency. The 54th Infantry Division which had been airlifted to Sri Lanka minus their heavy equipment, be brought to full strength and the 36th Division (Major General R. P. Singh) at full strength to replace the 76th Infantry Brigade in Trincomalee.

On October 7th, 1987 General K. Sunderji, Chief of Staff of the Indian Army, visited Jaffna enroute to Colombo where the Minister of Defence of India, K. C. Pant, was due to meet President Jayewardene. In Jaffna, General Depinder Singh convinced General Sunderji that the IPKF embark on military action against the LTTE. The recommendation was duly approved in New Delhi that week.

Jaffna symbolises the power and authority of the LTTE. It was for that reason that President Jayewardene had directed Operation Liberation against Jaffna in July 1987. For the same reason General Depinder Singh now planned to attack Jaffna. In essence his battle plan was as follows:

The 54th Infantry Division to capture Jaffna in four days as follows:

a) 18th Infantry Brigade at Kalladi, the 72nd Brigade at Palaly and 91st Infantry Brigade at Tellipalai, to commence the thrust on Jaffna.

b) One infantry battalion from the 91st Brigade to embark on naval assault craft at Kankesanturai and land to the west of Jaffna Fort, and link up with it.

c) Helicopter landing of one Company of infantry and one company of paratroop commandos in the Campus of the University of Jaffna which houses the Headquarters of the LTTE. Link up to be effected by 72nd and 91st Infantry Brigades.

d) 41st and 115th Infantry Brigades to stand by at Sendilippai and Atchuveli respectively. They would either reinforce existing thrusts or commence new initiatives, as necessary.

The attack on Jaffna by the IPKF commenced shortly before dawn on October 11th. The 18th Brigade from the East and the 91st Brigade from the North encountered fierce resistance. On October 12th, shortly after midnight helicopters began to land on the Campus of the University of Jaffna. The Task Force there consisted of 103 Para Commandos and a platoon of 30 soldiers from the 13th Sikh Light Infantry. Three of the four helicopters were hit by ground fire resulting in helicopter landings being suspended mid way. The ground fire was so intense that the entire platoon barring one soldier from the 13th Sikh Light was killed in action. In the meantime the 18th, 72nd and 91st Brigades were encountering very stiff resistance. In fact, Major R. Parameshwaram from Tamil Nadu who was serving with the 91st Brigade was posthumously awarded the *Param Vir Chakra*, the Indian equivalent of the Victoria Cross. Nevertheless the three Brigades made their way to Jaffna. They surrounded it on October 20th and finally captured it on October 22nd when LTTE cardes who had taken over the Jaffna Hospital and were shooting from there were silenced forever. The LTTE withdrew rapidly and the IPKF captured the entire Jaffna peninsula in the next few days.

Basically the LTTE took refuge in the Wanni, consisting of the District of Kilinochchi, Mullativu and Vavuniya and regrouped for battle. In the Eastern Province, where the Tamils account for 40% of the population as against a combined Muslim and Sinhalese population of 60%, the 36th Division established its supremacy without undue strain.

The Wanni accounts for 5% or the Northern Province in terms of population and 95% in terms of land surface which is by and large covered by jungle. As such it is ideally suited for guerilla warfare. As mentioned in Chapter II, the LTTE first established their training camps in the Wanni. Therefore General Depinder Singh sought additional troops with experience in guerilla warfare as opposed to conventional warfare. Accordingly the 57th Mountain Divison (Major General T.P. Singh) was transferred from Assam to Sri Lanka. According to General T.P. Singh,

> "Our strategy is to keep the LTTE in a continuous state of disruption and disorganization. If this pressure is eased and they are allowed to rest, they will attack the IPKF and then I cannot rest."

The basic strategy of General Depinder Singh was to bomb strategic targets in the Wanni using Canberra jet bombers based in Trivandrum and Bangalore and strafe using fighter aircraft based in Trivandrum and Tambaram (Madras) and helicopter gunships based in Palaly and Vavuniya in Sri Lanka. Then he would saturate the Wanni with ground troops, especially the troops brought in from Assam, whose numbers were steadily increased. In March 1988, General Depinder retired on superannuation. Regrettably the IPKF, then amounting to 100,000 troops, showed no tangible results in the Wanni. He was succeeded by Lt. General A.S. Kalkat who as a Major General had seen action with the IPKF in the Jaffna peninsula. He too could not show tangible results in the Wanni.

By July 30th, 1988 the IPKF had served in Sri Lanka for one year and over 600 Officers and men were killed in action. (In the Bangaladesh campaign in 1971 the corresponding figure was 1047 Officers and men). Besides the LTTE were experts in the art of placing mines. They claimed that they were taught these techniques by retired Indian Officers and men while they were receiving training in India from 1980-87. It resulted in many main battle tanks and armoured personnel carriers being knocked out and their crew killed in action.

While the IPKF and the LTTE publicly made claims and counter claims of their success, truth was that casualties were high on both sides and the overall scenario was like the Viet Cong fighting the military might of the United States and the Mujahudin errorists in Afghanistan fighting the military might of the Soviet Union.

As such, many knowledgeable people in India and Sri Lanka were wondering what the IPKF had achieved since the liberation of the Jaffna peninsula in October 1987. Some even advocated that the IPKF be withdrawn. One such advocate was the war hero Lt. General Jagjit Singh Arora, G-O-C Eastern Command, who in 1971 invaded East Pakistan and thereby caused the birth of Bangladesh. Since 1984, he was a Member of Parliament, as such the much respected General had a ready made forum to articulate his views.

On the other hand after the arrival of the IPKF in July 1987, the JVP, the Sinhalese terrorists, whose insurrection was ruthlessly crushed by Prime Minister Sirima Bandaranaike in 1971, had raised its ugly head again.

Against this background both the Opposition and the outlawed JVP were whipping up emotion amongst the normally volatile Sinhalese. It was also no secret that Prime Minster Premadasa was openly hostile to India in general and to the IPKF in particular.

At this juncture perhaps some reference is appropriate about J.N. Dixit, High Commissioner for India in Sri Lanka, since 1985. During his tour fo duty in Sri Lanka he was vilified by the Press, who still contemptuously refer to him as a Viceroy, loathed by the Opposition and disliked intensely by most members of the Cabinet of President Jayeardene especially by Prime Minister Premadasa. However his ability and integrity were much admired by President Jayewardene, Foreign Minister Hameed and others.

In the profession of diplomacy it is well established that the effectiveness of an Ambassador is inversely proportional to the publicity he gets. For that reason most Ambassadors who are professional diplomats keep a low profile. However High Commissioner Dixit, despite all his experience, kept a high profile even when he was forcing bitter pills down our national throat! Besides, he made a virtue of that evil streak in the Foreign policy of India ever since the time of Prime Minister Indira Gandhi, namely interfering in the domestic affairs of other countries, especially neighbouring countries!! To Mani Dixit Mother India was always correct or alternatively Mother India could not be wrong. For these considerations, High Commissioner J. N. Dixit was loathed, then and even now, in many quarters in Sri Lanka. However I will be less than honest unless I emphasize that he was an Ambassador of exceptional ability. In 1991, he superceded several able Ambassadors more senior to him in the Indian Foreign Service in being appointed Foreign Secretary of India. In May 2004 he was appointed National Security Adviser to the new Government of India.

In September 1988, President Jayewardene was 82 years old and in his last few months in office. A Presidential election was due by the end of the year. The Opposition had already nominated former Prime Minister Sirima Bandaranaike. She was indeed a powerful candidate and had led the SLFP to magnificent victrories at the General Elections of 1960 and 1970. In due course the, UNP nominated Prime Minister R. Premadasa as its candidate.

The Presidential Election of December 1988 was held under the most difficult of circumstances because of terrorist activitiy. The LTTE was operating in the North-Eastern Province and the JVP, which was just as barbaric, in the seven Sinhala speaking Provinces. Indeed it reflected much credit both on the Government and people of Sri Lanka that a Presidential Election could be held at all under these trying circumstances. Inevitably the polling was low, the turn out being around 55% as against the customary figure of 80 to 85% in any election in Sri Lanka at the national level.

Throughout the election campaigns of Prime Minister R. Premadasa (UNP) and former Prime Minister Sirima Bandaranaike (SLFP), it appeared that the result would be very close indeed. When the votes were finally counted Prime Minister Premadasa had taken 50.4% of the popular vote and the world's first lady Prime Minister 44.9%. Therefore Prime Minister Ranasinghe Premadasa was declared duly elected as the second executive President of Sri Lanka.

On January 2nd 1989, President R. Premadasa assumed the highest office in Sri Lanka. Since Independence the right wing UNP had produced five Heads of Governments. The other four were Prime Minister D. S. Senanayake, the architect of Independence, his son and successor Prime Minister Dudley Senanayake, Prime Minister Sir John Kotelawela, and President J. R. Jayewardene. They had one common factor, namely they were all scions of aristocracy. In direct contrast, the ascendancy of President R. Premadasa was cast in the same mould as that of President Abraham Lincoln, from the log cabin to the White House. Indeed in many quarters in Sri Lanka it was perceived that his different background would bring about a different sense of values to the consevative UNP. By the same token his views on India were very different from those of previous heads of Governments from the UNP. More pointedly President Jayewardene was a great admirer of India (though admittedly he was disenchanted with Prime Minister Indira Gandhi) while President Premadasa was anything but an admirer of India, as reflected in the previous chapter. The presence of the IPKF in terms of Sri Lanka Accord would be supplanted with an Indo-Sri Lanka Friendship Treaty and the IPKF sent home. On the other hand the SLFP manifesto also clearly spelled out that the Indo-Sri Lanka Accord would be abrogated and the IPKF sent home. Thus 95% of Sri Lankans who exercised their franchise at the Presedential Election in December 1989 wanted the IPKF to leave. New Delhi was not insensitive to these trends in Sri Lanka and made a token withdrawal of 2,500 of the 70,000 to 100,000 troops of the IPKF, in time for the inauguration of the new President.

President Premadasa inherited from President Jayewardene an open market economy which had averaged a growth rate of over 5% during the period 1977 – 1982 but had slowed down appreciably during the period 1983 – 1988, and had dropped to 2% in 1988. The decline was due to the rapidly deteriorating law and order situation with 1988 being the worst year in living memory. The Sinhalese terrorists, the JVP, had run amok in the seven Sinhalese speaking Provinces ruining the economy and above all killing innocent people at their whim and fancy. Thus the highest priority of President Premadasa was restoring law and order. This received his undivided attention following the General Elections of February 15th, 1989, which was also held in a terror-stricken atmosphere. The UNP won comfortably, taking 125 seats in an expanded Parliament of 225 seats, as against 67 seats won by the SLFP.

After his new Cabinet was appointed and new senior officials were duly posted, President Premadasa systematically launched his campaign to restore law and order. From every platform he stated that he was readily available for discussions to bring about constructive solutions to the problems of the coutry. Indeed he advocated a policy of consultation, compromise and consensus. Further, to coincide with the traditional Sinhala and Tamil New Year celebrations on April 13th and 14th, he declared a ceasefire on a unilateral basis.

The President was spending the New Year vacation at his estate in Ambanpola, some 100 kilometers from Colombo, when a fax message was received in the Presidential Secretaraiat from the LTTE office in London. It was a positive response and was promptly dispatched to Ambanpola in the middle of the night. Upon his return to Colombo, the President informed his confidantes that Dr. Anton Balasingham, the LTTE spokesman and theoretician, would be arriving in Colombo shortly for consultations. Dr. Balasingham and his Australian wife Adele called on the President on April 26th and thereafter it was announced that the LTTE would negotiate for peace. Accordingly on May 4th 1989, two Bell-212 helicopters from the SLAF left for a destination in the jungle north of Vavuniya. Dr. Balasigham who was on board one of the helicopters carried his own communication equipment with which he relayed messages to the LTTE once the helicopters were near their destination. Suddenly in the middle of the jungle a white marking appeared and the two aircraft made a safe landing on an improvised helipad. The Balasinghams were received with exuberance by the LTTE while the air crew and the accompanying media personnel were treated as guests. The LTTE delegation of nine personnel, all in battle dress and carrying automatic weapons, then boarded the helicopters whose next destination was the helipad at SLAF Headquarters in Colombo. The LTTE delegation which was given VIP treatment complete with maximum security was then taken to the Hilton. The following day they called on President Premadasa. Thereafter the negotiations began with the Government delegation led by A. C. S. Hameed, Minister of Justice, and consisting of four other Cabinet Ministers including Ranjan Wijeratne, Minister of Foreign Affairs and State Minister for Defence, and several key officials from the Presidential Secretariat, the Ministry of Defence and the Ministry of Foreigh Affairs. In May, there were nine meetings at which the LTTE berated the IPKF and accused them of all manner of atrocities. It resulted, amongst other things, in the dynamic and impatient Ranjan Wijeratne grumbling that he had come for a dialogue and had to listen to a monologue!

In the meantime the General Officer Commanding the IPKF, Lt. Gen. A. S. Kalkat, was reporting to Army Headquarters in New Delhi that the LTTE was on its last legs and that the IPKF would finish them off by the end of 1989. Whether this was fact or fiction is largely a matter of opinion.

India has the world's fourth largest Army, next to those of China, the Soviet Union and the United States of America. Besides, India has the largest Air Force and Navy in the Third World. The might of the Armed Forces of India had co-ordinated magnificently in 1971 to rout Pakistan in the war over East Pakistan. Since 1971, India was acutely conscious of her Military might in the context of South Asia. Therefore her experience in Sri Lanka was anything but a happy one. In October 1987, admittedly the IPKF had liberated the Jaffna peninsula in seven days at a cost of the lives of 253 Officers and men and 1047 wounded. Since then over 1000 Officers and men were killed in action and about 2500 wounded, yet there were no tangible results by the 70,000 to 100,000 strong IPKF in vanquishing "the boys". After this sterile periods of one and a half years which was a source of embarrassement to India from a viewpoint of prestige, somehow General Kalkat had become confident. In modern times India has had a history of intrigue with respect to all her neighbours, and since 1983 Sri Lanka had learnt of those machinations throught bitter experience. Whether the confidence shown by General Kalkat in 1989 was part of the designs of India or the professional opinion of a senior field commander will remain a mystery for years to come.

About that time the Sinhala speaking Provinces were experiencing violence on an unprecedented scale. The JVP terrorists were waging war on the newly elected Government and committing all manner of atrocities. The writ of the Government did not run in many areas outside Colombo and the Provincial capitals. At a personal level, I had assumed duties in Brussels as the new Ambassador of Sri Lanka to the European Community and was astonished that Human Rights organizations in Europe, who since 1983 had given a rough time to my predecessors, observed total silence while the JVP was butchering so many innocent people. For all intents and purposes the JVP wanted to overthrow the democratically elected Government of President Premadasa. However their rhetoric was that they wanted to rid the country of the IPKF.

President Premadasa was indeed pleased by the response he had received from the LTTE. Quite clearly the terrorist movements, both the LTTE and the JVP, wanted the IPKF to leave Sri Lanka. More importantly, so did the UNP and the SLFP. Weighing the pros and cons, he decided to ask the IPKF to leave. Accordingly on June 2nd 1989 he wrote to Prime Minister Rajiv Gandhi the following letter which was delivered personally by Foreign Secretary Bernard Tilakaratne, functioning as a Special Envoy.

> "My dear Prime Minister,
>
> "I am writing to you on some matter of urgent importance, the most immediate matter relates to the presence of Indian Forces in Sri Lanka. After I assumed the Presidency of Sri Lanka, the Government of India initiated the withdrawal of troops. We are grateful for your prompt action in this regard.
>
> "One of the important campaign pledges made by me at both the Presidential and Parliamentary Elections was the withdrawal of the IPKF on being elected to office. I assumed the office of President of Sri Lanka on the 2nd of January 1989. Five months have elapsed since then. The complete withdrawal of the IPKF will, hopefully, contribute to stabilizing the situation in Sri Lanka, where the presence of the IPKF has become a deeply divisive and resentful issue. It is also in keeping with your often expressed sentiments that the IPKF will be withdrawn when requested by the President of Sri Lanka.
>
> "I am thankful for the efforts of the IPKF during the time it has been in our country. I have often paid tribute to the bravery of the many officers and men who lost life and limb in the discharge of their duties. The tragedy of violence has not only affected your soldiers, it has also destroyed many Sri Lankans as well. Our Armed Forces and large numbers of civilians, innocent and uninvolved, have suffered beyond description. Their sacrifices must not be in vain. I am confident that a complete withdrawal of the IPKF will enable me to secure the trust and confidence of my people. Therefore, I would like all IPKF personnel to be withdrawn by July 31st 1989.

"The withdrawal of the IPKF will also enable Sri Lanka to host the SAARC Summit in November this year in a climate of tranquility. As you are aware, we could not undertake our obligation to do this in 1988. You will appreciate how difficult it is to host a regional gathering of this nature with foreign forces on our soil. Our people are most enthusiastic about welcoming leaders of our region, particularly our closest neighbour. However, their anxieties must also be satisfied especially in relation to their deep patriotic and nationalist sensitivities.

"In this context, we have submitted several proposals regarding an Indo-Lanka Friendship Treaty. I belive that, in the long term, such an agreement will further strengthen relations between India and Sri Lanka. I await your response to our proposals in this regard.

"We have always appreciated your sincere interest in the unity and the territorial integrity of our country. Our own efforts to this end need the understanding and goodwill of our neighbours. I believe, that your people and you yourself, share these objectives and will contribute to their realization.

"I have just seen the Aide Memoir which was handed over by yόur High Commissioner this evening. As the Aide Memoir refers to the need for consultations between our Governments, I am designating my Foreign Secretary to personally clarify our position on these matters.

With assurance of my highest consideration and esteem."

However in a totally unorthodox move the President made a public statement at a temple ceremony at Battaramulla on June 1st, the day before he wrote to Prime Minister Rajiv Gandhi, requesting that the IPKF leave Sir Lanka by July 29th, 1989, the second anniversary of the signing of the Indo-Sri Lanka Accord. This unorthodox move riled the Government of India in general and her Prime Minister in particular.

Notwithstanding the wealth of experience Foreign Secretary Tilakaratne had in Indian affairs, it was next to impossible for him to persuade Prime Minister Rajiv Gandhi to accede to the request of President Premadasa. The JVP anticipated this and stepped up their campaign, by wanton killing on the one hand and demanding a boycott of Indian goods on the other. Those who did not comply were summarily executed. Among such victims was Dr. (Mrs) Gladys Jayewardene, Chairperson of the State Pharmaceuticals Corporation. A sister-in-law of President Jayewardene, she had used her influence to obtain the services of the Sri Lanka Navy to unload consignments of medicine from India which were urgently needed in our hospitals and which were held up in the Port of Colombo due to the JVP inspired boycott on Indian goods.

The reply of Prime Minister Rajiv Gandhi to the letter from President Premadasa was delivered by the new High Commissioner of India in Sri Lanka, Mr. L. L. Mehrotra, on June 21st. It read as follows.

> "Dear Mr. President,
>
> "I have your letter of the 2nd of June, which was handed over to me by your Special Envoy, Foreign Secretary Tilakaratne.
>
> "India is committed to preserving the unity and integrity of Sri Lanka, under the terms of the Indo-Lanka Agreement. It was as a result of this commitment and our responsibility as a guarantor for the implementation of the Indo-Lanka Agreement that we responded to the request of the Government of Sri Lanka to send the IPKF. This was at a time when the situation seemed headed inexorably towards the break-up of Sri Lanka. During its presence, the IPKF has striven, with considerable success but at heavy cost to itself, to prevent such an outcome and safeguard the unity and integrity of Sri Lanka. Three successive elections have been held peacefully despite threats of terrorist violence in the North-East, and all Tamil groups barring one, have joined the democratic process. Std groups, barring one, had given up the demand for Eelam. If the process of devolution of powers to the Provincial Council had been implemented in time and had the deliberate attempt by the Sri Lankan Government to alter the population balance in the Tamil areas by the continued State sponsored colonization of Tamil areas been stopped, the extremists would have been further isolated and marginalized, and the violence ended.
>
> "As you have yourself stated, we had started the withdrawal of the IPKF even before you requested for it. A broad time frame for the IPKF's withdrawal was also discussed at our initiative, based on which your Foreign Minister had made a statement in your Parliament on the 31st March, 1989. All this was being done on the basis of assurances given by the Sri Lankan Government and on the assumption that the implementation of the Indo-Lanka Agreement – especially the devolution of powers of the Provincial Councils – would proceed simultaneously, so that the legitimate aspirations of the Tamils could be met within the framework of the

unity and integrity of Sri Lanka. It is pertinent to recall that it was precisely because these aspirations were not being met that a situation was created which threatened the unity and integrity of Sri Lanka.

"I have always maintained that the IPKF will not stay in Sri Lanka a day longer than necessary. But we cannot be unmindful of the responsibilities and obligations of the two countries under the Indo-Sri Lanka Agreement and to join the democratic process within the framework of a united Sri Lanka only on the basis of assurances of devolution of powers. Our two Governments are, therefore, morally and legally bound to ensure that the Tamils are given the autonomy they were promised, both in the 13th Amendment to the Sri Lankan Constitution, as also in the additional areas promised in the Agreement signed between former President Jayewardene and myself on the 7th November, 1987. Failure to do so will only lend credence to the claims made by the Tamil groups that Tamils cannot expect justice within a united Sri Lanka. We have to be fully conscious of the dangers of a return on a situation which may be worse that prevailing prior to the Indo-Sri Lanka Agreement.

"We believe that, in the spirit of traditional friendship between our two countries, we must jointly draw up a mutually agreed schedule for the full implementation of the Indo-Sri Lanka Agreement and the complete withdrawal of the IPKF. The two have to be joint, parallel exercises.

"We have no objection to your proposal for a friendship treaty. I had told your Special Envoy that we could set dates for commencing discussions with a view of finalizing the text of the proposed treaty."

The reply of Prime Minister Rajiv Gandhi hardly surprised astute observers of India, be they in Sri Lanka or elsewhere. Those who are openly hostile to India, like those from Pakistan and China, predicted that Indian troops would be in Sri Lanka for years under some pretext or another. Of late many Sri Lankans loathed India and they too shared that opinion. Admittedly India had disgraced herself in training Sri Lankan terrorists on her soil and thereby had immeasurably strengthened her well established reputation of intriguing against her neighbours, even those who bore no ill will whatsoever against India. That was indeed a tragic flaw in the Foreign policy of India for the past twenty five years or more. However there was some method in their madness in respect of Sri Lanka.

Prime Minister Jawaharlal Nehru, that great statesman won landslide victories at the General Elections of 1947, 1952, 1957 and 1962. However there were two untoward features in his splendid victory in 1957. In the State of Kerala, where unemployment was rife, the Congress Party was defeated by the Communist Party. In the Madras Presidency, now referred to as Tamil Nadu, the Dravida Munetra Kazagam (DMK) led by C. N. Annadurai campaigned on the basis that they wanted secession from India and polled over 25% of the vote. Prime Minister Nehru was disturbed by this trend and quickly brought in The Sixteenth Amendment to the Constitution of India whereby no recognized political party could advocate secession from India. The DMK then dropped the call for secession. In the anti-Congress swing of 1967 the DMK trounced the Congress Party in Tamil Nadu and the charismatic C. N. Annadurai became Chief Minister. Following his death in 1969, he ws succeeded by M. Karunanidhi. With the split in the DMK, his arch rival M. G. Ramachandran formed the All India Anna DMK. For two decades power in Tamil Nadu has oscillated between them and the Congress Party has been a minority element ever since their humiliating defeat in 1967. For this reason successive Governments of India by the Congress Party have found Tamil Nadu a difficult State to govern.

Though neither Karunanidhi nor his arch rival Ramachandran have advocated the secession of Tamil Nadu from India, they had been staunch supporters of Tamil Eelam in Sri Lanka. Whoever was in Opposition was more vociferous than one other in power in advocating a separate State for the Tamils in Sri Lanka. Such a secession would be a disaster for India as it could well result in Tamil Nadu eventually seceding from India. For this reason Prime Minister Indira Gandhi and Prime Minister Rajiv Gandhi and their respective Governments were never in favour of a separate State for Tamils in Sri Lanka. They both perceived that secession in Sri Lanka can be avoided only if redress is given to the Tamils who as a community have justifiable grievances against the Sinhalese. Having reached that logical conclusion, they both stooped to folly in allowing Tamil terrorists from Sri Lanka to be trained in India, be it by sympathetic Tamils in Tamil Nadu or by the Government of Tamil Nadu or by RAW. Now in June 1989, Prime Minister Rajiv Gandhi perceived that if the IPKF departed from Sri Lanka before a generous devolution package was arranged for the Tamils, their clamour for secession would persist and that in turn would have serious repercussions for India. It was for this reason that the Government of India was prepared to spend Indian Rupees 50 million per day and sacrifice the lives of nearly 1,000 Indian soldiers in Sri Lanka as against the 1,047 Indian soldiers killed in action in the Bangladesh campaign in 1971, and face all manner of humiliations in Sri Lanka. On the other hand the widespread opinion amongst the Sinhalese, that India has territorial designs over Sri Lanka was arrant nonsense, of the same magnitude as the claims of Prime Minister Indira Gandhi and Prime Minister Rajiv Gandhi that no Sri Lankan terrorists were trained on Indian soil.

Indeed a strange situation was developing in Sri Lanka with Prime Minister Rajiv Gandhi insisting that the IPKF remain, for the reasons already adduced, and President Premadasa persisting that they leave, because he had an electoral mandate on this sensitive issue. The Government of India from their Prime Minister downwards was livid that the LTTE whom they were fighting for two years was now enjoying the benedictions of President Premadasa. (Somehow they chose to forget who initially trained the LTTE). Therefore the IPKF was authorized to attack the LTTE fiercely and helicopter gunships and fighter aircraft strafed the jungle hideouts of the LTTE which appealed to President Premadasa for arms and ammunition to fight the IPKF, for cement for the construction of bunkers to protect themselves from the IPKF and for funds to finance their campaign. They were duly authorized by the President himself.

While these developments were taking place the exchange of dispatches between President Premadasa and Prime Minister Rajiv Gandhi were becoming more and more acrimonious, as reflected in the following dispatch from New Delhi on July 11th 1989:

> "Dear Mr. President,
>
> "I have your letters of 30th June and 5th July. I do not wish to enter into a debate on various interpretations of mutual obligations assumed by our sovereign nations. These are quite clear. I also do not wish to go into the validity of assertions like the LTTE having resumed violence on 2nd August, 1987 whereas the arms surrender started and the amnesty letter was handed over by the Sri Lankan Government to the LTTE three days later. We should let facts speak for themselves.
>
> "There is an Agreement between our two countries. This Agreement is meant to preserve the unity and intregrity of Sri Lanka and to ensure the safety, security and legitimate interests of the Tamils.

"Nearly a thousand Indian soldiers have made the supreme sacrifice in fulfillment of India's obligations as a guarantor of this Agreement. Since the signing of the Agreement, not only have the Provincial Council elections been held, but also the Parliamentary and Presidential elections. The situation in the North-Eastern Province is far more settled and peaceful than elsewhere in Sri Lanka. Despite all this, the devolution package promised to the Tamils has not been implemented. These are incontrovertible facts.

"Both of us agree that the IPKF should be withdrawn. Both of us agree that we had commenced the withdrawal even before you asked for it. A broad time frame for IPKF's withdrawal had in fact been discussed. Discussions on finalizing details were proposed by your Foreign Minister at Harare only a few days prior to your unilateral announcement of 1st June. I have repeatedly said that the IPKF's withdrawal schedule should be worked out through joint consulations along with a simultaneous schedule for the implementation of the Indo-Lanka Agreement. We are willing to resume discussions on this subject at any time and place of your convenience. Your collegue, the Honourable Mr. Thondaman, who met me here, would have conveyed to you our desire for friendly relations and our willingness to resolve any misunderstandings through mutual consulations. If, however, discussions for this purpose are not acceptable to you, we will have to decide the details of IPKF's withdrawal unilaterally consistent with our responsibilities and obligations under the Indo-Sri Lanka Agreement.

"While I reiterate Government of India's willingness to cooperate with your Government to resolve pending issues, I must emphasise to Your Excellency that India has traditionally been mindful of the sanctity of the Agreements it signs with other countries and of commitments solemnly undertaken under such Agreements. India will under no circumstances deviate from this policy affecting our concerns.

"It has been our practice to maintain the confidentiality of official correspondence, particularly between Heads of State or Government, unless otherwise agreed upon. However, the gist of your messages to me was more often than not made available to the media before they reached me. Now I find that all our recent official correspondence has been public made by the Sri Lanka Government.

I may thus be constrained to depart from tradition by authorising this communication being made public, after your receive it."

In the meantime President Premadasa was over generous to the LTTE and provided them with the following to fight the IPKF.

500 T-56 machine guns
500 AK-47 machine guns
5000 Chinese grenades
200,000 rounds of live ammunition
20 Jeeps
200 tonnes of cement
Rupees 20 million in cash.

According to many, President Premadasa had thereby committed an impeachable offence. In fact Generals who did not want to stain their professional reputations with accusations of treason, flatly refused to the associated with this operation.

As events were becoming more and more complicated, on July 13th the LTTE hit squads in Colombo assassinated A. Amirthalingam, former Leader of the Opposition, V. Yogeswaran, former TULF MP for Jaffna and narrowly missed assassinating M. Sivasithamparam, the President of the TULF and a Member of Parliament from 1960 to 1983. On July 16th another LTTE hit squad in Colombo murdered Uma Maheswaran, the leader of the rival terrorist group, the PLOTE. This confused the situation still more with the Government of India warning the LTTE and the people of Sri Lanka wondering what type of people their President was negotiating with!

In the meantime President Premadasa in his capacity as Commander-in-Chief of Sri Lanka issued an order to General Kalkat, General Officer Commanding the IPKF, that his troops either leave Sri Lanka by July 29th or be confined to barracks as of that date. The General never replied to that communication but it is alleged that he had told Indian reporters that the IPKF would open fire on any Sri Lanka troops that came out of their barracks, thereby violating the Indo-Sri Lanka Accord of 1987. In a war of nerves the Indian media claimed that the aircraft *INS Viraat* was cruising somewhere off Colombo and a squadron of Canberra jet bombers from the Indian Air Force was suddenly transferred from Trivandrum to the Palaly SLAF Base in the Jaffna peninsula. Propaganda and rumour apart, a crisis was brewing and it had to be defused.

Early in July 1989, at a meeting of Foreign Ministers of the Non-Aligned Movement held in Harare, Zimbabwe, Foreign Minister Ranjan Wijeratne had met Foreign Minister Narasimha Rao of India and had been invited to visit New Delhi. He seized the opportunity to visit India and left at short notice accompanied by Foreign Secretary Tilakaratne and several key officials from the Presidential Secretariat and the Ministry of Defence.

The resolve of India had by now been seriously undermined by V. P. Singh, who had defected from the Government where he was Minister of Finance, and was leading a conglomeration of parties which was opposing the Government at the forthcoming General Elections. He was openly campaigning for the immediate withdrawal of the IPKF from Sri Lanka. He was strongly supported by the much respected Lt. General Jagjit Singh Arora, General Officer Commanding the Eastern Command during the Bangladesh campaign. A national hero ever since 1971 and a Member of Parliament since 1984, his influence was decisive in swinging public opinion in favour of immediately withdrawing the IPKF from Sri Lanka. Against this background Foreign Minister Wijeratne and Foreign Minister Rao somehow reached a face saving solution for both countries which was sound in theory but was ambivalent in practice.

Having survived that ordeal in July, President Premadasa was facing another in August. The JVP which had been running amok for the past several months threatened all members of the Armed Forces and the Police. Either they resign or else their families would be executed. After two such families were executed, Ranjan Wijeratne, in his capacity as Minister of State for Defence, gave the Security Forces a free hand in dealing with the JVP. Within three months the JVP was exterminated while Human Rights organizations in the West, which were hitherto silent about atrocities by the JVP, howled in protest. As 1989, an extremely difficult year for Sri Lanka drew to its end, at the General Elections of India the joint Opposition led by V. P. Singh defeated the Congress Party led by Rajiv Gandhi. In keeping with his electoral mandate Prime Minister V. P. Singh authorized the immediate withdrawal of the IPKF. On the other hand, President Premadasa boasted that he got rid of the IPKF! His sycophants fell over each other in congratulating the President!!

With the JVP exterminated and the IPKF under orders to return home, Christmas and the festive season in 1989 was particularly merry. On January 2nd, 1990 President Premadasa celebrated his first year in office. He had every reason to be pleased with his performance in restoring law and order within one year of assuming office. His relations with the LTTE seemed particularly good, as reflected in his giving a personal gift to Prabhakaran of a desert falcon specially imported from the Middle East and according VIP treatment to his wife at the Colombo International Airport, when she arrived from Singapore and then transporting her to Jaffna in a SLAF helicopter. Kittu, the one-legged Commander of the LTTE in Jaffna was likewise given VIP treatment when he left for London to obtain an artificial leg. He was even met at Gatwick Airport by diplomats of our High Commission in London when he arrived there. In another outward manifestation of goodwill the Government resumed the services of "Yal Devi", the Colombo-Jaffna-Colombo express train, after the damaged track north of Vavuniya was quickly repaired. It would indeed have been marvelous had this rapprochement continued to grow.

The first note of discord, I observed, was during my dialogue with Foreign Minister Ranjan Wijeratne who for all intents and purposes was also Minister of Defence. He is justifiably credited with having saved the country from the JVP menace. He was a long standing personal friend of mine and whenever we met in Europe he used to grumble "I negotiate with the LTTE but can never trust them. The President not only negotiates with them but even trusts them."

President Premadasa and the LTTE shared one objective, they both wanted the withdrawal of the IPKF. The last contigent from the IPKF left Sri Lanka on March 24th 1990, the logistic arrangements for their transportation having taken over three months. Shortly after their departure the LTTE began to gradually increase the pressure on the Government of Sri Lanka. The first move was a public demand to revoke the Sixth Amendment to the Constitution of Sri Lanka whereby all public servants, including elected representatives, had to take an oath to preserve the unitary state of Sri Lanka. President Premadasa, when confronted with a delegation from the LTTE, side-stepped the issue claiming that to amend the Constitution he needed a two-thirds majority in the Parliament and that he did not have such a majority. Within a week of the departure of the IPKF, the LTTE was in total control of the North-Eastern Province, any opposition having been exterminated. On April 2nd 1990, Prabhakaran made the following public statement in Jaffna:

"Today, our liberation struggle is facing a new historical turning point. We have successfully foiled the Indian military intervention. Now, the Indian occupation forces have completely withdrawn from our homeland. The termination of the Indian invasion is a grand victory to our struggle.

The Indian forces were sent here specifically to crush our liberation struggle and to annihilate our organization which embodied the spirit of the struggle. It is for this specific reason, India unleashed a full fledged war against us. This war is a monumental event in the history of the world. For more than two years, we fought a ruthless war shedding our blood against a formidable military force, a mighty power in Asia. The supreme sacrifice made by our fighters, and by our people in this armed conflict has become a historical epic of heroism and courage. Our victory in this was has set an excellent example that the legitimate struggle of an oppressed people and their yearning for freedom could not be crushed by military force however formidable it may be.

"Our people have also learned a bitter lesson as a consequence of the Indian military intervention and the colossal damage it brought about. We have learned that we have to be self dependent and fight our own struggle to win our rights rather than depending on foreign powers. I am sure that all Tamil groups, who supported the Indian intervention would have realized this political truth. We are not a hostile force to the Indian Government or to the Indian people. We opposed the misguided policies of the former Indian administration and resisted the military intervention. We do not want the Government of India to interfere, politically or militarily, in our problems. The policy makers in Delhi should realise that the legitimate struggles of our oppressed people will not in any way contravene the geo-political concerns of India nor will it undermine the internal stability of the Indian State. We fervently hope that on the basis of this understanding, the new Indian Administration would make sincere efforts to restore friendly ties with our organization. We desire that the Indian Government and the people of India should support and recognize the legitimate struggle of our people.

"For nearly a year we have been involved in peace talks with the Government of Sri Lanka. I am very pleased to note that the talks have been cordial, constructive and have progressed on the basis of mutual trust and understanding. As a direct consequence of these talks there is peace and normality. The present Sri Lankan regime seems to have realized that racist oppression and military suppression will not bring about a solution to the problems of the Tamil speaking people. I should say that the courageous and the radical approach enunciated by President Premadasa has resulted in the present climate of peace and conciliation. We sincerely desire that the present atmosphere of peace should continue and that our people should live a life of freedom, dignity and security. The future depends solely on the perceptions and approach of the Sinhala political leaders and the Sinhala masses. The Sinhalese people should realize the blunders of the past and should be prepared to resolve our problems on the basis of human justice and righteousness. If on the other hand, justice is denied to our people and if oppression is unleashed against our people, we will not hesitate to resume the armed struggle to uphold the freedom of our people. For a long time we have been fighting an armed struggle to advance the cause of our people. But the forms of our struggle changed in accordance with the concrete conditions and historical compulsions. Such changes in the modalities of our struggle are inevitable. Now, we have decided to build up our Party structure and to embrace democratic politics as the mode of our struggle. We will expand our organization into a mass movement and prove to the world that the Liberation Tigers are the authentic representation of our people. We are not opposed to democratic norms and practices. We have been fighting to secure the fundamental political liberties and democratic rights of our people. Our political objective is to build a radical new society based on social and democratic freedoms.

"The Sri Lankan Government should eliminate all oppressive conditions pitted against our people so that genuine democratic traditions can be best enhanced in the political mainstream offering us a substantial framework that would be a basis for a permanent political settlement. Even though the Government of India utilized all its military might against our movement, it miserably failed in achieving its objective of disarming us. It is a tragedy that the Government of India completely disregarded the political aspirations, interests and security concerns of our people who have suffered long years of genocidal oppression but was primarily concerned about our arms, which constituted the shield of security of our people. This was the Himalayan blunder made by India and she has learned a bitter historical lesson for such a misguided policy. We sincerely hope that Sri Lanka will not make such a disastrous mistake again. There is peace and a cessation of hostilities between the Sri Lankan Armed Forces and the LTTE fighters. But the fundamental problems of our people have not been resolved. Our economy is in a shambles. The towns and villages have been reduced to graveyards as a consequence of prolonged wars. The conditions of oppression perpetrated against our people have not been fully eradicated. The wounds of State oppression have not been healed. Our people still live in fear and trepidation over their security in these circumstances.

"I feel sad to note that certain Sri Lankan newspapers are demanding that the LTTE should surrender arms. Instead, one should objectively study and understand the genesis of the armed struggle of the LTTE and the concerete historical conditions that led to the growth and development of the armed resistance. We wish to say that once concrete actions are taken to remove the causes and conditions that led to Tamil resistance, the question of arms will be settled forever. It is a misconception to assume that the ethnic issue would be resolved once the LTTE hands over its weapons.

> "It is the historical conditions of oppression which created the struggle for liberation and the armed resistance became the revolutionary expression of that struggle. The question of arms cannot be resolved unless the ethnic issue is resolved amicably. I hope that the Sinhala people and the Sri Lanka Government will understand our position. Our movement will continue to struggle to secure for our people a life of freedom, peace and a prosperous future. Our movement is the only light of hope of our people. I call upon the Tamil and Muslim people to rally around our movement to strengthen it as a powerful national force."

There was displeasure between the Government of Sri Lanka and the LTTE over the issue of the EPRLF. The EPRLF was a terrorist organization and had contributed significantly to the havoc in the North and the East. However the EPRLF, like the ENDLF and TELO, readily accepted the Indo-Sri Lanka Accord. Once the IPKF embarked on Military operations against the LTTE, the EPRLF, ENDLF and TELO under the banner "Three Stars" also waged war on the LTTE. However the "Three Stars" turned out to be more a hindrance than a help to the IPKF and was hence allowed to die a natural death early in 1988.

In mid-1988 the EPRLF and its junior partner the ENDLF formed a political alliance known as the EPRLF to contest the Provincial Council elections scheduled for September 1988. They fulfilled all election laws in Sri Lanka including the oath prescribed in the Sixth Amendment to The Constitution. In the North the EPRLF won all 36 seats and in the East 36 out of 71 seats. (The other 35 were won by the Muslim Congress, the UNP and Independents in that order). Thus the EPRLF was duly elected to office in the Provincial Council of the North-Eastern Province.

Once in office the EPRLF worked hand in glove with the IPKF. In fact the military arm of the EPRLF, the Tamil National Army was trained and financed by the IPKF. With the departure of the IPKF, the LTTE objected to the EPRLF continuing in office. On the other hand the Government of Sri Lanka saw no reason to dissolve the Provincial

Council of the North-Eastern Province which was duly elected less than two years ago.

On May 15th 1990 Dr. Anton Balasingham claimed that the Government of Sri Lanka was training EPRLF cadres in Trincomalee and that would necessarily sour the relations the Government had with the LTTE, because the LTTE was the sole representative of the Tamil people. Two weeks later LTTE hit squads in Madras killed Padmanaba, the leader of the EPRLF. In the meantime Ranjan Wijeratne, State Minister for Defence stated at a Press conference:

"If the LTTE claims that they are the sole representative of the Tamil people they should prove it by contesting elections. Elections will be held as soon as they lay down their arms because we are not prepared to hold elections at gunpoint."

Against this background, as an act of defiance the EPRLF decided to nominate Vartharaja Perumal, Chief Minister of the North-Eastern Province, as a Member of Parliament to fill the vacancy created by the death of Sam Tambimuttu, who together with Mrs. Tambimuttu had been gunned down by the LTTE, in Colombo.

As the detente between the Government of Sri Lanka and the LTTE was visibly deteriorating A. C. S. Hameed, the Minister of Justice, visited Jaffna on May 28th 1990 to discuss wide ranging issues with the LTTE. He met with no success. On the other hand, as the days rolled by there were an increasing incidences of skirmishes between the LTTE and the Police and even the LTTE and the Army. On June 1st, an LTTE delegation led by Dr. Balasingham called on President Premadasa. The President assured them that he was taking action to ensure that a free and fair election will be held in the North-Eastern Province as early as practicable. In turn the LTTE assured that they would not interfere with the law and order machinery of the State. However on June 7th, the LTTE opened fire at an Army patrol in Vavuniya killing one soldier and injuring several because they refused to stop at a LTTE checkpoint. This resulted in howls of protest from the SLFP who claimed that President Premadasa was desperately trying to appease the LTTE and had ceded the North-Eastern Province to them.

As tension mounted it became obvious that the LTTE was looking for some excuse to renew hostilities. On June 10th 1990, a Muslim tailor employed by the LTTE, trying to make advances to a Sinhalese woman in a refugee camp in Batticaloa was caught by her irate husband and assaulted. In the resulting fisticuffs both men were injured. They were marched off to the Police Station and later treated as out patients at the General Hospital. That night the LTTE cardes arrived at the Police Station and accused them of having assaulted their tailor. When the Police gave their version, the LTTE cadres visited the General Hospital but could not find their tailor. They then returned to the Police Station in an unruly state and captured two Policemen who were taken as hostages. In the morning over 200 terrorists from the LTTE in battle dress and armed to the teeth overpowered the Police Station. Later that night, June 11th 1990, the LTTE simultaneously attacked and overpowered all Police Stations in the Batticaloa District. The next day all Police Stations in the Trincomalee District were also captured. Two days later when Major General Denzil Kobbekaduwa was rushed to Amparai as General-Officer-Commanding the Eastern Command, every Police Station in the Eastern Province as well had been captured by the LTTE. The Sinhalese and Muslim Policemen amongst the captives, accounted for over 600. Almost all of them suffered the same fate. They were taken to the nearby jungle with their hands tied behind their backs. Thereafter, according to a few who managed to escape, there was machine gun fire. Some weeks later mass graves were found. Despite the wide publicity in the media there was not one word of protest from Human Rights organizations in Europe. In fact two weeks after these atrocities were made public in the international media, in the European Parliament at Strassbourg a nasty resolution was tabled at the behest of some Christian Human Rights organizations accusing the Government of Sri Lanka of atrocities against the Tamils! Of the eight Members of the European Parliament who had tabled that resolution two could not even spot Sri Lanka on the map of the world when I challenged them to do so!!

Indeed Sri Lanka was now fighting a civil war. Ranjan Wijeratne in addressing Parliament summed up the mood of the Sinhalese in saying.

"No half way house with me. Now I am going all out for the LTTE. We will annihilate them."

In Sri Lanka the military and political base of the LTTE is the Jaffna peninsula. However in the larger context the military and emotional base of the LTTE is Tamil Nadu in India. A very significant part of the people of Tamil Nadu and even parts of the Government of Tamil Nadu were covertly and sometimes overtly supporting the LTTE. Indeed on a global basis the power base of the LTTE is not the Jaffna peninsula but Tamil Nadu. During a period of eight years from 1979, when President Jayeweardene first committed troops to Jaffna, to 1987, when the IPKF arrived in Sri Lanka, the LTTE had organized 35 training camps in the districts of Anna, Coimbatore, Chengalpattu, Madurai, Pudukkotai, South Arcot, Salem, Tanjavur, Tiruchi and Ramanathapuram. The LTTE supply bases were in the districts of Atiruchi, Coimbatore, Dharmapuri, Madurai, Periyar, Pudukottai, Tanjavur and Rameshwaram. Coimbatore was the principal supply base for arms, ammunition and explosives, Dharmapuri for explosives, Periyar for uniforms. Tutticorin was their smugglers haven, Tanjavur had their communication center and Tiruchi the hospitals for the wounded. Nagapattam was the area where the bulk of imported arms and communications were surreptitiously unloaded for eventual transportation to the former Northern Province in Sri Lanka. One of the principal recruitment centers in Tamil Nadu was Rameshwaram where hordes of refugees arrived periodically from Sri Lanka. This formidable military base was established with the full knowledge of Chief Minister M. G. Ramachandran who was the Godfather of the LTTE and after his demise by his arch rival M. Karunanidhi, who also took over the role of Godfather for the LTTE. In the Federal set up in India the Chief Minister has complete jurisdiction over the Police whereas the Armed Forces are in theory under the President and in practice under the Prime Minister. It was common knowledge that the wrath of the Chief minister of Tamil Nadu, whoever it be, would descend on any Policemen who applied the law of the land on the LTTE. The plea of Prime Minister Indira Gandhi and Prime Minister Rajiv Gandhi that they they were powerless in Tamil Nadu was not untrue. In practice the AIADMK (M. G. Ramachandran) and the DMK (M. Karunanidhi) together controlled over 80% of the seats of the State Legislature.

Let alone the amazing supply base, both for men and material, which the LTTE has in Tamil Nadu, their efficiency was astonishing. Even when the IPKF was waging war against the LTTE in the North-Eastern Province and the Eastern Fleet of the Indian Navy was patrolling the Palk Straits, there was a continuous flow of supplies of arms and ammunition for the LTTE in Sri Lanka. The LTTE owned four ships, the *Sun Bird*, *Golden Bird*, *Illyana* and *Cauline* which were used extensively to transport arms and ammunition to Sri Lanka. A special unit of the LTTE The Sea Tigers operating in speed boats met these ships out at sea and surreptitiously brought ashore the lethal weapons. Alternatively these ships had a rendezvous off the coast of Nagapattam in Tamil Nadu and Indian fishermen and smugglers brought the cargo ashore. Thereafter, suitable arrangements were made to transport the cargo across the Palk Straits to Sri Lanka on routes best known to the smugglers, who during war or peace have enjoyed a lucrative trade between Tamil Nadu and Sri Lanka and vice versa.

Moreover the survival capabilities of the LTTE were also amazing. By November 1987, the IPKF had driven them out of the Jaffna peninsula into the jungles of what was once called the Northern Province. Lt. General Depinder Singh and his successor Lt. General Kalkat had at least 70,000 troops under their Command supported by 220 tanks and air cover of nearly 100 aircraft. MI-24 helicopter gunships, MIG fighters, Mirage-2000 fighters were regularly strafing the jugles of the former Northern Province and occasionally Canberra jet bombers were used in action. Yet not one of the top leaders of the LTTE, Prabhakaran, Mahattaya, Kittu and Pottu Amman (their Intelligence chief) were killed or captured by the IPKF despite their concerted action for over two years.

The management of the current war devolved on Ranjan Wijeratne, State Minister of Defence and Minister for Plantations. He had systematically incurred the wrath of the LTTE. Physically towering over others, he also towered over others in embodying the resolve of the Government of Sri Lanka in fighting terrorism. Consequently he was the most heavily guarded man in Sri Lanka next to President Premadasa. On Saturday 2nd March 1990 his Mercedes Benz complete with a tight Police escort left his residence en-route to the Ministry of Defence. Less than half a mile away as his car was passing by, a LTTE car bomb was detonated with pinpoint accuracy. The massive explosion hit the car broadside. Death was instantaneous to everybody in the Mercedes Benz. Thus Sri Lanka lost a patriot and a splendid Cabinet Minister.

Prabhakaran's capacity for leadership militarily has made him a hero to chauvinistic Tamils, be they in Sri Lanka, Tamil Nadu or anywhere else in the world. A high school drop out, he was active in the Tamil Youth Front and later in the Tamil New Tigers. Early in 1975 when he was 20 years old, he killed Chetti Thanabalasingham, leader of the Tamil New Tigers, to assume the leadership of that organization which was later named the Liberation Tigers of Tamil Eelam (LTTE). Later in 1975, he made its first public kill, Mayor Alfred Duraiappa of Jaffna who had joined the SLFP. (Prime Minister Sirima Bandarnaike was then in office). Since then he has displayed remarkable skill both in terrorism and survival. In keeping with his style he has exterminated all rivals. Among his numerous victims were Uma Maheshwaran, the leader of PLOTE, Sri Sabaratnam the leader of TELO and V. Padmanaban, the leader of the EPRLF. By the same token the LTTE decimated the cadres of those terrorist organizations. Thus by the time the IPKF left Sri Lanka the LTTE was for all intents and purposes, the sole terrorist organization amongst the Tamils. As the political ambitions of Prabhakaran grew, the LTTE exterminated some of the best known former Members of Parliament from the TULF. Thus the LTTE filled the power vacuum with Prabhakaran becoming the leader of the Tamil community in the absence of any other leader.

As his stature increased within the Tamil community for the manner in which the LTTE stood their ground against the might of the Armed Forces of India, the confidence of Prabhakaran grew tremendously. Following the assassination of the de-facto Minister of Defence, Ranjan Wijeratne, whom the LTTE loathed, Prabhakaran planned the assassination of former Prime Minister Rajiv Gandhi.

According to LTTE sources, Prabharakan felt that Rajiv Gandhi had cheated him in July, 1987. He was brought to New Delhi by RAW under the pretext of the Prime Minister wanting to have discussions with him on the deteriorating security situation in Sri Lanka. While in New Delhi he was virtually under house arrest at the plush Ashok Hotel and the Prime Minister merely met him to hand over a copy of the Indo-Sri Lanka Accord which he would be signing in Colombo the following day.

The consensus of opinion in the Jaffna peninsula and elsewhere in the North-Eastern Province was that the Tamil people suffered more under the IPKF than under Army. All of this was attributed to Rajiv Gandhi. With the fall of Prime Minister V P Singh in October 1990 and weak coalition Government of Prime Minister Chandrashekar in office, an early General Election was imminent and the return to power of Rajiv Gandhi was more than likely. Lately Rajiv Gandhi, like the late Ranjan Wijeratne, could not conceal his contempt for the LTTE and his pithy remarks often appeared in the media.

Prabhakaran soon took the decision to assassinate Rajiv Gandhi somewhere in Tamil Nadu. The decision was to be implemented by Pottu Amman, the Chief of Intelligence of the LTTE. A suicide bomber would be used to exterminate the likely next Prime Minister of India.

According to the Tamil Nadu Police, Pottu Amman assigned the operation to Sivarasan, a trusted confidante to Prabhakaran. He had lost an eye in a bomb explosion and was now based in Madras. The suicide squad consisted of Dhanu and Subha, both members of the LTTE women's wing. According to LTTE propaganda both girl come from families which were either raped or murdered by the IPKF in Sri Lanka. They prepared a belt bomb. It consisted of four grenades containing cyclonite explosives each filled with thousands of splinters to enhance the lethal effect at close range. This death dealing contraption complete with a battery and detonators were fitted into a ladies denim belt encased in TNT. The suicide bomber merely had to switch on the detonator and a massive explosion would result killing her and everybody around her. The LTTE leaves nothing to chance and Dhanu had a rehearsal on former Prime Minister V. P. Singh when he addressed a meeting in Tamil Nadu on May 12th 1991. She garlanded him and bowed low in making obeisance and pressed her stomach. That day she was not wearing her lethal denim belt but in attendance was Hari Babu, a free lance photographer who was filming the entire rehearsal for Prabhaakran. On May 20th, former Prime Minister Rajiv Gandhi was due to address a rally of the Congress Party at Sriperumbudur near Madras. When he arrived around 10 pm, well behind schedule, Dhanu approached him with a sandalwood garland. She was escorted by Hari Babu who was filming the entire operation and Sivarasan who was masquerading as a journalist. She garlanded Rajiv Gandhi, bowed low and respectfully and then switched on the detonator. The explosion killed Rajiv Gandhi, Dhanu, Hari Babu, nine Policemen and twenty five bystanders.

Once again Prabhakaran had it his way, but the aftermath of the assassination was indeed grossly detrimental to the LTTE. Firstly the wrath of the Government of India was directed against the LTTE. The Indian Police moved with amazing speed and by October 1991, an indictment for murder was filed in the Madras High Court against Prabhakaran, Pottu Amman and 36 others. Ironically the camera of the late Hari Babu had recorded the assassination in detail. It showed amongst others Sivarasan and Subha, the standby suicide bomber, Dixon their communication expert and several other key LTTE personnel in Tamil Nadu. They were hunted throughout South India and when surrounded by the Police committed suicide in the LTTE fashion by swallowing cyanide. The exception was Sivarasan who shot himself through his glass eye.

Secondly, for the first time Human Rights organization in the West turned against the LTTE. For once they looked upon the LTTE not as freedom fighters but as terrorists and murderers. The truth had dawned on them at last!

At the General Election of 1991, the Congress Party easily outstripped all other Parties, thought they lacked a simple majority in the Lok Sabha. Former Foreign Minister Narasimha Rao became the leader of the Congress Party and Prime Minister while L. K. Advani the leader of the

BJP, became Leader of the Opposition. Under Prime Minister Narasimha Rao, the Congress Party Administration turned hostile to the LTTE.

With immediate effect, the Military machine of the LTTE was systematically dismantled. The LTTE training camps were no longer in Tamil Nadu, they were relocated in the jungles in the North-eastern Province in Sri Lanka. Armament factories of the LTTE in Coimbatore were sealed and their staff arrested. Their explosive factories in Dharmapuri and uniform manufacturing factories in Salem suffered the same fate. Their communications center in Tanjavur was dismantled and the equipment confiscated. Even their hospitals in Tiruchi were under constant surveillance with patients under arrest and doctors under interrogation. Tuticorin was no longer a haven for smugglers working for the LTTE. However the smuggling of foreign arms and ammunition via the coastal stretch from Nagapattam to Rameshwaran in India to the numerous coves in districts of Mannar and Mullaitivu continued but on a reduced scale.

Prime Minister Narasimha Rao rescinded the previous pernicious policy of India in sanctimoniously interfering in the domestic affairs of Sri Lanka. Navy fired on LTTE launches crossing the Jaffna lagoon, a prohibited zone, and killing 29 civilians when Srilankan were killed. In the time of Prime Minister Indira Gandhi and Prime Minister Rajiv Gandhi, the Ministry of External Affairs would have not only have made a public protest but would have induced the media in India to accuse Sri Lanka of genocide. In this episode the Ministry of External Affairs said absolutely nothing and the media in India said next to nothing.

Down the ages there has been traditional friendship between India and Sri Lanka. In 1948 when Prime Minister D. S. Senanayake was on his first State visit to India, he suggested to Prime Minister Jawaharlal Nehru, truly one of the great statesmen of his times, that the relationship with India should be like between elder brother and younger brother. In my knowledge of Foreign Affairs there could be no better way of describing what the relations between our two countries should be. It was indeed a tragedy both for Sri Lanka and India that the daughter of the great Jawaharlal Nehru behaved in the way she did towards Sri Lanka. The price of her folly in giving succour to the LTTE was the assassination of her son by the LTTE. The price of her folly in giving succour to the Sikh extremists resulted in her own assassination.

India is truly a great nation and like all great nations learns quickly from the folly of their leaders after they have vacated high office. India has already learnt from the folly of meddling in the domestic affairs of friendly neighbours. Indeed there is overwhelming evidence not only in Sri Lanka but also in Bangladesh and in Nepal that India is no longer a meddlesome neighbour.

The burning question at this juncture is, was it wisdom or folly on the part of President Premadasa to have requested the withdrawal of the IPKF? To say the least that is an emotionally charged question, because Sri Lankans in general and the Sinhalese in particular were deeply offended when President Jayawardene invited the IPKF and were so relieved when the IPKF finally left. Against that background, earlier in this book it was stated that only history could judge whether it was wisdom or folly for President Jayewardene to have invited the IPKF. By the same token it must be stated that only history could judge whether it was wisdom of folly for President Premadasa to have demanded from India the immediate withdrawal of the IPKF.

Chapter V

THE PROTRACTED WAR

The period after the withdrawal of the Indian Peace Keeping Force was very difficult indeed for the Government of Sri Lanka. The LTTE was provoking the Government at every turn and skirmishes between the LTTE and our Armed Forces or Police were the order of the day. Finally on the night of June 11th 1990, the LTTE turned against President R. Premadasa. They overran all Police stations in the District of Batticaloa, and the President ordered all such Police personnel to surrender rather than risk their lives. All except the Tamil Policemen were executed by firing squad. Thus began Eelam War II, which was fought with savage fury with unusually high casualties. For example during the period June 1987 to March 1990, the IPKF recorded the loss of lives of 1,155 soldiers. In seven months of 1990 our Army lost a staggering 720 soldiers.

1991 began as a difficult year for the Government of Sri Lanka. There were no Military victories whatsoever. On the other hand, the LTTE had overrun the Army camps at Kokavil and Mankulam, in the Northern Province. Besides the territory north of Vavuniya and south of Elephant Pass was completely under the control of the LTTE. So was the bulk of the Jaffna peninsula barring the Army camp and Air Force Base at Palaly, Army camps at Elephant Pass, Thondamanar, Madagal and Pooneryn and the Naval Base at Karaingar. In July, the garrison at Elephant Pass under the command of Major Sanath Karunaratne of the 6th Battalion Sinha Regiment (6/SR) was under constant siege by the LTTE. As the pressure mounted the Governemnt launched Operation Balavegaya, a land, sea and air borne attack to save the garrison. Troops from the Second Division under Major General Denzil Kobbekaduwa were ferried to Pullimodai in the Mullaitivu district, where a detachment from the Navy under Rear Admiral Quintus Wickramaratne had in readiness a flotilla of mechanized landing craft (LCM), Chinese built Shanghai gunboats, and

Israeli built Dovra gunboats. General Kobbekaduwa travelled in the mother ship SLNS *Wickrema* with his troops, the 3rd Battalion Sri Lanka Light Infantry (Lt. Col. Gamini Jayasundera), 3rd Battalion Gajaba Regiment (Lt. Col. Seevali Wanigasekera). The Commander of the Task Force Brigadier Vijaya Wimalaratne was on board the SLNS *Edithara* with Captain H.R. Amaraweera who commanded the flotilla, and Group Captain Dick Sally who co-ordinated the air operations.

The first attempt at a sea borne landing at Vettilakerni scheduled for 1430 hours on July 15th 1991 met with stiff resistance. At the request of Brigadier Wimalaratne, the landing was delayed. At 1800 hours under cover of fire from Naval gunboats and air support from low flying Sia Marchetti SF-260 aircraft directed by Wing Commander Sunil Cabral, the first wave led by Major Angelo Peiris, waded ashore. Resistance continued to be stiff but the 3/SLLI and the 3/GR secured a beachhead that night. Within 24 hours the balance of the 1st Brigade under the command of Col. Anton Wijendra and the 3rd Brigade under Col. Sarath Fonseka arrived after overcoming all manner of logistic problems ranging from low tide to artillery and armour getting stuck in the soft sea sand. Thereafter arrived a holding Brigade under the command of Col. Devinda Kalupahana. Once the beachhead was securely established, General Kobbekaduwa authorized Brigadier Wimalaratne to commence the link up operation with Elephant Pass which was about ten kilometres away.

In the meantime Elephant Pass was under siege. Anti-aircraft batteries prevented any helicopter borne assistance and Sia Marchetti aircraft were used to relieve the pressure by strafing the hinterland. Nevertheless the forward platoons of the LTTE were approaching the garrison, their armour included tractors converted into armoured cars. Corporal Gamini Kularatne of the 6/SR then crawled out of the garrison under machine gunfire. With total disregard for his own safety he approached an improvised armoured car. As the garrison watched in disbelief he mounted it and lobbed in his grenades thus destroying the vehicle before he was mowed down by enemy fire. He was posthumously awarded the *Parama Weera Vibushanaya*, our equivalent of the Victoria Cross. Later his ashes were taken to Hasalaka where he was given a Military funeral befitting a hero. Today a statue at Hasalaka perpetuates the memory of this gallant soldier who joined the Army after the massacre of 27 Buddhist priests and noviciates at Arantalawa in 1987. They had their throats gruesomely slit by the LTTE.

In the meantime Brigadier Wimalaratne was leading two Brigades which were advancing at only 500 to 1,000 metres a day because the terrain was heavily mined and resistance was even more stiff than at Vadamarachchi in 1987. Casualities were heavy and among those killed in action was Major Angelo Peiris. By now General Kobbekaduwa had under him approximately 4,000 troops as against an estimated enemy strength of 5,000 to 6,000. Despite the complete air superiority which he had, his troops were severely taxed and at the end of one week they had advanced only three kilometres, to the Muliyan Kovil, after suffering heavy casualties. By this time Lt. Colonel Sanath Karunaratne commanding the garrison and given a battlefield promotion, was also under severe strain. The garrison had run out of fresh food and was running low on fresh water. Besides the casualties were heavy and any evacuation by helicopter abandoned after several attempted landings were aborted because of heavy ground fire. Against this background Sergeant Major Nanda Godamunne of the Medical Corps serving at Elephant Pass was inquiring on the radio from Army doctors at the field hospital at Vetteleikerni on how best to treat a soldier who was bleeding to death with his leg shattered below the knee. Instructions were relayed by radio on how to do an amputation. The Sergeant Major carried out the instructions successfully. He was given a battlefield commission.

The first sign of victory was in the third week when Major Shiran Jinasena of the 1st Recce Regiment of the Sri Lanka Armoured Corps, commanding a squadron of Saladin armoured cars, broke through enemy lines despite two of his vehicles being blown up by mines. General Kobbekaduwa who had received reinforcements earlier that week then regrouped his armour. Saladin and Saracen armoured cars from the 1/SLAC and 3/SLAC and the South African built Buffel APCs, which are normally assigned to infantry battalions, rehearsed as a armoured battle group at Vetteleikernai and were then brought into combat. On August 2nd the cavalry charge was led by Major Jinasena. He was followed by Major Roshan De Silva of 4/GR who commanded a squadron of Buffel APCs. Then the three infantry Brigades under Brigadier Wimalaratne, which included the newly arrived 7th Brigade under Colonel Gamini Angammana, went into action. On August 3rd 1991 the troops repeatedly intercepted LTTE messages such as,

> "These devils are pouring in from all sides"
> "We cannot resist them anymore"

On August 4th, the forward platoons in the Task Force reached the beleagured garrison singing their battle song '*Hela Jathika Abhimane*'. A few hours later General Kobbekaduwa came in on an armoured car from his old regiment the 1/SLAC to congratulate his troops. He was greeted with the lusty singing of the theme song of the war film '*Sandesaya*'

Of Lt. Colonel Sanath Karunaratne and his six hundred officers and other ranks from the 6/SR it could surely be said,

"Theirs was not to reason why,
Theirs was to but, do and die."

Indeed the Army could be justly proud of this battalion which held the beleagured garrison for four weeks under the most difficult of circumstance and gave the nation her first recipient of the *Parama Weera Vibushanaya*. By the same token the LTTE exhibited once again, as they did in Vadamarachchi in May 1987 and in Jaffna in October 1987 during the siege by General Depinder Singh, their magnificent skills in soldiering.

It is widely accepted that General Kobbekaduwa was one of the best field commander ever produced by our Army. A superb soldier, he was also the epitome of an Officer and gentleman in the true sense of the word. Indeed his humanitarian values were just as well a known as his skill in battle. Since 1990 the General-Officer-Commanding the Second Division based in the North, he had under him over 20,000 troops and had a front extending over 100 kilometers. Notwithstanding his legendary skill in leadership and the troops at his disposal, he was unable to push the front northwards. Such was the formidable enemy he faced.

Against that background his only option was an Inchon type of landing which the five-star General Douglas MacArthur of the United States planned and executed brilliantly in 1950 during the Korean war. General Kobbekaduwa advocated an amphibious landing on the Jaffna peninsula from the island of Kayts, which he would personally lead, and for Brigadier Vijaya Wimalaratne to lead another column into Jaffna from Palaly. The General hoped to capture the Jaffna peninsula in 15 days as against the 11 days taken by General Depinder Singh of the IPKF. He admitted that casualties would be heavy. After detailed discussions the three Service Commanders vetoed this plan because of the heavy casualties it would entail.

However President Premadasa saw political advantage in the liberation of the Jaffna peninsula and finally approved the operation in August 1992. General Kobbekaduwa was elated, though he was still mourning for his father who had died a few days earlier. To finalize plans he left his headquarters in Vavuniya for the Naval Base at Karainagar near Jaffna. On August 5th 1992, General Kobbekaduwa, Brigadier Wimalaratne and senior staff officers left Karainagar for Kayts. They were accompanied by Commodore Mohan Jayamaha, Naval Officer Commanding the Northern Area. After their reconnaissance mission, for some inexplicable reason all these senior officers got into one Land Rover. That vehicle was blown up by a mine. Everybody on board was killed except a batman who had both his legs amputated.

Promoted posthumously to the rank of Lt. General, the rank of the Commander of the Army, General Kobbekaduwa was honoured in death as he was in life. His death was mourned throughout the nation, even in Jaffna. His funeral was the largest Military funeral ever seen in Sri Lanka.

In October 1992, the LTTE stepped up their campaign both on land and by sea, using their new commandos, the Sea Tigers. The LTTE carried out a massive raid on the Janakapura camp in the Welioya sector. (Welioya is the confluence of the Northern Province, the Eastern Province and the North Central Province). They overran the camp completely, killed 251 soldiers and spirited away over Rs. 10 million worth of Military equipment. Immediately thereafter the Sea Tigers stepped up their activities, in direct response to the Naval blockade of the Jaffna peninsula enforced by Vice Admiral Clancy Fernando, the Commander of the Navy.

A suicide bomber laden with explosives rammed his motor cycle into the Mercedes Benz flag car of Admiral Fernando while he was traveling from his residence at Longden Place, to Navy Headquarters in Flagstaff Street. All on board the Mercedes Benz were killed instantaneously. Two months later in January 1993 a suicide bomber from the Sea Tigers rammed a boat full of explosives into a Fast Attack Craft of the Navy in the high seas off Point Pedro. The Israeli built Dovra sank with all on board. In rapid succession Sea Tigers in their explosive laden boats rammed the surveillance craft SLNS *Edithara* and SLNS *Abeetha* causing extensive damage to the vessels and killing many members of their crew. To add insult to injury the Sea Tigers captured an Inshore Patrol Craft in the Jaffna lagoon having killed her crew and sailed away in it.

In November 1993, a LTTE Task Force of nearly 1,000 troops, both Tigers and Tigresses, overran the new shore establishment at Sri Nagaventhurai near Kilali inflicting heavy casualties and capturing three Inshore Patrol Craft. They then went further afield to attack the Army Camp at Pooneryn, which had a strength of two battalions. The LTTE Task Force under Colonel Karikalan, their highest ranking military officer, directed artillery fire at Pooneryn. Then their infantry equipped with T-56 and AK-47 assault rifles stormed the camp with the Tigresses joining the Tigers in combat. The Army casualties were a staggering 525 officers and men killed in action or listed as missing. Besides the enemy captured over Rs. 50 million worth of military equipment and even drove away in three T-55 tanks! It resulted in the embarrassed Commander of the Army Lt. General Cecil Waidyaratne, who had spent the formative years of his career in the Armoured Corps, submitting his papers for retirement.

The battle at Pooneryn sent shock waves through the Sinhala speaking Provinces. For once even the foolish amongst the Sinhalese, there is a surprisingly high percentage of them in the context of the ethnic problem, admitted that the LTTE was a formidable force. Such fools who are fluent in English periodically advocate their pet theories such as:

"Bomb Jaffna"
"Flatten Jaffna"
"Wipe out Jaffna"

For once they accepted reality and accepted why an Army of 90,000 had over 15,000 deserters and why the youth no longer clamoured to join the Armed Forces. Following the assassination of President Premadasa by the LTTE, for once the naive advocated a negotiated settlement. In the meantime President D. B. Wijetunga advocated his own inane theory that there was no ethnic problem!

At the General Election of 1994 the architect of the victory of the SLFP led People's Alliance was unmistakably, Chandrika Bandaranaike Kumaratunge. Her principal election strategy was to pledge an open market economy, like what the UNP had successfully introduced in 1977 but without the attendant evils of corruption, to negotiate an honourable peace with the Tamils, there being no viable Military solution and to give the nation a clean Government, which the UNP had failed to do ever since it had taken leave of its senses. By and large the nation believed her.

On the ethnic issue Prime Minister Chandrika Bandaranaike Kumaratunga was influenced not by the thinking of her parents, who had both contributed to worsening it, but by the thinking of her husband, The late Vijaya Kumaratunga. Prime Minister S. W. R. D. Bandaranaike was the architect of the Official Language Act of 1956 which was a disaster. In 1970, Prime Minister Sirima Bandaranaike introduced the weighted system of marks to the University Entrance Examination which was another disaster. On the other hand Vijaya Kumarantunga was a visionary in the context of the ethnic problem and was more liberal towards the Tamils than even the Marxist leader Vasudeva Naayakkara M.P. In the perception of Vijaya Kumarantunga, the Tamil community, rightly or wrongly perceived that the Sinhalese had treated them unjustly. That had to be corrected as early as practicable.

On assuming duties as Prime Minister, Chandrika Bandaranaike Kumarantunga insisted on extending her hand of friendship to the Tamils. The Prime Minister gave the highest priority to negotiations with the LTTE, the *de facto* rulers of the Northern Province, north of Thandikulam. Correspondence was initiated by her with Prabhakaran, with the International Committee of the Red Cross (ICRC) functioning as the conduit. As a measure of goodwill all manner of restrictions on items banned in the North by the Army, were withdrawn.

In the last week of August 1994, when the new Prime Minister initiated action to solve the, problem the basic constraints she was subjected to were as follows:

The Bandaranaike – Chelvanayakam Pact of 1957, the Dudley Senanayake Pact of 1965, the District Development Councils Act of 1980 and the Provincial Councils Act of 1987, both initiated by President Jayewardene, had been written off as unmitigated disasters by the Tamil community. By the same token, the Ceasefires with the LTTE initiated by President Jayewardene in 1985 and initiated by President Premadasa in 1989-90 were written off as unmitigated disasters by the Sinhalese community. Consequently, the level of trust between the leadership of the two communities was at a low ebb. However the new Prime Minister was given the benefit of the doubt by both communities because of her idealism and because she belonged to a new generation of leaders.

Another factor in her favour was the exemplary role of India in the context of the tenuous relationship between the Sinhalese and Tamils. Since the assassination of Rajiv Gandhi in May 1991, the LTTE was looked upon by the Government and people of India, not as freedom fighters but as a band of terrorists and Prabhakaran, who earlier was looked upon as an idol, was now looked down upon as murderer who was absconding. The anger of the Government and people was self-evident and in whatever possible way the Government of India helped the Government of Sri Lanka, since 1991. For example in March 1993, the Indian Navy was tipped off by a defector from the LTTE that Kittu, perhaps the best known terrorist in the LTTE next to Prabhakaran, was on board the tramp steamer the M. V. *Ahat* somewhere in the Bay of Bengal. The *Ahat* was allegedly carrying a cargo of arms for the LTTE to be discharged into smuggler's *vallams* (canoes) somewhere in the Palk Straits. A flotilla from the Indian Navy then trailed the *Ahat* and fired a warning shot across her bows, whereupon the Captain and the crew jumped overboard having scuttled the ship. Kittu remained on board and swallowed his cyanide capsule. Indeed no commentary on the period of Eelam War II is complete without emphasizing that once again the High Commissioner of India in Sri Lanka, be it Ambassador N. N. Jha (1990-1993) or Ambassador Nareshwar Dayal (1993-1996) were highly respected and much loved in every sector of our society. Since Independence, every High Commissioner of India to Sri Lanka has visited the Island regularly on vacation after his tour duty was duly completed. The solitary exception was Ambassador Mani Dixit.

Yet another factor in favour of Sri Lanka, of which the new Prime Minister was a beneficiary, was the attitude of Human Rights organizations in the Western world. They had been critical of the Government of Sri Lanka ever since 1981, when the Army under Major General T. I. Weeratunge engaged the LTTE in open confrontation. In 1983, when the Sinhalese disgraced themselves during the racial riots of that year, the hostility of Human Rights organizations towards the Government of Sri Lanka increased to unbelievable levels, while they chose to conveniently ignore similar barbaric acts by the LTTE. For example, Human Rights organizations in the Western world said absolutely nothing in 1984 when the LTTE swooped on a Sinhalese encampment in the Northern Province named the Dollar and Kent farms and slaughtered over 100 rehabilitated prisoners who were farming there; in 1985 when the LTTE slaughtered over 140 by-standers while retreating after desecrating the *Sri Maha Bodhiya* in Anuradhapura; in 1986 when the LTTE detonated a bomb on board an Air Lanka Tristar while still on the tarmac at Colombo International Airport and killed 19 people including 14 European tourists en-route to the Maldive Islands; in 1987 when the LTTE detonated a huge bomb at the Pettah bus terminus resulting in 150 people perishing; in 1989 when the LTTE slaughtered in cold blood 29 Buddhist priests and novitiates at Arantalawa by slitting their throats with knives and machetes; in 1990 when the LTTE executed over 600 Sinhalese Policemen of the 700 who had surrendered to them when Eelam War II broke out on the night of June 11th 1990; in July 1990 when the LTTE slaughtered 120 Muslims performing their Jumma prayers at Kathankudi and in August 1990 when the LTTE slaughtered another 140 Muslims at the Jumma Prayers at Eravur. That deafening silence spoke for itself. These were a supreme examples of the duplicity of the West. This attitude changed when the LTTE assassinated former Prime Minister Rajiv Gandhi of India. The 180 degree turn by Human Rights organizations became more pronounced in 1992 when Amensty International amended their constitution at their General Assmebly held in Yokohama, Japan, whereby they could pontificate not only against sovereign nations but also against terrorist groups that violate Human Rights. Thus by 1994 when the UNP Administration began to fall apart, the attitude of Human Rights organizations to Sri Lanka was basically more balanced.

In negotiating for peace, a critical factor was the Eastern Province where the three major ethnic groups in Sri Lanka, the Sinhalese Tamils and Muslims, live in sizeable numbers. According to the Census of 1981, the breakdown of population of that Province was as follows:

Sri Lankan Tamils	-	40.9%
Muslims	-	32.2%
Sinhalese	-	24.9%
Indian Tamils	-	1.2%
Burghers	-	0.8%

At the Genneral Election of 1994 and the Presidential Election of 1994 the polling in the Tamil speaking Eastern Province was around 75% as against an average of around 85% in the seven Sinhala speaking Provinces. Thus the Eastern Province was now ready for a Referendum, in terms of The Thirteenth Amendment to the Constitution, to decide whether or not the temporary merger with the Northern Province should continue. It is common knowledge that it is difficult to find a single Sinhalese or Muslim who is in favour of such a continuation. Considering that the combined Sinhalese and Muslims population of the Eastern Province is 57.1% as against a Sri Lankan Tamil population of 40.9%, the verdict of the Province in such a Referendum is a foregone conclusion. However, for security reasons the Referendum originally scheduled for 1988, when President Jayewardene was in office, has been repeatedly postponed.

Indeed, Prime Minister Chandrika Bandaranaike Kumaratunga was very confident of her peace initiatives which she embarked upon in August 1994. Her first peace delegation was due to leave for Jaffna in mid-October. It was strategically timed for the Presidential Election where the principal candidates were herself and the Leader of the Opposition, Gamini Dissanayake from the UNP. However early in October 1994, a suicide squad from the Sea Tigers under the command of Lt. Commander Kalyani, rammed their explosive laden boat against the gunboat SLNS *Sagarawardene* which was anchored at night in the Gulf of Mannar. The massive explosion killed 16 sailors, 10 were listed as missing in action and the Captain of the gunboat Commander Ajit Boyagoda was taken prisoner before the *Sagarawardene* sank. Somehow the Prime Minister looked upon that episode as one caused by an over zealous suicide squad.

On October 13th 1994, a delegation of influential officials left for Jaffna. The delegation was led by Kusum Balapatabendi, Secretary to the President. They were given a rapturous welcome by the people of Jaffna, who had gone through hell for over ten years. Quite clearly the Prime Minister had captured the imagination and the mood of the people of Jaffna. The preliminary negotiations with the LTTE commenced in Jaffna that day and the delegation returned to Colombo the following day bringing with them as a gesture of goodwill from the LTTE, four Policemen who had been in captivity since June 1990. To complete formalities the following communique was issued in Jaffna on October 14th 1994.

"The first round of talks between the Government of Sri Lanka and the Liberation Tigers of Tamil Eelam was conducted in an atmosphere of cordiality and goodwill. The talks were very constructive and held in Jaffna on October 13th and 14th, 1994.

In his opening speech, Karikalan, the Leader of the LTTE delegation, said that the LTTE is committed to peace and a peaceful settlement of the Tamil question.

Ever since the outbreak of hostilities in June 1990, the LTTE leadership has been calling for a cessation of hostilities and peace talks. But the previous Government had failed to take any positive steps to bring an end to the war and to start negotiations. But we are glad to note that the new Governement of Chandrika Bandaranaike Kumaratunga has taken constructive measures to create congenial conditions for peace. We are also pleased to note that she is genuinely committed to political negotiations.

The collective aspirations of the Tamil people are to see an end to this war and the long standing suffering that resulted from this conflict. This war that was imposed on our people has caused tremendous suffering. The people are facing innumerable problems which are immediate and urgent. We think that the initial talks should address these problems. The LTTE fervently hopes that the Government will take urgent measures to redress the grievances of our prople."

Karikalan emphasised the importance of a ceasefire as a necessary condition for the creation of a peaceful environment and for the return of normalcy. He also said that the stoppage of an armed conflict would help promote peace talks.

Welcoming the Government delegation to the negotiating table, Karikalan said that the LTTE would participate in these talks with an open mind and make every effort to co-operate with the Government to ensure the talks are successful.

The leader of the Government delegation, K. Balapatabendi said, the existing situation in the North has become a national problem, and that requires for its definitive resolution the involvement of all concerned in peace and harmony. The Prime Minister therefore considered it important, that a negotiation process be quickly launched which could successfully lead to speedy establishment of peace and that she and the Government well understood that, in the prevailing circumstances of the condition of the Tamil people, the LTTE had an influential role to play.

He said that they would discuss how best the Government could ensure the adequate supply and equitable distribution of essentials commodities to all the people of the North. As a corollary of that, to discuss how best they sought to advance the fulfilment of the to State's overriding responsibility to provide to all segments of its citizens, the public utilities and services which are essential to the community's well being.

Though that was the primary focus and matter of most immediate concern, what was fundamental was that the Northern people's enjoyment of the necessities of daily life should stem from their acceptance at heart, that they are no longer less than equal in the eyes of the State. Their deliberations would concern the political aspirations of the Northern people. This is why they particularly looked forward to projected meetings with various citizen's groups and leading personalities of the Tamil community.

On the question of transporting essential items and distributing them at low prices to the people, the LTTE representatives explained in detail the delays and difficulties involved in the movement of traffic at Thandikulam. They also pointed out that the spiraling freight rates on goods transported by sea have increased the prices. The Government delegation assured that the impediments in the flow of traffic at Thandikulam would be removed and also that they would take action to reduce shipping charges.

On the question of opening up a land route between the peninsula and the mainland, the LTTE delegates requested the opening of the Sangupity causeway for which they argued that the troops stationed at Poonaryn needed to be withdrawn. The LTTE team further explained that the opening of this land route would facilitate the traffic of people and goods and that it would be considered as an act of goodwill towards the people of Jaffna. The Government delegates gave a sympathetic hearing and said that the matter would be taken into consideration.

On the question of economic reconstruction of the North, the Government delegates stated that the new Administration of the Prime Minister Chandirka Bandaranaike Kumaratunga had decided to take immediate steps to restore electricity, renovate irrigation schemes, and undertake urgent reconstruction work. The LTTE assured that it would fully co-operate with the Government in the deployment of administrative and technical staff involved in the task of economic reconstruction.

At the request of the LTTE delegation, the Government team agreed to set up a Commission of Inquiry to investigate and report on the destruction of the Jaffna library. The Government delegation also agreed to reconstruct the library.

The LTTE delegates emphasized the importance of a ceasefire to create a congenial condition of peace and goodwill. The Government delegates argued that the possibilities of the cessation of hostilities have to be explored before the declaration of a ceasefire. The Government delegates finally agreed to discuss the matter with the defence authorities.

In conclusion, both parties agreed to have a second round of talks within the next ten days.

On the night of October 24th 1994, a suicide bomber from the LTTE assassinated Gamini Dissanayake, the Leader of the Opposition and the Presidential candidate of the UNP, while he was campaigning. That dastardly act was carried out in masterly manner. The technique used was identical to that of the assassination of Rajiv Gandhi. That morning the delegation for the second round of talks in Jaffna was scheduled to leave Colombo. On a directive from the Prime Minister the departure of the delegation was stopped and the talks postponed. The second round of preliminary talks were held in November 1994, after the Prime Minister was elected as the new President. The third round of talks were held in December and the fourth in January 1995. That ended in a deadlock on preliminary objections to peripheral issues. The nature of the deadlock was such that the LTTE prevented the foreign observers from Canada, the Netherlands and Norway, who they had agreed upon, from becoming operational in the field. Besides, offers to mediate by Australia and France wre spurned by the LTTE. At that point many including the President began to suspect the LTTE and their motives, especially their requests for unrestricted fishing rights and for allowing armed terrorists to move unhindered in the Eastern Province.

The dialogue between the Government of Sri Lanka and the LTTE became a ritual in sophistry. By early 1995, there were many indications that the talks would collapse sooner rather than later.

The last of these talks took place in April 1995 just before the traditional vacation for Sinhalese and Tamil New Year. When the delegation of the Government of Sri Lanka returned to Colambo from Jaffna, the President and her children had already gone to Nuwana Eliya, the mountain resort, for their vacation. The President had a lengthy discussion with the delegation at the resort. on April 12th 1995 and she sent a confidential fax to Prabakaran through the good offices of the ICRC. Prabhakaran replied an April 18th as follows:

"We have carefully considered the fax sent by Your Excellency on April 12th 1995 and were shocked and disappointed.

The LTTE had placed our difficulties before the Government of Sri Lanka, and the only satisfactory outcome was the lifting of the economic embeargo. However in practice, even that was not implemented in time. These planned delaying tactics were resorted to beat the deadline we had placed before you. Your reply was an attempt at evasion. You were trying to make them issues that should be resolved in future talks.

A few concessions have been made on the issue of the ban on fishing but the ban itself continues in most parts of the sea. Even in the areas where the Government agreed to lift the ban, obstacles continue to be placed in our path. We are not in agreement with the decisions you took about the important issues of opening the Pooneryn road and the movement of LTTE cadres with arms in the East. We do not accept your position that they should be considered during future talks.

The Government does not seem to have any plan to bring normalcy and normal life in our areas. Instead, you seem to be interested in looking after the interests of the Army. Attention is being paid to building up the Army using the favourable environment created by the cessation of hostilities.

This action amounts to a breach of the cessation of hostilities. We are thus complled to take the painful decision to quit the peace talks and end the cessation of hostilities."

By 1 a.m. on April 19th 1995, just five hours after the LTTE handed over their letter to the ICRC in Jaffna for onward transmission by fax to the President, a suicide squad from the Sea Tigers attacked two gunboats which were at the moorings at the Two Fathoms jetty at Trincomalee. Twelve sailors fast asleep in their bunks were killed. The following day a STF patrol was attacked and five Policemen were killed at Uppuveli, in the Trincomalee district. On the day after, LTTE cadres from their base camp 4 - 6 surrounded the isolated Army camp at Kaddumuruvi Kulam which had 9 officers and 151 other ranks. Of those 160 soldiers, 28 were killed, 32 injured, and 20 were listed as missing in action. On April 27th on the island of Kayts, where General Kobbekaduwa, General Wimalaratne and Admiral Liyanage were killed in action in 1992, an Army outpost was subject to an amphibious attack and 18 soldiers were killed. Some of the dead and injured were transported to Colombo on a routine Palaly-Anuradhapura-Ratmalana Air Force flight on April 28th 1995. On board the Avro aircraft was Wing Commander Roger Weerasinghe, the SLAF Zonal Commander for the North, returning to his headquarters at Anuradhapura. Once airborne, the aircraft developed a fire on the under side of the port engine, which was not seen by the pilot but was visible to the ground crew at Palaly AFB. The pilot, Flight - Lieutenant Mahes Gamage, was instructed by the tower to return to Palaly. While making his final descent the Avro exploded, killing all 38 on board. The following day, Saturday 29th April, shortly after first light, another Avro took off from Ratmalana AFB on a routine Ratmalana-Anuradhapura-Palaly flight. As the aircraft was making its descent to Palaly, Wing Commander Shirantha Goonatilake, an experienced pilot and the son of Air Vice Marshall Harry Goonetileke, who had commanded the SLAF from 1976 - 1980, radioed the tower that his Avro was being attacked by a missile. Within a minute the Wing Commander radioed that two missiles were making a bee line towards his Avro. Then there was a huge fireball in the sky and all 52 on board were killed.

Ironically on board the second Avro was Wing Commander D. S. Wickremasinghe from the engineering branch of the SLAF. He was proceeding to Palaly AFB to investigate the crash of the previous day. Also on board were three journalists who were covering that tragedy for their respective newspapers.

Thus began Eelam War III with the LTTE having effectively deceived yet another Government of Sri Lanka. Prabhakaran who was neither seen nor heard of, for the entirety of 1995, suddenly surfaced and gave an exclusive interview to the BBC. He claimed triumphantly that the LTTE was ready to discuss peace and blamed the present calamity on President Chandrika Bandaranaike Kumaratunga for having unnecessarily delayed the offering of a peace package!

The President was then away in Paris at the annual meeting of the Aid Sri Lanka Consortium. Before dawn on Saturday 30th April 1995, she was woken up in her hotel suite in Paris by a telephone call from Colombo and duly apprised of the reverses suffered by the SLAF. She was scheduled to relax that Saturday in Paris, to travel to London on Sunday to look up her mother, Prime Minister Sirima Badaranaike who was in a nursing home in London, and then to leave for New Delhi to attend the annual conference of Heads of States/Heads of Governments of SAARC nations due to be held there commencing on Tuesday 2nd May. She immediately changed her itinerary and left for Colombo by the first available aircraft. An emergency Cabinet meeting was held the same day. Once again, she wisely opted for a negotiated settlement on the premise that there was no viable Military option.The State-owned media, which no person of consequence takes seriously, trumpeted that the President will negotiate directly with the Tamil people rather than with the LTTE. How that can be done is known only unto God.

To say the least, the President was livid. The UNP which constituted a powerful opposition in Parliament was openly laughing at her. So were her next-of-kin who had fallen out with her. In her anger she blasted the LTTE in an exclusive interview given to Shekar Gupta, Editior of *India Today* on May 1st just before leaving for the SAARC Summit in New Delhi. The relevant extracts are reproduced below:

Question : Do you now regret conceding so much?

Answer : No. We had to do all this even when the LTTE did not reciprocate. We sent shiploads of free rations and fuel for the people of Jaffna which the LTTE grabbed.

Question : How bitter are you?

Answer : Not at all. I did not expect anything else from the LTTE. They are the most ruthless and most effective guerrilla organization in the twentieth century. We tried our best, keeping in mind that we were dealing with a merciless megalomaniac who has killed every single person who was opposed to him. The LTTE was nurtured, fed, financed and armed by Indira Gandhi and Rajiv Gandhi. Yet Prabhakaran decided to bump off Rajiv. I am personally very much aware that if he did not get from me what he wanted, I would be the first person on his hit list.

Question : In hindsight, would you have handled the LTTE differently?

Answer : I have been asking myself this question last week. I cannot think of any other way I would have handled it given the commitments we had taken on. Except, perhaps, on one score which I cannot mention yet. But, politically, it would not have been possible to change that either, because we have an electorate in the South. We are not dealing only with Prabhakaran and the LTTE.

Question : When you started the peace process, a lot of people said the Government does not know who it is dealing with. That it is going out on a limb. Do you think they were right?

Answer : No, because every other kind of thing that was used had not succeeded. There is no other way possible apart from going for an all-out war against the LTTE with Armed Forces which are not the best trained and not at all equipped.

For eleven years, the past Government had waged a war and the Armed Forces were very badly equipped. The Tigers know all the details about this. As far as Military equipment goes, I do not know what happened to all the money that was spent, the billions and billions of rupees. A lot of it evidently had not gone into buying what was necessary.

Question : So you had no option?

Answer : We were certainly not going to go into an all-out war. Second, even if we wanted to, we were not properly equipped. And we thought, well, let us try something which nobody had tried till now.

Question : And you thought there was not very much to lose any way?

Answer : Yes. Exactly. But the feeling was that if it does not work out, well, then we cannot rule out other options. But we did not say it. We cannot say it. So we thought let us tell them that for the first time there is a Government that is willing to consider them as our equals and consider very favourably their requests, except the request for a separate State.

There was another calculation. The people of the North desired peace desperately, like never before, because they feel that this time if there is peace they will not get licked by the Government in power. You see, the chemistry had changed. We knew that the LTTE, and especially Prabhakaran, is paranoid about peace. He is terrified of peace.

Question : Are you saying the chemistry had changed but the psychology had not?

Answer : It seems like that. Then, you see, the psychology also changes when external factors play on it. We knew from our intelligence reports that the LTTE was very seriously divided. There was the Mahattaya group which was saying you should be flexible with this Government. This is why Mahattaya has disappeared now. Whether he is alive or not we don't know, but he's not allowed to operate.

Question : What is your analysis of Prabhakatan and his psychology?

Answer : Apparently he had stated, "I have killed so many of my own people; how can I live in a situation of peace?"

Question : It you look at it from his point of view, what guarantees does he have?

Answer : May be you are right. But there are solutions of these things and we wanted to discuss these with him within a framework of a devolutionary package while he could still keep his own security guards.

Question : But of course, in situation like this where a war has dragged on for 12 years, a people get tired of war. They want to live normal lives. He also has two young children. As I said, the pressure of his own people who want to live normally. Look at people like Anton Balasingham, his main spokesman, making statements like they are willing to go in for a Federal solution as an alternative to Eelam.

By now the LTTE had been condemned by the Government of the United States, the European Union and the Governments of Australia and Canada, all of whom had seen some justification in the LTTE during the of the eighties. The Western media which for over 15 years had portrayed Prabhakaran as some kind of popular outlaw like Robin Hood, now vilified him.

Indeed, President Chandrika Bandaranaike Kumaratunga had achieved a miracle in turning the Human Rights record of Sri Lanka through 180^0 within six months of coming to power. The only comparable example in the recent history of the world was Argentina following the overthrow of General Leopoldo Galtieri in 1982 in the aftermath of the Falklands War. The Human Rights record of Sri Lanka was indeed dreadful in the years 1983-1994 with one President of Sri Lanka being openly accused, both at home and abroad, of being a murderer!

During her two day visit to New Delhi on May 2nd and 3rd 1995, to attend the SAARC Summit, the President moved strategically and swiftly. Prabhakaran was the first accused and his Intelligence chief Pottu Amman the second accused in the Rajiv Gandhi assassination case currently being heard by the High Court of Madras. Under the laws of India, an accused cannot be tried *in absentia* for premeditated murder. Besides extradition procedures have to be initiated by a Court of Law. (Under the laws of Sri Lanka an indicted murderer can be tried *in absentia* and the Inspector-General of Police or the Attorney-General can initiate extradition procedures.) It was no accident that while in New Delhi, the President called on Mrs. Sonia Gandhi for *tete-a-tete* and called on Prime Minister Narasimha Rao in like manner. On June 1st 1995, the Government of India formally requested the Government of Sri Lanka for the extradition of Prabhakaran. On the international scene that had a devastating impact, with the powerful pro-Eelam lobbies in Australia, Canada, France, Germany and the UK unable to explain why Prabhakaran, who for some 15 years was portrayed by them as some kind of Robin Hood, was wanted for murder by the Government of India. The net impact of the LTTE scuttling the peace talks in April 1995 and Prabhakaran wanted for murder in India in June 1995 was that the credibility of their efficient propaganda machine was reduced to zero, a fate which befell the propaganda machine of the Government of Sri Lanka in the aftermath of July 1983.

Against this background, the Government of the United Kingdom withdrew the arms embargo imposed on the Government of Sri Lanka way back in July 1983. The Governments of France, Germany and above all that of the United States also initiated action to withdraw their arms embargo imposed on Sri Lanka.

Thus the LTTE which lost Tamil Nadu, its most powerful base worldwide, in 1991, following the assassination of Rajiv Gandhi, was now in the process of loosing their base in the Western world. For example Lawrence Thillagar their principal spokesman in the West, who is now a French citizen, was denied entry into Canada which then had 200,000 refugees and immigrants from Sri Lanka and now has 300,000. Nearly all such refugees and immigrants make substantial contributions to the LTTE, sometimes as a token of gratitude and at other times due to fear or coercion.

When the LTTE missiles brought down two SLAF Avros on April 29th and 30th 1995, panic set in amongst the Sinhalese. Indeed the Sinhalese panic easily, as reflected in their behavious on Friday 29th July 1983, when it was rumoured that the Tigers had come to Colombo. The scenario was indentical when on Sinhalese (and Tamil) New Year's day, 1971, when it was rumoured that the JVP under Rohana Wijeweera had captured the Army cantonment at Panagoda and was marching on to capture Colombo. One generation earlier the panic was even greater when a Japanese armada bombed Colombo on Easter Sunday 1942, with carrier borne aircraft.

After the missile attacks in April 1995, panic stricken Sinhalese attributed all manner of imaginary capabilities to the LTTE. For example, some claimed that Prabhakaran had kamikaze type pilots operating micro-light aircraft made in France, while others said he had bought a submarine from the Ukaraine. Of course, Prabhakaran is today the world's most efficient terrorist leader, having completely eclipsed Abu Nidal of the People's Front for the Liberation of Palestine and Paul Gussman of the Shining Path, who is currently in prison in Peru.

Contrary to popular opinion, the strategy of Prabhakaran is not to have a confrontation with the Armed Forces of Sri Lanka at their base camps, but lightining strikes against their outposts. The debacle at Mandaitivu in 1995, was a supreme example. It was a non-strategic outpost off the Jaffna peninsula manned by about 600 officers and men from a volunteer regiment. He timed the attack beautifully when half the strength of that garrison was away on leave and before replacements had arrived in Mandaitivu. By the same token the attack on Kayts, the day before the first missiles brought down an Avro, was also directed against an outpost. It was indeed significant that Prabhakaran has so far avoided a Military confrontation at Pooneryn, the scene of his spectacular victory in November 1993. That garrison, is heavily armed and had six battalians headed by a Brigadier.

According to the Census of 1981 the principal concentrations of Sri Lankan Tamils were as follow:

District	Tamil Population	Total Population
Jaffna	792,264	829,619
Batticaloa	234,348	325,471
Colombo	165,952	1,596,896
Wanni*	163,551	282,612
Tincomalee	86,341	256,714
Amparai	78,315	386,904

Not surprisingly the main thrust of the LTTE has been in the Jaffna peninsula and in the Wanni Batticaloa, Tincomalee and Amparai in that order, In the city of Colombo their targets were political. Hence the President, the Leader of the Opposition, the *de facto* Minister of Defence and the Minister of Foreign Affairs, who was a Tamil, were under maximum security. In all three districts of the Eastern Province the LTTE had operated from its jungle hideouts and had attacked either isolated Army outposts e.g. Kadumurvi Kulam, or Sinhalese settlements e.g. at Dimubalalagala where they killed a very courageous Chief priest, and at Karallawa where they exterminated an entire fishing village.

In fact, in the Eastern Province the Military strategy of the LTTE since April 19th 1995 was becoming clearer and clearer. Prabhakaran had transferred to the East his crack units from the North, yet all they could achieve were lightning strikes against lonely Military outposts and defenceless Sinhalese. When those crack units are withdrawn, in the event of the Armed Forces attacking the LTTE in the North of, otherwise, the *status quo* in the East will revert to what it was in 1994, when the General Election and the Presidential Election were peacefully conducted with the voter turn out being very nearly the same as in the seven Sinhala speaking Provinces.

The troops in the Jaffna peninsula were known to be restless since April 19th 1995. They yearned for battle, rather than face all manner of indignities from the nation at large, while Prabhakaran systematically attacked Army outposts both in the North and in the East. The Armed Forces of Sri Lanka have seven major bases in or around the Jaffna peninsula. Clockwise they are Palaly, with a huge Army camp and an Air Force Base and the Army camps at Thondamanar and Madagal Army base camps at Elephant Pass, Vetteleikerni and Pooneryn and the Naval base SLNS *Elara* at Karainagar.

The combined manpower of these basse camps was 32,000 combat troops and it came under the command of Major General Srilal Werasooriya. The much respected General was trained at the Pakistan Military Academy at Kakul and at the National Defence College in New Delhi, where he was in 1994, prior to taking up his present command. His Human Rights record is impeccable and since 1983, when he was a Major, he had insisted that all prisoners-of-war must be treated strictly in accordance with the Geneva Convention. He is a devout Christian, a lay preacher and implicitly believes that all mortals are the children of God.

The outbreak of an all out war in the Jaffna peninsula would result in huge casualities on both sides, especially as the LTTE was heavily armed, considerably more than in 1987 when General Depinder Singh of the IPKF cleared the Jaffna peninsula in eleven days after fighting several pitched battles. Therefore the Government of Sri Lanka decidecd to exercise the only option that was open, namely to wage war on a limited scale.

Operation Leap Forward, launched on July 8th 1995, was limited in scope. Initially 252 square kilometers held by the LTTE since 1990 was captured and the authority of the Army was secure within 78 square kilometers of the territory. With the Jaffna peninsula accounting for 1080 square kilometers, that initial thrust was therefore inconclusive.

By August 1995 it was more than obvious to the war weary citizens of the Jaffna peninsula that another military operation was in the offing. They could see that daily the Sri Lanka Air Force was flying five to six sorties, each sortie consisting of five to six aircraft. They were the Ukraine built Antonov – 32B aircraft and the Chinese built Y-8 aircraft of the SLAF and the Antonov – 24 aircraft of the private airline Lion Air. Thus daily, 1,000 troops and 30 tonnes of military cargo were ferried across to the Jaffna peninsula. This massive airlift was carried out under the direction of Air Vice Marshall Jayalath Weerakkody, Director of Operations of the SLAF, who, displayed conspicuous gallantry during Operation Leap Forward. Not surprisingly he was soon promoted toAir Marshall and appointed the new Commander of the Air Force, at the age of 46 years.

The bulk of the arms, ammunition and equipment for the troop was brought into Kankesanturai harbour by two merchant vessels m. v. *Mercs Komari* and *Mercs Hendala* chartered by the Sri Lanka Navy or alternatively in Landing Craft (Medium) of the SLN. That massive sea lift from Trincomalee was handled with exemplary skill by Commodore

* *Districts of Mannar, Mullaitivu and Vavuniya*

(now Vice Admiral) Daya Sandagiri, Commander of the Eastern Naval Area and now Commander of the Navy. By September 1995 the SLAF had moved their combat aircraft into their forward bases. A squadron of Ukraine built MI-17 helicopters were sent to the Anuradhapura Air Force Base where the last two Base Commanders, Group Captain Roger Weerasinghe and Group Captain Shirantha Goonetileke were killed in action on April 28th and 29th 1995 respectively when the LTTE fired their newly acquired SAM-7 missiles. The Chinese built F-7 fighter aircraft were moved into the China Bay AFB which during World War II was an operational base of the Royal Air Force. The MI-24 helicopter gunships were moved into Minneriya AFB or into Palaly AFB. Palaly also had Sia Marchett-260 ground attack, MI-17 helicopters and Y-12 light transport aircraft.

Major General Rohan De Silva Daluwatte, the Chief of Staff of the Army, was the Overall Operations Commander of our Armed Forces in the North and the East. General Daluwatte received his basic training at the Royal Military Academy at Sandhurst. In 1963 he was commissioned a Second Lieutenant in the Ceylon Armoured Corps, which regiment has product the highest number of Srilankan Generals. Brigadier Daluwatte served on the staff of Major General Denzil Kobbekaduwa legendary fame. When General Kobbekaduwa fell in battle in 1992, Major General Daluwatte took over his Command, namely the General-Officer-Commanding the 2nd Division.

General Daluwatte, as a young officer, represented Sri Lanka in basketball. So did his wife Jayanthi. It is said marriages are made in heaven. However, according to usually reliable reports, their marriage was made in and around basketball courts somewhere in Sri Lanka!

In systematically preparing for battle to liberate the Jaffna peninsula General Daluwatte anticipated heavy casualties. That assessment was based on the experience of the Indian Peace Keeping Force (IPKF) which liberated the Jaffna peninsula in eleven days of heavy fighting in 1987, when 245 officers and other ranks were killed in action. Therefore General Daluwatte ensured that the Military Hospital at Palaly and the Base Hospital at Anuradhapura carried more than their full complement of surgeons. In Colombo, Major General C. Thurairaja, the most senior Tamil officer in our Armed Forces, took similar action. Another Tamil officer of flag rank was Rear-Admiral J.R.G. Sundaram.

General Daluwatte had under him the largest Task Force ever assembled in Sri Lanka, even larger than the Task Force that General Depinder Singh,

General Officer Commanding the IPKF, had assembled for the liberation of the Jaffna peninsula in October 1987 or Admiral Sir Geoffrey Layton, Commander-in-Chief Ceylon, had assembled in Colombo in April 1942 in anticipating an amphibious landing by Japan, during World War II. In essence, the principal thrust would be by the Army, using heavy artillery and armour but a minimum of infantry because all routes of Jaffna were heavily mined. The Air Force would give the necessary air cover and the Navy would seal off the Northern coast, to keep off the Sea Tigers from bringing in men and material to augment the cadres of the LTTE deployed in the Jaffna peninsula. According to General Daluwatte, the liberation of the Jaffna peninsula was vitally important to the nation against the background of the increasing military capabilities of the LTTE. By 1995 the Sea Tigers, established in 1992, had grown into a formidable force in the high seas off the coast Kankesanturai-Mullaitivu-Trincomalee. In 1995 alone, the Sea Tigers had sunk three Israeli built Dovra Fast Attack Craft and six patrol boats of the Sri Lanka Navy. Besides in 1995 the newly acquired SAM-7 missiles had destroyed two Avro transport aircraft, one Puccara ground attack aircraft and badly damaged a MI-17 helicopter of the Sri Lanka Air Force.

Major General Daluwatte was then our most senior General barring the Commander of the Army, Lt. General G.H. De Silva. Indeed General Daluwatte was greatly disturbed by the increasing striking power of the LTTE both at sea and in the air. At meetings at Army Headquarters he often expressed his misgivings on whether or not the Army could defend itself at Elephant Pass or even at Palaly in the years to come, if the strength of the LTTE at sea and in the air was allowed to grow at the present rate.

General Daluwatte launched his attack, Operation Riviresa, at first light on October 15th 1995 when the 51st Division (Brigadier later Major General Neil Dias), the 52nd Division (Brigadier later Major General P.A. Karunatileke), the 53rd Division (Brigadier later Major General Janaka Pererea), the 512th Brigade (Brigadier Ananda Hamangoda), the 521st Brigade (Brigadier later Major General K.B. Egodawela), 531st Airmobile Brigade (Brigadier Hiran Halangoda) poured out from the Forward Defended Localities (FDL) at the Army camps at Palaly and Madagal. Task Force I (Brigadier R.P. Liyanage) held Palaly and Madagal and the liberated areas. Task Force II (Brigadier later Major General Vasantha Perera) was ready for battle at the FDL in Elephant Pass in the event of General Daluwatte wanting to open a second front, thus pinning down the LTTE both from the north and the south, in the context of the Jaffna peninsula. The air cover provided by the SLAF consisted of Puccara ground attack aircraft, Bell-212 helicopters and MI-24 helicopter gunships under the Command of Air Vice Marshall Weerakkody.

After the first day of "Operation Riviresa", General Daluwatte was of the opinion that either his battle plan was wrong or his troops were walking into a trap. All his formation commanders in the ranks of Major General, Brigadier and Lt. Colonel reported that they were not encountering any resistance as such by the enemy. The SLAF aircraft on reconnaissance missions confirmed those reports. In fact, based on all reports General Daluwatte came to the conclusion that all casualties were due only to mine explosions and sniper fire.

It was common knowledge that the LTTE supremo Vellupillai Prabhakaran had ordered all civilians to leave the Valikaman sector of the Jaffna peninsula. Accordingly, the majority of them sought sanctuary in the Tennamarachchi and Vadamarachchi sectors while others went further afield to the Wanni. It later transpired that Prabhakaran had taken a calculated risk after hearing of the massive Task Force under General Daluwatte. Prabhakaran himself had commanded the LTTE in the battle for Jaffna peninsula against the IPKF in 1987. In 1991, General Kobbekaduwa had defeated him in the battle for Elephant Pass. On the other hand Prabhakaran was more than happy that he had kept the IPKF at bay for more than two years of fierece guerilla fighting in the Wanni. It has an extensive forest cover and is thinly populated, thereby making it excellent terrain for a guerilla war. Therefore it was the Wanni, not the Jaffna peninsula, that was the battleground which Prabhakaran had selected for his inevitable confrontation with the Army.

In the meantime LTTE cadres went on the offensive in the border village off Dehiattekandiya, Maha Oya, Valachchenai and Welikande in the Eastern Province in a well orchestrated diversionary tactic. In the first three days of fighting, 14 soldiers were killed in action. In the meantime LTTE cadres including suicide squads made a lightning attack in the Colombo, on the storage installations of the Ceylon Petroleum Corporation at Kollonnawa and Orugodawatte. On the night of 20th/21st October 1995, dressed in Army camouflage fatigues, one squad approached the main gate at Orugodawatte. They were mistaken government our troops till they opened fire at the storage tanks of crude oil with rocket propelled grenades and mortars and disappeared into the night. Altogether, eight storage tanks were gutted with fire, sending leaping flames and fumes of thick smoke into the sky. At Kollonnawa another squad infiltrated the complex by cutting through the defence perimeter. Once inside, they used their rocket propelled grenades and mortars against the storage tanks of petrol and kerosene. Three such tanks were thus destroyed and three more due to a secondary fire sending more flames and thick smoke into the damaged sky. Air Force Commandos and Police were rushed to both installations resulting in a mini battle at Kollonnawa with LTTE cadres, four of whom opted for suicide and nine were killed in action. Two Air Force Commandos and one Policeman were also killed in action.

Thus the war had once again come to Colombo and at least one million citizens saw for themselves the night sky complete with flames and thick smoke. Many more saw it on television. According to many senior citizens, the fire was even greater than when the Carrier based aircraft of Japan bombed the city on Colombo on Easter Sunday in 1942* and scored many direct hits on Kollonnawa.

While the fires raged uncontrollably for several hours, the Government of Sri Lanka appealed to the Government of India for their expertise in dousing the flames. Within hours a transport aircraft of the Indian Air Force arrived from Bombay bringing experts in fire fighting, complete with their equipment and the latest chemical foam. Even with such assistance, so generously made available from India, it took three days to douse the flames. The nett damage was estimated to be around Rs. 2 billion (US $ 40 million.)

In the meantime General Daluwatte was moving the 51st, 52nd and 53rd Divisions on the route Palaly-Achuveli-Neeraveli en-route to Jaffna. He encountered no resistance as such except when the 51st Division (Major-General Neil Dias) was nearing Neeraveli, which had the Command bunker of Prabhakaran. It was a three storey underground building complete with a 22 bed hospital. The building was heavily fortified and General Dias re-grouped his Division for the battle. The 51th Brigade (Brigadier later Major General Mahendra Wijeratne) and the 513th Brigade (Brigadier later Major General Gamini Jayasundera) breached the defences following excellent reconnaissance work done by the 6th Battalion of the Sri Lanka Light Infantry under Lt. Colonel Daya Ratnayake.

Following their defeat the LTTE insisted that all civilians vacate the Valikamam sector. They also withdrew their cadres. Therefore after the capture of Neerveli, General Daluwatte experienced no serious opposition but moved his Task Force with the greatest of caution because all routes

---

* *Vice-Admiral (later Admiral of the Fleet) Chechi Nagumo attacked Ceylon on Easter Sunday 1942. The Naval aircraft were from his flagship the aircraft carrier "Akagi" from which he led the attack on Pearl Harbour on December 7th 1941.*

to Jaffna were heavily mined. The overall casualties were 673 killed in action and 3770 wounded in action, when the city of Jaffna fell on December 5th 1995.

There was much rejoicing in all Sinhaka speaking Provinces on the fall of the City of Jaffna and the Deputy Minister of Defence Anuruddha Ratwatte became a national hero. He was looked upon as the twentieth century version of the legendary warriror Sapumal Kumaraya who captured Jaffna in the fourteenth century, during the reign of his foster father King Parakrama Bahu VI of Kotte.

The victory ceremony in Jaffna was a flag hoisting ceremony outside the Fort. Anuruddha Ratwatte hoisted the National flag, the Service Commanders and the Inspector-General of Police their respective Service flags and a retired Assistant Government Agent Jaffna, hoisted the flag of Jaffna. Within weeks he was assassinated by the LTTE! The splendid victory parade was at Palaly two days after the ceremony outside the Fort in Jaffna. The victory ceremony in Colombo was held the following week at the Presidential Secretariat. It was very emotional and the Deputy Minister of Defence read the instructions given to him by the Commander-in-Chief, President Chandrika Bandaranaike Kumaratunga. He then announced that those instructions were carried out in full. The Commander-in-Chief promoted him to the rank of an honorary General. He and his two sons are currently being tried for murder in the High Court of Colombo.

The liberation of the Jaffna peninsula in December 1995 was the greatest victory of our Armed Forces over the LTTE since the Civil War began in 1983. Jaffna was the nerve centre of the LTTE network in Sri Lanka and in fact their infrastructure was at its best in the Jaffna peninsula and a microcosom of the State of Tamil Eelam existed there. Now Prabhakaran had to abandon all of that and withdraw into the Wanni. Indeed the Wanni was the scene of his greatest successes against the IPKF, when he kept at bay the fourth largest Army and the sixth largest Air Force in the world.

After the liberation of the city of Jaffna, the Task Force under General Daluwatte encouraged the civilian population of over 600,000 who were refugees in the Tennamarachchi and Vadamarachchi sectors and in the Wanni to return home as early as practicable, as otherwise they would form a readymade base for recruitment by the LTTE. Thereafter the victory was consolidated in the entirety of the Jaffna peninsula with "Operation Riviresa II" and "Operation Riviresa III", when the Vadamarachchi and Tenanamarachchi sectors respectively were duly liberated.

By the end of 1995 Army Intelligence was expecting Prabhakaran to strike strategically within the city of Colombo with suicide bombers. Therefore the security for President Chandrika Bandaranaike Kumaratunga, Minister Anuruddha Ratwatte and Foreign Minister Lakshman Kadiragamar (because he is a Tamil), was stepped up sometimes to absurd levels. For example when the President was traveling on Galle Road, the principal thoroughfare in Colombo, the parallel Duplication Road her alternate route was also closed, thereby causing traffic jams which were made even worse because the President was perpetually late.

Wednesday 31st January 1996 was just another working day in the city of Colombo where there had been no untowards incidents following the attacks on Kollonnawa and Orugodawatte. As usual the traffic was heavy in the Fort, the heart of the commercial area of the city, and there were many lorries carrying building materials. That was a familiar sight because the 35 - storey Bank of Ceylon Tower was recently completed and the 37 - storey twin Towers of the World Trade Centre were under construction.

Blending with that background a lorry carrying building materials negotiated the round about near the Presidential Secretariat, the Hotel Inter Continental and the five-star Hotel Galadari. It turned into President's Road and drove past the Bank of Ceylon Tower and the 14 - storey Ceylinco House, which prior to the ushering of the open economy in 1977 by President J. R. Jayewardene, was the tallest building in Colombo. The lorry stopped right opposite the Central Bank. There the LTTE Commandos on board in civilian dress got down from the vehicle and opened fire with their AK - 47 machine guns. It was purely a diversionary tactic, which allowed the driver of the lorry carrying some 300-400 kilogrammes of explosives, concealed under the building materials, to reverse his vehicle into the most damaging position. The suicide bomber at the wheel did so. The lorry was on the ramp at the Central Bank as close as possible to the vaults, when a massive explosion which was heard up to 10 kilometers reduced the splendid building of the Central Bank to a shattered and burning hulk. The secondary fire generated made the Ceylinco House across the road into an inferno. Many adjoining buildings were badly damaged by the explosion. Later that a shocked nation which had watched the aftermath of the explosion on Television learnt that 96 dead,the casualties were 120 seriously injured, and 1185 had received out patient treatment at the National Hospital in Colombo. The damage to buildings was initially estimated to be between Rs. 1,000 - -2,000 million (US $ 20 - 40 million).

Thus in the course of three months the LTTE twice attacked the economic centers of the city of Colombo, causing damage to property amounting to Rs. 3,000 - 4,000 million (US $ 60 - 80 million)

The National Intelligence Bureau (NIB) had repeatedly warned the Government of Sri Lanka that for the visit of Pope John Paul II to Colombo in 1995, the LTTE suicide squads had infiltrated into the city of Colombo under the guise of pilgrims. Consequently there were repeated warnings to the citizens to be aware of suspicious strangers and many lodgings of Tamils especially in Kotahena and Grandpass were raided in the teeth of opposition from Human Rights groups. Those raids were intensified after the attack on the oil installations at Kollonawa and Orugodawatta in October 1995.

By mid-1996 the new Commander of the Army Lt. General Rohan de Silva Daluwatte, the new Chief of Staff Major General A.M.U. Seneviratne, and the new Overall Operations Commander in the North and the East, Major General Srilal Weerasooriya, were mapping out their strategy for the Wanni. None of them under estimated the skill of the LTTE supremo Prabhakaran. All three Generals were more than aware that in 1990 the LTTE over ran the Army camps at Kokavil and Mankulam. In the former camp, Second Lieutenant Saliya Aladeniya of the 3rd Battalion of the Sinha Regiment defended it to the last soldier and was posthumously awarded the *Parama Weera Vibushanaya* (PWV). The gallant Second Lieutenant had under him only two Platoons to defend the Television relaying station at Kokavil. At Mankulam the Army camp consisted of a Company. Therefore what worried the Generals even more was that in 1993 the LTTE successfully attacked the Army camp at Pooneryn which had a sanctioned strength of one Brigade but in practice had only two Battalions and the Naval station at Nagathevanthurai. The casualties were 613 killed in action or missing in action and 923 wounded in action, whereas by their own admission the LTTE had 499 killed in action. The enemy captured all five Inshore Patrol Craft at Nagathevanthurai, much of the arms, ammunition and equipment at Pooneryn including two T-55 main battle tanks! During the peace talks with the LTTE in 1994, the Army camp at Pooneryn was one of the main stumbling blocks. The LTTE wanted it closed because it was an obstruction to civilians who illegally crossed the lagoon at Killali. The Army flatly refused to close that camp because of its strategic location. However with the fall of the Jaffna peninsula Pooneryn had lost its strategic value. All three Generals agreed that now Pooneryn no longer served any useful purpose and therefore it should be closed down. Minister

Anuruddha Ratwatte endorsed that recommendation. Therefore the Commander-in-Chief gave her assent.

There was another isolated but strategic camp at Mullaitivu. Whether the 25th Brigade at Mullaitivu should be strengthened or withdrawn was a matter of opinon. Before any definitive decision could be taken the LTTE struck there with devastating skill. The Army camp at Mullaitivu is flanked by the sea on the east, the lagoon on the west and is over six kilometers in length and two kilometer in breadth. The 25th Brigade stationed at Mullaitivu was commanded by Colonel Lawrence Fernando. A Brigade usually has three Battalions, each of them commanded by a Lt. Colonel. As of July 1996 this Brigade had only two Battalions, Major W.M.S. Gunaratne commanding the 9th Battalion of the Sinha Regiment and Major T.R.A.Aliba commanding the 6th Battalion of the Vijayaba Regiment Thus the 25th Brigade, which was isolated but of strategic value, was seriously understaffed. That was well known to our troops and for certain the LTTE would have been aware of it. On the other hand that Army camp was primarily a Military depot with its armouries well stocked with all types of arms, ammunition and equipment. Around July 15th 1996, both Colonel Fernando and Major Guneratne, left for Colombo on separate important official engagements. Thus the Brigade was temporarialy under the command of Major Aliba. That was probably when the LTTE decided to strike.

Around midnight on July 18th 1996 the Sea Tigers from across the lagoon and across the sea, launched their attack. The Tigers who had infiltrated the camp, then attacked it, artillery and motar positions from the north and the south. Thus the camp was under siege simultaneously from all four directions. After the communication centre was knocked out of action, the Brigade headquarters right in the middle was captured by the Sea Tigers who had launched a fierce amphibious attack. The battle raged for hours and the next day the entire camp was overrun, all armouries emptied and all buildings blown up by the LTTE to prevent the Army from ever using it. The casualties were 1187 Officers and men either killed or missing in action. The LTTE took with them almost a ship load of arms, ammunition and equipment. It must be emphasized that for the first time the LTTE overran an Army Camp where a Brigade was stationed.

At first light that day Major General Weerasooriya, the Overall Operations Commander, left Palaly for Trincomalee in a helicopter gunship. There he conferred with Rear Admiral D.K. Dassanayake, then Commander Eastern Naval Area and the Acting Base Commander at the China Bay AFB. Air Force reconnaissance missions quickly established that the Army Camp at Mullaitivu was still under siege. General Weerassoriya ruled out air support as our troops will also be killed in such an operation. Therefore he activated the Reserve Strike Force based in Batticaloa and under the Command of Major General Janaka Perera, the hero of many battles after whom Janakapura in the Weli Oya sector is named. It consisted of two crack Brigades, the Air Mobile Brigade (Brigadier Hiran Halangoda) and the Independent Brigade (Brigadier Percy Fernando) consisting of Commandos and Special Forces. The 1st Battalion Speical Forces (Lt.-Colonel Fazil Laphir) and the 2nd Battalion Special Forces (Lt.-Colonel Raj Wijesiri) were airlifted to the China Bay AFB and prepared for battle.

In the meantime Minister Anuruddha Ratwatte, General Rohan Daluwatte and the Commander of the Navy, Vice-Admiral Mohan Samarasekera, who arrived in Palaly on a previously scheduled operational visit made their own contingency plans. In essence it was to land troops in Mullaitivu and to re-capture the Army Camp at any cost. Accordingly Admiral Samarasekera directed Rear Admiral A.H.M. Razeek, Commander of the Northern Naval Area, to prepare to sea lift two Battalions to Mullaitivu. Admiral Samarasekera also directed Admiral Dassanayake in Trincomalee to dispatch three Landing Craft Medium (LCM) with a naval escort to rendezvous at sea off Mullaitivu.

The LTTE ships unloaded their weapons into their launches and fishing boats somewhere off the shores of Mullaitivu. Therefore the sea in that area is subject to intensive patrols by the Sea Tigers. Hence Admiral Dassanayake was cautious in his approach. The Naval escort he arranged was led by the gunboat SLNS "Ranaviru" (Lt.-Commander Prakrama Samaraweera) and six Dovra FACs to sail at sundown. In Palaly General Daluwatte selected the 6th Battalion of the Sri Lanka Light Infantry (Lt.-Colonel Upul Lanerolle) and the 7th Battalion Gemunu Watch (Lt.-Colonel Tilak Seneviratne), to undertake the landing at Mullaitivu. At Kankesanturai Admiral Razeek commandeered a Sri Lankan merchant vessel which was in harbour that day and by 1600 hours the troops boarded the ship. The transfer of the troops from the ship of the LCMs took place 30 nautical miles at sea and duly completed by midnight.

At first light on July 19th 1997 the three LCMs were to beach at Mullaitivu. However the enemy fire was so intense that no landing was possible. Therefore Lt.-Commander Prakrama Samaraweera was contemplating a landing elsewhere when two suicide craft of the LTTE laden with explosives rammed into the SLNS "Ranaviru". Following a deafening explosion the SLNS "Ranaviru" sank taking with her to a watery grave the Captain, 35 officers and sailors. Hence the three LCMs prepared for a landing near Alampil some twelve kilometers south of Mullaitivu. The enemy fire power there was even greater. Therefore Admiral Dasanayake aborted the mission.

In a few hours six MI-17 helicopters under Squadron Leader Royce Gunaratne escorted by two MI-24 helicopter gunships under Squadron Leader Thilina Kaluarachchi, with the entire formation under Wing Commander Ranil Gurusinghe were airborne. They flew several sorties and on board the first wave were Special Forces from the Reserve Strike Force led by Lt. Colonel Fazli Laphir. Shortly after the helicopter descended between the Mullaitivu lagoon and the Nayaru lagoon they established a beach head. Lt. Colonel Laphir stormed out of the helicoptr and led his troops with total disregard to his safety. Killed in action he was awarded the *Param Weera Vibushanaya*. With him 100 elite troops were killed in action. Lt.-Colonel Wijesiri who arrived with the second wave was lucky to survive with a bullet entering his torso near the shoulder and exiting near the waist. Nearly 200 elite troops were wounded in action, so were Colonel Lawrence Fernando and Major W.M.S. Gunaratne who had rushed back from Colombo and had volunteered to go into battle. By now the three LCMs had made a successful landing near the bech head and thereby the 6th Battalion of the Sri Lanka Light Infantry and the 7th Battalion of the Gamunu Watch went into action. Brigadier Percy Fernando of the Reserve Strike Force commanded ground forces at the Forward Operational Base near Mullaitivu. Had this battle continued no doubt the Army camp at Mullaitivu would have been re-captured in the next few days.

To minimize casualties General Weerasooriya halted operations and ordered the evacuation of troops. Then once again Wing Commander Gurusinghe, Squadron Leader Gunaratne, Squadron Leader Kaluarachchi and their air crew risked their lives in the brave performance of duty. Despite intense fire by the enemy, they evacuated the Special Forces. These pilots, were recommended for gallantry decorations which they so richly deserve. Unfortunately Squadron Leader Kaluarachchi was killed in action before he could receive the award. After our victory in Jaffna in December 1995, many refused to belive that our Armed Forces liberated the peninsula only by a walk over. It now it began to dawn on all that the real war was in the Wanni not in Jaffna and the defeat in Mullaitivu was the first battle in the current phase of a protracted war.

"The Protected War" was a series of brilliant lectures delivered by Professor Henry at Harvard Univercity, during the Vietnam war. I listened to those lectures with awe over thirty five years ago and the knowledge imparted is still fresh in my mind after all these years. Our protracted war was fought within the framework so aptly described by Professor Henry Kissinger,

"The guerillas win, when they do not loose
The Armed Forces loose, when they do not win".

In the Jaffna peninsula which was remarkably quiet in 1997 it was indeed disturbing that despite the rout of the LTTE, the citizens were not spontaneously co-operating with the Army. It was so different when the JVP terrorists in the Sinhala speaking areas were routed by the Army in 1989 and earlier in 1971. Perhaps events on July 4th 1996 were self-explanatory. Nimal Siripala De Silva, Minister for Housing and Construction, visited Jaffna to open the outlet of the Building Materials Corporation on Stanley Road, Jaffna. After the function when the Minister and his entourage had got into his Pajero, a woman apparently in an advanced state of pregnancy approached the vehicle. She was a suicide bomber and the explosion killed almost everybody in the Pajero barring the Minister. Two soldiers of his motor cycle escort also perished. Brigadier Ananda Hamangoda was one of the several victims.

Colombo was tense on July 24th 1996, the thirteenth anniversary of the racial riots of 1983, because Prabhakarn threatened the city with retaliation. That day the 5.10 p.m. train destined to Aluthgama left the Fort Railway station, as usual jammed packed with office workers. At the next two stations, Slave Island and Kollupitiya, more office workers got in. Thus the passengers were packed like sardines for their two hour journey home. At the Dehiwela station three brief cases somewhere in the carriages suddenly exploded. The casualties were 71 killed and 505 injured.

Indeed a huge deployment of troops was required to hold the Jaffna peninsula and a similar deployment in Colombo where the nerve centers of the economy in particular were becoming increasingly vulnerable to attacks by suicide squads. Thus the balance troops were thinly spread in the jungles of the Wanni and in the Eastern Province. The LTTE capitalized on the situation and struck decisively in the Eastern Province. Besides assassinating Upali Sahabandu, the Deputy Commandant of the Special Task Force (STF) of the Police, the LTTE repeatedly attacked isolated Army Camps in the Districts of Amparai and Batticaloa with increasing frequency. For example there were periodic forays off Eravur, Maha Oya, Vallachchenai and Welikanda, when those areas were brought under control fresh violence erupted in Batticaloa, Dehiattakandiya,

Kokkadicholai, Pottuvi and Samanturai. Then the LTTE stepped up their forays in the North.

By the end of 1996, one year after the capture of the city of Jaffna, the Sri Lanka Freedom Party (SLFP) was still boasting of their Military victory. In the Opposition the United National Party (UNP) jibed that significant portions of the Eastern Province were overrun by the LTTE. Both statements were a mixture of the truth, half-truths and untruths, so typical of politicians.

In the meantime the State-owned and controlled media, which has been reduced to ludicrous level of sycophancy by successive us. Administrations, were systematically misleading the nation with their sunshine stories. It is indeed a mystery to me why every Government of Sri Lanka since 1983, be it the UNP or the SLFP - led Coalition, has consistently deceived the people of Sri Lanka through the media on the vital issue of ethnic conflict. If their reports are true, then every man woman and child in the North and the East has been killed at least twice!!

When General Daluwatte mapped out his strategy for 1997, he had knew the Military capability of the LTTE. Clearly the next battlefield would be the jungles of the Wanni, where ten years ago the LTTE held at bay the IPKF. With the war to be fought fiercely in the Wanni splitting it right down the middle would be in the best interests of the nation. It was decided decided to open a Main Supply Route (MSR) to Jaffna by way of Vavuniya-Puliyankalam-Mankulum-Kilinochi-Elephant Pass. Kilinochi having fallen to General Weerasoriya in August 1996, in a retaliatory raid to atone for the fall of Mulliativu, in practice the MSR had to be opened only on the stretch Vavuniya-Puliyankulam-Mankulum-Kilinochi. Strategically it was a well conceived plan and it was duly approved by the Commander-in-Chief.

Accordingly there was another build up of men and material, this time in Anuradhapura and Vavuniya. Besides there was a change of key personnel in the higher echelons of the Army. As of November 1st 1996 the new Overall Operations Commander for the North and the East was Major General Asoka Jayawardhana who had recently returned from London after completing a course at the Royal College for Defence Services. As a precursor to launching "Operation Jayasikuru", to open the (Main Supply Route) General Jayawardhana launched "Operation Edibala" to clear the Mannar sctor which may become vulnerable once "Operation Jayasikuru" was launched. Therefore the Western flank of the Wanni was captured and the threat of sporadic attacks were duly eliminated. Besides the Army

Camp at Mannar under Brigadier Lawrence Fernando was fortified to ensure that it will never suffer the fate of the Army camps at Mullaitivu and Pooneryn.

Thereafter at first light on May 13th 1997, the 53rd Division (Major General Vasantha Perera) and the 55th Division (Major General Shantha Kottegoda) poured out of the FDLs at Vavuniya and moved in the direction of Vavuniya-Puliyankulum-Mankulum-Killinochi to open the MSR. The resistance by the enemy was unprecedented. Because of the fierce resistance General Jayawardhana encountered his Task Force reached the outskirts of Puliyankulum 18 kilometers away after two months. For example the LTTE used against his troops the 122 mm field guns and the 81mm mortars captured in Mullaitivu in July 1996. In fact on June 10th 1997 the LTTE attacked the troops behind forward lines at Thandikulum with those 122 mm field guns. That morning quite by accident I had arrived in Vavuniya around dawn to visit refugee camps. The crossfire that day reminded me of my wartime assignments with the UN in Nigeria and Bangladesh. Because of the long range weapons used against his troops General Jayawardhana called for air support. One sortie after another of MI-24 helicopter gunships under the Command of Group Captain Roshan Goonetileke, Zonal Commander for the North, went into action pounding enemy targets. The enemy repeated the attack at Periyamadu on July 24th 1997, and once again the Air Force played a decisive role with the skillful use of MI-24 helicopter gunships and Israeli built Kfir jet fighter based at the Katunayake AFB.

Torrential rain which brought in its wake hepatitis and typhoid, increased the woes of General Jayawardhana whose Task Force was in the outer periphery of Puliyankulum for weeks and months without being able to capture it. The LTTE then launched a massive attack behind the army lines at Karuppakutti on October 14th 1977. The fierce battle resulted in 64 officers and men being either killed in action or listed as missing and 342 wounded in action. Indeed both the Army and the LTTE badly needed reinforcements. The former received theirs but according to intercepted radio messages the LTTE just did not have any more reinforcements. They had extensive problems pertaining to recruitment after the liberation of the Jaffna peninsula. In fact many of their cadres from the District of Ampara and Batticaloa were deployed in the North, resulting in the East being relatively quiet in the latter half of 1997.

The day after the battle at Karuppakuti was the Vap Full Moon Poya holiday. Security arrangements in the Fort in Colombo were very tight ever since the explosion at the Central Bank on January 31st 1996. No lorry was allowed to enter the Fort between 6 am and 6 pm, the only exception being on Sundays and public holidays. Thus on that Poya holiday, the monthly Sabbath of the Buddhists, those rules were relaxed and around 7 am a lorry carrying bags of rice negotiated then round about at Lotus Road and turned towards the Hotel Galadari. At the service entrance to that five-star hotel, the lorry was stopped routinely by the security. At the point LTTE Commandos in the lorry in civilian dress opened fire killing the security guards. Then the suicide bomber at the wheel manoeuvred his lorry into the most damaging position while the LTTE Commandos fled from the scene while emptying their magazines in a diversionary tactic. The lorry, with at least half a tonne of explosives under the bags of rice, exploded causing damage though not structurally, to the brand new 37-storey twin towers of the World Trade Centre owned by the billionaire P.S. Tao of Singapore and ceremonially opened the President four days earlier. Similar damage was also caused to the Bank of Ceylon Tower and structural damage to the Hotel Galadari.

The overall damage was estimated at Rs. 1,000 million (US$ 20 million) and the message was loud and clear to prospective foreign investors in Sri Lanka. Thus the new strategy of the LTTE in the city of Colombo became clearer and clearer. They were targeting the nerve centers of the economy. On that basis their likely targets in the future would be the Kelanitissa Power Station, the Port of Colombo and the Free Trade Zones in Biyagama and Katunayake, all of which were therefore placed under maximum security. In fact an attack on the Kelanitissa Power Station on the Poya holiday of November 1997 was effectively stalled.

It was against this background that on November 1st 1997 General Weerasooriya replaced General Jayawardhana as the Overall operations Commander in the North and the East. The following week Prabhakharan withdrew his troops from Puliyankulum and the troops of General Weerasooriya entered the beleaguered town.

According to usually reliable intelligence reports, Prabhakaran was re-grouping his forces somewhere near Mankulum. In fact Israeli built UAV un-manned aircraft of the SLAF spotted a new LTTE camp near Mullaitivu,. Therefore that was the next logical target for General Weerasooriya, who sent Special Forces and Commandos to capture it. They did so but it turned out to be a perfect dummy. Then suddenly from nowhere the 122mm field guns and 81mm mortars captured by the LTTE in Mullaitivu opened fire and 147 of the crack troops perished. Such was the skill of the LTTE.

The international network of the LTTE is indeed far superior to that of the Governemnt of Sri Lanka. At a conservative estimate they collect every month US$ 2-3 million from the Tamil disapora which accounts for not less than 400,000 people as against a population of about 2,000,000 Sri Lankan Tamils living in Sri Lanka. Indeed the LTTE can influence Governments in such disparate countries such as Bulgaria, one of their suppliers of arms, Canada, where 200,000 Tamils live in Toronto alone, Netherlands and Norway, which by tradition are over generous to erfugees, Ukraine, another of their supplier of arms, and Zimbabwe, where forged documents were used to get hold of a shipload of arms.

With the fall of the Jaffna peninsula two-thirds of all Tamils in the North-Eastern Province live free of the LTTE. Therefore recruitment of new cadres became a major problem for them, against the background of fierce fighting and heavy casualties in the Wanni. In fact the ominous calm in the East was because the LTTE had no option except to divert their cadres in the East to the Wanni. To fight such a war, our Army will need at least 100,000 troops in the North-Eastern Province alone, which was the strength of the Indian Peace Keeping Force at peak. Therefore the envisaged strength of the Army will have to be of the order of 150,000. As of now the sanctioned strength of the Army is 100,000. It is saddled with a staggening 20,000 deserters. As the protracted war continues, especially in the Wanni, the favourite battlefield of the LTTE, the Army desperately needs additional manpower to achieve our basic Military objective, to marginalize the LTTE.

Therefore the nation must glamourise war and venerate our war heroes. Regrettably our State-owned media venerate not our war heroes but our politicians of whom the less said the better. Since the inception of the State-owned TV station *Rupavahini* or TV Sri Lanka as it is known abroad, it has been reduced to ludicrow levels of sycophancy. The time has come for *Rupavahini* to jettison its servile nature and to honour these to whom honour is due.

For example Second Lieutenant Saliya Aladeniya and his two platoons were mowed down while they were guarding the *Rupavahini* relaying station at Kokavil in 1991. Second Lieutenant Aladeniya defended Kokavil to the last soldier. When his Company Commander, Major Nihal Weerasooriya, who was at Mankulum requested him by radio to evacuate, he refused to do so saying that he had too many wounded and that he would never abandon them. Then he gave the option for all survivors to evacuate, if they wish to do so voluntarily. An hour later he informed his Company Commander by radio that the Camp was surrounded by the enemy and he would be killed soon. He therefore pleaded that the Air Force be sent to bomb the camp because then he will not only die but have the satisfaction of seeing the enemy killed. During the next hour his Company repeatedly tired to contact him but in response there was total radio silence. He was posthumously awarded the *Parama Weera Vibushanaya.*

From what I know of the details of that battle in Kokavil, it can be made into a splendid TV documentary to be telecast at prime time. However servility to the Government of the day being a way of life at *Rupavahini*, I doubt they have anybody on their staff who could write a script worthy of The late Second Lieutenant Saliya Aludeniya. If so, I shall volunteer to do so on a gratis basis but subject to one condition. Politicians and allied vermin must have nothing to do with that documentary.

With the advent of 1998, the focus of attention of the nation was on Independence Day, February 4th 1998, the fiftieth anniversary of Independence. The occasion was to be graced by the Prince of Wales, Prince Charles, who was deputizing for his parents, Queen Elizabeth II and the Duke of Edinburgh. The arrangements were on a lavish scale and the principal celebrations were to be in Kandy, where the last King of Kandy surrendered to the British way back in 1815.

About one week before the arrival of the Prince of Wales, the LTTE completed their reconnaissance of Kandy. Their Intelligence was amazed at how slack our security was on King Street. The street has the Remand Jail, the President's House and the Court House, however there was just one check point. That was outside the President's House. There were no mobile patrols and the solitary check point was manned by just two Policemen.

At 0600 hours on the morning of Sunday, January 25th 1998 there was a routine shift in security. At the Queen's Hotel, Kandy, they were preparing breakfast to a full house of foreign tourists. Kandy itself was a hive of activity, preparing for the celebrations on Independence Day. A common sight were lorries and half-trucks carrying building materials for the temporary constructions.

At 0605 hours a Isuzu Elf half-truck bearing number 43-1396 turned into King Street *en route* to the Temple of the Tooth some four hundred metres away. It had a cargo of three hundred kilograms of explosives and at the wheel was a Tiger Commando named "Master". On board were three Tiger Commandos armed with AK-47 repeater rifles. They were dressed in civilian clothes. When this vehicle approached the security check point in front of the President's House, Commando "Master" accelerated the vehicle while the other terrorists opened fire. Under a hail of bullets, the half-truck rammed through the check point. The vehicle drove past the Court House and turned into *Dalada Vidiya* on which stood the Temple of the Tooth, in all its majesty. When the vehicle was abreast of the main entrance of this world famous Buddhist shrine, there was a massive explosion.

The four Tiger terrorists perished with the explosion. So did eleven innocent pilgrims. Hundreads of pilgrims and foreign tourists were injured. Every building in the vicinity was damaged. Consequently the Queen's Hotel had to be closed down for one year.

Above all, the sacred Temple of the Tooth was damaged extensively. The explosion had ripped off the roof and in many areas broken rafters were hanging precariously. The Temple walls were cracked, the decorative wall on the perimeter smashed, and the entrance in smithereens.

The sacrilege was akin to the Irish terrorists causing explosions in Westminster Abbey in London or Islamic fundamentslists causing explosions in St. Peters' Basilica in Rome. The reaction amongst our citizens was predictable. The Buddhists were livid. The Christians, Muslims and Hindus were angry. They all condemned this cowardly attack by the Tigers. So did the international community, who some years ago naively thought the Tigers were freedom fighters and not terrorists.

In Parliament, for once the Sri Lanka Freedom Party (SLFP) in Government and the United National Party (UNP) in Opposition, joined hands to proscribe the Tigers. In The President's House, President Chandrika Bandaranaike Kumaratunga took the decision to transfer the Independence Day celebrations from Kandy to Sri Jayawardenapura, the capital of Sri Lanka situated on the outskirts of Colombo, and to have such celebrations on a limited scale.

Thus the Civil War raged on without an end in sight. The Chief of Staff of the Army, Major General Srilal Weerasoriya, was the Overall Operations Commander in the North. The battle scarred General was having the same experience with the Tigers as the Generals of the Indian Peace Keeping Force had ten years earlier. The Tigers could be driven out of the Jaffna peninsula but they could not be evicted from the Wanni.

In 1998 the successes of the Army were minimal and therefore early in 1999 some influential members of the clergy took upon themselves the task of negotiation for peace. A delegation of ten influential Buddhist monks accompanied by Bishop Kenneth Fernando, Bishop of Colombo of the Church of Ceylon, and Bishop Rajappu Joseph, Bishop of Mannar of the Roman Catholic Church went behind the forward defence lines in the quest for peace. At Mallavi they met the hierarchy of the LTTE led by S.P. Thamilchelvam, the Chief of the Political Wing and the trusted lieutenant of Prabhakaran.

At the outset the Tigers asked for forgiveness for having desecrated the Temple of the Tooth. The delegation of Buddhist priests were visibly shaken by this gesture. They were further shaken by 1130 hours when alms were offered to the Buddhist clergy with Buddhist protocol being observed to perfection. Some monks even candidly admitted that day that they had been offered alms with even freater finesse than devout Buddhists observe.

Thereafter the negotiations began on a relaxed note. Thamilchelvam wound up the session pleading with the Venerable monks to take their submissions direct to President Chandrika Bandaranaike Kumaratunga. She gave an appointment to the delegation to meet her in May 1999, three months away. When Prabhakran heard of this he was livid and the negotiations collapsed.

Then Prabhakaran took some far-reaching decisions. Those decisions were:

- The President to be assassinated using suicide bombers.
- To celebrate the Millenium with the liberation of Jaffna. As a first step to liberate Elephant Pass in 1999.

Thus the die was cast. The consequences would necessarily be drastic and Sri Lanka would bleed in 1999 to dangerous levels. That became abundantly clear in the last quarter of 1999 when Prabhakan launched his Operation Unceasing Waves.

The final phase of Operation Unceasing Waves commenced on November 1st 1999 with the crack Charles Anthony brigade in the vanguard, supported by the Kittu artillery brigade, the Victor armoured corps, the Black Tigers, the Soothiya Women's Corp, and last but not least the suicide squads. Prabhakaran had hand picked Balraj to be the field commander. He was assisted by Bhanu, Jeyam, Theepan, and Swarnam, all formation commanders with proven ability.

Then their Commandos infiltrated and took up positions behind our lines. Thereafter in a lighting strike, the LTTE breached the forward defence lines on the Oddusudan-Mankulam sctor. Their strategic objective was to safeguard their supply lines from their forward operational base in Mullaitivu, which is also an operational base of the Sea Tigers.

The lightning strike by the LTTE routed the 55th Division (Brigadier T.M. Boharan) at Oddusudan and the 56th Division (Major General Gamini Goonesekera), in a holding operation with their forward operational base at Kanagarayankulam. They fled rather ignonimously. After an exhaustive inquiry, both General Goonesekera and Brigadier Boharan were compulsorily retired.

In the meantime Major General Wasantha Perera, the new Security Forces Commander in the Wanni, worked out his own strategy. The youngest General in the Army and with the potential to be a future Commander of the Army, he had just returned to the Island after completing his training at the prestigious War College in the United States.

His strategy was to open new forward defence localities at Omanthai, because civilians were already fleeing from Vavuniya which had become a ghost town. However the LTTE using 130 mm long range artillery and highly sophisticated equipment such as Saggar Anti-Tank ground-to-ground missiles broke through our Army defences, despite fierece fighting by the 53rd Division (Major General Sisira Wijesooriya) which suffered heavy casualties.

On November 7th 1999 the LTTE struck again. Kanagarayankulam, Puliyankulam and Oneguthai fell within seven days. In 1997 Major General Asoka Jayawardhana then Overall Operations Commander and currently the Governor of the North-Eastern Provinces, took almost the entirety of that year to capture these towns in the course of fierece fighting. Now all was lost in just one week. Therefore Major General Wasantha Perera was relieved of his Command. After an exhaustive inquiry this highly talented officer was compulsorily retired.

Thus the main supply route: Omanthai-Puliyankulam-Karayankulam-Mankulam, captured during Operation Unceasing Waves in 1999 connecting with Kilinochchi-Paranthan captured earlier in 1999 was solidly under the control of the LTTE. Thus the Army could not attack the LTTE from the south. Then the LTTE prepared for a massive attack on Elephant Pass using Kilinochchi and Paranthan as their forward operational bases. They massed their infantry, armour and support artillery. Large consignments of ground-to-air missiles were brought in to neutralise the Sri Lanka Air Force from either strafing or bombing the strategic interests. The Sea Tigers began intensive patrolling in and around the seas at Vettalaikerni. Thus the LTTE was fully prepared for the batttle for Elephant pass.

One month before Operation Unceasing Waves, according to Government sources, President Chandrika Bandaranaike Kumaratunga was more popular than her Administration in the seven Sinhala speaking Provinces. The exact parallel in history was in 1982 when President J.R. Jayewardene perceived he was more popular than his UNP Administration. Therefore he decided to have the Presidential Election in 1982 to be followed by a General Election in 1983. By the same token in 1999, President Chandrika Bandaranaike Kumaratunga decided to have the Presidential Election first, to be followed by a General Election in 2000.

The Presidential Election was Gazetted on October 20th 1999 and duly fixed for December 21st 1999. The Presidential Election was relatively quiet by contemporary standards. (That necessarily includes incidents of thuggery, violence and murder.) As the Election campaign entered the final week it appeared to many an articulate observers that the result will be:

- The President – 48%
- The Leader of the Opposition (Ranil Wickremesinghe UNP) – 45%

On the final day of the campaign, Saturday 18th December 1999, I was woken up by an urgent telephone call by one of my best informants in the Police. His father had worked under my father and the two of us have maintained cordial relations for years. In fact I was his referee when he applied to join the Police, some twenty years ago. He said "Sir, please do not attend that giant rally of the PA today. According to the Special Branch of the CID there may be an attempt to assassinate the President." He rang off very abruptly even before I could ask him any questions.

I repeated that message to Godwin Fernando, my classmate at the Univercsity of Ceylon and the Director of Research for all my books. We were due to cover the final meeting of President Chandrika Bandaranaike Kumaratunga at the Town Hall and that of Ranil Wickremesinghe, the Leader of the Opposition, at the Sugathadasa Stadium, in Colombo later that night.

Two months earlier Godwin Fernando had actually passed on some confidential information, in writing, to the President after returning from a business visit to Singapore. He is a very successful Business

Consultant and had gathered information in Singapore that both the President and Sonia Gandhi were due to be assassinated by the Tigers during the respective Election campaigns in Sri Lanka and India. More specifically the President was due to be assassinated by a suicide bomber during the campaign.

I was against Godwin Fernando submitting such information because the standard technique in intelligence work is to double-check the veracity of the first intelligence report (FIR). That techniques is routinely adopted by the CIA, the KGB, the MI-5 and the RAW. Besides I doubted that the secrets of the LTTE will be known to anybody abroad. I wanted Godwin to double-check his FIR, if necessary to do another business visit to Singapore for that purpose. However Godwin insisted on sending a top-secret note to the President through his confidante, C.V. Gooneratne, the Minister of Industrial Development a close friend of mine ever since we were schoolmates.

Much to my surprise the President gave Godwin a personal interview within twenty-four hours. As he walked into the Presidential Secretariat with C.V. Gooneratne, he saw sitting outside Deputy Inspector-General of Police (DIG) National Intelligence Bureau, DIG (Special Branch) and DIG (Presidential Security Division). They were in readiness to attend the meeting, if called upon to do so. Godwin Fernando was with the President for over an hour and emphasised that according to his information the Tigers dreaded Sonia Gandhi coming into power in India and the President being simultaneously re-elected in Sri Lanka. He further added that Sonia Gandi would probably not be assassinated because polls forecasts in India had predicted that she will be badly beaten.

On the morning of Saturday, December 18th 1999, I attempted to contact my friend, O.K. Hemachandra, DIG (Special Branch). We both represented Sri Lanka in Athletics about the same time. Unfortunately, Hemachandra was neither in his office nor at his home. Therefore I telephoned T.N. de Silva, DIG (Colombo), whose father had served under my father and with whom I had a very cordial relationship ever since he joined the Police. As always he readily agreed to my request that I come over to his office immediately.

The DIG was astonished when I told him of the information I had received, which he himself had heard only an hour earlier. He was not too communicative but listened to me impassively. However when he realized that his information and mine tallied he decided to exchange Intelligence reports. I would like to be excused in divulging such information.

The DIG (Colombo) and I then discussed the recent unsuccessful attempts of suicide bombers, especially the attempt to assassinate Air Marshall Oliver Ranasinghe, Commander of the Air Force, outside Air Force headquarters in 1998 and the bus driver who blew up his vehicle at Maradana junction in 1999. We also spoke of the assassination of The late Dr. Neelan Thiruchelvan, MP (TULF-National List) in 1999 while he was on his way to office. We discussed the possibilities of such an attack on the Presidential Mercedes Benz or an attack like that on the one late Gamini Dissanayake. Such information is deliberately omitted from this book to safeguard our national security.

That evening the security arrangements were very strict at the Town Hall. Entrance to the meeting was only through the end facing Dharmapala Mawatha. Every man, woman and child going through that entrance was frisked by the Presidential Security Division (PSD). There was a light shower around 1830 hours when inevitably the frisking was reduced. During the shower two large and noisy processions came in. One was led by the son of Cabinet Minister A.H.M. Fowzie, who is himself a Provincial Councillor, and the other led by Bhartha Lakshman, MP (PA Colombo Dsitrict). It is widely believed that the suicide bomber from Baticoloa had come in one of these two processions. It is also believed that those enthusiastic PA supporters were not frisked by the PSD, because well known politicians from the PA in those processions had assured the PSD that those in the procession were ardent supporters of the PA. That explanation was indeed plausible.

As usual the President arrived late at the Town Hall. In a very real sense she is the late President even when she is very much alive. There was absolutely no attempt to blow up her Mercedes Benz or the identical empty Mercedes Benz on the way from her official recidence to the Town Hall. By 2030 hours she was addressing the meeting. Again her discourse was crude and unbecoming of a President and unworthy of a Bandaranaike.

During her long and fiery discourse, the message came through the Police network that retired Major General Lucky Algama of the UNP was assassinated at his last rally at Ja-Ela. Apparently security was tight at that meeting, besides nobody was allowed within twenty metres of the podium. Therefore the suicide bomber had used his supplementary weapon, a Chinese hand grenade routinely used by the Army in operational areas. Thereafter he detonated his suicide kit.

On the podium at the Town Hall the President was still breathing fire. After she ran out of steam, she bid goodbye to her Ministers.

Thereafter she received a hug and kiss from Mrs Lalith Athulathmudali, whom she had dropped from her Cabinet in 1996. Then forsaking standard security precautions, she walked towards the crowd for a final farewell!

The FIR submitted in writing by Assistant Superintendent of Police, S.A.D.S. Gunwardena, to the Special Branch around 1000 hours that day was not corroborated even late in the day. Though the Special Branch took that report very seriously and Senior Superitendent (later Deputy Inspector-General) Gaya Patikitikorale, even dispatched a posse of Policemen in plain clothes to mingle with the crowd apparently the PSD did not take the warning all that seriously. Consequently, the President was not informed about a possible attempt on her life. To say the least, that was a serious lapse in security by the PSD. Another blunder by the PSD was that there was no escape route for the President from the Town Hall, in the event of anything untoward. A standard security arrangement was therefore observed in the breach. The podium should never have been located behind the only by-road linking F.R. Senanayake Mawatha to the Town Hall. It should have been located in front of the by-road, thereby affording a safe exit for the President, routinely or otherwise.

The suicide bomber was waiting for the President right in front of her in the crowd, but outside the twenty metre range of the blast. The President unknowingly walked towards the assassin and was obstructed by a visiting British TV correspondent who asked her some question, which she answered. Then a quick-thinking member of the PSD deflected the path of the President towards the bullet proof Mercedes Benz. Only the head of the President appeared over the vehicle when the suicide bomber detonated the lethal weapon. That perhaps saved her life.

The President collapsed with shrapnel in the right eye, the rest of her body being shielded by the car. Her bodyguards carried her into her Mercedes Benz. The chauffeur was killed by the blast and hence another quick-thinking member of the PSD deputized as her chauffeur. She was rushed to the nearby Nawaloka Hospital, on her instructions.

The carnage at the Town Hall was dreadful. DIG T.N. de Silva, who was between the suicide bomber and the Mercedes Benz, was killed instantaneously. He was the highest ranking officer in the history of the Sri Lanka Police to be killed in the performance of duty. The chauffeur who breached standard security arrangements by alighting from the car while the engine was running paid for his subservience with his life. Three security guards from the PSD between the Mercedes Benz and the suicide bomber perished. So did three journalists in that location and two Budhist priests further afield. The final count was thirty three killed. Emergency surgery was performed on Cabinet Ministers Professor G.L. Peiris and Alavi Moulana. Altogether not less than one hundred people were injured and admitted to hospital or given outpatient treatment. Thus ended the Presidential campaign of 1999 for the People's Alliance. At the Sugathadasa Stadium Ranil Wickremesinghe abruptly ended the campaign for the UNP.

Therafter the outburst of emotion was so evident. Even in the District of Colombo, the power base of the UNP, there was a noticeable swing in favour of President Chandrika Bandandaranaike Kumaratunga. It was common knowledge that many women had wept on seeing the TV coverage of the injured President at the Nawaloka Hospital. Not surprisingly she polled 51.2% and easily defeated the Leader of the Opposition, Ranil Wickremesinghe, who polled 42.7%.

As the Civil War raged, in April 2000 the attack by the LTTE was spearheaded by their troops from the crack Charles Anthony Brigade, complete with 130 mm long range artillery captured from the Army camp at Mullaitivu in 1996. In the vanguard was a suicide squad. Those troops were under the command of Karuna, their most daring field commander barring Prabhakaran himself. The ground troops of Karuna were supported at sea by boat squadrons of the Sea Tigers off the coast at Vettilaikerni. They were under the command of Soosai, who had systematically built up the Sea Tigers as a viable threat to our Navy. The strategy of Prabhakaran was to prevent Elephant Pass receiving any reinforcements by sea.

The battle for Elephant Pass in the year 2000 began with a massive artillery barrage on April 15th, with the 130 mm guns which had a range of 25-30 kms and 140 mm heavy mortars. The 54th Division (Brigadier Percy Fernando) responded appropriately but he lacked air power to repulse the enemy.

On the night of April 17th 2000 the Sea Tigers off-loaded on the beach at Vettilaikerni two Companies of Commandos under Theepan who had commanded a similar amphibious operation at Mullaitivu in 1996. The following night, under cover of darkness, the Commandos made their way to the Army camp at Iyakatchi which was the supply base of fresh water to the Army camp at Elephant Pass (Major General K.B. Egodawela). Due to the salinity of the water at Elephant Pass, it was only fit for washing and bathing. That night the Commandos captured Iyakatchi.

Thus Elephant Pass lost its vital supply of fresh water. The consequences were disastrous. Our troops collapsed and died of dehydration. Amongst the dead was Colonel Bhatiya Jayatilleke, the son-in-law of General Hamilton Wanasinghe, former Commander of the Army and later General-Officer-Commanding the Joint Operations Command.

The relentless pounding of heavy artillery, mortar, the continuous bombardment of propaganda by the Tigers in fluent Sinhala over their public address system and the chaos caused by the dehydration, left Brigadier Percy Fernando with just one option. He had to make a strategic withdrawal and to re-group his forces in Chavakachcheri where the 52nd Division (Major General Parami Kulatunga) was based. In view of pressing problems he was compelled to carry out that withdrawal in broad daylight. Tragically, he was killed in action.

The names of The late Brigadier Bhatiya Jayatilleke and The late Major General Percy Fernando (both were promoted posthumously) are the 43rd and 44th to be inseribed on the new War Memorial at their *Alma Mater*, Royal College. That famous school has produced not only the highest number of Generals amongst all school in Sri Lanka but above all has produced the longest casualty list in our Civil War.

Neither the Tigers nor the nation could believe that Elephant Pass could conceivably fall within one week of fighting. Encouraged by this success Karuna deployed the crack Charles Anthony Brigade as follows:

1st Battalion to Chavakachcheri,

2nd Battalion to Chavakachcheri and beyond to Kaithadi,

3rd Battalion to Elephant Pass, in a holding operation.

The 1st Battalion was under Murali and the 2nd under Balraj. There was fierce confrontation with the 52nd Division at Chavakachcheri and at Kaithadi. The casualties on both sides were heavy. In the midst of this fighting the Sea Tigers stealthily transported across the lagoon from Pooneryn to Thannankilappu near Colombothurai, one Company of Commandos under "Johny". He had lost an eye but won a battlefield promotion on the successful attack on Mullaitivu in 1996. Moving behind our lines those Commandos quickly captured Colombothurai and were thus outside the gates of Jaffna. In the meantime the coloumn under Balraj captured both Chavakachcheri and Kaithadi, the bridge at Navathkuli, and crossed over to Ariyali. Thus they were also outside the gates of Jaffna. Therefore the city of Jaffna was partially encircled in an arc extending from Colombothurai in the east to Ariyali in the north. According to the

Tigers they were then militarily capable of completely encircling Jaffna, a certain precursor to the fall of the city. However Karuna opted otherwise and appealed to the civilians to evacuate, but the bulk of the civilians refused to evacuate and instead took refuge with the Army. That was confirmed by independent reports from the Roman Catholic Church.

In May 2000, in desperation the Government of Sri Lanka appealed to India for military assistance. In New Delhi military assistance to Sri Lanka is a sore subject, both with the Congress and the BJP. They bitterly complained that President Premadasa did all he could to humiliate the Indian Peace Keeping Force ever since his ascendancy to power in January 1989. For example he armed the LTTE and gave them huge donations in cash to evict the IPKF. The IPKF had lost 1,157 Officers and men killed in action as opposed to 1,047 in the War of Independence of Bangladesh in 1971. Both the Congress and the BJP are livid that neither UNP nor PA Administrations deemed it fit to build a war memorial to those Indiàn soldiers who made the supreme sacrifice on behalf of Sri Lanka. Therefore without assigning reasons Prime Minister Atal Behari Vajpayee turned down the request for Military assistance. Instead he offered us humanitarian assistance if and when the need arose. In practical terms it meant offering food and medical supplies to the civilian population and to evacuate 32,000 troops all but marooned in the Jaffna peninsula in the event of the city of Jaffna, the Palaly Air Force Base and the Kankesanturai Naval Base were captured. It was no accident that the aircraft carrier INS "*Viraat*" (formerly HMS *Hermes* which had seen action in the Falklands war) and several flotilla of ships from the Indian Navy sailed from their bases in Cochin and Vizagapatnam in the general direction of the Jaffna peninsula. By that time the United States also offered us humanitarian assistance. Accordingly, the USS *John F. Kennedy*, a nuclear powered aircraft carrier, and a flotilla of warships on operational duties in the Persian Gulf were diverted towards our waters. Later a troopship from Diego Garcia also joined that Rapid Deployment Force.

About this time the Commander-in-Chief of our Armed Forces, was concerned with the possibility of 32,000 troops being marooned in the Jaffna peninsula. Therefore she secretly sent a Special Envoy to New Delhi with a special request from her. The secrecy was so great that even the Ministry of Froeign Affairs did not know about the mission of Foreign Minister Lakshman Kadirgamar, in whom she had implicit trust. Besides he was held in high esteem in New Delhi and so many other key capitals.

Foreign Minister Kadirgamar was a distinguished product of Trinty College, Kandy, the Univercity of Ceylon and Oxford Univercity, where he was President of the Union. The special request from the President was that the Government of India order the Indian Air Force, operating from their bases in South India, to bomb the forward defence lines and the forward operational bases of the LTTE. The Government of India turned down that request but reiterated their offer of humanitarian assistance.

In the meantime Major General Janaka Perera, a distinguished product of Sandhurst and the Royal College of Defence Studies, London, with a most impressive combat record, was hibernating in Colombo as Deputy Chief of Staff. Allegedly he was too close to the UNP. However on April 20th 2000 he was appointed as Overall Operations Commander and rushed to Jaffna at a few hours notice. When he arrived in Jaffna, the link between Elephant Pass and the peninsula was effectively severed and the Army was thoroughly demoralized after of a series of defeats.

While General Janaka Perera prepared his battle plans he visited the 32,000 troops he commanded and exhorted the Armed Forces never to withdraw. He inherited a dispirited and demoralized Armed Forces. The proud all conquering Armed Forces of the vintage of 1995 was not in existence any more. His rallying cry was,

> "Either I win Jaffna or I become fertiliser to Jaffna soil. I will never abandon my troops. I have come here to win Jaffna and to save the nation for future generations."
>
> (Thunderous applause.)

His addresses to his troops was broadcast over the radio, shown on TV, and used by the State to induce all deserters, roughly twenty percent of the Army, to return to active service.

In the meantime Balraj and Paduman were trying a break through on the Palai-Muhamali-Nagarkovil-Kilali front and Swarnam simultaneously pushing from Ariyalai and Thanankilappu. When General Janaka Perera succeded in motivating and galvanizing his troops to fight, he began his offensive. Then the LTTE trained their long range 130 mm artillery on Palaly AFB and the Naval Base at Kankesanthurai in order to curtail replenishment of arms and ammunition and the evacuation of casualties. At this critical juncture General Janaka Perera used ingenuity and sent Special Forces and Commandos behind the forward defence localities of the LTTE at Muhamalai, Nagarkovil, Ariyalai, Thanakillappu and Pooneryn thereby threatening the LTTE from the rear. That restricted the LTTE to disjointed attacks, at a maximum. These special operational groups were so effective that the LTTE leaders feared to move forward because their reinforcements and replenishments were scuttled. General Janaka Perera proved his ability to turn defeat into victory as he had done at the battle for Welioya in July 1995 and Operation Thunder Strike in October 1995. By May 17th 2000 the bulk of the major battles were over with one last attempt by the enemy at Sarasalai on May 22nd and 23rd 2000 which resulted in the retreat of the LTTE.

In the meantime General Weerasooriya obtained the reinforcements he had wanted so desperately for over a year. With the string of victories for the Tigers at Kilinochchi, Paranthan, Oddusuddan, Mankulum, Periyankulam and Omanthai, the Army was desperately short of sophisticated arms. Now C-130 transport aircraft of the Pakistan Air Force roared off their bases, ferrying massive multi-barrel rocket launchers to Katunayake AFB. Such modern equipment was then rushed from Colombo to Kankesanturai by sea under a heavy escort our Navy.

Having retreated beyond Palai, Balraj consolidated his position at Sarasali pounded Palaly AFB and Kankesanturai harbour with 130 mm artillery. Therefore General Janaka Perera bombarded Sarasali and relieved the pressure. The multi-barrel rocket launchers reached Jaffna in the nick of time. Capable of firing forty rockets with one loading, this new equipment was a boon to the General in his final assault. The enemy retreated to live and fight another day.

Undoubtedly the hero of the battle to save Jaffna, General Janaka Perera, was promoted Chief of Staff of the Army. On retirement he was appointed High Commissioner for Sri Lanka in Australia, on the basis of an exceptional measure.

On July 26th 2001 the Tigers launched a massive attack to commemorate the holocaust of July 25th 1983 when the disgraceful ethnic riots erupted and many Sinhalese behaved like barbarians. That night some young people dressed in casual clothing alighted from a Mitsubishi micro-bus at the Major Raj Fernando playground right next door to the Sri Lanka Air Force Base at Katunayake. The young people appeared to be on a picnic and the Sinhala music emanating from their audio cassettes and their *baila* dancing strengthened that view. However some of the neighbours were suspicious but their warnings were duly ignored by the SLAF foot patrols. Soon the young people who were merry had finished their dinner and got into their Commando uniforms. They then proceeded to a lonely spot on the 700 acre Air Force Base and cut open the fence with their sophisticated pliers. They then did a leopard crawl through the coconut plantation to the runway. On one side was the No. 10 Jet Squadron, the pride of the SLAF, which consisted of Israeli built Kafir supersonic jet fighters, the No. 6 squadron consisting of Soviet built MI-17 helicopter gunships and No. 4 squadron of MIG-27 gropund attack aircraft. On the other side of the runway was the parking apron of Bandaranaike International Airport. This area, which includes the parking apron for military aircraft on one side of the runway and civilian aircraft on the other, is the nerve centre of Katunayake AFB and the Bandaranaike International Airport.

The LTTE Commandos, under Jegasothy, stealthily reached that area. As to how they got there while doing a leopard crawl is withheld from this book for reasons of national security. Around 0130 hours, an alert Air Force Sergeant had spotted some surreptitious movements. When he radioed the Operations Room he was assured that an ambush patrol was in the area he described. It is factually correct that an ambush patrol was operational that night, but elsewhere in the Katunayake AFB.

There was complete silence till after 0300 hours and the plausible explanation is that the Commandos waited till the scheduled departure of civilian aircraft from the Bandarnaike International Airport. That takes place on schedule between 0001 hours and 0230 hours and the scheduled arrival of Sri Lanka Airlines flights from Jakarta and Male, around 0300 hours. By 0300 hours, some of the Commandos took up their positions in front of the No. 6 helicopter squadron while others did so in front of the No. 10 Jet squadron. Then the Tiger Commandos opened rapid fire with Light Anti-Tank Weapons (LAWS) and Rocket Propelled Grenades (RPGs). While thick smoke billowed and the night lit up with flames, the aircraft destroyed on ground were:

2 Kafir supersonic jet fighters
1 MIG 27 jet fighter
3 K8 jet fighters
2 MI 17 helicopter gunships.

Thereafter the Tiger Commandos attacked the hangars where more jet fighters and helicopeters were parked. A bitter gun battle between the Tiger Commandos and Air Force Commandos ensued. The hangers were saved although many jet fighters and helicopters were damaged, some beyond repair. The casualties amongst the Tiger Commandos amounted to eight, whereupon they withdrew and instead attacked the Sri Lankan Airlines Airbus aircraft parked on the apron. The rapid fire from LAWs and RPGs set fire to four Airbus aircraft and damaged two more. That spread panic amongst ground crew and further afield amongst passengers and officials in the terminal building. Thereafter some Tiger Commandos attempted to take over the terminal bulding. They were mowed down by Air Force Commandos. By dawn all Tiger Commandos were exterminated, altogether fourteen of them. Thus fourteen Tiger Commandos successfully attacked largest Air Force Base which was located some two hundred kilometers from the battle front.

The damage caused at Katunayake was huge. Even leaving allowance for the comprehensive insurance coverage for the six Airbus aircraft of Sri Lankan Airlines which were damaged totally or partially, the loss suffered by the destruction of Air Force aircraft amounted to nearly US$ 80 million. Besides, the nation lost millions of dollars as a result of new insurance premia even for ships calling on Colombo and tourist earnings which abruptly dropped to zero commencing August 2000.

At a conservative estimate the damage was greater than that of the daylight raid conducted by Tiger Commandos on the Central Bank in Colombo on January 31st 1996 and the attack on the oil storage tanks at Kolonnawa and Orugodawatte on the night of October 20th 1995.

As our Civil War dragged on without an end in sight, there was an event of great significance on the international scene on September 11th 2001. Arab terrorists based in the United States hijacked four Boeing aircraft on domestic flights originating from Logan Airport in Boston, Newark Airport in New Jersey, Dulles Airport in Washington and crashed them into strategic targets in New York and Washington. The target in New York was the twin towers of the World Trade Centre and in Washington the target was the Pentagon. Another crashed in Pennsylvania *en route* to Washington, with the target possibly the White House.

Outraged Americans reacted the same way their ancestor reacted on December 7th 1941 when the Imperial Japanese Navy attached Pearl Harbour. All this attack achived was to wake a slumbering giant and fill him with terrible resolve.

Thus the war against terrorism took a new dimension.

Chapter VI

THE QUEST FOR PEACE

The General Election of December 5th 2001 resulted in a clear victory for the UNP. Therefore President Chandrika Bandaranaike Kumaratunge invited the former Leader of the Opposition Ranil Wikremesingha to become Prime Minister and form his Cabinet. The LTTE responded by offering the new Prime Minister a truce for Christmas.

While the truce for Christmas was operative, a Press release issued by the Office of the Prime Minister stated,

> "Yesterday, the Prime Minister spoke on the telephone to Prime Minister Kjell Mangue Bondevik of Norway. He indicated that the Government of Sri Lanka would make a formal request to the Government of Norway to continue their work to resolve the ethnic conflict in Sri Lanka."

On the following day at a Press conference held in Colombo, Prime Minister Ranil Wickremesinghe explained that Norway is acceptable to the Government of Sri Lanka as a facilitator. The Prime Minister said,

> "I want the first steps to be both slow and steady. It is only then we can build a firm foundation for the peace process. Of course there will be many obstacles, but the challenge is to overcome them."

The same day the LTTE stated through their spokesman in London, Dr. Anton Balasingham, that they have confidence in the Government of Norway as a facilitator and would welcome their intervention.

Thus, as the year was drawing to its end, there was every indication that a serious effort was being made to negotiate a settlement. For example at the Ministry of Defence the war hero General Rohan Daluwatte, Chief of Defence Staff, was very pleased with the incoming security reports. He was constantly in touch with his field commanders in Amparai, Batticoloa, Jaffna, Trincomalee and Vavuniya. All reports indicated that the truce was effective. Then he contacted his erstwhile colleague the Governor of the North-Eastern Province, the war hero retired Major General Asoka Jayawardhana. By sheer force of habit, General Jayawardhana was following closely Intelligence reports which he was now receiving from civilian sources. The reports he received from the Government Agents of Amparai, Batticoloa, Jaffna, Trincomalee and Vavuniya indicated that everywhere the Sinhalese, Tamils and Muslims welcomed the truce and observed it.

However, many had misgivings. The well established pattern of the LTTE was to use a truce to strengthen themselves militarily and then to resume hostilities. Their track record could not be worse.

In 1985 President J. R.Jayewardene accepted an invitation from the King of Bhutan to send a delegation to Thimpu to have discussions with the LTTE at a Peace negotiation held under the patronage of the Government of India and organised by Foreign Secretary Romesh Bhandari. The President accepted the invitation and as a measure of goodwill declared a Ceasefire. In Thimpu the LTTE was filibustering while their troops were re-grouped and reinforced once that was achived they attacked the Armed Force with renewed vigour.

Perhaps a worse example of the LTTE reneging on their responsibilities was in respect of the truce initiated by President R. Premadasa for *Wesak* in 1989. President Premadasa offered them a Ceasefire and an offer to negotiate for peace. The LTTE accepted this Ceasefire and their principal negotiator, Dr. Anton Balasingham arrived in Colombo in a blaze of publicity. One week later he left for the Wanni in a SLAF Bell-412 helicopter, and returned with six LTTE Commandos in battle dress, once again with a blaze of publicity. The negotiations commenced immediately with the Commandos of the LTTE being treated as State guests and accommodated at the Colombo Hilton.

The negotiations went on for over six months and President Premadasa even provided arms, ammunition and money to the LTTE to evict the Indian Peace Keeping Force, which he loathed. In the meantime, at the General Election of India in November 1989, V.P. Singh defeated Prime Minister Rajiv Gandhi. In keeping with his election pledge, Prime Minister V.P. Singh withdrew the IPKF. According to President Premadasa, he sent them away. Either way, the last contingent of Indian troops left Sri Lanka in March 1990. Thereafter the LTTE found some convenient excuses to quarrel with the Government of Sri Lanka. Fighting commenced in June 1990 and went on endlessly. On May Day 1993, President Premadasa was assassinated by a suicide bomber of the LTTE. To this day there is no definitive evidence of why the LTTE assassinated President Premadasa who in 1989 and in early 1990 was bending over backwards to accommodate them.

Another outrageous example was how the LTTE responded to offers of peace by President Chandrika Bandaranaike Kumaratunga. At the General Election of 1994 her campaign was oriented towards accepting reality in the context of the LTTE being in full control of the Jaffna peninsula and the bulk of the Wanni. That was indeed a most wise policy though not necessarily a popular policy. Following her victory, she had the courage to negotiate for peace with the LTTE even before the Presidential Election held four months later. The negotiations collapsed within six months, and within a year fighting commenced and the Army captured the Jaffna peninsula. In 1999 the LTTE attempted to assassinate President Chandrika Bandaranaike Kumaratunga. It was a miracle that she escaped.

Therefore it is understandable that millions of citizens did not expect much from thus Ceasefire. On the other hand, many perceived that with the mighty United States waging war on terrorism throughout the world since September 11th 2001, there was some hope for Sri Lanka. That was the dichotomy of the thinking while the year 2002 was ushered in. It was aptly described by President Chandrika Bandaranaike Kumaratunga and Prime Minister Ranil Wickremesinghe in their respective messages to the nation for the New Year.

The President said, *inter alia* :

> "The path to peace is not an easy one. It is hazardous and painful. We have to be convinced of this reality. What we next need is not a peace that is a victory to one community and a defeat to another. Our aim is an honourable peace for both communities."

The Prime Minister said, *inter alia* :

> "The path open to us to traverse is extremely hazardous. Yet we have to make that journey. We are holding in our hands not a beautiful bouquet but a thorny branch. Yet we are compelled to grip it. Let us tread the hazardous terrain and make the thorny branch bloom."

By now the Government of Sri Lanka and the LTTE had one common objective. Both wanted the Christmas truce to be extended to an enduring Ceasefire. The Christmas truce began on December 24th 2001 and now both sides were negotiating for a Ceasefire, with the Government of Norway functioning as a facilitator. That involved shuttle diplomacy between Oslo, London and Colombo undertaken by Eric Solheim, former Member of Parliament and currently Advisor to the Ministry of Foreign Affairs of Norway. In addition, Deputy Foreign Minister, Vidar Helgesen was visiting London, where Anton Balasingham lived, and Colombo to meet Prime Minister Ranil Wickremesinghe and key Cabinet Mnisters.

The first official statement, indicating that the negotiations were progressing satisfactorily, was issued in Colombo on January 11th 2002. That was after the delegation from Norway had left. Professor G.L. Peiris, a key Cabinet Minister and the spokeman for the Government, said at a Press conference in Colombo:

> "We are keen to ensure the Christmas truce, due to end on January 24th 2002, be extended beyond that date. We have to put together the necessary mechanisms to ensure that the truce will lead to a permanent Ceasefire, without being prejudicial to our national interests. Accordingly, the Government has decided to lift the embargo of goods to the Wanni, barring a few restricted items, with effect from January 15th 2002."

The contents of this statement were confirmed by statements issued in London by Anton Balasingham, on behalf of the LTTE.

By mid-January 2002 there was one sensitive issue to be resolved. The LTTE wanted their proscription removed as a pre-condition for negotiations. They even indiscreetly claimed that the de-proscription was a first step towards removing the ban on the LTTE imposed in chronological order by the Governments of India, Malaysia, the United States, the United Kingdom, Canada and Australia. Prime Minister Ranil Wickremesinghe made discreet inquires from the Ambassador of the United States and the High Commissioners of Australia, Canada, India, Malaysia, the United Kingdom. He was assured that even if the Government of Sri Lanka removes the ban on the LTTE for whatever reason, those nations will not do so. They will do so only if the LTTE renounces terrorism in word and deed and meets the exacting standards enforced by each of those nations.

Therefore the Prime Minister publicly announced his desire to remove the ban on the LTTE. The LTTE hailed his statesmanship, quite unaware of the guarantees the Prime Minister had received from Australia, Canada,

India, Malaysia, the UK, and the US. The LTTE then extended their Christmas truce, due to end on January 24th 2002, by a further one month. It was promptly reciprocated by the Prime Minister.

On January 23rd 2002 the Prime Minister addressed Parliament. He said the LTTE had failed to set up a State of Eelam and the Government of Sri Lanka had failed to militarily crush the LTTE. Already 64,000 citizens had perished and many more were either disabled or wounded. So far the Civil War had cost the nation over Rupees 500 billion, with the expenditure in 2001 alone over Rupees 80 billion, (any of the larger headworks of the Mahaweli Scheme cost around Rupees 50 billion) and 800,000 citizen internally displaced. Therefore he emphasized that the Government will not allow this last chance for peace to slip way.

In ths first week of February, with the assistance of the Government of Norway, a Memorandum of Understanding (MOU) to establish a permanent Ceasefire was being formulated. In the course of their shuttle diplomacy, the delegation from Norway visited both Colombo and Kilinochchi. In Colombo they conferred with the President, the Prime Minister and two key Cabinet Ministers, Professor G.L. Peiris and Milinda Moragoda, as also with Foreign Minister Tyronne Fernando. In Kilinochchi, they met Velupillai Prabhakaran and S.P. Thamilchelvan, Chief of the Political Wing of the LTTE. (Earlier he was a field commander and was seriously injured in the battle at Pooneryn in 1993.)

The Norwegian delegation, consisting of Deputy Foreign Minister Vidar Helgesen, Special Envoy Eric Solheim and Ambassador Jon Westbourg, Ambassador of Norway to Sri Lanka, were very pleased at the progress. They were reticent when meeting the media. However, in private conversations they were optimistic that the MOU will be signed on or before February 24th 2002, by the Government of Sri Lanka and the LTTE. In the meantime, Prime Minister Kjell Mangue Bondevik of Norway said in an interview with the BBC,

> "The only realistic approach to any lasting peace in Sri Lanka would be for the LTTE to give up their long standing claim for the establishment of a separate State of Eelam."

That was a clear indication of the predilections of the Government of Norway.

In February 2002 there was tangible evidence to show the mutual co-operation between the LTTE and the Government of Sri Lanka. The stretch of highway Thandikulam-Omanthai-Puliyankulam-Mankulam-

Kilinochchi-Paranthan-Elephant Pass-Chavakachcheri-Jaffna on the A-9 (Kandy-Jaffna) was to be cleared of mines. Thereafter civilian traffic would be permitted to travel freely on highway A-9 from Vavuniya to Jaffna, commencing April 2002. There was also the release of prisoners both by the LTTE and the Government of Sri Lanka. Finally on February 22nd 2002 the MOU was signed in respect of a permanent Ceasefire commencing immediately. Prime Minister Ranil Wickremesinghe signed on behalf of the Government of Sri Lanka in Vavuniya, in the presence of Ambassador Jon Westbourg of Norway. Later in the day Velupillai Prabhakaran signed on behalf of the LTTE, also in the presence of Ambassador Westbourg, in Kilinochchi.

With immediate effect the Government of Norway appointed retired Major General Trond Furuhovde as the Head of the Sri Lanka Monitoring Mission (SLMM) to observe that the Ceasefire was properly implemented. General Furuhovde, who was the Head of the UN Ceasefire team in Lebanon ten years ago, was indeed well qualified for this post by virtue of his past experience. The SLMM would be based in six different locations, Amparai, Batticoloa, Jaffna, Kilinochchi, Trincomalee and Vavuniya.

On March 3rd 2002 Prime Minister Ranil Wickremesinghe made a statement to Parliament on the MOU. He said:

> "Mr Speaker, I thank you for having summoned this House to enable me to make a statement on the Ceasefire. It is the policy of this Government to keep this House informed of each new development in our search for a political solution to the ethnic crisis. That is why I readily agreed to the request of the Leader of the Opposition, for an adjournment debate.
>
> All of us who are citizens of this country are stakeholders in the Peace process. What we say and do here has an impact on 18 million people. It is the same people who gave this Governemnt a mandate to bring a negotiated political solution to the ongoing North-East conflict.
>
> Our approach to finding a political solution is based on the past experiences of negotiating with the LTTE. I have had the opportunity commencing from the Thimpu talks, to participate in or to observe all developments at close quarters either from the side of the Government or from the Opposition.
>
> I have also had time to analyse and reflect on the mistakes we have all made. Therefore this time, our approach is going to be a

step-by-step process, where each step stands on its own but is sequentially connected to the next.

The first step was to deal with the humanitarian issues that concerned the Tamil people. The previous rounds of negotiations with the LTTE broke down on the humanitarian issue. We have tried a different approach. The UNF made a pledge to the electorate to resolve the humanitarian issues. As the new UNF Government, we gave priority to implementing this pledge.

What we signed on the 22nd of February was a Ceasefire. It was not aimed at arriving at a political solution to the important national problem. But this Agreement takes us half way down the road to not only meeting the concerns of the LTTE but also towards addressing important issues raised by the Tamil population reagarding discrimination. Humanitarian issues associated with the Ceasefire address several day-to-day problems faced by the Tamil people by ensuring free movement of people and goods throughout the country. This would present the people in the North and East with the opportunity of freely engaging in their livelihoods; be it farming, fishing, public service or businesses. This is a right that should be available to all Sri Lankans. Therefore, we as a Government will ensure that all Sri Lankans are given access to the same quality of life regardless of race, sex, religion or where they live. When we achieve this and the people of this country believe they can live in security without discrimination or harassment, we as a nation and society would have traveled half way down the road to peace. What remains thereafter would be to determine a Constitutional framework that would ensure equality of treatment and the extent to which powers should be devolved to the Provinces so as to enable the people in those areas to determine their own economic and social future and cultural advancement.

The Agreement is based on the recognition that civilians, who are not directly a party to the conflict, are also suffring and as such, requires both parties to take confidence building measures with the aim of restoring normalcy to all inhabitants of Sri Lanka. It also prohibits both parties from engaging in illegal and hostile actions such as abductions, extortions and harassment. This Agreement is wide enough to cover the unacceptable incidents that occurred during the period when the two unilateral declarations were in force. This includes extorition of money from traders, especially. Muslims, and the abduction of people in the East. The Ceasefire is also wide enough to cover forcible recruitment of children by the LTTE. The Police have to maintain law and order in all these areas. One of the groups who were most affected by the hostile acts against civilians, are the Muslims and this Agreement specifically refers to the Muslim population in this context. The Governemnt is committed to ensuring that the Muslim population can live in safety and security in their villages in the North and East. Furthermore, we have taken steps to strengthen the Police in some of the troubled areas.

Under this Ceasefire the free movement of armed cadres of the LTTE is limited to the areas presently dominated by the LTTE. Outside these areas, the LTTE members have to be unarmed and are to be governed by this Agreement. While the Governemnt is responsible for the civil administration throughout the country, we have no control over law and order, in significant portions of land in the North and East. The armed units of the LTTE dominate these areas. The Armed Forces have so far been unable to regain control. We all know this is the reality but we do not want to sepak about it. We have been fooling the people and in the process we have fooled ourselves.

The forward defence lines in the Northern Province deamcrate the areas dominated by the armed units of the LTTE. The then Government for the first time admitted to the areas in which we have no control in the Eastern Province. In the Report on Census of Population in 2001, in the Districts of Trincomalee and Batticoloa, the Census was carried out fully in 12 *Grama Sevaka* (GS) Divisions, partially in 8 GS Divisions and could not be carried out in 3 GS Divisions. If the writ of the Government ran in all parts of the Eastern Province, we would have been able to carry out the Census without excluding any GS Divisions.

In the Northern and Eastern Provinces the two parties have to draw up lines of demarcation by D Day + 30 days. The Monitoring Mission will assist the two parties in drawing up the demarcation lines. Without such as exercise, separation of combatants in the Eastern Province, where there are no bunker lines (as in the case of the Northern Province), will not be possible. Therefore, it is incorrect to say that the Norwegian facilitators, have been given the final responsibility for demarcating. Another important aspect of this Ceasefire is that there is provision for monitoring. The Agreement for cessation of the hostilities signed in 1995 also made provision for monitoring though circumstances did not allow this to be implemented. The Draft Agreement to permit free movement of goods to the Wanni prepared in April 2001 also contained provision for monitoring by the Government of Norway and this is now included in this Agreement. The monitoring provisions are important to the Government of Sri Lanka which has always complained of the LTTE having violated previous agreements. This is not the first time a foreign country is helping to bring the two parties together in this long drawn conflict. India did this in 1987. The Indo-Lanka Accord further provided for a Peace Keeping Force. We sent them away. What was said of India then, is now being said of Norway by the same detractors. I tell them, do not make the same mistake again.

This Ceasefire has been welcomed by a vast majority of people in the country. However, many are still concerned as to the true intentions and motivation of the LTTE. Given the history of this conflict, it is not surprising that there is a high level of mistrust between the two parties. Therefore while we go forward to implement this Ceasefire we will continue to keep our Armed Forces on constant alert. Most Sri Lankans want us to move ahead with the peace process cautiously and a step at a time, while keeping our guard up at each stage. With this in mind, I have spoken to our soldiers and our Military leaders and explained to them our thinking and our approach. This dialogue has reaffirmed my belief, that all Sri Lankans want a lasting peace. While moving ahead on the peace process we will entrust our Armed Forces with the responsibility of safeguarding any threat to our national security. In this context, I will do what is necessary to strengthen, reform and re-train our Armed Forces. I have already begun work on this important task. Through this process, on an incremental basis, we would be able to build confidence on a solid foundation based on mutual respect. Then we can correspondingly disengage Military involvement as the ground situation improves.

The Government has acted in a responsible and prudent manner in drafting the Agreement. It should be seen as a reasonable and practical foundation on which a political solution to this seemingly intractable problem can be built upon and not as an end in itself. Often our stands on an issue depends on where one sits at that particular time and this is especially the case in Sri Lankan politics, where parochial opportunistic and divisive politics often overwhelm statemenship and a united national outlook. Having engaged in politics for over two decades, I realise that this attitude is an intrinsic part of the Sri Lankan political process. This has been the very reason why this conflict has become almost impossible to solve. My intention is to seek a viable consensus for this most critical national issue bearing in mind the fact that the Government has a clear mandate from the people to search for a political solution.

We have to be mindful of the fact that this is the first instance in which the LTTE has accepted the alternative of a negotiated political solution to the crisis. That position was amply reflected in the statement made by the leader of the LTTE in November last year.

We also have to be mindful of the fact that the international community has fully backed the policy of my Government at every stage. They too have called for political negotiations with a view to resolving this crisis.

Finally, My Speaker, I would like to warn this House and the nation, as it has been the case with other peace processes around the world, the road to peace will have more pitfalls and setbacks than successes. Our collective character and resolve as a nation and society will be tested and challenged at every turn. Every setback will be criticized by our detractors, with an "I told you so" and successes, more often than not, will be trivialized or ignored. But our people yearn for peace and they plead that we unite as a nation to address this important cause ignoring political and philosophical allegiances.

Today, we are living in a fractured and a fragmented country. It is important to unite the country, which has been fragmented over the years and put it back. In the words of Abraham Lincoln, let me quote,

"Let us strive on to finish the work we are in; to bind up the nation's wounds."

(Source : Hansard)

In March 2002, I began my travels to Jaffna, initially by air. I was amazed at the kindness extended to all Sinhalese visitors. For example, I had a habit of introducing myself in pidgin Tamil, saying:

"*Naan Colomba Sinhalavar. Perre Dissanayaka.*"

(I am a Sinhalese from Colombo. My name is Dissanayaka.)

The spontaneous reaction was people greeting me in traditional Sri Lankan style or shaking my hand. Of course I have many friends in the North and East, who are not without influence. However, this example pertains exclusively to the man in the street. To me it was a heart warming experience. Above all, it was clear evidence that the Tamil-speaking people in the North and the East, like the Sinhala speaking people elsewhere in the Island, yearned for peace.

Indeed the ethnic problem has taken a totally different configuration since December 2001 when Prime Minister Ranil Wickremesinghe was sworn-in. By a stroke of his pen the cumbersome check points in Colombo were removed, except round the President's House in deference to the wishes of Her Excellency. It was later replicated throughout the nation, wherever the Governemnt of Sri Lanka was in control. Apart from this, the Prime Minister has a habit of picking up independent reports. For example, at the Royal-Thomian cricket match of 2002 he spotted me sitting a few rows behind him. He summoned me to sit next to him and spoke to me at length on my visit to the Jaffna peninsula earlier that week. To those who overhead that conversation, despite the band playing *baila* music rather loudly and the atmosphere of *bonhomie*, it was obvious that every question was based on the quest for peace. That indeed was the preoccupation of the Prime Minister.

The first official visit of the Prime Minister to Jaffna was in the following week. He was warmly welcomed wherever he went in the peninsula, be it to the Jaffna District Secretariat, the General Hospital, or the Buddhist temple *Naga Vihare*. That was more evidence that the people of Jaffna wanted peace, not war.

As March 2002 drew to its end, there was one factor which was ignored by the media, both print and electronic. The Sri Lankan Monitoring Mission (SLMM) completed their first month in Sri Lanka. There is no Ceasefire anywhere in the world which is devoid of minor violations. The parallel is that there is no licensed driver of a motor vehicle anywhere in the world who does not commit minor violations of motor traffic laws. As such the first requirement of the SLMM was to determine whether the violations were minor or major. There was complete unanimity in the thinking of General Furuhovde and his staff on this issue. The violations made by the Government of Sri Lanka and the LTTE were essentially of a minor nature, notwithstanding the disproportionate publicity in the Press.

However there was one feature which puzzled the SLMM in the Districts of Amparai and Batticoloa. The LTTE under the local leadership of war hero Karikalan was acting in a strange manner. He was recruiting pre-teenage children into the LTTE to be trained as soldiers. That was a gross violation of UN based regulations, for which the LTTE had been warned in the past. Besides, on the direction of Karikalan, the LTTE was imposing all manner of unauthorized taxes on the citizens be they Muslims, Sinhalese or Tamils. General Furuhovde made these observations in his report to the Government of Sri Lanka and the LTTE. The wrath of Prabhakaran descended on Karikalan, who was almost suspended from duty. He was subsequently replaced by the war hero Karuna in September 2002.

On April 3rd 2002, Anton Balasingham and his wife arrived in style in Kilinochchi. They did so by Maldives Air Taxi sea plane from Male which landed in the Iranmadu lake. They were greeted warmly by Prabhakaran and his wife.

However, the LTTE was running into serious problems abroad. India and the Maldives rejected outright the request of the LTTE to hold Peace talks on their soil. India in particular was livid that the LTTE which had assassinated Rajiv Gandhi, had the audacity to propose Peace talks to be held on their soil. The Leader of the Opposition, Sonia Gandhi publicly stated that when the Congress returns to power, India will seek the extradition of Velupillai Prabhakaran, the first accused in the Rajiv Gandhi assassination trial. (In that trial twenty six accused were sentenced to death by the High Court of Madras in 1998. In appeal, the Supreme Court of India commuted to life imprisonment the death sentence on twenty two accused and affirmed the death sentence on the other four). Chief Minister Jayalalitha Jayaram of Tamil Nadu went a step further and wanted Prabhakaran extradited immediately.

The LTTE had no illusions of the displeasure they had evoked in the immediate neighbourbood of Sri Lanka. It was against that background that the LTTE prepared for the first public TV interview that Prabhakaran was to give. It was scheduled for April 8th 2002 in Kilinochchi.

Despite rigorous security checks enforced by the LTTE it was attended by nearly three hundred journalists and TV cameramen, technicians, etc. They represented all major wire services such as Associated Press, AFP and Reuter, all major international TV networks such as BBC and CNN and all major newspapers with international standing such as "The New York Times", "The Washington Post", "The London Times", "Le Monde" from Paris, etc. Besides, leading newspapers and leading radio and TV stations in Bangladesh, India, Indonesia, Pakistan, the Maldives, Malaysia, Singapore and Thailand were well represented.

It was a great opportunity for the LTTE to show the world that they have changed for the better. For example they could have announced that they have rejected terrorism, as a means of achieving their objectives. Such a statement would have earned for the LTTE new friends in the West, especially in the United States. Regrettably, Dr.Anton Balasingham as the principal spokesman, made no such statements. Of course Velupillai Prabhakaran was the *prima donna*. Anton Balasingham was flattering him, calling him both the Prime Minister and President of the State of Eelam. No mention was made as to when Prabhakaran was elected Prime Minister and President. The foreign journalists laughed at this sophistry. Thus the first public TV interview arranged by the LTTE turned out to be a pantomime. Not surprisinglythe LTTE never repeated such TV interviews publicly.

There was exhilaration on April 10th 2002 when the route A-9 was opened for civilian traffic on the stretch Vavuniya to Jaffna. It was a joyous occasion for the people of Jaffna because their relatives in Colombo could visit them for the Tamil New Year, on April 14th 2002 after a lapse of so many years. The civilian traffic using this route initially amounted to 1,000 travellers per day in each direction. With the availability of more buses on the routes Colombo-Jaffna-Colombo and Kandy-Jaffna-Kandy, the civilian traffic reached a figure of 3,000 travellers per day in each direction. The current figure is 4000. That included 500 Sinhalese per day in each direction. I myself traveled on this route by car. It was amazing to see what goodwill the opening of route A-9 generated. Once again, I used to stop my car and speak in pidgin Tamil to the people on the wayside, saying:

> "*Naan Colomba Sinhalavar. Perre Dissanayaka.*"

(I am a Sinhalese from Colombo. My name is Dissanayaka.)

Once again the spontaneous reaction was that they greeted me in traditional Sri Lankan style, claimed how happy they were to meet a Sinhalese and offered me a cup of tea. Thus as April 2002 was drawing towards its end, the goodwill generated by the Peace process was immense. So was the popularity of Prime Minister Ranil Wickremesinghe.

However the intransingence of the LTTE was clearly visible. This resulted in a noticeable reaction in the Sinhala-speaking Provinces. President Chandrika Bandaranaike Kumaratunga sneered at the strenuous efforts made by Prime Minister Ranil Wickremesinghe and his Cabinet. The JVP, accounting for sixteen seats in Parliament and basically representing the protest vote, was hyper-critical both of the intransigence of the LTTE and the efforts of the UNP to break through the present impasse. The extremist Sinhala Urumaya, which accounted for less than one per cent of the vote in the last two General Elections, were more vocal than ever

Notwithstanding these reservations, the Sri Lanka Monitoring Mission, now expanded to twenty four Scandinavians, reported that there were only minor violations of the ceasefire. They also stated that both the Government of Sri Lanka and the LTTE were co-operative in obviating such minor violations.

After the Ceasefire was operating satisfactorily for one month, it was appropriate to pay some attention to our Armed Forces stationed in the Jaffna Peninsula now amounting to 28,000.

The civilian population of Jaffna ignored the troops with unconcealed disdain. At the Rolex Restaurant, the best café in Jaffna as of 2002, the Tamil clientele who were so kind to Sinhalese visitors from Colombo, ignored the Officers in uniform who droped in there for a good meal. Sinhalese Christians from Colombo attending Church services in Jaffna were most cordially received by the regular congregation, not however Sinhalese Christians in uniform. To say the least, the rape and murder of the saucy schoolgirl Krishanthi Cumaraswamy and her mother is no isolated incident in the Jaffna peninsula. Besides, Chavakachcheri is not the only town where every conceivable building, including outhouse toilets, were completely devastated, in total violation of all concepts of noble warfare.

The Armed Forces stationed in the Jaffna peninsula, ranging from Generals or Privates, had all the time to reflects on their performance. In April 2001 they were humiliated in Operation *Agne Khehela* (Rod of Fire) designed to drive away the enemy from Muhamali to Elephant Pass. On the first day of that battle, 441 Officers and men were killed in action and 2,011 wounded in action. On the second day the Army abandoned the battle! In April 2000, in even more dramatic style the LTTE captured Elephant Pass, the second largest Military establishment in the Jaffna peninsula. It is now their largest Military establishment. In the past ten years the Armed Forces had lost all their battles barring two, the battles for Jaffna in 2000 and in 1995.

Down the ages it has been said, "There is nothing called a bad soldier. There are only bad Officers." The Army admits that their desertion rate is an appalling twenty per cent and that the *graffiti* on the Camp walls against Officers was shocking. If so, why have our Officers failed so badly?

I still remember that meeting in the Ministry of Defence in 1985 presided over by The late Lalith Athulathmudali Minister for National Security. The participants were Officers of the Armed Forces at the highest level and civilian officials at the highest level. (I represented the Foreign Secretary). So many awkward questions were asked as to why the LTTE was winning so many battles. At one point General Sepala Attygalle, the Secretary of Defence and earlier the Commander of the Army, thumped the table angrily and said,

> "Gentlemen, are you trying to tell me that those sarong buggers from Jaffna and elsewhere can outmanoeuvre my Officers who were trained at Sandhurst, Camberley and the Royal College of Defence Studies or alternatively in Dehra Dun, Wellington and the National Defence College in New Delhi?"

Indeed it is time that the Government of Sri Lanka sets up a Commission to investigate why those sarong clad yokels from Jaffna and elsewhere outmanouvred and outclassed its Officers even in conventional warfare!

By May 2002, there were some reports that the LTTE was responding positively to the advice of the Government of Norway. The first reliable reports I had were from Ambassador Jon Westbourg of Norway. He and I were regular worshippers at the Cathedral of the Church of Ceylon in Colombo. He is deeply religious and the son of a Chrisian priest. Besides, he is reticent by nature, much more reticent than most good Ambassadors. After the Ceasefire was operational, he repeatedly told me that the Government of Norway was giving the highest priority to persuading the LTTE to abandon the quest for a State of Eelam and instead opt for a Federal solution. The first corroborative report I had was from the CIA. All American Ambassadors I know are in my age group. We have known them either since our days at Harvard or since our days as young diplomats or since our days as Ambassadors. Now we are in our mid-sixties. As such they have all retired and so have I. Somehow many of them are in touch with the CIA, hence they continue to be an invaluable source of information to me.

According to these sources, the CIA had repeatedly warned the LTTE that after September 11th 2001 the United States would not tolerate any terrorist activity by the LTTE. They explained to the LTTE that they have excellent freedom fighters and that the United States greatly admires freedom fighters, ranging from George Washington to Nelson Mandela. Thus the LTTE would be acceptable to the United States as freedom fighters, if they abandon terrorism. However according to the Pentagon, the Military capability of the LTTE was to establish a State of Eelam confined only to the Northern Province. That would not be a viable State unless oil is discovered there. Previously, repeated explorations revealed the absence of oil. Therefore the United States also persuaded the LTTE to abandon their quest for a separate State of Eelam.

Somehow these reports to me from the States became increasingly frequent when Prime Minister Ranil Wickremesinghe was due to visit Washington in mid-July 2002 for discussions with President George W. Bush, General Colin Powell, Secretary of State, James Wolfenshon, President of the World Bank and Horst Kohler, Managing Director of the International Monetary Fund (IMF).

In Washington, President George Bush himself assured Prime Minister Ranil Wicremesinghe that terrorism is anathema to the United States. Therefore the United States will use its resources to assist Sri Lanka to combat terrorism. Besides, President Bush assured that the United States would make a generous grant to assist in the rehabilitation work in the war-torn areas. Accordingly, Deputy Secretary of State Richard Armitage would be making a visit to Sri Lanka to make an assessment of the rehabilitation aid required by Sri Lanka.

By the same token, in Washington the President of the World Bank and the Managing Director of the IMF assured Sri Lanka a generous package of rehabilitation aid. That subject was discussed in great detail.

However, the negative factor was that the Peace talks scheduled for May 2002 in Thailand, were repeatedly postponed. Such repeated delays were indeed irritating and it was a heaven sent opportunity for the Opposition to ridicule the Government.

Besides, there were many reports from the Navy and the Air Force that mysterious freighters were periodically anchored outside our territorial waters and in the vicinity of the coast of Mullaitivu and Batticoloa. Based on past experience, there was definitive evidence that the LTTE was smuggling arms and ammunition through their well established modality of discharging from freighters to small boats interspersed amongst thousands of *bona fide* fishing vessels. The Government was helpless.

The Prime Minister was convinced the LTTE wanted Peace not war. He knew that most Sri Lankans were skeptical of the forthcoming Peace talks and the Opposition sneered at him. Now he sneered at the Opposition.

The first week of September 2002 was indeed most interesting. Cabinet Minister Rauf Hakeem, the President of the Sri Lanka Muslim Congress(SLMC), visited Anton Balasingham in London. Cabinet Minister Milinda Moragoda and Ambassador Bernard Goonetilleke, the Director – General of the Peace Secretariat in Colombo, visited Oslo. By this time the Government of Norway announced that the Peace talks between the Government of Sri Lanka and the LTTE will be held in Sattahip, Thailand from September 16th to 18th, 2002. Sattahip is a Naval base and these crucial talks, barring the ceremonial opening, were to be held in the luxury guest house of the Admiral. In the next few days the respective delegations were duly announced:

Government of Sri Lanka

- Professor G.L. Peiris, Cabinet Minister (Leader of the Delegation)
- Milinda Moragoda, Cabinet Minister
- Rauf Hakeem, Cabinet Minister
- Ambassador Bernard Goonetilleke, Director-General of the Peace Secretariat

LTTE

- Dr Anton Baalsinghm (Leader of the Delegation)
- Mrs Adele Balasingham, Secretary (She was necessary because her husband is a patient suffering from a serious kidney ailment)
- Vishwanathan Rudrakumar, Legal Advisor
- Dr Jay Maheswaran, Rehabilitation Expert.

At this juncture it must be emphasized that the SLMC was unhappy about an Interim Council being established in the North-Eastern Province and brought under the authority of the LTTE. The SLMC has complained bitterly that the cuirrent breakdown of the population of the former Eastern Province is as follows:

Muslims	39.6%
Sinhalese	26.2%
Tamils	33.1%

(Source : Census of 2001 Supplemented with District secretarial figures for early 2002).

Before the outbreak of the Civil War, which resulted in so many Tamils in the former Eastern Province fleeing to Canada, the ethnic breakdown in that Province as per 1981 census was:

Muslims	35.1%
Sinhalese	23.0%
Tamils	40.9%

(Source: Census of 1981)

At the advent of Independence the ethnic breakdown in the former Eastern Province was:

Muslims	40%
Sinhalese	11%
Tamils	49%

(Source: Census of 1946)

At the beginning of the twentieth century the corresponding figures were:

Muslims	39%
Sinhalese	3%
Tamils	58%

(Source: Census of 1901)

Rauf Hakeem insisted that the former Eastern Province is now dominated by the Muslims, not the Tamils. On the other hand the LTTE insisted that the Tamil-speaking former Eastern Province is an integral part of the North-Eastern Province. Somehow the LTTE is oblivious to the fact that the North-Eastern Province was created as a temporary measure in 1987 under The Thirteenth Amendment to the Constitution and is subject to a Referendum in the former Eastern Province to decide whether or not their citizens prefer to merge with the former Northern Province. With the combined strength of Muslims and Sinhalese of over 65%, there is no doubt of the outcome of such a Referendum, which was scheduled for 1988 and has been postponed indefinitely due to security reasons.

Thus there was much evidence in favour of the conflicting viewpoints of both the LTTE and the SLMC, as to who should rule the former Eastern Province. Resolving that would indeed be a thorny problem because the Sinhalese are averse to the concept of the North-Eastern Province being one unit. The Sinhalese fear two-thirds of the coastline of Sri Lanka will be given to the LTTE, under the guise of the North-Eastern Province. Therefore it will be next to impossible for a Peace package, which concedes the North-Eastern Province to the LTTE, to survive a Referendum.

No commentary on the recent political development in the former Eastern Province is complete without reference to the rising tide of expectations amongst the Muslims. Gone are the days when the Muslims in the Districts of Amparai, Batticoloa and Trincomalee were a pliant community. M.H.M. Ashraff, the first President of the SLMC, made the first critical impact on the politics of the nation, by the Muslims. In the 1988 campaign for the Presidential Election, he was with Sirima Bandaranaike, the leading Presidential candidate from the Opposition. However he demanded too much and was jettisoned by her. Then he went into the camp of Prime Minister R. Premadasa of the UNP, who won by 50.4% to 44.9%. In the General Election of February 1989, the SLMC won 3.6% of the popular vote. Thus, had M.H.M. Ashraff remained in the fold of the SLFP, the results of the President Election may have been different.

In June 2001 President Chandrika Bandaranaike Kumaratunga was so annoyed with Rauf Hakeem, the successor to M.H.M. Ashraff who was killed in a helicopter crash in 2000, she sacked him from her Cabinet. That resulted in the SLMC gravitating towards the UNP and the PA Administration facing defeat in Parliament. Thus the SLMC has a critically important role to play in our political evolution at the national level. To say the least, they do not accept the supremacy of the LTTE in the former Eastern Province.

In the Peace talks too the Muslims will play a critically important role. They are hyper-critical of the LTTE for having driven out Muslims from their traditional homes in the Jaffna peninsula and in the Wanni. They will also never forgive the LTTE for the massacres in 1990 at the mosques in Eravur and Kathankudi, during Jumma prayers.

Indeed a new political force is emerging in the former Eastern Province. All members of Parliament from the SLMC in the District of Amparai, Batticoloa and Trincomalee are both emotional and vocal on the issue that the Tamils and Muslims are two distinct races, notwithstanding the fact that they have the common language of Tamil. They admit that in the twentieth century the Tamils were in the majority, however they emphasise that in the twenty first century the Muslims are in the majority. Therefore the Muslims must now be given pride of place in the former Eastern Province.

According to the Census of 2001 supplemented with the District Secretariat figures for early 2002, the exact breakdown of the population of the former Eastern Province is as follows:

Race	Districts		
	Amparai	Batticoloa	Trincomalee
Muslims	245,089	113,473	94,349
Sinhalese	231,771	4,439	77,312
Tamils	110,180	195,319	68,947

The migration of Tamils, especially to Canada, is so heavy that Greater Toronto has more Sri Lankan Tamils that Greater Colombo. Scarborough has more Sri Lankan Tamils than Wellawatte. Therefore in a few years from now, under existing conditions, the Tamils inhabiting the former Eastern Province would be only marginally more than the Sinhalese.

The plaintive cry of the Tamils for years was that they wish to live in security, with dignity and self-respect and not be marginalized by the Sinhalese. By the same token, now the plaintive cry of the Muslims is that they too want to live in security, with self-respect and dignity and not be marginalized by the Tamils. Thus the Peace talks will take years before these problems are resolved.

Much to my surprise on Friday 13th September 2002, the LTTE invited me to spend the week end with them in Kilinochchi. In keeping with their standard security arrangements, I had less than twelve hours to leave Colombo for Kilinochchi by car, a journey of seven hours. I left before dawn in my car with a professional driver from the Church of Ceylon at the wheel. He was a Tamil familiar with the road to Kilinochchi.

That was a weekend I will never forget. The VIP treatment extended to me in Kilinochchi was no less than the VIP treatment extended to me abroad, during my years as an Ambassador of Sri Lanka. The LTTE guest house was the most comfortable I have ever stayed in Sri Lanka. The food was unbelievable, it was Jaffna cuisine at its very best.

On Saturday I had long discussions with Daya Master and S. Puleedevan, senior officials of the Political Wing of the LTTE. Both are fluent in English and both had read all my previous books on our ethnic problem. On Sunday I had long discussions with S.P. Thamilchelvan, Head of the Political Wing of the LTTE, who understands English but speaks through an interpreter. My courtesy call on Velupillai Prabhakaran was scheduled for Monday, before my departure for Colombo. I was invited for another weekend in Kilinochchi and Prabhakaran himself told me that I may report to Prime Minister Ranil Wickremesinghe what we discussed.

Prabhakaran had said:

(1) The LTTE wants peace, not war.

(2) The LTTE trusts Prime Minister Ranil Wickremesinghe and the Government of Norway. They do not trust President Chandrika Bandaranaike Kumaratunga because her credibility is so low.

(3) The LTTE is prepared to shelve its long standing claim for a State of Eelam and instead opt for a Confederation on the lines of Switzerland. However the LTTE insists that in this envisaged Federal set up, the unit of devolution must be the North-Eastern Province on the one hand and the seven Sinhalese-speaking Provinces, either individually or collectively, on the other.

I was truly amazed that the LTTE was prepared to shelve its claim for a State of Eelam. To my mind it was as radical a decision as the decision of the British Labour Party, to reject Socialism altogether, though that was the very basis for their existence for years.

During the long journey by car from Kilinochchi to Colombo, I was continuously tuned to the World Service of the BBC. Their coverage of the opening day of the Peace talks on Monday, 16th September 2002 at the Sattahip Naval Base in Thailand, was extensive. The morning session was ceremonial but the opening addresses by both delegations, the Government of Sri Lanka and the LTTE, was indicative of a strong desire for peace. The first working session held that afternoon was held *in camera* and later both leaders of the delegations, Professor G.L. Peiris and Dr Anton Balasingham, briefed the media. Once again, both delegation re-affirmed their commitment to peace. They further added that the *camaraderie* between the two delegations was a new dimension. That was transparently clear on TV. Such *camaraderie* was conspicuously absent at the previous Peace talks held in Thimpu, Bhutan (1985), Colombo (1989/90) and in Jaffna (1994/95).

As for me, my highest priority was to convey to Prime Minister Ranil Wickremesinghe who was then at the UN General Assembly the gist of my discussions with Prabhakaran. That was done from Vavuniya.

At the media briefing on September 18th 2002, Anton Balasingham dramatically announced,

“We now reject our earlier claim to a separate State of Tamil Eelam. Instead we opt for our traditional homelands within the Republic of Sri Lanka so that we may live with self-respect and dignity.”

That stunning statement was given extensive media coverage, both in Sri Lanka and internationally. The new policy of the LTTE was hailed by all political parties but one, in Sri Lanka. The JVP alone was not convinced.

To have a stable peace in Sri Lanka, three miracles are necessary:

(1) The LTTE has to renounce its desire to establish a State of Eelam.
(2) The Government of Sri Lanka has to renounce the unitary form of Government and replace it with a Federal form of Governemnt.
(3) The LTTE has to renounce terrorism, both in theory and practice.

The first step in such a venture is to educate people. Federalism has never resulted in secessation anywhere in the world; it is a mechanism to share power. Such education will take several years. The biggest problem is to overcome the well established popular misconceptions about Federalism. It is akin to the popular misconceptions in Sri Lanka three decades ago, about birth control. Once that barrier was overcome, the family planning programmes became effective in all strata of our society.

In addressing the UN General Assembly, the Prime Minister said *inter alia*:

> “Our discussions and debates in this Assembly often reach heady heights and seek great objectives, but ultimately they are about the future lives, the well-being and security of the people we are privileged to represent.
>
> It is with such thoughts in my mind that I recall the horrendous events of September 11th last year which claimed the lives of so many Americans and people of other nationalities, from all over the world. As we are only too painfully aware, they are not the only victims of terror.
>
> The attack confirmed what we in Sri Lanka have long known that terrorism had also long been globalised. As President Bush acknowledged. ‘September 11th 2001 was not the beginning of global terrorism: it was the beginning of the World’s concerted response.’
>
> We, in Sri Lanka, perhaps know better than most nations the tragedies that conflict and terrorism create. My country has been

ravaged by a twenty year conflict. It has caused over 65,000 deaths. 800,000 are internally displaced. Tragic stories abound. Children who will never see their fathers return home, mothers who have lost their sons, and children who, even today innocently, fatally step on anti personnel mines. I have talked to the disabled soldiers and the dispossessed, the people who have no homes and those who return to the North-East to find war torn ruins and once productive fields sown with land mines.

The election victory last year of the Government I represent, was a clear national mandate to end the conflict in the North-East. The Government has since moved swifty towards the fulfillment of this mandate. A ceasefire with the LTTE group was signed on 22nd February this year. The Ceasefire has held.

Confidence building measures have encouraged the free movement of people throughout the country and have revived economic activity. Peace talks with the LTTE, facilitated by Norway, commenced two days ago in Sattahip, Thailand. The LTTE has been unilaterally de-proscribed by the Sri Lanka Government to facilitate the talks, to give peace a chance and the LTTE a chance for peace. A flexible approach is necessary in the negotiations, a warm heart and a cool head. An understanding of the other side, their aspirations and their concerns is essential. Negotiations are complex and will take time.

In the early stages of our talks with the LTTE, we are trying to resolve some of the immediate practical needs of the people that can bring relief and normalcy to our society. Economic re-construction and development of the affected areas will be a deciding factor in sustaining the momentum of political negotiations. Development is part of the healing process in a wounded, divided society. The pressing day-to-day problems of the people need to be settled as early as possible. Indeed at the discussions in Thailand, there was strong endorsement of the urgent need for resources to ensure early dividends of the peace process. The role played by Norway in facilitating this process and most recently, at the peace talks is deeply appreciated. I extend my sincere gratitude to them for all their efforts.

Already, following the Ceasefire, there are signs of people enjoying their re-discovered freedom. The people want more. Exchange visits between schoolchildren and other groups from the south and north and *vice versa* have revealed to many that the 'other side' is not so different after all. Last week our capital Colombo came to a standstill as people from all over the country, from every religion and every ethnic group in society flocked to a Peace rally.

These are all encouraging signs. But with them comes a risk. The imperative for Peace is growing. The people demand Peace and the politicians and negotiators on both sides had better deliver. Peace is people driven. The conflict had dragged our economy to near bankruptcy and last year, for the first time in independent Sri Lanka, we recorded negative growth. Resources must flow into developing the areas ravaged by war. Opportunities should be created. The momentum of growth must be re-established. The people want to see normalcy restored, not tomorrow, but today. The farmers want their damaged irrigation canals repaired today. Their harvest cannot be delayed until the final agreement is reached. This imperative is driven evermore by young people among Sri Lankan armed forces and LTTE cadres whose weapons lie silent. Without international support and help with resources to build a peace dividend, the gloss on peace can be dulled. With the re-creation of opportunities for people and for growth, politicians and negotiators will be driven even harder to stabilize, advance and sustain the peace. From there, we can approach the complex constitutional issues. Those questions will take time. Yet we believe that the way forward is through a clearly representative interim administration within a united Sri Lanka in which the rights of all communities, Tamil, Muslim and Sinhalese are safeguarded. This allows us to carry forward an initiative to empower local people by decentralizing governmental authority and establishing five regional economic development zones. Through such initiatives we intend to encourage local people to be responsible for driving economic growth in their regions. These measures, along with the liberalization and de-regulation of our economy will generate wealth.

Meanwhile an immediate security dimension is pressing. Hundreds of thousands of mines need to be removed from tracts of land to make it safe and arable for the internally displaced persons to return to their homes and farms. Sri Lanka is reviewing the position on the Ottawa Convention on Anti-Personnel Mines, with a view to becoming party to it as confidence in peace accrues. We are grateful for the help we are receiving from the UN, members of the international community and NGOs, in our de-mining programme.

My Government is resolved to ensure that the people of the North and East of our Republic should also enjoy the same security, the same quality of life, democratic governance and human rights which people in other parts of the country enjoy. Sri Lanka has a high rating on the Human Development Index of the UNDP with our per capita income figures, our life expectancy and literacy amongst the highest in the region. Peace will enhance all this further but its devidend must be credited to all the shareholders in Sri Lanka's future.

Sri Lanka welcomes the support our peace process has received from members of the international community and the United Nations. On a request made by me to Secretary-General Kofi Annan, a UN Inter-agency Needs Assessment Team visited Sri Lanka in April-May this year. The team reached a strategic overview of the current situation that can guide immediate, mid to long term action by UN Agencies in Sri Lanka. We thank the Secretary-General for his efforts.

(Source: Ministry of Foreign Affairs)

In the coming years, the unitary form of Government being supplanted by a Federal form of Government, will become inevitable. However any Government of Sri Lanka will find it a difficult package to sell to the Sinhalese, if the North-Eastern Province remains as one entity thereby having two-thirds of the entire coastline of the nation. Firstly, the Sinhalese are a majority with a minority complex because of the huge Tamil population across the narrow Palk Strait in Tamil Nadu, India. Secondly, rousing communal passions is a way of life in the politics of Sri Lanka.

In the decade of the thirties of the last century, G.G. Ponnambalam, a brilliant product of Cambridge University, advocated the 50-50 policy which was inane to say the least. In the decade of the fifties S.W.R.D. Bandarnaike, a brilliant product of Oxford University, advocated the Sinhala. Only policy which was just as inane. One generation later, the only one of my friends whom I thought would one day be President, was Lalith Athulathmudali. He was one year my senior at Royal College, two years my senior at Harward were truly brilliant. I was so happy for Sri Lanka when a man of his high calibre took to politics in 1972. His elevation to Cabinet rank after the General Election in 1977 was inevitable. Thereafter he developed a trait he never had before; he become a Sinhalese chauvinist. Repeatedly I cautioned him,

" Lalith, I well remember when you returned from Oxford and Harvard some fifteen years ago, you had such a mature and balanced view on or ethnic problem. What nonsense are you talking now? How will you ever win a Presidential Election if 25% of our people who speak Tamil look upon you as a disaster?"

Such advice had the same impact on him as water poured on a duck's back. It was a matter of time before he would blunder. It happened in 1984, his first year as Minister for National Security. He paroled some Sinhalese prisoners and rehabilitated them in the Doller and Kent farms in Kokilai near Mullaitivu, in the heart of thc Northcn Province. Within a few months the LTTE carried out a dawn raid and slaughtered all prisoners, their wives, mistresses and children!

Such was the deterioration in Lalith Athulathmudali due to communal politics. One generation earlier, G.G. Ponambalam and S.W.R.D Bandaranaike deteriorated the same way due to communal politics. All three were products of world famous Universities and all three displayed tremendous ability. The temptations of communal politics are indeed great; too great even for these three famous leaders. Other leaders who disgraced themselves on the ethnic issue, included J.R. Jayewardane in 1943 and in 1957 and Sirima Bandarnaike1966. In 1943 within one month of entering the State Council (the Legislature) J.R. Jayewardene, without telling a soul, suddenly introduced the first ever Sinhala Only resolution. In 1956 after the Sinhala Only Bill was passed, to mollify the Tamils, Prime Minister Bandarnaike proposed a new Act, The Resonable Use of Tamil. It was fireely opposed by J.R. Jayewardene who launched a protest march from his residence in Colombo to Kandy, to pray at the Temple of the Tooth to prevent the Prime Minister betraying the Sinhalese! In 1966, when Prime Minister Dudley Senanayake proposed a similar Act, his version or The Resonable Use of Tamil, Sirima Bandarnaike, the Leader of the Opposition, launched a protest march from her residence to Parliament to prevent the Prime Minister betraying the Sinhalese! The March went out of control and the Police opened fire killing a Buddhist monk!!

The temptations of communal politics are indeed great; too great even for famous leaders. Concessions by the Sinhalese to the Tamils is anything but popular but in the context of reality today, it is inevitable. Otherwise the Civil War could start all over again.

To make a Peace package feasible in operation, the UNP and the SLFP, the only two Parties capable of forming a Government, must actively co-operate with each other. Regrettably they are at each others throats and fighting their own internecine war.

Politics is basically the art of the possible in the realm of the unknown. Today the highest priority is to engage in confidence building exercises between the Government of Sri Lanka and the LTTE. Already there has been an exchange of prisoners of war. Route A-9 is now open by day. The rehabilitation of roads in the North-Eastern Province was given the highest priority and the results are visible. Providing electricity is being given the second highest priority. The next priority will be accorded to re-settling the 800,000 internally displace Sri Lankans. In October 2002, the World Bank allocated an initial US$30 million for this project. Similar grants were made by the European Union, Japan and the United States. An international pledging conference was to be held in Oslo, in November 2002, to raise funds for rehabilitation work in Sri Lanka. The fiscal allocation required for 2003 alone was of the order of US$500 million. It was a staggering figure but it was achieved.

The LTTE of course had to reciprocate on confidence building measures. The first need was the removal of permits for passengers traveling to Jaffna via the Wanni and tax on commercial goods transported through the Wanni but they did not. Such permits and taxes are applicable for travel from one sovereign nation to another, not from one Federal state to another. Moreover, the LTTE will have to abandon its pernicious policy of abducting people, be they soldiers or civilians and holding them as hostages. The LTTE has to learn to protest within a framework of a democratic nation. The recourse to violent protests, as demonstrated in October 2002 in Amparai, Delft, Point Pedro, Trincomalee and Valachchenai and the consequential opening of fire by the Special Task Force of the Police, was a disaster. That certainly did not help the cause of peace. To say the least, it is a penny wise pound foolish adventure on the part of the LTTE, which must be abandoned with immediate effect.

Another aspect is that the Sinhalese and Tamils must grow up and stop basking in their glory of ancient times. What is more pertinent now is how greatly the Sinhalese and Tamils have failed since Independence.Sri Lankans be they Sinhalese, Tamils or Muslims, have a poor capacity in governing themselves. What is politically expedient is economically suicidal and what is economically expedient is politically suicidal.

As the months rolled by Dr Anton Balasingham arrived in Sri Lanka where he was scheduled to have extensive discussions with Velupillai Prabhakaran himself, before proceeding to Thailand for the next round of Peace talks due to begin on October 31st 2002. Another delegation which arrived in Colombo, to have discussions with Prime Minister Ranil

Wickremesinghe and with Velupillai Prabhakaran in Kilinochchi, was that from Norway led by Deputy Foreign Minister Vidar Helgesen. They too were proceeding to the next round of Peace talks in Thailand, later in the week. In 2002 the greater part of the negotiations were on the Ceasefire. Later sessions focussed attention on the Joint Task Force to strengthen the ceasefire by obviating skirmishes. Accordingly, each side has included a high ranking Military officer with extensive combat experience. The Government of Sri Lanka nominated the war hero Major General Sharta Kottegoda, now Lt. General and Commander of the Army. The LTTE nominated the war hero Colonel Karuna. By 2003 the focus of attention was to be on rehabilitating 800,000 internally displaced citizens, reconstructing roads, supplying electricity, repairing irrigation networks and promoting the fisheries industry. It will only be in late 2004 or later, when core issue will dominate the Peace talks. In the intervening period much work has to be done to improve the estranged relationship between the Sinhalese and Tamils.

Notwithstanding the level of distrust between Sinhalese and Tamils, the second round of Peace talks held in Nakorn Pathom, Thailand, from October 31st to November 3rd 2002 was conducted in a remarkable friendly atmosphere. Both delegations agreed on the concept of the Joint Task Force being mutually beneficial but recognised the views of those who knew no better and hence opposed it. To circumvent such obstacles, it was decided to implement it at the District level. Both delegations further agreed that high ranking civilian officials and high ranking Army Officers on bothe sides meet in Omanthai within a week and high ranking Naval Officers on both sides meet in Muhamalai during the next week.

The LTTE had correctly assessed the militancy of the Muslims in the former Eastern Province. Against that background the LTTE wisely dropped their request for an Interim Council for the North-Eastern Province, much to the relief of the Government of Sri Lanka. Thus the power struggle in that Province would climax when the next Provincial Council Elections scheduled for 2004, are held.

There was complete agreement on the joint approach at the next session to be held in Oslo, Norway, to be held in conjuction with the pledging Conference for rehabilitation and scheduled for November 2002. Besides both delegations agreed to give the highest priority to rehabilitating the 800,000 internally displaced Sri Lankans from all communities.

To diffuse the political pressure being brought by President Chandrika Bandaranaike Kumaratunga and the SLFP, core issues were to be an item on the agenda for future peace talks. Accordingly a Sub-Committee for Political Affairs jointly chaired by Professor G.L. Peiris and Dr Anton Balasingham was formed.

There were two important events in Oslo immediately before the third round of Peace talks. They were the official visit of Prime Minister Ranil Wickremasinghe to Norway from November 20th to 22nd 2002 and the Pledging Conference for aid to Sri Lanka hosted by the Royal Norewegian Government on November 25th 2002. The visit by Prime Minister Ranil Wicremesinghe helped to cement the growing friendship between Sri Lanka and Norway. On the other hand, the Pledging Conference was contentious. Norway had invited the LTTE. Professor G.L. Peiris, the head of the delegation of the Government of Sri Lanka, enthusiastically supported that invitation. In direct contrast the Opposition in Sri Lanka took strong exception to the LTTE being invited to a Pledging Conference where all other invitees were sovereign nations. India endorsed these sentiments and flatly refused to participate in that conference. The United States and the United Kingdom, which have banned the LTTE as a terrorist organization, were also critical of the invitation extended to the LTTE. Both the United States and the United Kingdom played a very constructive role at the Pledging Conference. By the same token they were conspicuous absentees when Dr Anton Bakasingham, the head of the delegation of the LTTE, addressed the conference. Thus, it was crystal clear that, whereas the Government of Sri Lanka was bending over backwards to accommodate the LTTE, the Governments of India, the United Kingdom and the United States were hostile to the LTTE. All three nations have banned the LTTE as a terrorist organisation. Australia, Canada and Malaysia have also banned the LTTE. They too were so hostile.

Thus it was more than clear to the LTTE in general and to Dr Anton Balasingham in particular, that his strategy of refusing to negotiate with the Governemnt of Sri Lanka unless Sri Lanka revoked the ban on the LTTE had achieved absolutely nothing. Firstly, Prime Minister Ranil Wickremasinghe had clearly out maneuvered the LTTE. Besides it was more than clear to the delegation of the LTTE that the six nations were treating their organization as a *pariah* in the contemporary world.

The Pledging Conference served two useful purposes. Firstly, the participating nations had an opportunity of coming together to discuss how best they could help Sri Lanka, both in respect of rehabilitation aid and development aid. Secondly, it carried a clear message to the LTTE of what other nations thought of their terrorist organization. It was against this background that the third round of the Peace talks were held in Oslo in December 2002.

The third sessions of Peace talks were held in Oslo, Norway, from December 2nd to 5th 2002. Both the delegations were cautiously optimistic. The first two sessions of Peace talks had clearly shown, that both sides were clamouring for Peace. Besides these talks were held in a remarkably friendly atmosphere. Indeed that was self-evident in the TV footage on news programmes.

In direct contrast, the serious misgivings expressed by so many citizens of Sri Lanka was most disturbing. Most citizens could not trust the LTTE, because their track record could not be worse. A few argued that September 11th 2001, a day of infamy in the United States, had irrevocably changed the fortunes of the LTTE. I myself belonged to that school of thought in 2002. I had seen for myself the change in the thinking of the LTTE during the calender year 2002.

At the second round of Peace talks held in Nakorn Pathom, Thailand, from October 31st to November 2nd 2002 many useful decisions were taken. One of the most important decision taken was the establishment of the Sub-committee for Immediate Humanitarian and Rehabilitation Needs in the North. The immediate priorities was:

(a) Stepping up mine clearing operations
(b) Accelerating the rehabilitation and resettlement of internally displaced persons This amounted to 865,000 citizens of Sri Lanka, consisting of 738,000 Tamils, 92,000 Muslims, and 35,000 Sinhalese.

(Source: Ministry of Rehabilitation)

At the third sessions of Peace talks held in Oslo, this subject was dealt in great detail with near unanimity between the two parties. On the other hand a very significant difference of opinion arose on the issue of resettling displaced Tamils in their homes within the High Security Zones in the Jaffna peninsula. As a token of goodwill, the Government of Sri Lanka agreed to appoint a retired Indian General, Lt. General Satish Nambiar, who had served in Bosnia with the UN, to give expert advice to Sri Lanka on this subject. The move was appreciated by the LTTE who knew that our Generals stationed in Jaffna, in particular Major General Sarath Fonseka. Security Forces Commander, Jaffna, were intrasigent on this sensitive issue.

Another key issue taken up in Oslo was the setting up of the Sub-committee for Political issues, jointly chaired by Professor G.L. Peiris and Dr Anton Balasingham. That was to off-set the pressure brought to bear by President Chandrika Bandaranaike Kumaratunga, Dr Sarath Amunugama, Lakshman Kadirgamar and Mangala Samaraweera, all senior Cabinet Ministers in her last Administration. They wanted this issue included in the agenda in December 2002 itself. The plan of the Government was to solve urgent problems first, such as rehabilitating 800,000 citizens who were internally displaced and political issues to be taken up in due course, perhaps in 2004.

Both the Government of Sri. Lanka and the LTTE were quite pleased with the third sessions of Peace talks held in Oslo in December 2002. On the other hand there were dissenting reports which of necessity had to be taken seriously.

Firstly, our Military Intelligence was consistently reporting that the LTTE was smuggling in arms and ammunitation in huge quantities while negotiating for Peace. According to the LTTE, they had to smuggle in arms and ammunition after the Ceasefire was signed to ensure their fighting capability remains on par with the Armed Forces of Sri Lanka who were modernizing Navy and Air Force while negotiating for Peace.

Secondly, the CIA operatives based in Colombo produced irrefutable evidence that in 2002 the LTTE had done absolutely nothing to change its structure as a terrorist organization. Admittedly there were some cosmetic changes such as the LTTE abandoning the policy of recruiting children. More importantly, no decision was taken to dismantle the suicide squads. In fact some death squads were operating in Colombo and exterminating Tamils who were informants of the Governemnt! This opinion was shared by the RAW, the Indian equivalent of the CIA. RAW has an extensive coverage in Sri Lanka, by virtue of the fact that Sri Lanka is a neighbour of India. For sheer ability the RAW is truly splendid when operating in the neighbourhood of India. I saw this for myself while stationed in Bangladesh, Burma and Nepal and therefore gave much weightage to the reports from RAW.

In January 2003 in preparing for my first visit to the Jaffna peninsula and Kilinochchi in the New Year, I studied carefully our Military Inteligence reports and whatever Inteligence reports I could get from CIA and RAW. Besides I had indepth discussions with Professor G.L. Peiris, Rauff Hakeem and Milinda Moragoda, the three Cabinet Ministers on the Sri Lanka delegation to the Peace talks. All three are personal friends of mine and I do admire their unquestioned ability and integrity.

By and large my visit to the Jaffna and Kilinochchi was most rewarding. The information I gathered in Colombo from our Military

Intelligence was correct and the information I obtained from the three Cabinet Ministers did not reflect the harsh realities at the grass roots level. The day of reckoning was February 5th 2003, when for the first time since the Ceasefire the LTTE launched a campaign throughtout Jaffna to recruit young people in the age group of 18 years and more. Around the time the schools closed that day, the LTTE propaganda units arrived outside St. John's College, Chundukuli, Jaffna right opposite the Vicarage in which I stayed. In no uncertain terms they said that the Peace talks were a farce and war will break out soon. They said the LTTE will capture the Jaffna peninsula in three days of fighting because General Janaka Perera is not in the Army any more. The LTTE now has very efficient supply lines from nearby Elephant Pass as opposed to the supply lines in April 2000 from relatively far away Kilinochchi. The LTTE propaganda units claimed that with the assistance of the Sea Tigers, large consignments of arms had been smuggled in. Thus the LTTE now had enough and more arms and ammunition. Therefore what they wanted now was enough manpower. Apparently the LTTE had recruiting squads like this outside all major schools in Jaffna that day.

Therefore I telephoned Ravi Karunanayake, the Minister for Commerce and Consumer Affairs who is son my sister's son and my God son. I deliberately spoke to him in Sinhala, which I rarely do, and the conversation was as follows:

> "Ravi, this is Uncle Al, speaking to you from Chundikuli, Jaffna. While I am speaking to you the LTTE is across the road and outside St. John's College, Chundikuli, Jaffna. They are attempting to recruit schoolboys of eighteen years and more. They claim.........................
>
> "Uncle Al, how do you know what they are saying. You do not understand or speak Tamil"
>
> "Hold on Ravi. My interpreter will now speak to you. He is a priest from the Church of Ceylon.
>
> After their conversation was over, I spoke again,
>
> "Ravi, at a confidential briefing I had from the Church of Ceylon in Jaffna I was informed that (deleted due to security considerations) ....
> ...."
>
> "My God, Uncle Al, you are frightening me".
>
> "Ravi, in a confidential briefing I had from the powerful Roman Catholic Church in Jaffna I was informed that (deleted due to

security considerations) ....
...."

"Uncle Al, this is very very serious. Can I quote you?"

"Of course. Please convey what I have now told you to the Prime Minister and the three Cabinet Ministers on our delegation to the Peace talks."

"Any other info for me to pass on"

"Please tell Aunty Marlyn (my wife) that my departure from Jaffna is postponed indefinitely. She need not know repeat she need not know what is delaying my departure for Colombo."

"Okay, Uncle Al. What you want conveyed will be conveyed to those who matter. Message to Aunty Marlyn will be conveyed immediately."

"That's all for now, Ravi. Cherio".

That evening Marlyn telephoned me to inquire what was delaying my departure from Jaffna. I said something vague but plausible. She telephoned me again the following morning. That time she was crying because a very dear cousin of hers who was ailing had passed away during the night. He had been so kind to me and the least I could do was to attend his funeral.

After the funeral I rushed back to my base at Chundikuli, Jaffna, and into the vortex of another storm. The previous day the Navy had detected a trawler with Indian registration marks being towed by a boat of the LTTE within Sri Lankan territorial waters. The Navy observed that there were twelve LTTE cadres on board their boat, including two famales, and three LTTE cadres, all males, on board the trawler. The LTTE refused to allow the Navy the right to search the vessels. The Navy Fast Attack Craft (FAC) which made this detection was assisted by other FACs which sailed in and surrounded the two LTTE vessels. When the Sri Lanka Monitoring Mission (SLMM) arrived on the scence, they made a meticulous search of the boat and advised the Navy that there was no incriminating cargo on board. Therefore the LTTE boat and their crew of twelve were allowed to sail away. On the other hand a painstaking search of the trawler revealed the following contraband:

One	23mm anti-aircraft gun
One	AK 47 rifle
Two	boxes of 23mm ammunition
Three	hand grenades

When confronted with these arms and ammunition, the three LTTE cadres advised the SLMM that they would set the trawler on fire and thereafter they would commit suicide by taking cyanide. Therefore they advised the SLMM personnel to jump overboard and save their lives. Then the LTTE cadres carried out their threat!

The Government of Sri Lanka and the LTTE hierarchy in Jaffna and Kilinochchi traded insults on this debacle. Besides student unrest began in Jaffna and the LTTE called for a boycott of the opening of the refurbished Jaffna Public Library scheduled for the following week. (The original Library was set on fire in 1981 by Sinhalese goons). Besides, the Sea Tigers undertook a retaliatory raid off Trincomalee and by error sank a Chinese trawler. Seventeen Chinese lost their lives and that incurred the wrath of the Government of China. However, Dr Anton Balasingham magnanimously announced at the fifth sessions of Peace talks held in Berlin from February 8th to 10th 2003, that the LTTE was at fault and that this incident should not derail the Peace talks.

On March 10th 2003 a shocked nation heard the following communiqué issued by our Ministry of Defence and broadcast by all radio and TV stations in Sri Lanka.

> "Yesterday The Sri Lanka Navy received credible information that a LTTE cargo vessel carrying arms and ammunitions was approaching the coast at Mullaitivu with the aim of unloading weapons at mid-sea into small boats. The Sri Lanka Navy ship *"Sayura"* which was on a routine patrol in the areas was directed to investigate. The *"Sayura"* challenged the suspicious ship 185 nautical miles east of Mullaitivu in international waters.
>
> "The LTTE ship had no name, no registration number, no flag. The Navy therefore tried to communicate with the ship through the international maritime communications channel. Since the response received was vague and contradictory, the Navy ordered the ship to stop to verify that it did not pose a security threat to Sri Lanka. The suspicious ship did not respond to this command, instead attempted to escape. The Navy then gave chase whereupon at close range the LTTE ship opened fire on the SLNS *"Sayura"* causing injury to one Officer and three sailors on board.
>
> "The SLNS *"Sayura"* then took appropriate retaliatory action whereupon the LTTE ship caught fire and sank approximately 180 nautical miles east of Mullaitivu. There were no survivors"

In subsequent news bulletins, the Sri Lanka Monitoring Mission confirmed that the LTTE had informed them that one of their ships was sunk in international waters when fired upon by the Sri Lanka Navy. Thereafter there was the incessant trading of insults between the LTTE and the Government of Sri Lanka. More importantly, it was obvious that the Ceasefire, which had withstood the vicissitudes of life for over one year, was now in jeopardy.

After this episode it was a miracle that the sixth sessions of Peace talks scheduled held in Hakone, Japan, from March 18th to 21st 2003 was actually held on schedule. In terms of the Agreed Statement (Vide Annexure III), the parties met amid growing security concerns following recent incidents on land and at sea. While they acknowledged that parallel progress is needed in negotiations on security, economic and political issues, the parties left no doubt that they must now give top priority to improving the security situation, in particular at sea. The parties undertook to enforce better compliance of the Ceasefire by their personnel.

The international community was most appreciative of the leadership of Prime Minister Wickremasinghe but was puzzled by the leadership of Vellupillai Prabhakaran. In the eyes of the international community Prime Minister Wickremasinghe had consistently taken decisions to promote Peace. On the other hand Velupillai Prabhakaran had taken some decisions to strengthen Peace, for example to stand by the Ceasefire come what may. By the same token he had taken many decisions, which were grossly detrimental to the cause of Peace. For example as of February 22nd 2003 death squads of the LTTE had exterminated nineteen citizens, some Tamils others Muslims, some living in the North-Eastern Province others living in Colombo, who were suspected to be informants of the Government.

The United States Embassy in particular was dismayed by this consistent trend which was growing from bad to worse. For example during the six months February 22nd to August 22nd 2003, LTTE death squads had accounted for an additional twenty four murders, the most dramatic being the murder of Inspector Sunil Thabrew of the Dehiwela Police who was gunned down in the Police Station itself. Thereafter the assailant attempted to commit suicide the LTTE way by swallowing a cyanide capsule which somehow did not work. He was promptly arrested and is being tried for murder in the High Court of Colombo.

According to CIA operatives in Sri Lanka, the worldwide network of the LTTE has been persuaded by the worldwide network of CIA to scuttle their suicide squads and death squads. This was the first meaningful step towards being acceptable to the international community. There is not a shred of evidence of this being achieved in the first year of the Ceasefire Agreement.

In direct contrast, the Embassy of the United States, the British High Commission, the Australian High Commisssion and the Embassy of the Netherlands all of whom were so critical of the Human Rights record of the last UNP Administration under President R. Premadasa were so appreciative of the Human Rights record of the current UNP Administration of Prime Minister Ranil Wickremasinghe. Of course they admired even more the excellent work done by President Chandrika Banadaranaike Kumaratunge in bringing the Human Rights record of Sri Lanka to acceptable levels, ever since she came to power in 1994.

Besides, the Embassy of the United States and the British High Commission were convinced that the Government of Sri Lanka under Prime Minister Ranil Wickremasinghe was in no way preparing for war. They were aware of the ground realities, for instance when the Army advertised for 5,000 vacancies for Privates in January 2003 only 427 applied! Besides, in the first year of the Ceasefire the Army accounted for an additional 8,000 deserters! The Army did not even pursue them through the local Police. They merely wrote them off!!

Periodically there were statements issued by the Department of State in Washington which were very complimentary of the progress made by the Government of Sri Lanka in the quest for Peace. Frequently such compliments were paid by Richard Armitage, Deputy Secretary of States and sometimes by General Collin Powell, Secretary of State himself.

On the economy, the encomiums came from the World Bank and the International Monetary Fund, both situated in Washington. They were impressed by the financial discipline enforced in Sri Lanka by Prime Minister Ranil Wickremasinghe. Both the World Bank and the International Monetary Fund predicted that Sri Lanka will achieve a 6% growth in Gross National Product by 2004, a most impressive growth from a negative growth rate in 2001.

On the other hand the World Bank and the International Monetary Fund looked upon with a mixture of amusement and amazement the antics of the LTTE. Initially they refused to believe that the LTTE arbitrarily imposed a 5% "Development tax" on the US$ 6 million contract awarded by the Asian Development Bank to rehabilitate the A-9 highway from Thanadikulam to Jaffna, a distance of 140 kilometers most of which is in LTTE controlled areas. A good road Colombo-Thandikulam-Jaffna would be the main artery linking Colombo with the Jaffna peninsula. It would be the life line for the Tamil people yet the LTTE chose to place obstacles. It later transpired that the "Development tax" was devised by Velupillai Prabhakaran himself.

The emerging pattern in the Eastern Province was so different from that in the Northern Province. In the Eastern Province, the influence of the LTTE was waning visibly since the Ceasefire which was duly signed on February 22nd 2002. (I was in Batticoloa for the first anniversary).

According to the District secretariat figures, as of early 2004, the population or the Eastern Province is:

Muslims	40%
Sinhalese	27%
Tamils	32%
Burghers	1%

Thus for the first time in living memory in terms of population, the Tamils are not the leading community in the Eastern Province. More importantly the Muslim population is so conscious of their new role, as a majority. The LTTE knows there figures are correct sbut finds it difficult to accept that the Tamils are no longer the majority in the Eastern Province. They merely pretend that they control the levers of power.

Admittedly the Muslim Members of Parliament in the Eastern Province are from several Parties, which are involved in internecine political activity. They are badly divided on all manner of issues pertaining to personalities and not policies. However, they are united splendidly on one crucial issue, the Muslims are now the dominant partner in the Eastern Province. They complain bitterly, both individually and collectively, of the atrocities of the LTTE such as in 1990 exterminating Muslims at Jumma prayers at Eravur and Kathankudi, periodic forays into Muslim towns by the LTTE and leaving behind a trail of death and destruction in 1985 Akkaraipattu, Kalmunai, and Samanturai, in 1986 in Muthur and Valaichchenai, in 1987 in Eravur and Kathankudi, in 1990 in Nintavur and Samanturai, in 1991 in Akkaraipattu *et cetera* and after the Ceasefire was signed in 2002 in Valaichchenai and Muthur, and again in 2003 in Muthur. In the Eastern Province the Muslims portray the LTTE as nothing more than a murderous gang of extortionists who make life intolerable.

Besides, the Muslims are very proud of their achievements in the field of economic development. In the twenty first century our biggest single source of foreign exchange is expartiate earnings, not tea. Now nearly one million Sri Lankans work in the Middle East and Muslims in their hundreds of thousands from the Eastern Province and elsewhere find gainful employment there on a preferential basis. The impact of the petro-dollars on the economy of the Eastern Province is evident even to a tourist. For example the Muslim towns of Eravur, Kalmunai and Kathankudi are visibly more prosperous than the Tamil town of Batticaloa.

Of late the Muslim towns, especially Eravur, Kathankudi, Kalmunai, Oluvil, Nintavur and Samanturai display unmistakably Muslim architecture. Besides, the ladies wear not sarees but traditional Muslim dress, *shalwar kameez* and *abayas* complete with *hijabs* (head dress). Indeed now these towns, amongst others, look so similar to towns in Bangladesh and Pakistan.

Against this background the pertinent question asked by the Muslims is, what can the LTTE offer the Muslims now? Whenever I went behind LTTE lines in Chenkaladi and Vakarai in the District of Batticaloa, and Muthur, in the District of Trincomalee, I asked the LTTE this question. Now they are tongue tied. Of course the LTTE curse the Sinhalese. By the same token, the Muslims curse the LTTE often using the same colourful epithets which the LTTE uses to condemn the Sinhalese. Thus my conclusion is that the LTTE is no longer a potent political force in the Eastern Province. Their only power is the power that emanates from the barrel of a machine gun!

The Naval action by the SLNS *"Sayura"* on March 10th 2003 left an indelible mark on the Ceasefire. No longer could the detractors of Prime Minister Ranil Wickremasinghe accuse him of bending over backwards to be helpful to the LTTE at the expense of the nation. For example he authorized the Navy to sink any LTTE vessels suspected to be transporting arms and ammunition. It happened a second time when the SLNS *"Nandamithra"* sank another LTTE vessel on June 14th 2003. Now the burning question was, how will the Ceasefire be affected by the Naval action? Will the Ceasefire itself last?

On the issue of the options open to the Government of Sri Lanka, an expert, in the true sense of the word, is retired Foreign Secretary Bernard Tilakaratne, now 78 years old. He had five postings in India accounting for half of his distinguished career. I have a habit of doing a walk in the morning and frequently dropping in at his home for a chat. I once asked him in 2003,

> "Bernard, if the LTTE decides to abrogate the Ceasefire and go to war what will India do".

"Jungle" it is a difficult question you ask me. The crux of the problem is what Prime Minister Atul Behari Vajpayee will do, especially against the background of his present problems with Pakistan and with the next General Election less than one year away.

"Can you remember you asked me the same question when Jaffna was on the verge of falling to the LTTE in April 2000? Even when the President sent Foreign Minister Lakshman Kadirgamar as a Special Envoy to plead that the Indian Air Force bomb Elephant Pass and other forwad operational bases of the LTTE, Prime Minister Vajpayee only promised us humanitarian assistance in the event of Jaffna falling to the LTTE. That was the moment of truth. He then ordered the Indian Navy to stand by to evacuate our troops if Jaffna fell. There was never a question of Canberra jet bombers being alerted at their base in Bangalore or Mirage fighters standing by at their base at Trivandrum for operational missions over the Jaffna peninsula.

"The situation was very different in the time of Prime Minister Rajiv Gandhi. He repeatedly told me that if the LTTE captured Jaffna he will send the Indian Air Force to bomb Jaffna. He repeatedly sent messages to President J.R. Jayewardena through our friend Mani Dixit to the effect that the Indian Air Force will bomb Jaffna if the LTTE captured the peninsula. That was well and good in theory. In practice, in 1987 when General Kobbekaduwa won the battle at Vadamarachchi and was poised to capture Jaffna the next week, Prime Minister Rajiv Gandhi almost sent the Indian Air Force against us. That was the huge difference between theory and practice. In theory, the entire scenario changed after the Indian Peace Keeping Force (IPKF) was sent here in 1987 and left in humiliation in 1990. Firstly they left without victory. Secondly President Premadasa wanted them to leave. Thirdly Prime Minister V.P. Singh made it an election issue to withdraw the IPKF.

"Rightly or wrongly, India perceives herself as a major regional Military power in this part of the world, ever since the Indo-Pakistan war of 1971 which gave birth to Bangladesh. Therefore to India the end result of the expedition to Sri Lanka was a humiliation".

"Bernard, the situation is very different now, be it in theory or in prctice. As of February 22nd 2002 there is a Ceasefire signed in public. What will India do against the background of all these new developments?

"India will give us humanitarian assistance. That is the Foreign Policy of India, as of now. Remember India will do what is good for Mother India. That is the Foreign Policy of India. In India personalities do not come into the equation on issues of Foreign Policy.

"Jungle", what do your powerful colleagues at Harvard have to say"?

"So many of my American colleagues at the Harvard Centre for International Affairs became famous Ambassadors. They are now in retirement but still in touch with the CIA. They all tell me the same story.

"According to the Pentagon, the Military capability of the LTTE is at a maximum, the ability to capture the Jafna peninsula despite the likelihood of heavy casualities on both sides. All the victories of the LTTE were in the North, namely Elephant Pass (2000), Kilinochchi (1999), Mullaitivu (1996), Pooneryn (1993) and Mankulam (1990). They did not fight one battle in the East in twenty years. The Jaffna peninsula and the Wanni put together makes the Northern Province. That is just not enough to make a State of Tamil Eelam".

"So "Jungle" what you imply is that the LTTE will not risk a war, because they have so little to gain and so much to lose".

"Correct. That is my perception as of now. However the possibility of another bout in the Civil War can never be written off or taken lightly. We now have 27,000 to 28,000 troops in the Jaffna peninsula. Besides, we have more troops in Vavuniya and Minneriya. They can be flown in at short notice either in fixed wing aircraft to Palaly Air Force Base or by helicopter to the battle front itself. Remember the battle at Alampil near Mullaitivu in 1996. Lieutenant Colonel Fazil Laphir commanding a battalion of Special Forces fought with total disregard for his own safety. He was posthumously awarded the *Parama Weera Vibushanaya*. Lieutenant Colonel Raj Wijesiri commanding another battalion of Special Forces was seriously wounded with a bullet entering his torso under the shoulder and exiting through his waist. Then Lieutenant Colonel Prasanna de Silva also from the Special Forces volunteered to replace his brother officers, one killed in action and another wounded in action. He also fought with total disregard for his own safety. Somehow he survived the battle and was also recommended for the *Parama Weera Vibushanaya* which so far has been awarded only posthumously. Therefore he was awarded the *Weera Wickrema Vibushanaya,* our second highest decoration for gallantry. According to Colonel Karuna, Commander of the LTTE forces in the East in succession to Colonel Karikalan, the Special Forces are the best troops in the Island, including those of the LTTE. He himself told me so in Vakarai, when I was his guest.

"Bernard, few people know this. At the battle for Mullaitivu the LTTE was under the command of Colonel Karikalan, one of their best field commanders. He had under him the crack Charles Anthony Brigade and supported by the crack Kittu Brigade of Artillery. It was Colonel Karikalan himself who realized it was futile to battle with our Special Forces and Commandos. Therefore he ordered his crack troops to withdraw into the jungles after sunset and after blowing up our Camp in Mullaitivu which they had captured the previous night with all personnel, 1187 Officers and men, killed in action. Such is the respect the LTTE has for our *elite* troops, the Special Forces and the Commandos. On the other hand the LTTE ridicules our under-trained troops who become cannon fodder. They refer to them contemptuously as *Shingalaya modaya* (Sinhalese fools). Their favourite camp song is the Sinhala ditty,

> *Sinhalaya modaya*
> *Kavun kanna yodaya*
> (The Sinhalese fools,
> They are only good to eat oil cakes.)

sung with a Tamil accent!

"But Prabhakran is a thoroughly irrational fellow. His most irrational decision was to assassinate Rajiv Gandhi. Overnight the entirety of India, turned against the LTTE. What will happen if this mad fellow decides to go to war? What do your high powered friends from Harvard say?

"The US will never send ground troops to Sri Lanka like they sent to Afghanistan after September 11th 2001. They will never fire a Cruise Missile at Kilinochchi. Instead they may embark on a Naval blockade of the North and the East coasts of Sri Lanka while operating in international waters. The massive Seventh Fleet of the US Navy operating out of Subic Bay and Diego Grarcia may undertake the blockade. A solitary ship from the Royal Navy and the Royal Australian Navy may come in but that will constitute only a token presence. In six months Prabhakaran will be starved of ammunition even if he has the arms to sustain the war.

"Have you noticed that of late the United States is helping our Navy, not the Army nor the Air Force. For example in the midst of the crisis of the SLNS *"Sayura"* sinking a tramp steamer of the LTTE, the US Embassy suddenly released photographs of the USNS *"Courageous"* a Coast Guard ship recently sold for a song to our Navy. I understand more such ships are on their way. Besides every month a US warship now visits either Colombo or Trincomalee. Right now the aircraft carrier USS *"John F. Kennedy"* is in Colombo.

"Jungle", I have learnt the hard way that conflic resolution is a very slow process, more often than not an agonizingly slow process. President Jayawardene knew this but not President Premadasa. As Foreign Secretary he sent me to New Delhi on six occasions in my first year in office. I functioned more as a Special Envoy of the President than as the Foreign Secretary of Sri Lanka.

"The LTTE is now in a new phase in their evolution. They have to prove to the Tamil community on the one hand and the international community on the other, that the LTTE is searching for a new identity.

Smuggling of arms and exterminating informants of the Government is part and parcel of their old trade mark. The LTTE did well in rushing humanitarian aid to Ratnapura and Galle during the recent floods. Are they changing fast enough? I remember when you were our Ambassador to Egypt and her neighbouring Arab nations you wrote several Special Reviews on the Civil War in Lebanon. You always reported that the combatants met quietly at some holiday resort on the Suez Canal and discussed peace. Did they change fast enough from prosecuting a war to serching for peace?"

"Bernard, those who negotiated for peace in Lebanon moved at the speed that made a snail pace look fast!. Those negotiations began in 1975 and ended in 1995!! I well remember the brilliant Ambassador of Lebanon to Egypt, my classmate at Harvard, telling me that he dreaded attending those meetings because they were so boring. He confided in me that he was tipped to be the next Ambassador of Lebanon to the United States. He feared that he may fall asleep at those negotiations and thereby ruin his chances of promotion to Washington. Therefore he made all manner of excuses and finally sent his Minister-Counsellor instead. That poor fellow not only fell asleep but snored rather loudly!"

"Jungle" listening to you I well remember our very dynamic Foreign Minister Ranjan Wijeratne telling me that he felt so bored and so sleepy attending the Peace talks with the LTTE in Colombo in 1990. Therefore whenever the LTTE came to Colombo he took to the hills! Ranjan Wijeratne was indeed so bold and so courageous. He dreaded not the LTTE, he dreaded falling asleep before the LTTE!" (Loud laughter)

Late in March 2003, I left for Jaffna fully briefed by our Intelligence. In Jaffna the mood was very different from what I had seen one month earlier. The students were volatile, sometimes violent, however the LTTE was subdued. The LTTE was no longer talking in terms of capturing Jaffna in three days of fighting. The LTTE cadres I met in Jaffna, for instance in their office, were significantly quiet and so mature in their approach. In fact they chose to speak to me about cricket, especially the performance of the Sri Lanka team in the recent World Cup.

It appeared that, the LTTE was not preparing for war, as of now. That was also evident in Kilinochchi. Even my friend S.P. Tamilchelvan, who is sometimes emotional, was cautious about what the LTTE will do next. I left Kilinochchi for Thandikulam, the border check point near Vavuniya, in one of their Jeeps which was captured from the Army some years ago and still carried Army number plates!. At Thandikulam I took the night train for Colombo. The train was complete with a sleeping car in the first class configuration. I slept so soundly because I was thoroughly convinced, that as of now, the LTTE was not preparing for war!

The Peace talks which began in September 2002 went on for six sessions till March 2003. Therefore it is pertinent to analyse what was achieved in tangible terms during these six months.

The de-mining process went on smoothly during the six months under review. That was a source of joy for both the Government of Sri Lanka and the LTTE and clearly showed people the tangible benefits from the Ceasefire Agreement.

The rehabilitating of 865,000 citizens of Sri Lanka was a lead project in ushering in Peace to Sri Lanka. Much spade work was undertaken. However, the success story was anything but, spectacular. For example, the LTTE itself was particularly keen that the 92,000 Muslims are rehabilitated in their traditional homes as early as practicable and the LTTE for once admitted that the ethnic cleansing policy which was enforced in 1990 was their mistake. However, at the end of the first six months not a single Muslim who was classified as a internally displaced person was rehabilitated in the North. The corresponding figure for the Tamils was 101,000. Thus regrettably the Government of Sri Lanka was both slow and fumbling in handling the rehabilitation of the 865,000 internally displaced persons.

There was just one bone of contention between the Government of Sri Lanka and the LTTE in this entire exercise of rehabilitation. There were approximately 50,000 internally displaced persons from the Tamil community who had their original homes in the High Security Zones in the Jaffna peninsula. Major General Sarath Fonseka, Security Forces Commander in Jafna, justifiably objected to resettling them in the High Security Zones because the LTTE had long range artillery and sophisticated weapons at short range and hence our Military establishments in the peninsula were vulnerable. Lieutenant General Satish Nambiar upheld that objection but arrived at a lower figure of approximately 45,000 who could not return home. Thus altogether over 700,000 Tamil refugees could return home safely. That programme was not properly implemented and as of this writing a further 360,000 have to return home. Much worse the Government did not implement their decision to withdraw the Army from occupying publicly and privately owned building within the Municipal limits of Jaffna. For example Gnanam Hotel, Jaffna, continues to be a Brigade Headquarters.

The signing of the Ceasefire on February 22nd, 2002 necessarily entailed a drastic reduction in the authority of the LTTE even in the Northen Province, let alone the Eastern Province. With the Ceasefire the guns became silent. Some never could comprehend this very significant change. One such was the war hero Colonel Karikalan, their field commander in Batticaloa. After several warnings issued by Prabhakaran himself, he was removed from his Command in October 2002, just after the first sessions of Peace talks. He was replaced by another war hero, Colonel Karuna. On the other hand the strategy of Prabhakaran was a disaster in another sensitive field. At the first sessions of Peace talks in September 2002 the LTTE publicly renounced its claim for a separate State of Tamil Eelam and instead opted for a Federal solution. However, the LTTE levied a "Customs Duty"on imports. It is an irritant to passengers at Thandikulam and Muhamalai. The Sinhalese and Muslim passengers openly criticise the LTTE and the Tamil passengers remain silent but resentful. Besides the LTTE imposes "a turn over tax" on businessmen wherever they have influence, for example in the city of Jaffna and in the towns of Batticaloa and Trincomalee. This has natural effect of increasing the cost of living. For example "the turn over tax" on the three wheel taxies in the District of Batticaloa is Rs. 2,000/- per month. It results in the three wheeler fares in Batticaloa being twice to thrice the fares in Colombo. In the predominantly Muslim town Eravur and Kathankudi three wheeler operators openly refuse to pay this tax to the LTTE, hence the fares are appreciably less. Throughout the District of Batticaloa, Muslims and Tamils live side by side. The Muslims openly condemn the LTTE for their "taxes". According to the Muslims and the Sinhalese, who now account for approximately 67% of the population of the Eastern Province, the LTTE consists of not merely brigands but also of anti-social elements.

It was foolhardy for the Government of Sri Lanka to have been bending over backwards to accommodate the LTTE in September 2002. After the euphoria of the first sessions of Peace talks, the LTTE applied to the Government of Sri Lanka to operate a radio station in Kilinochchi. Permission was duly granted. Then the Government of Sri Lanka outrageously violated the Vienna Convention which governs the conduct of diplomacy, by requesting the Embassy of Norway to import this equipment on a duty free basis on behalf of the LTTE. In my entire career in diplomacy covering eight foreign posting in four continents and over a period of twenty five years, never have I heard of the host nation so flagrantly violating the Vienna Convention. In Sri Lanka the documentation for duty free imports is routinely handled by the Ministry of Foreign Affairs and outraged officials leaked the news to the media. Justifiably the Government of Sri Lanka was hauled over the coals.

As usual the Sinhalese and Hindu New Year was celebrated joyfully on April 13 and 14th 2003. The LTTE was still silent about the Naval action by the SLNS *"Sayura"* one month earlier. Finally their verdict was delivered on April 21st 2003. The LTTE unilaterally suspended the Peace talks and refused to attend the Pleadging Conference to be held in Tokyo, Japan on June 10th and 11th 2003. In the open letter addressed to Prime Minister Ranil Wickremasinghe, Dr Anton Balasingham stated:

"In accordance with the decision of our leadership, I am advised bring nto your urgent attention the displeasure and dismay felt by our organization on some critical issues relating to the on-going peace process.

You are well aware that the Ceasefire that has been in force for more than one year and the six rounds of peace negotiations between the principal parties has been successful, irrespective of the occurrence of some violent incidents that endangered the peace process. The stability of the Ceasefire and the progress of the peace talks, you will certainly appreciate are the positive outcome of the sincere and firm, determination of the parties to seek a permanent resolution to the ethnic conflict through peaceful means.

The cordial inter-relationship, frank and open discussions and the able and wise guidance of the facilitators fostered trust and confidence between the negotioators and helped to advance the talks on substantial levels. The negotiating teams were able to form important sub-committees on the basis of the equal and joint partnership. During the early negotiating sessions it was agreed that the Government of the Sri Lanks and the LTTE should work together and approach the international community in partnership. The Oslo donor Conference held on 25 November 2002 turned out to be an ideal forum for such joint endeavour.

The LTTE had acted sincerely and in good faith extending its full co-operation to the Government of Sri Lanka to seek international assistance to restore normaly and to rehabilitate the war affected people of the north-east. The LTTE to date has joined with the Government and participated in the preparation of joint appeals and progammes. In spite of our goodwill and trust, your Government has opted to marginalize our organization in approaching the intenational community for economic assistance. We refer to the exclusion of the LTTE from the crucial international donor conference held in Wahington on 14th April 2003 in preparation for the major donor conference to be held in Japan in June. We view the exclusion of the LTTE, the principal partner to peace and the authentic representatives of the Tamil people from discussions on critical matters, affecting the economic and social welfare of the Tamil nation, as a grave breach of good faith. Your Government, as well as our facilitator Norway, are fully aware of the fact that the United States has legal constraints to invite representatives of a proscribed organization to their country. In these circumstances an appropriate venue could have been selected to facilitate the LTTE to participate in this important preparatory aid conference. But the failure on the part of your Government to do so gives us cause for suspicion that this omission was deliberate. The exclusion of the LTTE from the conference has severely eroded the confidence of our people in the peace process.

As you are aware, considerable optimism and hopes were raised amoung the people when your Government, shortly after assuming power, entered into a ceasefire agreement with our organization, bringing to an end twenty years of savage and bloody conflict. Expectations were further raised when both sides began direct negotiations with Norwegian facilitation. In particular, there was a justifiable expectation that the peace process would address the urgent and immediate existential problems facing the people who are internally displaced by the conflict and are languishing in welfare centers and refugee camps.

As such, the Ceasefire included crucial conditions of restoring normalcy which required the vacating, by occupying Sri Lankan troops, of Tamil homes, schools, places of worship and public buildings. Despite the agreed time frame for the evacuation of troops, which has since passed, there has been no change in the ground situation. We have repeatedly raised the issue of continuing suffering of our people at every round of talks with your Government. Your negotiators repeated assurance that the resttlement of the displaced people would be expedited have proven futile.

The negotiations have been successful in so far as significant progress has been made in key areas, such as the agreement to explore federalism on the basis of right to self-determination of our people. But this progress has not been matched by any improvement in the continuing hardships being faced by our people as a result of your Government's refusal to implement the normalization aspects of the Ceasefire and subsequent agreements reached at the talks. As a result, considerable disillusionment has set in amongst the Tamil people, and in particular the displaced, who have lost all hope that the peace process will alleviate their immense suffering.

Though there is peace due to the silencing of the guns, normalcy has not returned to Tamil areas. Tens of thousands of government troops continue to occupy our towns, cities and residential areas suffocating the freedom of mobility of our people. Such a massive military occupation of Tamil lands, particularly in Jaffna a densely populated district during peace times denying the right of our displaced people to return to their homes, is unfair and unjust.

In our view, the condition of reality prevailing in Tamil areas are qualitatively different from southern Sri Lanka. The Tamils faced the brunt of the brutal war. Twenty years of intense and incessant war has caused irreparable destruction to the infrastructure in the North and East. This colossal destruction augmented by continued displacement of the people and their inability to pursue their livehood due to military restrictions and activities have caused untold misery and extreme poverty amoung the people of the North and East. Continued displacement has also depleted them from regaining their lives on their own. The war-affected people need immediate help to regain their dignity. They need restoration of essential services to re-establish their lives. Reconstruction of infrastructure such as roads, hospitals schools and houses are essential for them to return to normal life.

The poverty that is prevailing in southern Sri Lanka is a self-inflicted phenomenon, caused by the disastrous policies of the past Governments (both the UNP and the SLFP) in dealing with the Tamil national conflict. In its fanatical drive to prosecute an unjust war against the Tamil people, the Sinhalese wasted all national wealth on a futile cause. The massive borrowings to sustain an absured policy of 'war for peace' by the former Government caused huge international indebtedness. The economic situation of the south has been further worsened by the mismanagement of state funds, bad governance and institutional corruption. Therefore, the conditions prevailing in the South are distinctly different from North-East where the scale and magnitude of the infrastructure destruction is monumental and the poverty is acute. Ignoring this distinctive reality, your Government poses poverty as a common phenomenon across the country and attempts to seek a solution with a common approach. This approach grossly understates the severity of the problems faced by the people in the north-east.

The "Regaining Sri Lanka" document completely lacks any form of identified goals for the North-East. Statistics presented for substantiating the policy totally ignore the North-East and solely concentrate on the South. However, this has been promoted as the national strategy to the international community to seek aid. It is evident from this that the Government lacks any comprehensive strategy for serious development of the North-East. The Poverty reduction Strategy fails to address the poverty of the North-East as distinct from the rest. In seeking international assistance your Government disingenuously speaks of reconstruction being needed in all areas, thereby making the total destruction of the infrastructure of the North-East which has resulted from the militarist policies of the past three decades.

As we pointed out above, the exclusion of the LTTE from critical aid conference in Washington, the non implementation of the terms and conditions enunciated in the truce document, the continuous suffering and hardship experienced by hundreds of thousands of internally displaced Tamils, the aggressive. Sinhala military occupation of Tamil cities and civilian settlements, the distortion and marginalisation of the extreme condition of poverty and deprivation of the Tamils of the North-East in the macro economic policies and strategies of the Government have seriously undermined the confidence of the Tamil people and the LTTE leadership in the negotiating process. Under these circumstances the LTTE leadership has decided to suspend its participation in the negotiations for the time being. We will not be attending the donor conference in Japan in June. While we regret that we were compelled to make this painful decision, we wish to reiterate our commitment to seek a negotiated political solution to the ethnic question. We also urge the Government of Sri Lanka to restore confidence in the peace process amongst the Tamil people by fully implementing, without further delay, the normalization aspects of the Ceasefire Agreement and permit the immediate resettlement of the internally displaced people of the North-East.

We also request the Government to re-evaluate its economic developments strategy to reconstruct the Tamil nation destroyed by war"

That comprehensive statement on behalf of the LTTE issued by Dr Anton Balasingham was indeed a tale of woe. Admittedly, the Government of Sri Lanka is to be blamed in a few instances, for example for fumbling on the withdrawal of troops from the Municipal limits of the city of Jaffna, and locating them elsewhere in the Jaffna peninsula. This involves less than ten percent of troops based in the Jaffna peninsula.

The LTTE must be blamed for having heaped calumny upon themselves ever since the Ceasefire was signed publicly on February 22nd 2002, by Prime Minister Ranil Wickremasinghe and Vellupillai Prabhakaran.

Prabhakaran himself has made a colossal error in embarking on a policy of negotiating for Peace and simulataneously smuggling arms and ammunition in huge quantities. According to Military Intelligence as many as six shiploads have been smuggled into the Northern Province in the twelve months after the singing of the Ceasefire Agreement. I well remember during the Christmas and New Year festivities in December 2002-January 2003, the Commander of the Army and his Chief of Staff, the Commander of the Navy and the Chief of Staff of the Air Force, complaining loudly at parties that the smuggling of arms and ammunition was being carried out rampantly by the LTTE. Of course something had to be done and the SLNS "*Sayura*" did the needful on March 10th 2003 and the SLNS "*Nandamithra*" repeated it on June 14th 2003.

The Government of the United States insisted in hosting that Preparatory Conference in Washington in April 2003. It is common knowledge that the Spring Conference was held every year in the month of April. Somehow the LTTE, even the learned Dr Anton Balasingham, was unaware of this. It is a separate issue that Washington is hyper-critical of the LTTE for not showing any evidence whatsoever in dismantling their terrorist infrastructure especially their death squads and suicide squads, in the first year of an effective Ceasefire. Therefore, it was the pleasure of Washington to rub salt into the wounds of the LTTE and keep them away from the meeting in Washington. They merely quoted their Immigration laws which forbid the entry into the United States of any member of an organization banned by the United States.

The loud complaint made by Dr Anton Balasingham about the slow progress made in rehabilitation work in the North and East, is true. It is just as true, that this is due to the "Development tax" imposed by Velupillai Prabhakaran himself in the LTTE controlled areas. In the example already discussed seven local road construction companies were duly awarded ADB contracts worth US$ 6 million to reconstruct 140 kilometers of the highway A-9 on the stretch Thandikulam to Jaffna in six months ending June 30th 2003. All contractors were way behind schedule, because of the "Development tax" which they cannot absorb. In Batticaloa the LTTE have asked for a "Development tax" of Rs. 15 million to normalize the railway service Colombo-Batticaloa-Colombo on the stretch Valaichchenai-Eravur-Batticaloa and *vice versa.* On three occasions during the year 2003 the railway service Colombo-Batticaloa-Colombo was re-opened. On all three occasions after a few days the LTTE surreptitiously removed sleepers, thus the service had to be suspended. On one occasion I was on board the first class sleeping car. At Valaichchenai after a long wait we passengers bound for Batticaloa were told that the train could not proceed further. Some angry passengers pounced on the helpless Station Master. They wanted an immediate refund and Government regulations precluded that being done immediately. I was also angry for a different set of reasons. I had a ten o'clock appointment in Batticaloa. The only option open to me was to hire a three wheel taxi and I was surrounded by such operators who quoted an exorbitant fare of Rs. 600 for the 30 kilometre journey. (The hire from Colombo to the Bandaranaike International Airport which is also 30 kilometers away is Rs. 300). My knowledge of Tamil is very limited and I deliberately spoke in Sinhala and thereby found just one three wheeler operator, a Muslim who could speak a smattering of Sinhala. While traveling in his three wheeler to a nearby Church, I asked him why taxi fares were so exorbitant in Valaichchenai. All he said was "Aiyar, LTTE tax", "Aiyar LTTE tax" Then he spontaneously used some choice four letter words in Sinhala and Tamil to describe the LTTE.! Anyway he took me to the Church on time. From there I telephoned my friends in Batticoloa. They apologized profusely and sent me a vehicle all the way to Valaichchenai. They were my gracious hosts from the LTTE!!

Norway as the facilitator and Japan as the principal donor of aid to Sri Lanka made every conceivable endeavour to pursuade the LTTE to participate in the Pledging Conference to be held in Tokyo on June 10th and 11th 2003 even if they abstain from the seventh sessions of Peace talks scheduled for April 29th to 2nd May 2003. The galaxy of VIP's who came to Kilinochchi included Deputy Foreign Minister Viday Helgessen of Norway, who normally heads their delegation to the Peace talks, Ambassador Jon Westborg from the Ministry of Foreign Affairs of Norway and Special Advisor Eric Solheim from Norway. Japan sent her roving Ambassador Yasushi Akashi who was a regular visitor to Kilinochchi, and Ambassador Seiichiro Otsuka, the Ambassador of Japan to Sri Lanka. By the end of April 2003 it appeared that the LTTE was firm on the suspension of Peace talks but there was still a possibility that the LTTE would participate in the Pledging Conference of aid to Sri Lanka to be held in Tokyo, six weeks hence.

It was against this background that Prime Minister Ranil Wicremasinghe issued his formal response of May 1st 2003 address to Dr Anton Balasingham.

"I write further to my letter of April 22nd 2003 in response to yours of April 21st 2003, in which you had expressed your organisation's concern in relation to some critical issues on the ongoing peace process.

I must at the outset express my complete agreement with you that during the 14 months in which the Ceasefire Agreement has been consolidated as a result of the sincerity and determination shown by both sides, there has been substantial progress towards peace and development throughout the country. For instance. The Ceasefire has held for a period of 14 months, the daily toll of dead and maimed combatants and civilians has been brought to a halt.

- SLMM procedures have been strengthened and its activities and coverage, expanded: critical situations which would earlier have led to conflict have been defused and resolved.
- Places of worship and schools occupied by the Military have been handed over.
- The Government and LTTE have established SIHRN an institution for decision making in which both have equal participation.
- Through a joint approach by the Government and the LTTE to the Donors, a funding mechanism NERF has been established.
- Some of the issues pertaining to the Muslims have been addressed.
- Detailed study of Federal and Government structures has been undertaken by both sides.
- The Joint Gender Committee has been set up.
- Positive working relationships have been established between the parties at operational level.
- The international donors, both multilateral and bilateral, have already disbursed substantial funding (in excess of US$ 30 million) for humanitarian and rehabilitation work in the North-East.
- Although it has not been possible to reach agreement on all matters our joint resolve to cooperate has provided the space and confidence for the international community participate in rehabilitation and development. The 14 month period of peace has therefore been one of steady progress and hope to our people.

Let me take up one by one, the various reasons which appear to have led your organization to take what you have termed as a "painful decision",

1. Exclusion of the LTTE from the Preparatory Seminar in Washington.

As you would know, the Government of Japan suggested preparatory seminars in Washington, Brussels and Oslo prior to the Tokyo Conference. The Government of Norway later felt that it would forego this opportunity since the Oslo meeting last November had virtually served this purpose. Subsequently for various logistical reasons mainly connected with the Iraq crisis, the decision to hold a meeting in Europe was changed and it was proposed to have a preparatory meeting in Colombo in May. These arrangements were discussed at the meeting at Hakone.

There were two other significant reasons for going ahead with the Washington seminar in April. The first, was the fact that such a seminar would enable the gathering of major Donors who would be present in Washington as participants in the important Spring meetings of the World Bank and IMF. The other reason was that it was important to obtain commitment of the Donors to this process before their attention as absorbed by the needs of Iraq as a consequence of the situation following that conflict.

The Washington preparatory seminar was not a pledging conference. The multilateral organizations present at the seminar announced their indicative figures under their Country Programme at the meeting.

The LTTE's inability to attend the seminar was due to the fact that the organization still remains a banned organization under the United States Law. I regret the LTTE could not participate and you will appreciate that the Government cannot be blamed for this situation.

From the inception the Government was committed to working with the LTTE in rebuilding the North-East. In fact the Tokyo Conference offered by the Government of Japan as a pledging conference for the Reconstruction and Development of Sri Lanka took this fact into consideration. The conference is to be opened by the Prime Minister of Japan.

2. The non-implementation of the terms and conditions enunciated in the truce document. Both sides have obligations to fulfil the terms of the Ceasefire. While there has been increasing compliance, I agree with you that there is yet much to be done to implement fully, the provisions of the Ceasefire. Our view is that both parties should commit themselves to doing so. The presence of the Sri Lanka Monitoring Mission has undoubtedly helped in ensuring to the extent possible the observances of the Ceasefire in all its aspects. The final objective of course is

normalization of the ground situation. However in view of the fact that the conflict has been long drawn out, normalization is bound to be a difficult process. Both sides, I know, have been impatient at the pace at which normalization has taken place an it would be necessary to renew our joint commitment to make progress.

3. The suffering and hardship experienced by hundreds of thousands of internally displaced Tamils. The highest priority has been given by the government, your organization and the international community to alleviate the conditions of the internally displaced, as quickly as possible. We ourselves have pledged at the last election to:

(a) Take steps to made life easier for the people of the North and East, and
(b) Solve the problems of people who have been displaced and rendered helpless by war. In fact there has been progress. The Government has taken substantial loans from the World Bank and ADB for re-settlement of internally displaced persons and the numbers have been reduced significantly.

There is also the further question of de-mining of the lands in which internally displaced persons would be settling and an effective programme is underway with several international donors committed to humanitarian mine action. Indeed the work of your own TRO and its humanitarian de-mining unit working in the Vanni in this endeavour, is highly appreciated.

Of course there is much more to be done to make life better for the people. There have been delays in implementation due to the breakdown in government administration as a result of the twenty year conflict. In the last few weeks we have been discussing the masures to strengthen the effectiveness of implementation and to establish an effective coordination mechanism for administration in the Northern districts.- the districts worst affected by the war. The Government will keep the LTTE briefed on these proposals prior to implementation.

We will also convey to you our views on making SIRHN more effective and look forward to reaching agreement on the modification that are needed. As Mr Bernard Goonetilleka's letter of 28th April 2003 would have informed Mr S P Tamilchelvam, we have formulated procedures to commence the 15 approved projects with the formal arrangements for NERF are being finalized. The Norwegian facilitator will be apprising you of the manner in which we are overcoming this problem.

4. The aggressive Military occupation of Northern cities and civilian settlement:

Ever since the Ceasefire, the policy of the Government has been to restore normalcy in order that the civilian population would be enable to carry on their customary livelihood. The visible signs of this are, the increased production in fisheries and the bumper paddy harvest that has been experienced in the recent Maha season in the Vanni.

Though there are yet steps to be taken to reduce the constraints now necessitated by security consideration, the differences in people's lives over the past year is, I believe quite evident. The Government is committed, as I mentioned earlier, to resolve the issues of the persons displaced by the war. Mr Austin Fernando, Secretary Defence by his letter dated 27th April 2003 informed Mr S P Tamilchelvam the intention of the Army to release the two Hotels in Jaffna town and the surrounding houses. Prefabricated buildings to house the troops have already been ordered. The report prepared by General Nambiar on the review of the High Security Zones, as mentioned in the Talks of 6-9th January 2003 will also be available when the talks resume.

5. The marginalisation of the people of North-East in the macro economic policies and strategies of the Government:

A careful reading of the "Regaining Sri Lanka" document which contains the vision and strategy for acceleration of development will indicate the degree to which conflict related development has been emphasized. "Regaining Sri Lanka" is the National Economic Policy Framework of the Government. Its objective is to achieve and sustain a high rate of growth for a decade or so which will enable:

(a) The creation of employment opportunities and
(b) Generation of sufficient economic resources for long-term development of the North East.

The specific strategies and plans for promoting economic development in the North East will be worked out in consultation with the LTTE. There is no intention to exclude the LTTE from the process.

One of the achievements for the Government and the LTTE was the ability to cooperate in commissioning the Multi Agency Needs Assessment to identify the rconstruction and rehabilitation requirement of the North East. Once the two parties agree on the Report, it will become the official planning framework for the rebuilding of the North-East. Reference to the planning framework will be included in the Regaining Sri Lanka documents. This planning framework will also be submitted to the Tokyo Donor Meeting in addition to the Regaining Sri Lanka document.

In the face of these very positive developments, albeit not at the pace which we might have desired, it is currently unfortunate that the LTTE leadership has decided to suspended its participation in the negotiations for the time-being.

I am however, encouraged by the reiteration of your commitment to seek a negotiated political solution to the question, and in furtherance of this, hope that you would at this decisive time, review your present stance, and continue a partnership which has as you have conceded already achieved considerable success.

I believe finally that this would be in complete accord with the firm desire of all our people that the peace process continues without interruption"

That was the official view point of The Government. It was matched with the official viewpoint of The Opposition, which had serious reservations about the Ceasefire ever since its inception. These views were articulated by Lakshman Kadirgamar, Foreign Minister from 1994-2001 in which capacity he rendered yeomen service to Sri Lanka. Many look upon him as a personification of a patriot, the only Tamil who has publicly condemnet the terrorism of the Tamils.There was pin drop silence when he addressed the Parliament on May 8th 2003. He spoke from a carefully prepared text. That itself was unusual for this former President of the Oxford Union, who is such an eloquent speaker in English. He said:

"In January 2002, I had the privilege of opening the debate for the Opposition on the Prime Minister's policy statement. On that occasion I said that the Opposition would do nothing to disturb the peace process that was just being resumed. The new Government must have time to settle in. we have kept that pledge. The Prime Minister was generous enough, during one of our routine consultations, to say so. I also said that the time comes when the substantive issues will have to be addressed. We reserved our opinion on those issues. That time has come. Hard issues have surfaced. They must be addressed. The Opposition owes a duty to the people to raise them and address them.

Our contention is that from the very signing of the Ceasefire Agreement on 22nd February 2002 the sovereignty of Sri Lanka has been steadily and visibly eoded to the point where Sri Lanka is in danger of being reduced to a nominal soverign shell, the major attributes of a sovereign state the capacity to govern, to resolve justifiable issues to enforce the law, to protect its citizens throughout the entirety of its territory as being drained away by stealth, fractured by assault and worn down by attrition.

This process commenced with and is being facilitated by the Ceasefire Agrement (CFA) itself a structurally flawed document whose imperfections have now been clearly revealed and are being deeply felt, as the weeks and months go by. The Prime Minister himself recently said that the CFA is not a perfect document and that if he strives for perfection there might have been no Ceasefire at all. Yes I agree. But if the Prime Minister had thought it fit to consult the President about the CFA before it was signed which did not happen some of the imperfections could have been removed, and a better balanced document drawn up, not only to serve the interest of the LTTE, but the interests of the nation as a whole. A bipartisan approach to the problem could have been established at an early stage. However, while the Prime Minister was prepared to extend his trust and confidence unreservedly to the LTTE, even to the extent of dismantling with unnecessary alacrity, the security structures that had been erected to protect the City of Colombo the consequences of which the public are now beginning to understand, his Government did not extend an iota of trust and confidence to the Head of State, the Head of the Govrnment, the Head of the Cabninet and the Commander in Chief of the Armed Forces over the so-called peace process. Instead the Governemnt embarked upon a campaign vituperative abuse against the President and harassment of Opposition supporters which receded only when it became clear that a two third majority in Parliament was not forthcoming for certain Constitutional amendments.

Within a few days of the signing of the CFA the President outlined in a letter to the Prime Minister some of the flaws in the Agreement. They were as follows:

(1) The question of naval operations Article 1.2 of the CFA itemizes a number of prohibited military operations, including "offensive naval operations" Article 1.32 graciously permits the Sri Lanka Armed Forces to continue to perform their legitimate task of safeguarding the sovereignty in offensive naval operations" How is the Navy to safeguard the sovereignty and territorial integrity of Sri Lanka if it is prohibited from engaging in offensive operations against the LTTE if required?

If a suspicious ship approaches our shores laden with arms, defies challenge and inspection and opens fire on the Navy, and the Navy sinks that ship, is that a prohibited offensive operation? If not, is it a defensive operation? If it is a defensive operation then what is an offensive operation? If the Navy gives chase in the open seas to an LTTE ship carrying arms in exercise of the right to of hot pursuit, to prevent if from lading those arms on our shores, is that an offensive or defensive operation? Why was this grey area created in the CFA? In the course of a statement made by the Prime Minister at Vavuniya on 22nd February 2002 when he signed the CFA-Mr Prabhakaran having signed it the same day in the presence of the Norwegian Ambassador he said"The Army, Navy and the Air Force will have the right to intercept the illegal movement of arms into Sri Lanka". What does "intercept" mean? Could there be interception by offensive naval operations, in which case there is a contradiction between the CFA and the Prime Ministr's statement. The Prime Minister's oral statement in Vavuniya have been incorporated into the CFA itself? Did the LTTE object? What was the Norwegian position on this issue? The Prime Minister's statement in Vavuniya being outside the CFA naturally does not bind the LTTE. Did the Prime Minister seriously believe that the LTTE could be trusted not to smuggle arms by sea into Sri Lanka so that meaning of the expression "offensive naval operations" would never have to be tested?

(2) Under Article 3.2 of the CFA if a dispute arises on a question involving the interception of illegal arms (for instance what is the offensive naval operation?) it will be the Head of the Monitoring Mission, a foreign national, who will be the final authority regarding the interpretation of the Agreement? Thus the jurisdiction of the Courts of Sri Lanka has been ousted on a question so vital to national security and the protection of the territorial integrity and sovereignty of Sri Lanka.

(3) Articles 1.4, 1.5 and 1.6 of the CFA deal with the drawing up of demarcation lines regarding defence localities in all areas of contention. The parties are required to provide information to the Monitoring Mission about their defence localities. In the event of disagreement between the parties the demarcation lines will have to be drawn by the Head of the Monitoring Mission who is the final authority regarding the interpretation of the Agreement.

Article 2.7 refers to the establishment of checkpoints to facilitate the flow of goods and the movement of civilians on the "line of control". The line of control is highly evocative expression in our region and elsewhere in the world where lines of control and demarcation have been source of confusion, bitterness and tragedy. Inevitably, a line of control becomes a line of division and of separation. This is the first time in the history of post independence Sri Lanka that a foreign government has been authorized to draw demarcation lines on the soil of Sri Lanka. The submission of such matters to the binding authority of a single individual appointed by a foreign Government is wholly inconsistent with the sovereignty of Sri Lanka which is vested in its People and is declared by the Constitution to be inalienable.

(4) The powers and functions which by this Agreement are vested in the Norwegian Government travel far beyond the role of a facilitator of the envisaged negotiations toward a political agreement. The Norwegian Government has now been cast in the role of a mediator or arbitrator and the Monitoring Mission has been given the role of a Judge in the resolution of disputes between the parties which is not the basis on which Norwegian assistance was sought in the first place. The nature of the Norwegian government's mandate has changed to such an extent and its role has become so inflated as to make it incompatible with the sovereign status of Sri Lanka.

(5) In the light of the verified evidence coming in from various LTTE controlled areas, especially in the East, relating to extortion, intimidation, abduction and harassment of civilians, much of it against members of the Muslim community but extending also to the Tamil and Sinhalese communities in these areas, we surely have to ensure that our people are protected by the strict application of Article 2.1 of the CFA which expressly prohibits such acts. Among the six districts (Jaffna, Mannar, Vavuniya, Trincomalee, Batticaloa and Amparai) in which the Monitoring Mission maintains a presence and local monitoring committees have been established. Kilinochchi and Mulaitivu, which are LTTE-controlled, are not included. This means that if "hostile acts against civilians population including such acts as torture, intimidation, abduction, extortion and harassment" referred to in Article 2.1 are committed in those two districts the Monitoring Mission and the local communities cannot intervene to help our citizens who live in these areas. We have thus recognized and legitimized an enclave in those two areas where the Govrnment's writ does not run. What does this do to our sovereignty over the entirety of our territory?

(6) What about the plight of children forcibly recruited by the LTTE? This odious practice is continuing. The evidence gathered by

reputable national and international sources is irrefutable and depressing. Sri Lanka has been in the forefront of the intrnational campaign against the conscription of child combatants. There are so many treaties and international resolutions on this subject. This is a matter which gravely troubles the conscience of mankind. The LTTE has given to the United Nations, but disregarded in practice, assurances that they will not recruit under-age children. Can we, I ask the House, be so cllous, so cynical that in the pursuit of peace, we are willing to compromise the rights of these children, to condone the brutal treatment meted out to them and their parents?

(7) The extensive freedom of movement for "political work" in Government controlled areas in the North and the East granted to LTTE members under Article 1.13 is not afforded to others (political parties, for instance) who might wish to do "political work" in LTTE controlled areas in the North and East. In a democratic society this is a totally indefensible distinction, violative of the Constitution, between one group of political parties and another. Democratic parties like the EPDP which entered the main stream of national politics many years ago now find themselves at a considerable disadvantage in relation to the LTTE. Disarmed by the CFA they are at the mercy of the LTTE. They have lost a number of cadres. The government appears to be unconcerned with these terrible violation of the CFA. Is the Governemnt unwilling or unable to help the EPDP to protect its cadres? Has the Government abdicated its sovereign right, its duty, to the bring the culprits to justice even if they be the LTTE?

(8) This erosion of sovereignty to which I have referred must also be viewed against the backdrop of the significant omission in the agreement of any reference to any assurance given the negotiations for a political settlement will be commenced by the parties by a fixed date and concluded by an agreed date. Even the apparent suspension of the authority of the State reflected in this document could lead to the accentuation of the movement towards secession on which the Agreement is singularly silent despite the innumerable "confidence building measures" which have been explicitly stated with great particularity. In his statement to the House in January 2002 the Prime Minister said "After formalizing the basic Agreement as regards peace talks, the talks should be held within a definite timeframe between the

government and the LTTE. Nearly 15 months have passed. Where is the time frame? It is nowhere in sight.

The structural flaws in the Ceasefire Agreement to which I referred at the opening of my speech are now being dramatically revealed as events unfold on the ground and at sea. The burning issue of the day is the question of the sea. In its so-called initial discussion paper the Head of the Sri Lanka Monitoring Mission made a series of proposals which the Opposition parties, in their press release of 25th April 2003, have described as "preposterous" One of them was that "in the spirit" of the CFA the Governemnt of Sri Lanka and especially its Navy, should recognize the LTTE Sea Tigers as a de facto naval unit". Another was that "the LTTE should be excluded from the law concerning limitations on the horse power of outboard motors". Yet another was that "the Sri Lanka Navy and the LTTE Sea Tigers should have specific marked exercise and training areas at sea, designed for navigation training and for live firing exercise as well".

These propositions can be faulted on a number of grounds.

1. Is it "in the spirit of the CFA" that the LTTE should systematically smuggle arms into the country? If not, why should it be "in the spirit of the CFA" that the Navy should recognize the LTTE as a de facto naval unit?

2. the SLMM has cited the Oxford English Dictionary meaning of de facto ("existing as a fact, although it may not be legally accepted as existing") to justify its proposal. A criminal gang may exist as a fact. Does the Police force have to "recognize" it? and having "recognized" it what is the Police Force expected to do? Ignore it or pursue it and bring it to justice? The plain fact is that the LTTE naval unit is an illegal entity. No country in the world has two navies. To which country does the LTTE's naval unit belong? De facto recognition by a sovereign State of an illegal entity which mounts a challenge to the authority of the state is only a whisker away from the achievement of *de* jure status by that officially recognized illegal entity.

3. When the CFA was entered into there were no areas marked out at sea for training exercises and live firing by the LTTE and the navy. The Navy made no such concessions to the LTTE. The preservation of the balance of forces is said to be one of the principal concepts underlying the Ceasefire Agreement. If that

be so, does not the delimitation one of these zones at sea disturb that balance.

4. In any event, why should a sovereign State hand over to an illegal entity an exclusive zone that derogates from its sovereignty? The real problem is that the Govrnment of the day is by its conduct, its palpable anxiety to accommodate even the most unreasonable demands of the LTTE, encouraging the LTTE to believe that it is a legal entity with legal rights.

5. Even if the exercise and live firing areas are within our teritorial waters in large numbers. What would happen it they enter the LTTE zone during live firing practice? There could be a major rapture in our relations with India, especially with Tamil Nadu. The Chief Minister of Tamil Nadu has clearly made known her deep concern that LTTE craft are capturing Indian fishermen. A shooting incident in a LTTE zone recognized by the Government of Sri Lanka could have a disastrous consequences to on our relations with India and Tamil Nadu. Moreover, fishing craft belonging to other countries China, Japan, South Korea enter our waters on legitimate business. We must remember what recently happened to a Chinese trawler. If the "armed criminal gang unknown to Sri Lanka" which is said by the Head of the Monitoring Mission to be prowling our coastal waters enters the LTTE zone will there be a shoot-out between these two illegal entities? We would be encouraging gang warfare at sea.

6. Live firing could be with short-range long-range weapons. The LTTE has 23 millimetre guns mounted on their naval craft with a range of 6 kilometres. If these guns are fired within the execise zone the bullets could go beyond the zone and hit innocent ships fishing or cruising just outside our territorial waters.

7. We allow India to use our air space above our territorial waters. When LTTE live firing is going on are we to tell the Indian Government that our air space will be closed to them? Would this not be an unfriendly, hostile act towards a neighbour that has proscribed the LTTE?

8. When the CFA was entered into the LTTE was limited to outbound motors of 40 horse power maximum. The Nordic proposal is that they be allowed the use of outbound motors of unlimited capacity. This allows the LTTE legitimately to secure inshore craft, gunboats, fast attack craft and off shore patrol craft

which are used by blue water Navies. During the British colonial period there was only one Navy in our region. With the independence of India and Sri Lanka two Navies emerged, the Indian and Sri Lankan. Now is there to be a third Navy with a licence to expand at will? Again I ask the question, to which sovereign State does that Navy belong?

Our Navy Commander has reacted strongly to the Nordic proposals. He said: The Sea Tigers arm of the LTTE is not a legitimate organization of force to carry weapons and ammunitation at sea according to international laws at sea and also in the territory of Sri Lanka which are controlled by the Sri Lanka Navy as per 1.7 of the CFA. "At the time the MOU was signed it was very clear that the Sri Lanka Navy was in total control of the sea and is the only legitimate force at sea. Hence the issue of a de facto force is of no relevance. At the end of peace talks some day, even if Federal status is given to the North and East, there will be only one Navy and that is the Sri Lanka Navy. Therefore excluding the Sea Tigers from the normal law of the country is unacceptable and out of the question." The Monitor's proposal that the parties' vessels should be marked in accordance with the UN Convention on the Law of the Sea (1982) implies, according to the Navy Commander, that "LTTE Sea Tigers" are on par with the Sri Lanka Navy which is not so. Therefore the proposal is totally unacceptable". "As for the proposed confidence building measure that the Sri Lanka navy and the LTTE Sea Tigers should prmit observers from the other party on board their vessels while conducting exercise and training", the Navy Commander says the "proposal is not possible. Refraining from the violation of the CFA, while at sea off Iranativu on 17th July 2002 and Delft on the 6th February 2003, by the LTTE itself would be a confidence building measure between the parties". With regard to the Nodric proposal that "neither the SLN nor the LTTE Sea Tigers and that the minimum distance between the parties vessels should be kept to one nautical mile". The Navy Commander says the "Sri Lanka Navy has the right to dominance and to free movement, at sea because it has to safeguard the sovereignty and territorial integrity of the country and also in conformity with Article 1.3 of the CFA". With regard to execise and training areas, the Navy Commander says the territorial waters and the contiguous zone up to the economic zone is under Sri Lanka Navy control. No other party can be allowed to conduct military training at sea since it is against the Constitution and sovereignty of the country and Article 1.3 of the CFA.

The Government presenting its response to the SLMM paper, modified the Navy Commander's response in several respects, important among them being the Government's willingness to allow the LTTE to conduct training exercise within a designated area (which the Navy commander was opposed to) but without the right to live firing. The SLMM's adjusted proposal return to its initial working paper. It reposes a training and exercise area for the LTTE with live firing rights and prohibits both the SLN and the LTTE Sea Tigers from "offensive or aggressive operations and movement at sea".

The Opposition has already made it clear in its press release of 25th April and now reiterates its position on the floor of the House, that the Opposition parties wholeheartedly support the Navy Commander in his opposition to the proposal of the Monitoring Mission with regard to the status of the LTTE's Sea Tigers. The Opposition has already stated that and now repeats, that it has no confidence in the competence and impartiality of the Monitoring Mission. The Opposition proposes that the Monitoring Mission should be recomposed.

I turn now, Mr Speaker, to that other major security question of the day the High Security Zones, The LTTE wants the Army to withdraw from these zones to accommodate internally displaced persons (IDP's). Major General Fonseka, the Northern Security Forces Commander, supported by the Army Commander, has said in a report last December that while appreciating the urgent need to resettle civilians in these zones that process should go hand in glove with a de-escalation process agreed between the government and the LTTE; no risks should be taken to weaken the safety environment by making the zones vulnerable; security can be relaxed only in stages i.e. disarming of LTTE cadres and decommissioning of LTTE long range weapons. The Ministry of Defence has confirmed that the 152 Army camps in the peninsula have been reduced to 88.

The Government has hired the services of a retired Indian General, General Nambiar, to advise it on security matters. In his report of last December he has said that Sri Lanka Army field commanders and their commanders at headquarters, appear to be unanimous in the firm conviction that if civilians are allowed unrestricted re-entry in these areas, LTTE cadres would infiltrate, establish their control even if only convertly in the initial stages, and seriously compromise the ability of the Sri Lanka Army to conduct operations, should the peace process break down. Any vacation of these areas is therefore perceived as dereliction of their responsibility towards the troops and security of the nation. General Nambiar has proposed that "as things stand it would appear that any review of the scope and content of the High Security Zones will only come about if the LTTE deposits its weapons to neutral supervision and initiates measures to withdraw from frontline positions into nominated areas. Such a step would provide a measure of reassurance to the Sri Lanka Army that surprise LTTE attacks may be discounted. Similarly, there would need to be some reassurance that there would be no coercion of civilians and officials by the LTTE cadres given access to areas on dismantling of the Zones. General Nambiar in his first report has completely supported General Sarath Fonseka's position. Indeed the last Head of the SLMM also stated, supporting General Fonseka, that during a Ceasefire the balance of forces should not be disturbed, that if the Army were to withdraw from the Zones it would place the Army at a disadvantage. General Nambiar has also said that there are rumours that in a Federal structure the LTTE might be allowed a separate Army. He says: "In my view any such rumour should be scotched at this very stage by the Prime Minister or the Minister of Defence making it absolutely clear that no matter what constitutional system is finally agreed upon there can only be one Army for the nation, namely the Sri Lanka Army.

For mysterious reasons the Governemnt commissioned General Nambiar to prepare a second report even before the first report had been discussed with the relevant security authorities. I understand that the second report is ready. General Nambiar has returned to Colombo, between the two reports General Nambiar has been visited more than once by important Government personalities. If there are any substantial changes in the second report serious questions will arise. General Nambiar is not the representative of the Government of India. He is a private consultant engaged by the Government of Sri Lanka in his private capacity.

Mr Speaker, Sri Lanka has become a carnival ground for international players, a sort of Hawkers Street for foreign experts peddling their wares. Do we really need foreign excperts to advise us on how to protect the territorial intergrity and sovereignty of the State? Surely our own Service Commanders, native to our soil, know best what needs to be done.

What we in the Opposition say to these worthy experts, there are many from different nationalities, who come to advice the Government is this: Please remember that the sovereignty of Sri Lanka is precious to us, its citizens to the members of this House, to our people. It may be a play thing in the hands of others; to us it is not a marketable commodity; it is not negotiable; it cannot be compromised if any of these expert reports make recommendations that impinge on our sovereignty. We of the Opposition will be duty-bound by our people to denounce such reports whoever the author may be. He who pays the piper call the tune.

The Prime Minister in his statement referred to a "safety-net of the international community" and a "a firm expression of views by our friendly countries including the United States, UK, Japan, France and India". They have certainly made, and with the United States and India, in particular strongly made statements in support of our territorial integrity and sovereignty. The United States has warned the LTTE that it must renounce violence, abandon the notion of separate State and embrance the concept of a plural society if it is to gain international legitimacy and acceptance. Is it not a great shame that our Government has never made a statement of the nature? How does the Government expect other countries to uphold our sovereignty when it is shy of doing so itself? But what is this safety net? The Prime Minister must tell the House what it is? It is important for the House to know. Are there any secret understandings? Will an aircraft carrier come our way if hostilities break out again?

The Prime Minister has said that in consultation with all parties the government will proceed to develop a "road map" towards the objective of devolution and that it is open to wideranging discussions on many

the core issues. We seem to have heard this before. Is it true? If so it is welcome. The hour is late but not too late to make the process of consultation inclusive which it is not at the moment. In the meantime the Opposition is of the view that we are moving inexorably toward the day when Sri Lanka will no longer be a sovereign State." (Applause)

(Source : The Hansard)

By mid-May 2003 the LTTE was becoming intrasigent and in keeping with their usual strategy they were asking for the impossible. Now their thinking was that if they do not participate in the Pledging Conference in Tokyo, it will dilute the importance of the conference on which the Government of Sri Lanka in general and Prime Minister Ranil Wickremasinghe in particular were depending so heavily. Therefore the LTTE was placing conditions, the first being the Government of Sri Lanka agree to an Interim Council to handle the North-Eastern Province till such time as the future of the North-Eastern Province is worked out permanently. It was a very dangerous proposition because any temporary solution could damage the very foundation of a permanent solution. Also an Interim council may be unrealistic because the creation of the North-Eastern Province itself was an interim solution subject to a Referendum, as clearly spelled out in The Thirteenth Amendment to the Constitution duly passed in October 1987.

Besides, as explained earlier in this book the ascendancy of the Muslims in the Eastern Province makes the very concept of the North-Eastern Province altogether unrealistic. To my mind, reality is essentially the reestablishment of the Northern Province and the Eastern Province as two distinct entities. Admittedly to the LTTE this a preposterous proposition, by the same token two-thirds of the coastline and one third of the nation being handed over to the LTTE is a preposterous solution to the Sinhalese. Everybody is clamouring or Peace. Therefore, the burning question is Peace : At what cost?

Even as late as in the first week of June 2003 the delegation of Norway, barring their astute Foreign Minister Jan Petersen, was hoping the LTTE will send at least a token delegation to Tokyo. To all of us who are familiar with the thinking of the powers that be in Kilinochchi (I was based in Kilinochchi for one week in May 2003) predicted that the LTTE will never participate in the Pledging Conference in Tokyo.

By early June 2003 the Government of Sri Lanka was hopeful of the Pledging Conference yielding US$ 3,000-3,5000 million for a planning cycle of four years. Our key Embassies, in the context of obtaining aid, listed alphabetically, namely China, the Eurepean Community, Germany Japan, Neitherlands, United Kingdom, United Nations, United States were all confirming this figure. It was indeed a most impressive figure because the record for any calendar year was US$ 700 million in 1990 (aid was annualized then) when President R. Premadasa was negotiating for peace with the LTTE.

In recent years the world record for any nation was US$ 4,500 million for Afghanistan, for the four year planning cycle commencing 2000. Therefore Sri Lanka had every reason to be jubilant when the commitment in Tokyo was US$ 4,500 million for the four year planning cycle commencing 2003 with Japan alone pledging a staggering US$ 1,000 million. The Asian Development Bank pledged US$ 960 million, World Bank US$ 875 million, International Monetary fund US$ 563 million, the European Union 250 million euros (US$ 289 million), United Kingdom US$ 70 million, United States US$ 54 million, Germany $51 million and The Netherlands US$ 50 million.

It was truly triumph for Prime Minister Ranil Wickremasinghe for his inspired leadrship in the cause of Peace. Even his detractors conceded that his sincerety for the cause of Peace was beyond dispite.

No lasting solution can be found to our ethnic conflict without establishing peace and rconciliation among the Tamils and Muslims who constitute two distinct and separate communities, although they speak the same language.

The Government of Sri Lanka, the LTTE and even the facilatator, the Government of Norway, continues to describe our ethnic problem as being between the Sinhalese and the Tamils. That is certainly true in the Northern Province. It is anything but true the Eastern Province.

The Muslim renaissance in the Eastern Province has resulted in Muslim politics in the Eastern Province being qualitatively different from conventional Muslim politics elsewhere. For example Muslim nationalism in the Eastern Province has evolved in response to Tamil nationalism in the Northern Province. As such the conflict in the Eastern Province is essentially tripartite and hence so different from the conflict in the Northerns Province where the Civil War is basically the Government of the day versus the Tamils.

During the past ten years I had to travel extensively in all nine Provinces, to write my books "The Politics of Sri Lanka" Volumes I to VI. In my judgement, in the past ten years no Province has changed so much as the Eastern Province. That has been due to four factors:

(a) The political thinking of The late M. H. M. Ashraff, who was a visionary.
(b) The influx of foreign exchange remittances from the Middle East, the biggest source of income in the Eastern Province.
(c) The emancipation of the Muslim community in the Eastern Province, which is modernizing itself so rapidly after a slow start in the decade of the nineteen fifties, sixties and seventies.
(d) The Muslim community becoming the largest of the three communities in the Eastern Province, due to the mass exodus of the Tamil community because of the Civil War.

M.H.M. Ashraff made his first indelible mark on the national political scene at the closely contested Presidential Election of 1988 where the SLMC proved that they held the balance of power between the giants the UNP and the SLFP. The SLMC proved it again in 2001 when Cabinet Minister Rauf Hakeem was sacked and the Government of Sri Lanka collapsed.

Tamil nationalism on the one hand and the LTTE on the other have a well orchestrated campaign publicizing the concept of a Tamil-speaking Province. That was certainly valid in the time of The late S. J. V. Chelvanayakam. In contemporary times it bears no relevance to reality in the Eastern Province.

There is overwhelming evidence that under the hegemony of the LTTE, the Muslim community has been subject to extortion, abduction and murder even after the Ceasefire was signed on February 22nd 2002. Even today, sudden death at the hands of the LTTE, is a way of life for the Muslims in the Eastern Province today.

In the face of these provocations, the Sri Lanka Muslim Congress, currently the most powerful political party in the Eastern Province, has negotiated a settlement with the LTTE but without avail. The sudden decision of the LTTE to keep away from the Peace talks has placed the Muslim community in a precarious position. The justifiable apprehension of the Muslim community is all that what the LTTE is attempting in the Eastern Province is to force a decision through recourse to arms.

The LTTE decided to respond to the public statement made by Prime Minister on May 1st 2003. Gone were the days when Prabhakaran made an arbitary *ex-cathedra* statement on behalf of the LTTE. After the Aid talks in Tokyo boycotted by the LTTE, Prabhakaran directed key officials of the LTTE in Sri Lanka and abroad and also invited influential LTTE sympathizers living abroad to meet somewhere abroad, and to formulate a suitable reply.

Among the influential sympathizers who attended those meetings was Siva Pasupathi, former Attorney General of Sri Lanka under Prime Minister Sirima Bandaranaike and President J.R. Jayewardene, who now lives in retirement in Australia. Another was Professor R. Sornarajah, my schoolmate, Dean of the Faculty of Law of the University Singapore. They met early in July 2003 in Switzerland for nearly two weeks. They decided to meet again in Ireland in August. In the meantime some sympathisers visited Kilinochchi for discussions with Prabhakaran himself because he is not in a position to attend conferences abroad. Under the laws of Sri Lanka he is an absconder because he was convicted by the High Court of Colombo on fifty one counts under the Penal Code and given twenty years jail to run consecutively and notionally summed up for two hundred years! Therefore there is no question of his being transported like other LTTE delegates from Kilinochchi to Bandaranaike International Airport in a helicopter of the Sri Lanka Air Force, and then take an international flight.

In August 2003 the LTTE delegates met in Ireland, exactly like they did in July and once again a few visited Kilinochchi to meet Prabhakaran. The third such meeting was in Norway in September, followed by even more sessions *in camera* in Kilinochchi. After all these sessions the LTTE prepared their proposals for the necessary conditions to commence the Peace talks which had stalled as of April 2003.

The formal letter of the LTTE addressed to Prime Minister Ranil Wockremesinghe dated October 31st 2003 and signed by Dr. Anton

Balasingham, was dispatched the day left for Washington to meet President George W. Bush. The Government of Sri Lanka and the LTTE gave much publicity to that document which contained the proposals to have an Interim Self Government Authority (ISGA), as a precussor to resuscitate the Peace talks (The full text is given as Annexure IV).

The proposal drafted by Siva Pasupati, former Attorney General who earlier had drafted the Thirteenth Amendment to the Constitution in 1987, was indeed a splendid document. The Thirteenth Amendment was perhaps the most the Sinhalese can conceivably concede to the Tamils. For example the North-Eastern Province was essentially a temporary feature. It would become permanent only if a Referendum held in the Eastern Province approves of it. President J.R. Jayewardene was convinced that the combined Sinhalese and Muslims population amounting to approximately 59% according to the Census of 1981 (and amounting to approximately 66% according to the Census of 2001) would ensure that the *status quo* of Northern Province and Eastern Province would be restored. The Internal Self Government Authority (ISGA) proposed by the LTTE was using the North-Eastern Province as the very basis for the negotiation. I for one doubt whether the UNP in power as of 2003 and the SLFP in power as of 2004 can accommodate the ISGA in any meaningful sense, though admittedly the ISGA does not conflict with the current Constitution of Sri Lanka.

Both the Government of Sri Lanka and the LTTE have realized the futility of war. Therefore we can hope for a permanent Ceasefire, like the Good Friday Agreement of 1998 in Ireland. However a stable Peace is still way beyond the horizon.

Considering the highly calibre of professionals who worked for over three months to draft the Internal Self Government Authority (ISGA), it was a pity that Prime Minister Ranil Wickremasinghe could not devote the time be should have to the proposals for the ISGA. Due to resons beyond his control, he received the document just before he left for Washington for discussions with the President of the United States. On the morning of that appointment, the President of Sri Lanka sacked the Cabinet Ministers for Defence, Internal Security and the Media and appointed herself to those three posts. The reasons attributed by her were derisory but in reality it ruptured the tenuous relationship between the Prime Minister from the UNP and the President from the SLFP.

The Norwegian delegation which had weathered so many storms and suffered so many indignities from the emotional Buddhist elergy and the vitriolic JVP, left in anger a week later when Prime Minister Ranil Wickremesinghe rushed back to Colombo and clashed heavily with

President Chandrika Bandarnaiake Kumartunga. The Norwegian delegation publicly stated that the in-fighting between the President and the Prime Minister made their position untenable.

Another General Election was likely although the President had assured the Speaker in writing that she would not dissolve Parliament while the UNP had a majority. However, she reneged and Parliament was dissolved as of February 6th 2004 and a General Election fixed for April 2nd 2004.

The new Parliament produced a minority Government that is also a Coalition Government. As of this writing, it is producing results which are partly novel and partly comic. However there is one silver lining in this dark cloud. The current Parliament reflects accurately the political realities pertaining to the vexed ethnic problem.

The JVP is in Parliament in significant numbers. The *Maha Sangha* (Buddhist priests) are in Parliament for the first time in history. It is widely debatable, whether the *Maha Sangha* should be in Parliament or they should be confined to their temples from where where they have traditionaly influenced the Buddhist laity. Both the JVP and the *Maha Sangha* are inveterate haters of the Tamils in general and the LTTE in particular. The LTTE is not yet in Parliament but are well represented by their surrogates, the Tamil National Alliance, who account for over 95% of the seats in the Northern Province. Thus for once the LTTE can decisively affect our national life, not through the crudity of terrorism but through the sophistication of Parliament.

Since April 2004, the Norwegian delegation consisting of Deputy Foreign Minister Vidar Helgesen Special Advisor Eric Sothein are once again frequent visitors to Colombo and Kilinochchi. In Colombo the Embassy of Norway is often surrounded by noisy members of the *Maha Sangha*, some of whom are in Parliament and more importantly, in Opposition. They jibe and chant that the JVP now in Governemnt has allowed their backbone to be supplanted by their wishbone. Indeed the sudden silence of the JVP is deafening, to say the least. To make matters worse, there have been ugly incidents in Parliament when members of *Maha Sangha* who are Members of Parliament have had their modesty outraged. Recently the speaker has adjourned Parliament for one month and invited the Police to investigate into this incident. As of now, one Cabinet Minister, two Deputy Ministers and one Member of Parliament are suspected for offences under the Penal Code.

Indeed the President, who is a prisoner of politics is maneuvering to stabilize her Governemnt. In doing she has been rebuffed by the LTTE according to whom their Internal Self Government Authority (ISGA) is non-negotiable. The President is more than aware that the ISGA is anathema to the JVP. Nevertheless she insists on negotiating for Peace with the LTTE.

The LTTE is also in a precarious position. In February 2004, the war hero Karuna led a rebellion against Prabhakaran and lived to tell the tale after he was defeated militarity. Down the ages not much love was lost between the Tamils in Batticaloa and Tamils in Jaffna. That enmity has surfaced again, hence the abortive rebellion by Karuna. Pottu Aman, who master minded the assassination of Rajiv Gandhi, is now exterminating the rivals of the LTTE in Batticaloa. Thus Tamils are killing Tamils and the old wounds between Jaffna Tamils and Batticaloa Tamils are becoming a festering sore. It has become such a serious problem that its merit a detailed analysis, at his juncture.

During the year 2003, I visited Kilinochchi and Chenkaladi (near Batticaloa) every two months and enjoyed the hospitality of the LTTE. I have meet all the leaders of the LTTE at least once personally and the most impresive of them was Colonel Karuna, the field commander of the LTTE in Amparai and Batticalos. Colonel is the highest military rank in the LTTE and he has the bearing os a young General, a born leader who gives crisp orders. Repeatedly I have asked him,

"Colonel, I see you are expanding your camps? Whom are you training to fight?"

"Please Sir, rest assured we are not going to fight the Armed Forces of Sri Lanka. The LTTE has passed the stage of attacking lonely outposts of the Army or indulging in terrorism. We now want to negotiate with the Government of Sri Lanka."

He never could convince me because the expansion programme of the LTTE in and around Chenkaladi, was self-evident. Then on February 15th 2004 Colonel Karuna turned his troops against the troops of his supremo, Prabhakaran. In my judgement Colonel Karuna chose the correct movement to strike, when Parliament was suddenly dissolved on February 6th and the nation was embroiled in an unexpected General Election. Prabhakaran promptly appointed Colonel Ramesh as his new field commander for Amparai and Batticaloa to replace Colonel Karuna, who was summarily dismissed. In due course he applied to the Sri Lankan Monitoring Mission (SLMM) for permission to move his troops across our lines, in conformity with the Ceasefire Agreement of February 22nd 2002. The Commander of the Army, Lieutenant General Lionel

Balagalle, mistook it for a routine transfer of troops of the LTTE from Kilinochchi to Trincomalee and *vice versa.* Such permission was therefore routinely granted.

Fighting broke out in the first week of April. When Prabhakaran moved his troops from Trincomalee, across the river Veragul. He then proceeded southwards in the general direction of Batticaloa. The first of the major battles was on Good Friday. Colonel Karuna had systematically built up his forces to 5,000 - 6,000 and therefore had a numerical advantage over the forces in the Wanni. However, the clite troops of the LTTE were stationed in the Wanni. During the battle of Good Friday, Colonel Karuna realized that he was fighting against the Charles Anthony Brigade and the Kittu Artillery Brigade, the elite troops he commanded in the battle for Jaffna in 2000. It later transpired that Colonel Sornam, whom he admired so much during the battle for Jaffna had by now crossed the river Veragul. In the face of the formidable enemy Colonel Karuna decided to retreat. He carried out a scorched earth policy in the Amparai - Batticaloa sector and fled. Thereafter he took refuge with the Sinhalese and was briefly in Colombo having taken escape route via Polonnaruwa. That is when I last met him.

Within a month he returned to the District of Batticaloa and now as a guerilla is battling the LTTE under Colonel Ramesh. Reportedly he wields considerable influence in the District of Batticaloa, which accounts for the second largest concentration of Tamils in Sri Lanka. It is common knowledge that of the eight candidates from the Tamil National Alliance (TNA), the surrogate for the LTTE, at the General Election of 2004, seven openly backed Colonel Karuna against the LTTE.

At the General Election of 2004, the results in the Eastern Province were as follows:

		Seats
The SLEP -JVP -SLMC (Ferial Ashroff wing)	-	4
The UNP -SLMC (Rauf Hakeem wimg)	-	6
Tamil National Alliance	-	7
Others	-	0
		17

At the critically important General Election of 1977, when the basic issue was the Vadamarachchi Resolution initiated by S.J.V. Chelvanayakan and G.G Ponnambalam, and seeking to create a State of Ealam through Parliamentary methods. The voting in the Esastern Province then was:

		Seats
UNP	-	5
SLAP	-	0
Tamil United Liberation Front	-	3
Others	-	0
		8

In direct contrast in 1977, in the Northen Province all 14 seats went to the Tamil United Lineration Front which took 68.3% of the popular vote, a record for any Province since Independence.

The figures for the Eastern Province speak for themselves in the context of the division of political power in that Province, both now and one generation ago. Thus if a Referendum is held in the Eastern Province in conformity with the Thirteenth Amendment of the Constitution. There is no doubt the Eastern Province will opt to exist as a separate Province where the current population now is:

		%
Muslim	-	39.6
Sinhales	-	26.2
Tamils	-	33.1
Burghers	-	1.1

(Source: Census of 2001 supplemented with District Secretariat figures for early 2002)

This result is so obvious that the burning question now is not whether or not a Referendum will be won or lost but whether the LTTE will allow a Referendum to be held or not. In my judgement that is indeed a serious problem which can be solved by bringing in a contingent of troops from Norway (or all Scandinavian nations) amounting to one Brigade and for a duration of two weeks, to supervise the Referendum. Scandinavian troops have helped in Referenda in Bosnia and Cyprus in such a manner in recent years.

After the Ceasefire signed on February 22nd 2002, The LTTE is learning fast of their limitations. They know that they too are under the vigilant eye of the international community. For example there is no nation anywhere in the world which supports their terrorism. They are vilified for their well established technique of exterminating their rivals. For example last week a sucide bomber was sent to assassinate the former terrorist leader Douglas Devananda of the Eelam Peoples Democratic Party who has eschewed terrorism, entered the Parliamentary process and is now a Cabinet Minister. In the nick of time the sucide bomber was apprehended by the Police. She then detonated her sucide kit, killing herself and four Policemen on duty. It resulted in many a nation condemning the LTTE, publicly.

Both Douglas Devanaada and Colonel Karuna assured me that Prabhakaran will never ever give up his clamour for Eelam.The propaganda by Douglas Devnaada has been most effective on the international community. Indeed his credentials are impeccable. He was a leading terrorist. Then he eschewed terrorism and took to Parliamentary democracy. Now he is a Cabinet Minister and the LTTE has on ten occassions attempted to assasinate him.

It is abundantly clear even to the LTTE that they have to eschew terrorism if they are to achieve acceptability within the international community. However, in direct contrast Prabhakaran makes no secret of his thinking that he will renounce terrorism and abolish the sucide squads, when the Sinhalese renounce their discrimination against the Tamils. Prabhakaran himself told me so in May 2004. Thus the spiral of violence will continue for several years to come or till Prabhakaran himself is exterminated.

Indeed Prabhakaran himself has to live with him ignominious past which troubles him from time to time. This year such trouble has come unexpectedly. While in Opposition, Sonia Gandhi repeatedly informed those who wield power in Sri Lanka, that when the Congress returns to power, as surely as day follows night the Government of India will request for the extradition of Prabhakaran. Now the Congress has unexpectedly returned to power and woe be unto Prabhakaran!

Sri Lanka is a nation which since Independence, has sown the wind and reaped the whirlwind. A separate Eastern Province for the Muslims is the cost of peace for the LTTE, which can win in war but cannot win in Peace. A separate Northen Province for the Tamils is the cost of Peace for the Sinhalese, who cannot win in war but can win in Peace. Unfortunately neither the Sinhalese nor the Tamils have the wisdom, as of now, to understand this equation. As the years roll by Sri Lanka has to learn that the only just and equitable solution to our vexed ethnic problem is to create a Federal Republic of Sri Lanka, with seven Provinces for the Sinhalese, one Province for the Tamils and one Province for the Muslims. Only then can all live in peace.

APPENDICES

APPENDIX I

The Indo- Lanka Accord

The President of the Democratic Socialist Republic of Sri Lanka, His Excellency Mr. J. R. Jayawadene, and the Prime Minister of the Republic of India, His Excellency Mr. Rajiv Gandhi, having met at Colombo on 29th 1987,

Attaching utmost importance to nurturing, intensifying and strengthening the traditional friendship of Sri Lanka and India, and acknowledging the imperative need of resolving the ethnic problem of Sri Lanka, and the consequent violence, and for the safety, well being and prosperity of people belonging to all communities in Sri Lanka, Have this day entered into the following agreement to fulfil this objective. In this context.

1.1 desiring to preserve the unity, sovereignty and territorial integrity of Sri Lanka:

1.2 acknowledging that Sri Lamka is a multi-ethnic and multi-lingual plural society consisting, *inter alia*, of Sinhalese, Tamils, Muslims, and Burghers,

1.3 recognising that each tethinic group has a distinct cultural and linguistic identity which has sto be carefully nurtured;

1.4 also recognizing that the Northen and the Eastern Provinces have been areas of historical habitation of Tamil speaking peoples, who have at all times hitherto lived together in this territory with other ethinic groups;

1.5 concious of the necessity of strengthening the forces contributing to unity, sovereignty and territorial integrity of Sri Lanka, and preserving its character as a multi-ethnic, multi-lingual and multi-religious plural society, in which all citizens can live in equality, safety and harmony, and prosper and fulfil their aspirations:

2.0 Resolve that :

2.1 Since the Government of Sri Lanka proopeses to permit adjoi9ning Provinces to join to form one administrative unit and also by a referendum to separate as may be permitted to the Northen and Eastern Provinces as outlined below;

2.2 During the period, which shall be considered an interim period, (i.e. from the date of the elections to the Provincial Council, as specified in para 2.3,) the Northen and Eastern Provinces as now constituted, will from one administrative unit, having one elected Provincial Council. Such a unit will have one Governor, one Chief Minister and one Board of Minister.

2.3 There will be a referendum on or before 31 December 1988 to enable the people of the Eastern Province to decide whether:

(a) The Eastern Province should remain linked with the Northen Province as one administrative unit, and continue to be governed together with the Northen Province as specified in Para 2.2, or

(b) The Eastern Province ahould constitute a separated administrative unit having its own distinct provincial Council and a separate Governor, Chief Minister and Board of Ministers.

The President may, at his discretion, decide to postpone such a referendum.

2.4 All persons who have been displaced due to ethnic violence, or other reasons, will have the right to vote in such a referendum. Necessary conditions to enable them to return areas from where they were displaced will be created.

2.5 The referendum, when held, will be monitored by a committee headed by the Chief Justice, a member appointed by the President, a member nominated by the Government of Sri Lanka: and a member appointed by the President, nominated by the representatives of the Tamil speaking people of the Eastern Province.

2.6 A simple majority will be sufficient to determine the results of the referendum.

2.7 Meetings and other form of propganda, permissible within the laws of the country, will be allowed before the referendum.

2.8 Elections to the Provincial Councils will be held within the next three months, in any event before 31 December 1987. Indian observers will be invited or elections to the Provincial Council of the North and East.

2.9 The Emergency will be lifted in the Eastern and Northen Provinces by August 15, 1987. A cessation of hostilities will come into effect over the Island within 48 hours of the signing of this agreement.

All arms presently held by militant groups will be surrendered in accordance with an agreed procedure to authorities to be designated by the Government of Sri Lanka.

Consequent to the cessation of hostilities and the surrender of arms militant groups, the Army and othersecurity personal will be confined to barracks in camps as on May 25 1987. The process of surrendering of arms and the confining of security personnel moving back to barracks shall be completed within 72 hours of the cessation of hostilities coming into effect.

2.9 The Government of Sri Lanka will utilize for the purpose of law enforcement and maintenance of security in the Northen and Eastern Provinces the same organizations and mechanisms of Government as are used rest of the country.

2.10 The President of Sri Lanka will grant a general amenesty to political and other prisoners now held in custody under the Prevention of Terrorism Act and other Emergency laws, and to combatants, as well as to rehbilitate militant youth with the view of bringing them back to the mainstream of national life. India will co-operate in that process.

2.11 The Government of Sri Lanka will accept and abide by the above provisions and expect all others to do likewise.

2.12 If the framework for the resolution is accepted, the Government of Sri Lanka will implement the relevant proposals forthwith.

2.13 The Government of India will underwrite and guarantee the resolutions, and co-operate in the implementation of these proposals.

2.14 These proposals are also conditional to an acceptance of the proposals negotiated from 4-5-1986. Residual matters not finalized during the above negotiations shall be resolved between India and Sri Lanka within a period of six weeks of signing this Agreement. These proposals are also conditional to the Government of India co-operating directly with the Government of Sri Lanksa in their implementation.

2.15 These proposals are also conditional to the Government of India taking the following actions if any militant groups operating in Sri Lanka do not accept this framework of proposals for a settlement , namely,

(a) India will take all necessary steps to ensure that Indian territory is not used for activities prejudicial to the unity, integrity and security of Sri Lanka.

(b) The Indian Navy/Cost Guard will co-operate with the Sri Lanka Navy in preventing Tamil Militant activities from affecting Sri Lanka.

(c) In the event that the Government of Sri Lanka requests the Government of India to afford military assistance to implement these proposals th Government of Inia will co-opcratc by providing to the Government of Sri Lanka such military assistance as and when requested.

(d) The Government of India will expedite repatrition from Sri Lanka of Indian citizens to India who are there, concurrently with the repatriation of Sri Lankan refugees from Tamil Nadu.

(e) The Goverments of India and Sri Lanka will co-operate in enduring the physical security and safety of all communities inhabiting the Northen and Eastern Provinces.

2.17 The Governments of India and Sri Lanka shall ensure free, full and fair participation of voters from all communities in the Northen and Eastern Provinces in electoral processes envisaged in the Agreement. The Government of India will extend full co-operation to the Government of Sri Lanka in this regard.

2.18 The official language of Sri Lanka shall be Sinhala. Tamil and English will also be official languages.

3. This Agreement and the Annexure thereto shall come into force upon signature.

In witness wherof we have set our hands and seals hereunto

Done in Colombo, Sri Lanka, on this Twenty Ninth Day of July of the Year one Thousand Nine Hundred and Eighty Seven, in duplicate, both texts being equally authentic.

Rajiv Gandhi Prime Minister of India	Junius Richard Jayewardene President of Sri Lanka

ANNEXURE TO THE AGREEMENT

1. His Excellency the Prime Minister of India and His Excellency the President of Sri Lanka agree that the referendum mentioned in paragraph 2 and its sub-paragraphs of the Agreement will be observed by a representative of the Election Commission of India to be invited by His Excellency the President of Sri Lanka.

2. Similarly, both Heads of Government agree that the elections to the provincial council mentioned in paragraph 2.8 of the Agreement will be observed by a representative of the Government of India to be invited by the President of Sri Lanka.

3. His Excellency the President of Sri Lanka agrees that the Home Guards would be disbanded and all para-military personnel will be withdrawn from the Eastern and Northen Provinces with a view to creating conducive to fair elections to the Council. The President, in his discretion, shall absorb such para-military forces, which came into being due to etheniv violence, into the regular security forces of Sri Lanka.

4. The Prime Minister of India and the President of Sri Lanka agree that the Tamil militants shall surrender their arms to authorities agreed upon to be designated by the President of Sri Lanka. The surrender shall take place in the presence of one senior representative each of the Sri Lanka Red Cross and the Indian Red Cross.

5. The Prime Minister of India and The President of Sri Lanka agree that a joint Indo-Sri Lanka observer group consisting of qualified representatives of the Government of India and the Government of Sri Lanka would monitor the cessation of hostilities from 31 July, 1987.

6. The Prime Minister of India and The President of Sri Lanka agree that in terms of paragraph 2.14 and paragraph 2.16 (c) of the Agreement, an Indian Peace Keeping contigent may be invited by the president of Sri Lanka to guarantee and enforce the cessation of hostilities if so required.

His Excellency Mr. J. R. Jayewardene
President of the Democratic Socialist Republic of Sri Lanka.

29 July 1987
Colombo

Excellency,

1. Conscious of thee friendship between our two countries stretching over two millennia and more, and recognizing the importance of nurturing this traditional friendship, it is imperative that both Sri Lanka and India reaffirm the decision not to allow our respective territorist to be used for activities prejudicial to each other's unity, territorial integrity and security.

2. In this spirit, you had, during the course of our discussions agreed to meet some of Inida's concerns follows:-

(i) Your Excellency and myself will reach an early understanding about the relevance and employment of foreign military and intelligence personnel with a view to ensuring that such presence will not prejudice Indo-Srilanka relations.

(ii) Trincomalee or any other ports in Sri Lanka will not be made available for military use by any country in a manner prejudicial to India's interests.

(iii) The work of restoring and operating the Trincomalee oil tank farm will be undertaken as a joint venture between India amd Sri Lanka.

(iv) Sri Lanka's agreements with foreign broadcasting organizations will be reviewed to ensure that any facilities set up by them in Sri Lanka are used solely as public broadcasting facilities and not for any military of intelligence purposes.

3. In the same spirit, India will:

(i) Deport all Sri Lankan citizens who are found t be engaging in terrorist activities or advocating separatism or secessionism.

(ii) Provide training facilities and military supplies for the Armed Forces of Sri Lanka.

4. India and Sri Lanka have agreed to set up a joint consultative mechanism to continuously review matters of common concern in the light of the objectives stated in para 1 and specifically to monitor the implementation of other matters contained in this letter.

5. Kindly confirm, Excellency, that the above correctly sets out the agreement reached between us.

Please accept, Excellency the assurances of my highest consideration.

Yours sincerely,

Rajiv Gandhi
Prime Minister of India

29 July 11987

His Excellency Mr. Rajiv Gandhi
Prime Minister of the Republic of India

Excellency,

This is to confirm that the aforesaid correctly sets are the understanding between us.

Please accept, Excellency the assurances of my highest consideration.

J.R. Jayewardene
President of Sri Lanka

APPENDIX II

The Memorandum Of Understanding for the Ceasefire

Preamble:

The overall objective of the Government of the Democratic Socialist Republic of Sri Lanka (hereinafter referred to as the GOSL) and the Liberation Tigers of Tamil Eelam (hereinafter referred t as the LTTE) is to find a negotiation solution to the ethnic conflict in Sri Lanka.

The GOSL and the LTTE (hereinafter referred to as the Parties) recognize the importance of bringing an end to the hostilities and improving the living conditions for all inhabitants by the conflict. Bringing an end to the hostilities is also seen by the Parties as a means of establishing a positive atmosphere in which further steps towards negotiations on a lasting solution can be taken.

The Parties further recognize that groups are not directly party to the conflict are also suffering the concequences of it. This is particularly the case as regards the Muslim population. Therefore, the provisions of this Agreement, regarding the security of civilians and their property apply to all inhabitants.

With reference to the above, the Parties have agreed to enter into a ceasefire, refrain from conduct that could undermine the good intentions or violate the spirit of this Agreement and implement confidence- building measure as indicated in the Articles below.

Article 1: Modalities of a Ceasefire :

The Parties have agreed to implement a Ceasefire between their armed forces as follows :

1.1 A jointly agreed ceasefire between the GOSL and the LTTE shall enter into force on such date is notified by the Norwegian Minister of Foreign Affairs in accordance with Article 4.2 hereinafter referred to as D-day.

Military Operations :

1.2 Neither party shall engage in any offensive military operation. Thus requires the total cessation of all military action and includes, but is not limited, to such acts as :

The firing of direct and indirect weapons, armed raids, ambushes, assassinations, abductions, destruction of civilian or military property, sabotage, sucide missions and activities by deep penetration units;

(a) Aerial bombardment;

(b) Offensive naval operations.

1.3 The Sri Lankan armed forces shall continue to perform their legitimate task of safeguarding the soverginity and territorial integrity of Sri Lanka without engaging in offensive operations against the LTTE.

1.4 Where forward defence localities have been established, the GOSL's armed forces and the LTTE's fighting formations shall hold their ground positions, maintaining a zone of separation of a minimum of six hundred (600) meters. However, each Party reserves the right of movement within one hundred (100) meters of its own defence localities, keeping an absolute minimum distance of four hundred (400) meters between them. Where exsting positions are closer than four hundred (400) meters, no such right of movement applies and the Parties agree to ensure the maximum possible distances between their personnel.

1.5 In areas where localities have not been clearly established, the *status quo* as regards the areas controlled by the GOSL and the LTTE respectively, on 24the December 2001 shall continue to apply pending such demarcation as is provided in Article 1.6.

1.6 The Parties shall provide information to the Sri Lanks Monitoring Mission (SLMM) regarding defence localities in all areas of contention, of Article 3. The SLMM shall assist the Parties in drawing up demarcration lines at the latest by D-day + 30.

1.7 The parties shall not move munitions, explosives or military equipment into the area controlled by the other Party.

1.8 Tamil paramilitary groups shall be disarmed by the GOSL by D-day + 30 at the latest. The GOSL shall offer to integrate individuals in these units under the command and disciplinary structure of the GOSL armed forces for service away from the Northen and Eastern Province.

Freedom of Movement :

1.9 The Parties' forces shall initially stay in the areas under their respective control, as provided in Article 1.4 and Article 1.5.

1.10 Unarmed GOSL troops, shall as of D-day + 60, be permitted unlimited passage between Jaffna and Vavuniya using the Jaffna-Kandy road (A9). The modalities are to be worked out by the Parties with the assistance of the SLMM.

1.11 The Parties that as D-day individual combatants shall, on the recommendation of their area commander, be permitted, unasrmed and in plain clothes, to visit family and friends residing in areas under the control of the other Party. Such visits shall be limited to six days every second month, not including the time of travel by the shortest applicable route. The LTTE shall facilitate the use of the Jaffna-Kandy road for this purpose. The Parties reserve the right to deny entry to specified military areas.

1.12 The Parties that as D-day individual combatants shall, notwithstanding the two-month restriction, be permitted, unarmed and in plain clothes, to visit immediate family (i.e. spouses, children, grandparentsm parents and siblings) in connection with weddings or funerals. The right to deny entry to specified military areas applies.

1.13 Fifty (50) unarmed LTTE members shall as of D-day + 30, for the purpose of political work, be permitted freedom of movement in the areas of the North and the East dominated by the Gosl. Additional one hundred (100) LTTE members shall be permitted freedom of movement as of D-day + 60. As of D-day + 90, all unarmed LTTE members be permitted freedom of movement in the North and the East. The LTTE members shall carry indentity papers. The right of the GOSL to deny entry to specified military areas applies.

Article 2 Measures to restore normalcy :

The Parties shall undertake the following confidence-building measures with the aim of restoring normalcy for all inhabitants of /sri Lanka:

2.1 The Parties shall in accordance wuth internatuional law abstain from hostile acts from the civilian population, including such as acts of torture, intimation, abduction, extortion and harassment.

2.2 The Parties shall refrain from engaging in activities or propagating ideas that could offend cultural or religious sensitivities. Palces of worship (temples, churches, mosques and other holy sites, etc.) currently held by either of the Parties shall be vacated by D-day + 30 and made accessible to the public. Places of worship which are situated in " high security zones" shall be yacated by all armed personnel and maintained in good order by civilian workers, even when thry are not made accessible to the public.

2.3 Beginning on the date of which this Agreement enters into force, school buildings occupied by either party shall be vacated and returned to their intended use. This activity shall be completed by D-day + 160 at the latest.

2.4 A schedule indicating the return of all other public bnuildings to their intended use shall be drawn up by the Parties and punlished at the latest D-day + 30.

2.5 The parties shall review the security measures and the set-up of checkpoints, particularly in densely populated cities and towns, in order to introduce systems that will prevent harassment of the civilian population. Such systems shall be in place from D-day + 60.

2.6 The Parties agree to ensure the unimpeded flow of non-military goods to and from the LTTE-dominated areas with the exception of certain items as shown in Annex A. Quantities shall be determined by market demand. The GOSL shall regularly review the matter with the aim of gradually removing any remaining restrictions on non-military goods.

2.7 In order to facilitate the flow or goods and the movement of civilians, the Parties agree to establish checkpoints on their line of control at such as are specified in Annex B.

2.8 The Parties shall take steps to ensure that the Trincomalee-Habarana road remains open on a 24-hour basis passenger traffic with effect from D-day + 10.

2.9 The Parties shall facilitate the extension of the rail service on the Batticoloa-line Welikanda. Repairs and maintenance shall be carried out by the GOSL in order to extend the Service up to Batticloloa.

2.10 The Parties shall open the Kandy-Jaffna road (A9) to non-military traffic of goods and passengers. Specific modalities shall be worked out by the Parties with the assistance of the Royal Norwegian Government D-day + 30 at the latest.

2.11 A gradual easing of the fishing restrictions shall take place starting from D-day. As of D-day + 90, all restrictions on day and night fishing shall be removed, subject to the following exceptions:

- Fishing will not permitted, within an area of one (01) nautical mile on either side along the coast and two (02) nautical miles seawards from all security forces camps on the coast;
- Fishing will not be permitted in harbours or approaches to harbours, bays and estuaries along the coast.

2.12 The Parties agree that search operations and arrests under the Prevention og Terrorism Act shall not take place. Arrest shall be conducted under due process of law in accordance with the Criminal Procedure Code.

2.13 The Parties agree to provide family members of detaines access to the detainees with D-day + 30.

Article 3 The Sri Lanka Monitoring Mission :

The Parties have agreed to set up an international monitoring mission to enquire into any instance of violation of the terms and conditions of this Agreement. Both Parties shall full co-operate to rectify any matter of conflict caused by their respective sides. The mission shall conduct international verification through on-site monitoring of the fulfillment of the commitments entered into this Agreement as follows :

3.1 The name of the monitoring mission shall be the Sri Lanka Monitoring Mission (hereinafter referred to as the SLMM).

3.2 Subject to acceptance by the Parties, the Royal Norwegian Government (hereinafter referred to as the RNG) shall appoint the Head of the SLMM (hereinafter reffered to as the HoM), who shall be the final authority regarding the interpretation of this Agreement.

3.3 The SLMM shall liaise with the Parties and report to the RNG.

3.4 The HoM shall decided the date for the commencement of the SLMM's operations.

3.5 The SLMM shall be composed of representatives from Nordic countries.

3.6 The SLMM shall establish a headquarters in such places as the HoM finds appropriate. An office shall be established in Colombo and in the Wanni order to liase with the GOSL and the LTTE, respectively. The LTTE shall maintain a presence in the districts of Jaffna, Mannar, Vavuniya, Trincomalee, Batticoloa and Amparai.

3.7 A local monitoring committee shall be established in Jaffna, Mannar, Vavuniya, Trincomalee, Batticoloa and Amparai. Each committee shall consist of five (05) members, two (02) appointed by the GOSL, two (02) appointed by th LTTE and one (01) international monitor appointed by the HoM. The international monitor shall chair the committee. The GOSL and LTTE appoints may be selected from among retired judges, public servants, religious leaders or similar leading citizens.

3.8 The committee shall serve the SLMM in an advisory capacity and discuss issues relating to the implementation of this Agreement in Their respective districts, with a view to establishing a common understanding of such issues. In particular, they will seek to resolve any dispute concerning the implementation of this Agreement at the lowest possible level.

3.9 The Parties shall be responsible for the appropriate protection of and security arrangements for all SLMM members.

3.10 The Parties agree to ensure the freedom of movement of the SLMM members in perfprming their tasks. The members of the SLMM shall be given immediate access to areas where violations of the Agreement are alleged to have taken place. The Parties also agree to facilitate the widest possible access to such areas for the local members of the six above-mentioned committees, of Article 3.7.

3.11 It shall be the responsibility of the SLMM to take immediate action on any complaints made by either Party to the Agreement and to enquire into and assist the parties in the settlement of any dispute that might arise in connection with such complaints.

3.12 With the aim of resolving disputed at the lowest possible level, communication shall be established between commands of the GOSL armed forces and the LTTE area leaders to enable hem to resolve problem in the conflictzones.

3.13 Guidelines for the operations of the SLMM shall be established in a separate document.

Article 4 Entry into force, amendments and termination of the Agreement:

4.1 Each Party shall notify its consent to be bound by this Agreement through a letter to the Norwegian Minister of Foreign Affairs signed by Prime Minister ranil Wickremesinghe on behalf of the GOSL and by leader Velupillai Prabhakaran on behalf of the LTTE respectively. The Agreement shall be initialed by each Party and enclosed in the above-mentioned letter.

4.2 The Agreement shall enter into force on such date as is notified by the Norwegian Minister of Foreign Affairs.

4.3 This Agreement may be amended and modified by mutual agreement of both Parties. Such Amendments shall be notified in writing to the RNG.

4.4 This Agreement shall remain in force until notice of termination id given by either Party to the RNG. Such notice shall be given fourteen (14) days in advance of the effective date of termination.

APPENDIX III

The Peace Talks and theAgreed Statements

16 – 18 September 2002 at Sattahip, Thailand.

The first round of formal peace talks between the Government of Sri Lanka (GOSL) and the Liberation Tigers of Tamil Eelam (LTTE) was held in Sattahip, Thailand, between 16 and 18 September 2002. The negotiations were facilitated by the Royal Norwegian Government.

The parties agreed that in their determination to bring the peace process forward, they are responding to the overwhelming call of the peoples of Sri Lanka to bring an end to the ethnic conflict, and create the conditions for lasting peace, prosperity, and respect for human rights.

Both parties expressed their resolve to address the full range of issues pertaining to a lasting political settlement of the ethnic conflict in Sri Lanka, fully realizing that this can best be achieved by pursuing a step-by-step approach to the negotiation process. This approach has proven successful in the establishment and implementation of the Ceasefire Agreement already in force since February. The parties recognized the need for sustaining the Ceasefire Agreement, with the continued assistance of the Sri Lanka Monitoring Mission, which the parties commended for its impartial conduct in the fulfilment of its important mandate.

The parties affirmed their determination to continue upholding the Ceasefire Agreement and expanding the range of confidence-building measures over the period ahead. Building on the achievements of the Ceasefire Agreement, the parties agreed to establish promptly a Joint Committee to deal with the issues relating to High Security Zones, with the aim of enabling the return of larger numbers of displaced persons to their areas of origin, thereby facilitating the restoration of normalcy. This Joint Committee will consist of senior representatives of both sides, including military personnel.

The parties discussed in depth the urgent need to address the difficult humanitarian situation in the north and east of Sri Lanka. To this effect, the parties agreed to establish a Joint Task Force for Humanitarian and Reconstruction Activities. The Joint Task Force will constitute a partnership between the Government of Sri Lanka and the LTTE, and will have responsibility for the identification, financing and monitoring of urgent humanitarian and reconstruction activities in the north and east. The task force will operate with due participation of Muslims, and its work will benefit all ethnic communities of the North and East. The details relating to the mandate and structure of the Joint Task Force will rapidly be finalized between the parties with the assistance of the Norwegian facilitators. The two immediate priorities of the parties are

(1) stepping up humanitarian mine action, and

(2) accelerating resettlement and rehabilitation of internally displaced persons.

The parties expressed their gratitude for the extensive goodwill of the international community toward the peace process. They urged donors to provide immediate funding for humanitarian priorities. This will enhance public confidence in the peace process and thus contribute to the further progress in the quest for peace in Sri Lanka.

The parties agreed that the establishment of the Joint Task Force is a sign of the increasing level of trust between the parties, and of their willingness to work together towards the establishment of a provisional administrative structure for the north and east.

Recognizing that the way forward is a long and demanding one, the parties agreed to continuing rounds of negotiations. The next three rounds of negotiations will take place on the following dates:

31 October – 3 November 2002

2 – 5 December 2002

6 – 9 January 2003.

The parties as well as the Norwegian facilitators reiterated their appreciation to the Royal Thai Government for their kindness in providing the venue for the negotiations as well as the generous hospitality shown to the delegations.

31st October to 3rd November

at Rose Garden, Thailand.

The Government of Sri Lanka (GOSL) and the Liberation Tigers of Tamil Eelam (LTTE) initiated the second session of the peace talks in Thailand at Rose Garden, Thailand from 31st October to 3, November 2002.It began with an evaluation of the implementation of the Ceasefire

Agreement over the past eight months. In their determination to consolidate the ceasefireand advance the peace process, the parties agreed to a set of measure to improve the security situation, inter-ethnic cooperation and respect for human rights in the North and Eastern Provinces.

In this context, the parties emphasized in particular their commitment to accommodate the needs and aspirations of all three communities in the east-Tamils, Muslims and Sinhalese. The parties set out specific measures to improve relations between the Muslim and Tamil communities.

The parties agreed to continuously monitor the implementation of each of the agreed measures and to report on progress at future sessions of the peace talks.

In light of the principal challenges in implementing the Ceasefire Agreement at this stage, the parties agreed to reconstitute the SLMM Local Monitoring Committees, establish in accordance with paragraph 3.7 of the Ceasefire Agreement. To this end, the parties agreed to replace a number of their appointees to the Committees with senior representatives from both the sides.

The parties are pleased to note that the SLMMhas established Points of Contact (POCs) in the north and east as sub-office of the SLMM district offices, in orders, in order to improve access to SLMM for local communities. The parties agreed to request the SLMM to consider establishing additional sub-offices, particularly in Batticaloa and Ampara districts.

The parties agreed to establish direct communications between the commanders of the LTTE and the GOSL Special Task Force in the east, in order to improve the security situation.

- The parties agreed to establish a process of regular consultation between LTTE leaders and Muslim political leaders.
- Mr. Hakeem and Mr. Karuna agreed to work together in the east to meet with local communities and address their specific concerns and aspirations, including matters relating to the occupation and cultivation of land. They will work in accordance with the Memorandum of Understanding reached between the leader of the LTTE, Mr. Velupillai Pirapaharan, and the leader of the Sri Lanka Muslim Congress, Mr. Rauf Hakeem, on 13 April 2002. The parties further agreed to rmove any impediments to the pursuit of traditional

economic activities of the Tamil and Muslim communities, such as fishing, farming and trading.

- The parties took special note of the need to address fully and cater for the interest and concerns of the Sinhala community in the Eastern Province, in the context of the ongoing peace negotiations.
- The parties agreed to establish peace committees at the community level in order to facilitate the resolution of local problems, contribute to inter-ethnic communication and reconciliation, and promote respect for human rights. The committeeas may include local community leaders, such as religious, political, business and civil society leaders. The committees will include local LTTE and GOSL leaders.

The parties demonstrated a positive, pragmatic and concillatory approach in siscussing a wide of issues, including present challenges as well as matters relating to long-term solutions. The parties thereby continued the dual approach of moving step by step towards a lasting political settlement, while remaining fully focused on the ground situation. The parties reconfirmed their strong commitment to the Ceasefire Agreement and their support for the Sri Lanka Monitoring Mission.

Against the backdrop of recent among the ethnic communities in the east, the parties agreed on immediate measures to improve the security situation, inter-ethnic co-operation and respect for human rights in the north and east. Acknowledging that peac e belongs to all peoples of Sri Lanka, the parties are committed to accommodate the needs and aspirations of all three communities in the east – Tamils, Muslims, and Sinhalese. The agreed measures are outlined in a separate statement issued by the Royal Norwegian Government on 1 November 2002.

In the determination to move the peace process forward, the parties reiterated that the process will be a long and demanding one. Throughout the process, the parties will continuously monitor the ground situation, thus enabling necessary action to be taken at all stages to ensure further progress.

In the quest for a final settlement, a broad range of issues must be addressed with considerable attention to detail For this purpose, the parties agreed on establishing, whenever needed, sub-committees to act on specific matters under the auspices of the negotiation teams. The sub-committees will be continually active and report at the sessions of the talks, in order to accelerate progress and give in-depth attention to issues.

Following the agreement at the first session of talks to set up a joint task force, the parties agreed to establish this in the form of a Sub-Committee on Immediate Humanitarian and Rehabilitation Needs in the North and East. The role of the Sub- Committee will be to

- Identify humanitarian and rehabilitation needs
- Prioritize implementation of activities to meet these needs
- Decide on the allocation of the financial resources for such activities
- Determine implementing agencies for each of the activities.

The Sub-Committee will ensure the involvement of sll ethnic communities so that their needs and aspirations are considered, and it will give priority to the mobilization of local labor and local institution in the implementation of activities initiated by the Sub-Committee will be financed by a fund, which will be set up in accordance with arrangement to be agreed upon with donor governments.

The Sub-Committee will consist of four members selected by the LTTE and four by the GOSL. Two members of the respective negotiating teams, Mr. Tamilselven of the LTTE and Mr. Bernard Goonetilleke of the GOSL, will be leading members of the Sub-Committee. Other GOSL representatives will include Mr. M.D.D. Peiris, Mr. M.I.M. Rafeek, and an additional member of the Muslim community. Other LTTE representatives will include Mr. Jay Maheswaran. The Sub-Committee will be assisted by a secretariat to be located in the Government Agent's Office in Killinochchi. Meetings of the Sub-Committee will be held in Killinochchi, Colombo, Batticaloa, and Kalmunai at the discretion of the committee.

As its first task the Sub-Committee will assist the Royal Norwegian Government in preparing for a political-level meeting of key governments to take place in Oslo, Norway on 25 November 2002. As the first ever of its kind, the meeting will demonstrate the unprecedented level of international support to Sri Lanka and to the parties in their present peace efforts. The meeting will aim at mobilizing financial support for immediate humanitarian and rehabilitation action in three priority areas agreed by the parties:

- Resttling and rehabilitating Internally Displaced Persons
- Rehabilitating war-affected women and children
- Providing livelihoods for war-affected people in the North and East.

The international community will further be encouraged to increase investment in Sri Lanka and respond positively to new challenges in the south resulting from the peace process.

In line with the overall objective of facilitating the resettlement of internally displaced persons, the parties acted on the decision made at the first session of peace talks to address matters relating to high security zones and other areas made inaccessible to the public. To this end, a Sub-Committee on DE-Escalation and Normalization was set up as a mechanism for a structured dialogue between the parties. While accommodating the security concerns of each party, the Sub-Committeen will examine ways and means to ensure resettlement, the return of private property and the resumption of economic activities in these areas. This Sub-Committee will include high-level civilian and military personnel on both sides, including Mr. Austin Fernando of the Ministry of Defence and Mr. Karuna of the LTTE.

As another issue relating to the restoration of normalcy, the status of Tamil prisoners held under the Prvention of Terrorism act was discussed.

The parties remain committed to building peace on the ground through practical steps to improve security and opportunity in people's daily lives. At the same time, the parties acknowledged that the peace talks must address a series of complex political questions in order to reach a negotiatied solution to the ethnic conflict, including constitutional, legal, political and administrative issues. Following discussions, the parties agreed to establish a Sub-Committee to commence work in connection with relevant political matters. The parties agreed that access to expertise on political matters will be important in order for them to enter into negotiations on issues central to the peace process. The parties will jointly and separately address in depth, at the current stage of the peace process, relevant subjects such as other peace processes, political solutions to ethnic conflicts, models and systems of government, issues of post-conflict transition, co-ordination of international assistance, and reconciliation processes. To this end, the parties will interact with relevant experts and practitioners in these fields, as a basis for the fomulation of approaches to the critical political issues for consideration in the future sessions of the peace talks.

The Sub- Committee on Political Matters will be chaired by the heads of delegations t the peace talks, Mr. Anton Balasingham and Mr. G.L. Peiris. Other government representatives will include Mr. Rauf Hakeem, leader of the Sri Lanka Muslim Congress.

The third session of talks will take place on 2 – 5 December 2002 in Oslo, Norway. The following sessions will be held on 6 – 9 January 2003, 7 – 10 February 2003, and 18 – 21 March 2003.

2-5 December 2002

at Oslo, Norway

The third session of peace talks the Government of Sri Lanka (GOSL) and the Liberation Tigers of Tamil Eelam (LTTE) was held in Oslo, Norway on 2 to 5 December 2002. in a frank, open and constructive manner, the parties focused on three ,ajor areas:

- Consolidation of the ceasefire
- Humanitarian and rehabilitation action
- Political matters

The parties agreed on a working outline defining the objective as well as a number of substantive political issues for negotiation.

Responding to a proposals by the leadership of the LTTE, the parties agreed to explore a solution founded on the principle of internal self-detmination in areas of historical habitation of the Tamil-speaking peoples, based on a federal structure within a united Sri Lanka. The parties acknowledged that the solution has to be acceptable to all communities.

Guided by this objective, the parties agreed to initiate discussions on substansive political issues such as, but not limited to:

v Power-sharing between the center and the region, as well as within the center

- Geographical region
- Human Rights protection
- Political and administrative mechanism
- Public finance
- Law and order

The parties recognized that progress on political issues bust be supported by the continued consolition of the Ceasefire Agreement. New concretemeasures will be taken to facilitate further de-escalation and to improve normalcy:

- The GOSL will shortly return one of the hotels in Jaffna to its original use
- The LTTE will ensure that all future transportation of area commanders will take place under the supervision of the Sri Lanka Monitoring Mission (SLMM)
- The LTTE will accept the right of political groups to carry out political work, including in the Jaffna peninsula and the islands,

provided that they are unarmed, as stipulated by the Ceasfire Agreement.

- The GOSL will, in consultation with all relevant parties and groups, envolve a solution to the problems arising from recent developments in the Delft island
- The parties will facilitate resolution and rehabilitation of places of worship in the north and the east belonging religious communities.

On the basis of their firm conviction that the maintenance of law and order in the north and east is of paramount importance, the parties agreed to request the Sub-Committee on De-escalation and Normalization to propose a comman approach to setting cases involoving the disputed use of private property, where such use has been impeded by the conflict. Furthermore, the LTTE will ensure that the activities of their law and order mechanism will not be extended beyond the areas dominated by the LTTE.

The parties strongly underlines the need to move rapidly on humanitarian and rehabilitation efforts in the north and east. For this purpose, the early establishment of the North-East Reconstruction fund 3will be critical. The parties agreed that the custodian of the fund should be selected and modalities for its operation agreed at the next meeting of the Sub-Committee on Immediate Humanitarian and Rehabilitation Needs. The parties expressed their appreciation of the strong support extended by several governments to the peace process at the Sri Lanka Support Meeting held in Oslo on 25 November, and urged these governments to rapidly release funds needed for humanitarian and rehabilitation efforts

The parties acknowledged the need to ensure that the priorities and needs of women are taken into account in all aspects of the peace process. To this effect, they agreed to establish a permanent advisory committee which will, on a regular basis, submit proposals relating to women's interests to the session of negotiations and to the sub-committees of the peace process. The committee will consist four representatives of each party.

As a priority area indentified by the parties for humanitarian action, the parties stressed the need to improve the situation for children affected by armed conflict. Inspired by the international norms protecting the rights of the child, the parties underlined the children belong with their families or other custodians and not in the workplace, whether civilian or military. The LTTE will engage in a partnership with the United Nations Children's Fund (UNICEF) to draw up an action plan for restoring normalcy to the lives of children, and the parties called on the international community to provide financial support for such an action plan.

The GOSL will, in order to arrive at the broadest possible consensus, establish an appropriate mechanism for consultation with all segments of opinion as part of the ongoing peace process.

6-9 January 2003

at Rose Garden, Thailand.

The Government of Sri Lanka (GOSL) and the Liberation Tigers of Tamil Eelam (LTTE) held the fourth session of peace talks at the Rose Garden in Thailand 6 – 9 January 2003.

Deliberations were conducted in a frank and constructive atmosphere, with both parties demonstrating their conviction that the peace process must be sustained even when difficult issues are addressed.

The main focus of the parties was on the need to ensure implementation of urgent humanitarian priorities. It was strongly emphasized that the significant political breakthrough made at the third session of talks in Oslo in December 2002, at which the basic principles for a political settlement were outlined, will be sustained through continued discussions on political matters. At the same time, political progress must be underpinned by tangible improvements in the daily lives of people. To this end, there is a need for more effective implementation by the parties as well as the speedy provision of funds by donor governments.

The parties recognized that the situation with regard to the High Security Zones involves major humanitarian and security concerns for both parties. Recent controversies surrounding this matter were discussed in depth. The parties did not reach agreement on the continuation of the work of the Sub-Committee on De-Escalation and Normalization (SDN).

Notwithstanding the disagreement on this particular issue, the parties emphasized the need for progress in resettling the hundreds of thousands of displaced persons. To this effect, the parties agreed on an "Action Plan for an Accelerated Resettlement Programme for the Jaffna District." As the clear majority of resettlement cases relate to areas outside the High Security Zones, the first phase of the Action Plan will focus on such areas.

The plan sets out four specific tasks and corresponding deadlines:

- A preliminary physical assessment to be completed by 7 February 2003
- The formulation of project recommendations and identification of potential implementing agencies by 14 February 2003
- The identification of available resources from appropriate funds by 20 January 2003
- A plan to release premises presently used by the Security Forces to the original owners or intended purposes, to be submitted by 31 January 2003.

Members of the Sub-Committee for Immediate Humanitarian and Rehabilitation Needs (SIHRN), representing both the GOSL and the LTTE, will meet with the United Nations High Commissioner for Refugees (UNHCR) shortly to discuss UNHCR participation in effectuating this plan. The particular needs of the displaced Muslim population will be duly accommodated in the resettlement process.

The second phase of the Action Plan will focus on resettlement of IDPs and refugees in areas within the High Security Zones, as and when they are released by the Security Forces for resettlement. For this purpose, the GOSL will carry out a review with the assistance of an internationally recognized military expert, taking into account relevant humanitarian and security needs.

Following the strong political and financial support pledged by the international community at the Sri Lanka Support Meeting held in Oslo on 25 November 2002, the parties stressed the need for moving from planning to implementation of humanitarian and rehabilitation programmes. The rapid establishment of the North East Reconstruction Fund (NERF) will be decisive for the speedy disbursement of international assistance. The parties welcomed a decision by the Sub-Committee on Immediate Humanitarian and Rehabilitation Needs (SIHRN) to select the World Bank as the custodian of the NERF. Furthermore, the parties confirmed the SIHRN as the prime decision-making body for meeting immediate humanitarian and rehabilitation needs in the north and east. The GOSL in particular undertook to ensure that the respective roles of government institutions engaged in the north and east are properly clarified and co-ordinated with the SIHRN.

In line with the agreement on basic principles for a political settlement, in which a number of issues were identified for discussion, the parties will commence a process for discussion of human rights issues. Human rights will constitute an important element of a Final Declaration. As first steps in furthering human rights issues in the process, the parties agreed on the following:

- A schedule on human rights issues will be worked out following discussions at the next session of peace talks. For this purpose, the assistance of the agreed human rights adviser to the parties will be sought.
- An independent verification mechanism will be established for persons Missing in Action (MIA) and Involuntary Disappearances, with the assistance of the International Committee of the Red Cross (ICRC).

As a means to reinforce respect for the provisions of the Ceasefire Agreement, monthly meetings will be held between the GOSL, the LTTE and the Sri Lanka Monitoring Mission (SLMM) in order to discuss issues arising from the regular SLMM summary of total recorded complaints and violations of the Ceasefire Agreement. Mr. Fernando (GOSL) and Mr. Karuna (LTTE) will be responsible for organizing these meetings and will report on progress made and any outstanding problems at each session of the peace talks.

The government expressed serious concerns related to the recent incident involving transportation of prisoners through Vanni. The LTTE gave assurances that the case will be examined and that appropriate action will be taken as a matter of urgency. More generally, the parties agreed to ask the facilitator to propose procedures to ensure rapid corrective action by the parties in cases of incidents that are or can be perceived as disrupting the peace process.

Following an agreement made at the third session of talks, a committee was established to ensure the effective inclusion of gender issues in the peace process. The terms of reference for the committee will be formulated by the members at their first meeting. The committee will be facilitated by the Royal Norwegian Government, which will seek to provide a senior Norwegian resource person and necessary financial resources. The committee will consist of the following five representatives of each party:

- LTTE: Ms. Sivahimi Subramaniyam, Ms. Renuga Sanmugaraja, Ms. Mathimalar Balasingam, Ms. Sridevy Sinnathampi, Ms. Vasanthapireminy Samasundaram.

- GOSL: Dr. Kumari Jayawardena, Dr. Deepika Udagama, Ms. Kumuduni Samuel, Ms. Faizoon Zakariya, Dr. Fazeela Riyas.

The parties agreed that a Muslim delegation will be invited to the peace talks at an appropriate time for deliberations on relevant substantive political issues.

The parties confirmed that subsequent sessions of peace talks will take place on 7 – 10 February and 18 – 21 March 2003. The parties also agreed that additional sessions will be held on 29 April – 2 May, as well as at an appropriate time in June to be determined once dates for the International Donor Conference in Japan are established.

8 February 2003 at Berlin, Germany

The Government of Sri Lanka (GOSL) and the Liberation Tigers of Tamil Eelam (LTTE) held the fifth and shortened session of peace talks at the Norwegian Embassy in Berlin on 7 – 8 February 2003. The discussions focused on complex isssues in a spirit of cooperation and conciliation.

The parties expressed their concern about the situation at sea and their strong commitment to ensure that an incident such as the one which resulted in the tragic loss of three lives on a Sea Tiger vessel near the Delft islands on 7 February 2003 does not recure. Recognising the gravity of the consequences of incidents of this kind, the parties agreed that a meeting will be held soon between the GOSL, LTTE and Sri Lanka Monitoring Mission (SLMM), to work out effective safeguards.

The parties reviewed progress reports on the work of the Sub-Committee on Immediate Humanitarian and Rehabilitation Needs in the North and East (SIHRN). Both parties underscored the urgent need to commence humanitarian and rehabilitation activities in the north and east. The parties reported that the agreement on World Bank custodianship of the Northeast Reconstruction Fund (NERF) is close to finalisation and will be signed within the next nweek. The parties once again appealed to the international community to make funds rapidly available for immediate humanitarian and rehabilitation needs in the north and east.

The parties reported that the implemantation of the Action Plan for Accelerated Resttlement in the Jaffna district (ARP) is ahead of schedule. The seven Assessment Teams, comprising representatives from the GOSL, LTTE and UNCHER, have completed preliminary needs assessment and are identifying the activities required to facilitate resettlement. The parties also reported that the concept papers approved at the previous meeting of SIHRN at the last meeting, the report on the return of displaced Muslims in the Northen Province has been submitted for their consideration.

The parties agreed to establish three committees, one in each district of the Eastern Province, to address land issues and other areas of mutual concern. The committees will consist of six representatives of the Muslim population and six representatives of the LTTE. The work of the committees will start immediately. Similar committees will be appointed to address such issues relating to other communities as and when required.

Following a through discussion of human rights, the parties agreed to ask their international Human Rights Adviser, Mr. Ian Martin, to draw up a roadmap for human rights issues relating to the peace process. The draft roadmap will be prepared for discussion in the sixth session of talks in Japan in March and will include

- substantive human rights activities and commitments to be implemented throughout the negotiation process.
- Effective mechanisms for the monitoring of human rights
- Training of LTTE cadres and GOSL officials in human rights and humanitarian law
- Trainng of police and prison officers.

Both parties agreed that children living in the east of Sri Lanka have been the most seriously affected by the war between the GOSL and the LTTE. UNICEF estimates that there are 900 000 children in the north east, all of whom have been seriously affected. Many of these children are faced with malnutrition, poor health care and education facilities, continued displacement, loss of parents and families, and land mines. The LTTE has agreed to work with UNICEF to draw up an action plan for children affected by the armed conflict in the north east. Such an action plan will include an intensified effort by the LTTE to stop underage recritment. The LTTE restated its pledge to bring the practice to an end. The action plan will include a credible review mechanism. The LTTE has agreed toa complete cessation of recruitment of, and recruitment campaigns aimed at, persons under 18 years of age. In this context, the LTTE has handed over 350 children who had joined the organization, for reunification with their parents or guardians. The plan will also include rehabilitation assistance, including provisions for schooling, vocational training, employment facilitation, and health and psychosocial care, with the active support of the government.

The parties intend to commence a discussion on the fiscal aspects of a federal structure at the next session. It was noted that the LITTE has already taken action to set up a Political Affairs Committee with a view to addressing in depth issues pertaining to alternative structures of Powersharing.

The parties confirmed that sixth session of peace talks will take place on 18 – 21 March 2003 in Japan and that seventh session will be held on 29 April – 2 May

18 to 21 March 2003 at Hakone, Japan.

The Government of Sri Lanka (GOSL) and the Liberation Tigers of Tamil Eelam (LTTE) held the sixth session of peace talks at Hakone, Japan from 18 to 21 March 2003.

The parties met amid growing security concerns following recent incidents on land and at sea. While they acknowledged that parellel progress is needed in negotiations on security, economic and political issues, the parties left no doubt that they must now give top priority to omproving the security situation, in particular at sea. The parties undertook to enforce better compliance with Ceasefire Agreement by their personnel.

The Government of Sri Lanka and the LTTE are deeply concerned about the latest incident at sea, including on 10 March. To prevent future incidents at sea that could threaten the stability of the ceasefire, the parties have agreed to convene senior naval and political representatives from both sides within three weeks to work out effective arrangements for the operation of naval units in keeping with existing treaty obligations. The meeting will be convended by the Royal Norwegian Government and the Head of the Sri Lanka Monitoring Mission (SLMM) and will immediately start preparing the meeting with military leaders on both sides. The parties agreed to instruct their naval units exercise restraint, as required by the Ceadefire Agreement, and to avoid provocative actions in the crucial period prior to the establishment of appropriate procedures.

In this context, the parties agreed to strength the mandate and capacity of the SLMM to undertake preventive measure to avoid serious incidents at sea and on land. As a fundamental precondition for the SLMM to take on a stronger role, the parties pledged to endure full compliance with the rulings of the SLMM, guarantee the security of its personnel in all situations, and take disciplinary action against anyone endangering the lives of SLMM personnel.

The parties also agreed to take steps to further strength the security situation on land, including the establishment of procedures with the cooperationnof the SLMM or handling soldiers and carders by the other party.

In their political discussions, the parties reiterated their commitment to develop a federal system based on internal self-determination within a united Sri Lanka. As the point of departure for planning how to give effect to the general principles of federalism in a final settlement of the ethnic conflict, the parties discussed the elements of fiscal federalism.

The parties discussed prilimanary issues and a framework for political matters and agreed to expand this into a complete plan at the seventh session of talks. The plan will outline the next steps to be taken by the parties and the topics that must be addressed in order to negotiate a federal solution for Sri Lanka. The parties recognize that a considerable amount of time will be required to addressed this wide range of topics, which will include geographical regions and the division of powers between the center and regions. In this context, the parties decided to invite the Forum of Federations, a Canadian-based international organization, to participate as consultants at seventh session of talks.

The LTTE reported on the formation of a Politicak Afairs Committee consisting of twenty one leading members of the organization. This committee will undertake an intensive study of federalism over the course of the next three months to build the LTTE's capacity for political transformation. The committee will study federal systems in other parts of the world, arrange seminars for LTTE cadres, consult Tamil parlimetarians and academics and seek advice from lawyers and constitutional experts, to prepare the ground for the process of establishing internal self-determination within a united, federal Sri Lanka.

Following a proposal by the GOSL to prepare for local government elections in the North and East, the LTTE will favorably consider supporting the holding of such elections.

It was agreed that the rescheduled meeting between the LTTE and the Muslim representatives in Batticaloa be convened on 27 April 2003. Furthermore, the LTTE and Mr. Rauf Hakeem agreed to arrange a sepoarate meeting between Muslim leaders and the leadershipof the LTTE in Kilinochchi to discuss political matters and the participation of a Muslim deligation in negotiations at plenary sessions.

The parties approved the proposals submitted by the Sub-Committee on Gender Issues to establish secretariats in Kilinochchi and Colombo.

Following up on the discussions in Berlin in February on human rights, the parties asked their international human rights adviser, Mr. Ian Martin, to develop three aspects of the proposed roadmap for adoption at the seventh session of talks:

1) The drafting of a Declaration of Human rights Humanitarian Principles. This would reflects aspects of fundamental international human rights and humanitarian standards, which both parties would undertake to ensure are respected in practice by their personnel, pending the full entrenchment of human rights standards in the eventual constitutional arrangements and in federal and local law.

2) The planning of a programme of human rights training for LTTE cadres and government officials, police and prison officials, which would contribute to the respect of these principles in practice, and of human rights education and awareness for other sections of the population. This programme would include specialized training offered by UNICEF in relation to the rights of the child, UNCHER in relation to rights of internally displaced persons and refugees, and ICRC in relation to international humanitarian law. The Office of the UN High Commissioner for Human rights would be invited to coordinate this programme.

3) Proposals for the Strengthening of the Human Rights Commissions of Sri Lanka to enable it to develop the capacity for increasingly effective monitoring throughout the country. These proposals would involve international advice and assistance to the HRC from the Office of the UN High Commissioner for Human Rights and other sources, and close coordination with the roles of UNICEF in relation to child protection, UNHCR in relation to the protection of returning internally displaced persons and refugees, and SLMM in relation to acts against the Civilian population.

The parties agreed to hold the seventh session of talks from 29 April to 2 May in Thailand, the eighth session from 12 to 15 June in Japan and the ninthe session from 15 to 18 July in Europe (Venue to be determined).

21 March 2003

Royal Norwegian Ministry of Foreign Affairs -PRESS RELEASE

The Government of Sri Lanka (GOSL) and the Liberation Tigers of Tamil Eelam (LTTE) held the sixth session of peace talks at Hakone, Japan from 18 to 21 March 2003.

The parties met amid growing security concerns following recent incidents on land and at sea. While they acknowledged that parallel progress is needed in negotiations on security, economic and political issues, the parties left no doubt that they must now give top priority to improving the security situation, in particular at sea. The parties undertook to enforce better compliance with the Ceasefire Agreement by their personnel.

The Government of Sri Lanka and the LTTE are deeply concerned about the latest incidents at sea, including on 10 March. To prevent future incidents at sea that could threaten the stability of the ceasefire, the parties have agreed to convene senior naval and political representatives from both sides within three weeks to work out effective arrangements for the operation of naval units in keeping with existing treaty obligations. The meeting will be convened by the Royal Norwegian Government and the Head of the Sri Lanka Monitoring Mission (SLMM) and will immediately start preparing the meeting with military leaders on both sides. The parties agreed to instruct their naval units to exercise restraint, as required by the Ceasefire Agreement, and to avoid provocative actions in the crucial period prior to the establishment of appropriate procedures.

In this context, the parties agreed to strengthen the mandate and capacity of the SLMM to undertake preventive measures to avoid serious incidents at sea and on land. As a fundamental precondition for the SLMM to take on a stronger role, the parties pledged to ensure full compliance with the rulings of the SLMM, guarantee the security of its personnel in all situations, and take disciplinary action against anyone endangering the lives of SLMM personnel.

The parties also agreed to take steps to further strengthen the security situation on land, including the establishment of procedures with the cooperation of the SLMM for handling soldiers and cadres apprehended by the other party.

In their political discussions, the parties reiterated their commitment to develop a federal system based on internal self-determination within a united Sri Lanka. As the point of departure for planning how to give effect to the general principles of federalism in a final settlement of the ethnic conflict, the parties discussed the essential elements of fiscal federalism.

The parties discussed preliminary issues and a framework for political matters and agreed to expand this into a complete plan at the seventh session of talks. The plan will outline the next steps to be taken by the parties and the topics that must be addressed in order to negotiate a federal solution for Sri Lanka. The parties recognise that a considerable amount of time will be required to address this wide range of topics, which will include geographical regions and the division of powers between the center and regions. In this context, the parties decided to invite the Forum of Federations, a Canadian-based international organization, to participate as consultants at the seventh session of talks.

The LTTE reported on the formation of a Political Affairs Committee consisting of twenty-one leading members of the organization. This committee will undertake an intensive study of federalism over the course of the next three months to build the LTTE's capacity for political transformation. The committee will study federal systems in other parts of the world, arrange seminars for LTTE cadres, consult Tamil parliamentarians and academics and seek advice from lawyers and constitutional experts, to prepare the ground for the process of establishing internal self-determination within a united, federal Sri Lanka.

Following a proposal by the GOSL to prepare for local government elections in the North and East, the LTTE will favourably consider supporting the holding of such elections.

It was agreed that the rescheduled meeting between the LTTE and the Muslim representatives in Batticaloa be convened on 27 April 2003. Furthermore, the LTTE and Mr. Rauf Hakeem agreed to arrange a separate meeting between Muslim leaders and the leadership of the LTTE in Kilinochchi to discuss political matters and the participation of a Muslim delegation in negotiations at plenary sessions.

The parties approved the proposal submitted by the Sub-Committee on Gender Issues to establish secretariats in Kilinochchi and Colombo.

Following up on the discussions in Berlin in February on human rights, the parties asked their international human rights adviser, Mr. Ian Martin, to develop three aspects of the proposed roadmap for adoption at the seventh session of talks:

1) The drafting of a Declaration of Human Rights and Humanitarian Principles. This would reflect aspects of fundamental international human rights and humanitarian standards, which both parties would undertake to ensure are respected in practice by their personnel, pending the full entrenchment of human rights standards in the eventual constitutional arrangements and in federal and local law.

2) The planning of a programme of human rights training for LTTE cadres and government officials, police and prison officials, which would contribute to the respect of these principles in practice, and of human rights education and awareness for other sections of the population. This programme would include specialised training offered by UNICEF in relation to the rights of the child, UNHCR in relation to rights of internally displaced persons and refugees, and ICRC in relation to international humanitarian law. The Office of the UN High Commissioner for Human Rights would be invited to coordinate this programme.

3) Proposals for the strengthening of the Human Rights Commission of Sri Lanka to enable it to develop the capacity for increasingly effective monitoring throughout the country. These proposals would involve international advice and assistance to the HRC from the Office of the UN High Commissioner for Human Rights and other sources, and close coordination with the roles of UNICEF in relation to child protection, UNHCR in relation to the protection of returning internally displaced persons and refugees, and SLMM in relation to acts against the civilian population.

The parties agreed to hold the seventh session of talks from 29 April to 2 May in Thailand, the eighth session from 12 to 15 June in Japan and the ninth session from 15 to 18 July in Europe (venue to be determined).

APPENDIX IV

The Interim Self-Governing Authority (ISGA) A proposal by the LTTE

Consistent with the principles of the rule of law, the human rights and equality of all persons, and the right to self-determination of Peoples,

Determined to bring lasting peace to all persons of the island of Sri Lanka,

Acknowledging with appreciation the services of the Royal Norwegian Government, the Norwegian People, and the international community in attempting to bring peace to the island,

Recognizing that a peaceful resolution is a real possibility, despite the challenging history of the peace process between the Tamil people and the Sinhala people.

Determined to establish an interim self-governing authority for the NorthEast region and to provide for the urgent needs of the people of the NorthEast by formulating laws and policies and, effectively and expeditiously executing all resettlement, rehabilitation, reconstruction, and development in the NorthEast, while the process for reaching a final settlement remains ongoing.

Being aware that the history of the relations between the Tamil People and the Sinhala People has been a process of broken promises and unilateral abrogation, by successive governments of Sri Lanka, of pacts and agreements solemnly entered into between the government of Sri Lanka (GOSL) and the elected representatives of the Tamil People,

Bearing in mind that successive Governments of Sri Lanka have perpetrated persecution, discrimination, State violence and State-orchestrated violence against the Tamil People,

Noting that the Tamil people mandated their elected representatives to establish an independent sovereign, secular State for the Tamil people in the elections subsequent to the Vaddukoddai Resolution of 1976,

Bearing in mind that the Tamil armed struggle as a measure of self-defense and as a means for the realisation of the Tamil right to self-determination arose only after more than four decades of non-violent and peaceful constitutional struggle proved to be futile and due to the absence of means to resolve the conflict peacefully,

Recalling that the Liberation Tigers of Tamil Eelam (LTTE) first took measures towards peace by unilaterally declaring the ceasefire in December, 2000 and again in December, 2001, opening highways, facilitating trade and the free movement of people, and entering into peace negotiations in good faith in the hope of creating an environment conducive to the return of normalcy and a just resolution of the conflict,

Taking Note of the political courage of the present GOSL in reciprocating to the 2001 cease-fire,

Realizing that the war in the island of Sri Lanka was principally confined to the NorthEast, resulting in the destruction of the social, economic, administrative, and physical infrastructure of that area, and that the NorthEast still remains the region in the island of Sri Lanka affected by war,

Recognising that the majority of the Tamil People in the NorthEast, by their actions in the general elections held in the year 2000, gave their mandate acknowledging the LTTE as their authentic representative,

Knowing that the LTTE exercises effective control and jurisdiction over the majority of the NorthEast area of the island of Sri Lanka,

Realising that reaching a final negotiated settlement and the implementation thereof is expected to be a long process,

Affirming the necessity for the safe and free return of all refugees and displaced persons and their urgent need for unimpeded access to their homes and secure livelihoods at land and sea in the NorthEast,

Mindful that institutions and services provided by the GOSL have proved to be inadequate to meet the urgent needs of the people of the NorthEast,

Recognising the failure of the Sub-committee on Immediate Humanitarian and Rehabilitation Needs (SIHRN) and other Sub-Committees formed during the peace negotiations, which failure was due to the composition of such Sub-Committees, which repeatedly led to inaction,

Acknowledging the recognition by the GOSL of the necessity for an Interim Authority, as mentioned in its 2000 election manifesto,

Realising that maintenance of law and order is an essential pre-requisite for a just and free society,

Recognising the need for raising revenue to meet the urgent needs for the Resettlement, Rehabilitation, Reconstruction and Development of the NorthEast region, which has been devastated by war, and for the carrying out of any function of Government,

Recognising the importance of control over land in resettlement, rehabilitation, reconstruction and development,

Mindful that the Tamils did not participate in the making of the 1972 and 1978 constitutions, which institutionalized discrimination and denied them an effective role in the decision-making process,

Noting the practice in international relations over the last decade of solving conflicts between Peoples through agreement between the parties to the conflict on terms of equality and through innovative and imaginative measures,

Relying on international precedents for establishing interim governing arrangements in war-torn countries having the force of law based solely on pacts or agreements between the warring parties recognized by the international community,

Noting that measures such as the Ceasefire Agreement, including the role of the Sri Lanka Monitoring Mission (SLMM), and, the establishment of the SIHRN and the NorthEast Reconstruction Fund (NERF) constitute valid precedents for making such arrangements,

Wherefore, the Parties, namely the Liberation Tigers of Tamil Eelam and the Government of Sri Lanka, hereby agree to the following provisions:

1. Interim Self-Governing Authority

An Interim Self-Governing Authority (ISGA) shall be established comprised of the eight districts namely: Amparai, Batticaloa, Jaffna, Kilinochchi, Mannar, Mullaitivu, Trincomalee and Vavuniya in the NorthEast, until a final negotiated settlement is reached and implemented.

Representatives of the Muslim community have the right to participate in formulation of their role in the ISGA.

2. Composition of the ISGA

2.1. The ISGA shall consist of such number of members as may be determined by the Parties to this Agreement.

2.2. The composition of the ISGA shall be:

- **2.2.a.** Members appointed by the LTTE,
- **2.2.b.** Members appointed by the GOSL, and
- **2.2.c.** Members appointed by the Muslim community in the NorthEast.

2.3. The number of members will be determined to ensure:

2.3.a. An absolute majority of the LTTE appointees in the ISGA.

2.3.b. Subject to (a) above, the Muslim and Sinhala Communities in the NorthEast shall haverepresentation in the ISGA.

2.4. The Chairperson shall be elected by a majority vote of the ISGA and shall serve asthe Chief Executive of the ISGA.

2.5. The Chairperson shall appoint the Chief Administrator for the NorthEast and suchother officers as may be required to assist in the performance of his/her duties. The Chairperson shall have the powers to suspend or terminate any such appointment.

3. Elections

The provisions of Clauses 2.2 and 2.3 shall continue until elections for the ISGA are held. Such elections shall be held at the expiry of five years of the coming into force of this Agreement, if no final settlement has been reached and implemented by the end of the said period of five years. An independent Election Commission, appointed by the ISGA, shall conduct free and fair elections in accordance with international democratic principles and standards under international observation.

4. Human Rights

The people of the NorthEast shall be accorded all rights as are provided under international human rights law. Every law, regulation, rule, order or decision of the ISGA shall conform to internationally accepted standards of human rights protection. There shall be an independent Human Rights Commission, appointed by the ISGA, which shall ensure the compliance with all such human rights obligations. The Commission will seek the assistance of international human rights bodies to facilitate the rapid establishment of an effective regime for protecting human rights. The Commission shall be entitled to receive petitions from any individual person, award compensation to any such affected person, and ensure that such person's rights are restored.

5. Secularism

No religion shall be given the foremost place in the NorthEast.

6. Prohibition against Discrimination

The ISGA shall ensure that there is no discrimination on grounds of religion, race, caste, national or regional origin, age or gender in the NorthEast.

7. Prevention of Bribery and Corruption.

The ISGA shall ensure that no bribery or corruption is permitted in or under its administration.

8. Protection of All Communities

No law, regulation, rule, order or decision that confers a privilege or imposes a disability on any community, which is not conferred or imposed on any other community, shall be made concerning culture or religion.

9. Jurisdiction of the ISGA.

9.1. The ISGA shall have plenary power for the governance of the NorthEast includingpowers in relation to resettlement, rehabilitation,reconstruction, and development,including improvement and upgrading of existing services and facilities (hereinafterreferred toas RRRD), raising revenue including imposition of taxes, revenue, leviesand duties, law and order, and over land.

These powers shall include all powers and functions in relation to regional administration exercised by the GOSL in and for the NorthEast.

9.2. The detailed modalities for the exercise of such powers and the performance of suchfunctions shall be subject to further discussion by the parties to this agreement.

10. Separation of Powers

Separate institutions for the administration of justice shall be established for the NorthEast, and judicial powers shall be vested in such institutions. The ISGA shall take appropriate measures to ensure the independence of the judges.

Subject to Clauses 4 (Human Rights) and 22 (Settlement of Disputes), of this Agreement, the institutions created under this clause shall have sole and exclusive jurisdiction to resolve all disputes concerning the interpretation and implementation of this agreement and any other disputes arising in or under this agreement or any provision thereof.

11. Finance

The ISGA shall prepare an annual budget.

There shall be a Financial Commission consisting of members appointed by the ISGA. The members should have distinguished themselves or held high office in the fields of finance, administration or business. This Commission shall make recommendations as to the amount out of the Consolidated Fund to be allocated to the NorthEast. The GOSL shall make its good faith efforts to implement the recommendation.

The ISGA will, giving due consideration to an equitable distribution, determine the use of funds placed at its disposal. These funds shall include the NorthEast General Fund, the NorthEast Reconstruction Fund (NERF) and the Special Fund.

The GOSL agrees that any and all of its expenditures in or for the NorthEast shall be subject to the control of the ISGA.

11.1.a NorthEast General Fund

The NorthEast General Fund shall be under the control of ISGA and shall consist of: 11.1 .a. The proceeds of all grants and loans made by the GOSL to the ISGA and theproceeds of all other loans made to the ISGA.

11.1.b. All allocations by the GOSL from agreements with states, institutions and/or other organizations earmarked in any such agreements for the NorthEast. 11.1.c. All other receipts of the ISGA, other than the funds specified below.

11.2. NorthEast Reconstruction Fund

The NERF shall continue to exist in its present form except that control over it will be transferred to the ISGA.

All grants given for the reconstruction of the NorthEast, will be received through the NERF. Utilization of resources from NERF will be directly determined and supervised by the ISGA.

11.3. Special Fund

All loans and any grants which cannot be channeled through the NERF for the specific purpose of RRRD will be received into the Special Fund. As in the case of other Funds, the ISGA shall control the Special Fund.

12. Powers to Borrow, Receive Aid and Trade.

The ISGA shall have powers to borrow internally and externally, provide guarantees and indemnities, receive aid directly, and engage in or regulate internal and external trade.

13. Accounting and Auditing of Funds.

13.1. The ISGA shall appoint an Auditor General.

13.2. All Funds referred to in this Agreement shall be operated, maintained and audited inaccordance with internationally acceptedaccounting and auditing standards. Theaccounts will be audited by the Auditor General. The auditing of all moneysreceived from international sources shall be subjected to approval by aninternationally-reputed firm appointed by the ISGA.

14. District Committees.

14.1. In the effective exercise of its legislative and executive powers, the ISGA maycreate District Committees to carry out administration in the districts and delegate to such Committees, such powers as the ISGA may determine. The Chairpersons ofsuch committees shall be appointed by the ISGA from amongst its members in orderto serve as a liaison between the ISGA and the Committees.

14.2. The other members of the Committees shall also be appointed by the ISGA, which shall have the powers to suspend or terminate any such appointment. In appointing such members, due consideration shall be givento ensure representation of allcommunities.

14.3. The Committees will function directly under the ISGA.

14.4. The Chief Administrator of the ISGA shall appoint Principal Executive Officers inthe districts, who shall also function as the Secretariesto the Committees. The Chief Administrator shall have the powers to suspend or terminate any such appointment.

14.5. All activities and functions of the Committees shall be coordinated through therespective Secretaries to the Committees.

14.6. Sub-committees may also be appointed to facilitate administration.

15. Administration

As part of the exercise of its executive powers the ISGA shall have direction and control over any and all administrative structures and personnel in the NorthEast pertaining to the powers set out in Clause 9 of this Agreement.

The ISGA may, at its discretion, create expert advisory committees in necessary areas. These areas will include but are not limited to Economic Affairs, Financial Affairs, Judicial Affairs, Resettlement and Rehabilitation Affairs, Development of Infrastructure, and Essential Services.

16. Administration of Land

Since land is vital to the exercise of the powers set out in Clause 9 (jurisdiction of the ISGA), the ISGA shall have the power to alienate and determine the appropriate use of all land in the NorthEast that is not privately owned.

The ISGA shall appoint a Special Commission on Administration of Land to inquire into and report on the rights of dispossessed people over land and land subject to encroachment, notwithstanding the lapse of any time relating to prescription.

The ISGA shall determine the term of competencies of the Special Commission.

17. Resettlement of Occupied Lands

The occupation of land by the armed forces of the GOSL, and the denial to the rightful civilian owners of unfettered access to such land, is a violation of the norms of international law. Such land must be immediately vacated and restored to the possession of the previous owners. The GOSL must also compensate the owners for the past dispossession of their land.

The ISGA shall be responsible for the resettlement and rehabilitation of displaced civilians and refugees in such lands.

18. Marine and off-shore resources

The ISGA shall have control over the marine and offshore resources of the adjacent seas and the power to regulate access thereto.

19. Natural Resources

The ISGA will have control over the natural resources in the NorthEast region. Existing agreements relating to any such natural resources will continue in force. The GOSL shall ensure that all monies due under such agreements are paid to the ISGA. Any future changes to such existing agreements should be made with the concurrence of the ISGA. Future agreements shall be entered into with the ISGA.

20. Water Use

Upper riparian users of river systems have a duty to ensure that there is a fair, equitable and reasonable use of water resources by lower riparian users. The GOSL and the ISGA shall ensure that this internationally recognized principle is followed in the use of water resources.

21. Agreements and contracts

All future agreements concerning matters under the jurisdiction of the ISGA shall be made with the ISGA. Existing agreements will continue, but the GOSL shall ensure that all proceeds under such agreements are paid to the ISGA. Any changes to such existing agreements should be made with the concurrence of the ISGA.

22. Settlement of Disputes

Where a dispute arises between the Parties to this Agreement as to its interpretation or implementation, and it cannot be resolved by any other means acceptable to the Parties including conciliation by the Royal Norwegian Government, there shall be an arbitration before a tribunal consisting of three members, two of whom shall be appointed by each Party. The third member, who shall be the Chairperson of the tribunal, shall be appointed jointly by the Parties concerned. In the event of any disagreement over the appointment of the Chairperson, the Parties shall ask the President of the International Court of Justice to appoint the Chairperson.

In the determination of any dispute the arbitrators shall ensure the parity of status of the LTTE and the GOSL and shall resolve disputes by reference only to the provisions of this Agreement.

The decision of the arbitrators shall be final and conclusive and it shall be binding on the Parties to the dispute.

23. Operational Period

This Agreement shall continue until a new Government for the NorthEast, pursuant to a permanent negotiated settlement, is established. The Parties will negotiate in good faith to reach such a settlement as early as possible.

Provided, however, that at the end of four years if no final agreement has been reached between the Parties to this agreement, both Parties shall engage in negotiations in good faith for the purpose of adding, clarifying, and strengthening the terms of this Agreement.